THE ZION
COVENANT
BOOK 4

Jerusalem
Interlude

THE ZION
COVENANT
BOOK 4

BODIE & BROCK
THOENE

TYNDALE HOUSE PUBLISHERS, INC. • WHEATON, ILLINOIS

Visit Tyndale's exciting Web site at www.tyndale.com

TYNDALE is a registered trademark of Tyndale House Publishers, Inc.

Tyndale's quill logo is a trademark of Tyndale House Publishers, Inc.

Edited by Ramona Cramer Tucker

Designed by Julie Chen

Published in 1990 as *Jerusalem Interlude* by Bethany House Publishers under ISBN 1-55661-080-7.

First printing by Tyndale House Publishers, Inc. in 2005.

Scripture quotations are taken from the *Holy Bible*, King James Version or the *Holy Bible*, New International Version®. NIV®. Copyright © 1973, 1978, 1984 by International Bible Society. Used by permission of Zondervan Publishing House. All rights reserved.

Library of Congress Cataloging-in-Publication Data

Thoene, Bodie, date.
   Jerusalem interlude / Bodie & Brock Thoene.
p. cm. — (The Zion covenant ; 4)
   ISBN 1-4143-0110-3 (sc)
   1. Holocaust, Jewish (1939-1945)—Fiction.   2. Holocaust survivors—Fiction.   3. Jerusalem—Fiction.   4. Jews—Fiction.   I. Thoene, Brock, date.   II. Title.
PS3570.H46J47 2005
813'.54—dc22   2004019780

Printed in the United States of America

11   10   09   08   07   06   05
7   6   5   4   3   2   1

*With much love
we dedicate this story
to Luke,
who has a heart for God
and a talent
to match!*

Acknowledgments

Our special thanks to Joseph Samuels, whose extensive knowledge and experience earn him the title of our honorary Rebbe! After a lifetime of building great synagogues across America, Joe has brought the same dedication to the monumental task of helping with the research of this series.

Joe, we thank the Lord daily for bringing you into our lives and work.

THE EUROPE THEATRE

GERMANY

POLAND

•Prague

CZECHOSLOVAKIA

SUDETENLAND

(ONCE AUSTRIA)

HUNGARY

FINLAND

SWEDEN

NORWAY

ESTONIA

NORTH
SEA

DENMARK

BALTIC
SEA

LATVIA

LITHUANIA

GREAT
BRITAIN

London

NETHERLANDS

•Hamburg

•Berlin

Warsaw

GERMANY

POLAND

SOVIET UNION

BELGIUM

•Paris

Prague•

CZECHOSLOVAKIA
(before Munich Agreement)

FRANCE

Munich

Vienna •

SWITZERLAND

(ONCE AUSTRIA)

HUNGARY

RUMANIA

SPAIN

ITALY

YUGOSLAVIA

BULGARIA

CORSICA

•Rome

ADRIATIC
SEA

ALBANIA

SARDINIA

MEDITERRANEAN
SEA

GREECE

Prologue

Outside the ornate facade of the Far East Café, the neon lights of San Francisco's Chinatown blinked and shimmered a bright reflection on the rain-slick street.

Dr. Charles Kronenberger loved this street. Ever since Murphy and Elisa had brought him and Louis here as children, the place had reminded him of a set for a Charlie Chan mystery movie. He had never shed the little-kid excitement of those days, and tonight he felt it again, stronger than ever. He hefted Tikvah Thurston's cello case and pulled her beneath the awning as rain pelted from the sky.

It was almost midnight, yet a few souvenir shops remained open. Through plate-glass windows, Charles and Tikvah could see round-faced clerks reading Chinese newspapers behind cluttered counters.

A clique of die-hard tourists shouted and laughed as they trudged from one shop to the next in search of some elusive bargain.

A yellow cab splashed by, and Tikvah smiled up at Charles. Her eyes were warm, happy—familiar to Charles, although he had never met her before tonight.

"What is it?" he asked, sensing there was something this beautiful woman wanted to say.

Her smile became shy. She looked away at the pools of color and light mirrored on windshields and hoods and bumpers. "I . . . I love . . . San Francisco. That's all."

He felt an urge to stoop and kiss her, but he did not. Instead he brushed a damp strand of hair from her forehead. Even that small touch seemed to startle her. "Yes." He averted his eyes quickly, glad he had not followed his first impulse. "Me too. I love this place. It doesn't matter if it's midnight. Chinatown is on Hong Kong time. It's lunchtime in Hong Kong. Are you hungry?"

She nodded, moving toward the doorway of the restaurant. She seemed to have recovered from his too-familiar touch. A diminutive and ancient Asian in a headwaiter's tuxedo shuffled toward them, worn menus cradled in his arm. He bowed slightly and gestured toward a carved teakwood arch. Beyond lay a long corridor lined with private dining rooms with curtains across the doors.

Tikvah craned her neck upward as she gazed in astonishment at enormous bronze chandeliers suspended above them. Several decades of dust coated the massive fixtures. She grinned back over her shoulder at Charles. "I hope this is not the night the big quake happens!" She laughed, and Charles knew she felt in this place the sense of mystery that had always captivated him. Even if he had not been sent to find her, even if he were not carrying the letters he must deliver to her, he would have wanted to be here with her.

The waiter paused halfway down the corridor and drew back a curtain to reveal a round table in the center of a small cherry-paneled room. Tikvah entered, and Charles followed. Before they could turn around, the curtain was drawn and they were alone.

Tikvah did not meet his eyes as she unbuttoned her coat. Charles propped the precious cello in the corner. Strange. Never had he thought of this wonderfully sinister place as *romantic*—until now!

"All these years in Frisco, and I've never been here." Tikvah's voice betrayed her excitement. "Private dining rooms—perfect for musicians. It's the same size as a practice room, so I won't have withdrawal being away from the concert hall."

The clatter of dishes drifted over the partition.

"A bit noisier than the practice room," she added.

"Maybe next time we can order takeout and eat back at the hall." *Next time!* He could not believe he had said that. *Too quick. Too sure. Too hopeful.*

He had not felt this way about any woman since Edith had died. He had not wanted to see anyone. He had almost forgotten what it was like to have a woman smile at him.

Once again the urge to kiss her swept over him. He fumbled with the buttons of his overcoat, then frowned as he reached into the deep inside pockets to retrieve two bound packets of letters. He placed the packets on the table between them. He had meant to give them to her after dinner, but he needed the distraction from this unexpected jumble of emotions.

Her smile was curious as she reached out to touch one packet of yellowed envelopes. In faded ink, the address read:

Mrs. Elisa Murphy
#36 Red Lion Square
London, England

The postage stamp bore the emblem of the British Mandate of Palestine and the postmark of Jerusalem, dated October 1938.

Charles saw Tikvah's smile fade as realization flooded her. She looked from the packets into Charles's eyes.

He answered the unspoken question. "A gift for you. From my mother. From Elisa."

"From . . ." Tikvah's fingers trembled as she picked up a packet and turned it to reveal the return address written in delicate hand:

Leah Feldstein
Post Office Box 679
Jerusalem,
British Mandate Palestine

She gasped and held the packet against her cheek as if Charles had presented her with a priceless treasure. Indeed he had. "Elisa," she managed to say. "My mother wrote her."

"Of course. They were friends. Best friends. Elisa kept these in a shoe box. Sometimes she would take them out and read them over and over again. Especially aloud. And she would tell Murphy that someday the story must be published—you know, all the early struggles in Jerusalem. What it was really like. Leah was a wonderful writer. She recorded all of it."

Tikvah's tears spilled over, and she carefully wiped the drops from the frail envelopes lest the ink run.

"There was nothing left, you know," she whispered. "After the Arab Legion captured the Jewish Quarter of Jerusalem where she lived, everything was destroyed. Everything. It was a miracle the cello survived. And then for nineteen years the Arabs would not let any Jew go home. No one to visit her grave." She faltered. "Or my father's."

"Elisa knew you would want her letters."

"All my life I have longed for some word from my mother. All . . . no matter how wonderful others may be—" she touched her hand to her heart—"I never stopped wishing for her! Sometimes in the music I heard her voice. In the music I thought I could almost feel her holding me." Tikvah brushed away her tears, appearing embarrassed by her emotion. "I never told anyone that before. Silly. I am older now than she was when she died. But still—I long for her!"

Charles nodded, saddened at the years that were lost to Tikvah. "Elisa and Murphy were told your mother died in the siege. Elisa knew Leah was expecting a child, but no mention was made of the baby . . . of your survival. As soon as she found out, we traced you. Traced you here to San Francisco." He paused awkwardly as a waiter slipped in with a steaming pot of tea.

Tikvah looked away, hiding her emotion in silence until the man left the room. Then the emotion returned with a rush. She grasped Charles's hand. "If only I had known!"

Charles nodded. "Yes. My real father was a journalist in Germany. When I grew up I made my way back to Hamburg and dug up everything he had written that had not been destroyed by the Nazis. Every word . . . a gift." His eyes lingered on the packages of letters, then rose to meet hers. "Everything you heard in her music, Tikvah—it's all there. So full. From the day she arrived in the Holy Land with your father. Ah, such a story she told! It is *your* story, Tikvah! Maybe she sensed that one day you would need to know."

Tikvah carefully unwrapped the first packet, fanning dozens of letters out on the table before her. Here and there was an envelope addressed to Charles and Louis as well. She glanced up at him as she let her fingers rest on his name. The name her own mother had penned! "I have never even seen her handwriting before now. And you were growing up in the same house where these letters were sent." A tone of awe entered her voice. "She loved you, Charles. Do you think she would have . . . how would she have felt about *me*?"

His reply was a gentle laugh. The question was so poignant, so filled with longing and self-doubt. Charles knew the certain answer to her query, but he would let the living words of Leah Feldstein answer a question that had lingered for thirty-seven years.

"We watched for the postman every day. We waited for her letters. Laughed and cried with Elisa over the news of this and that." Charles pressed his lips together in thought. "There was so much happening then. I can tell you our side of it. But Leah alone must answer your questions. Read the letters and *know her*, Tikvah! Then you will know how she would have loved you. How proud she would have been."

Charles leaned forward and kissed her softly. She did not resist his gentle hand against her cheek.

1

The Parting

Good-bye.

Was there a more painful word in any language? Today, in the ache of their parting, Elisa Murphy and Leah Feldstein could not remember any word that had ever cut deeper.

The beauty of the afternoon somehow made it harder. Warm sunlight bathed the ancient houses of Marseilles. Browns and yellows, soft blues and rusty oranges—the pastel facades glowed like a patchwork quilt on a clothesline. Windows of the houses were shining squares within the squares that reflected the vivid blue of the sky and the movement of the clouds.

Such beauty was meant to be shared over coffee at a sidewalk café. Such a day should have been savored leisurely with laughter and conversation. But all that was ending forever.

The two friends clung tightly to each other as the ship's whistle split the air. Their final words were drowned in the commotion of boarding passengers and shouting dockworkers.

Leah kissed Elisa lightly on the cheek. *More than sisters.* Warm brown eyes held the gaze of intense blue eyes. All was spoken in that long last look: *I will miss you. Thank you for everything. Be careful. I will pray for you. Please write . . . I love you!*

These silent words were heard by both hearts and answered by a nod. Elisa shook her head and brushed away the tears on Leah's cheek. Leah managed a smile and did the same for Elisa. *One more hug . . . the whistle again! Lord, why must it be so hard to leave her now?*

Shimon and Murphy looked on self-consciously. There was no way to make this easier. They had spent a week longer together on the crossing from New York to France, thanks to Murphy. He had found some excuse to stop over in France instead of traveling directly to London with Elisa and the boys. The extra week had been a time of peace and elegance, like the old days in Vienna. The women had learned to laugh again. The heartache of the recent months had at least receded from the center stage of their lives. Little Charles and Louis had explored every corner of the ship while Murphy and Shimon had played chess and talked politics and watched the friendship of their wives with a sort of envy. Such friendship was rare, and yet they made it look so *easy*—that is, until now.

Now it suddenly became hard. Painful. Almost cruel to know that the daily familiarity must stop at the edge of the Marseilles quay.

The whistle. Insistent, unforgiving, calling Leah to leave for Palestine, while Elisa must travel to London.

Shimon cleared his throat. He touched Leah's shoulder.

Elisa turned and hugged him too. More tears. "Take care of her, Shimon!" Elisa cried as she thumped his arm and stepped back.

Shimon nodded and shook Murphy's hand. Leah hugged Murphy hard, then patted his cheek. "Take care of her, Murphy," she likewise admonished the tall handsome American.

Elisa handed her a handkerchief. "Blow your nose," she instructed.

Leah laughed and obeyed.

Then it was time to gather up belongings. Handbag. Cello case. Always the cello . . .

Elisa captured the picture in her mind like the afterimage of a bright light: *Clouds of confetti fluttering down from the decks of the ship. Shimon and Leah together at the rail on the last leg of their journey to Zion. And beside Leah, leaning against her like a well-loved child, was the cello.*

Now Leah was on the ship. She tossed down a long red streamer to Elisa. The two friends held each end as the mooring lines were cast off.

"Next month in Jerusalem!" Elisa called.

Leah must have heard her. Or at least she read the message on Elisa's lips because she nodded as she tossed loose her end of the streamer. It floated down like a final embrace.

The air of Jerusalem smelled of rain. As if the population sensed a coming downpour, most of its residents had taken shelter indoors. The Arabs gathered in the gloomy coffeehouses of the Old City to smoke their water pipes and sip thick Turkish coffee. Jews of all sects gathered beneath the domes of their synagogues for Sabbath services. Armenian shopkeepers stood in the doorways of their empty shops and stared bleakly up at the clouds that kept the tourists away.

Here and there, small groups of British soldiers hurried through the crooked lanes of the Old City. Some would stop and browse, looking for a memento to send home to England. A few would bargain and buy to-day, but most would return empty-handed to the Allenby barracks to play cards and bemoan the fact that they had been stationed in such a godforsaken place as Jerusalem. In India, at least there were brothels. In Jerusalem there were only pious Jews and fanatic Muslims and shy Armenian girls who attended convent school.

A truly brave and desperate Englishman might find a female companion among the veiled women in the Arab Quarter. But lately the Arabs had been killing as many British soldiers as Jews. It was not wise to seek solace beyond the Damascus Gate. Many a man had met his end on the curved blade of a Muslim dagger.

On this gloomy day only a handful of the twenty thousand British soldiers in Palestine passed through Jaffa Gate into the souks and bazaars where Dr. Hockman walked. They passed him without noticing the scuffed leather briefcase beneath his arm. Homesick guardians of the great British Empire, they never suspected that this tall stoop-shouldered man carried within that case what was perhaps their own death warrants. Certainly it was the death warrant of the British Mandate in Palestine, and the command for the destruction of every Jew who lived there.

Hockman observed these sad-faced young men with the same emotion with which he examined the piles of oranges in the produce market. *If these are the best England has to offer,* he thought, *then certainly the Führer is right in his predictions about their destruction of the British Empire.*

He opened a shopping bag and counted out six oranges, oranges grown on the trees of the Zionists. Planting fruit trees was one thing the Jews had done for Palestine. But soon not even a trace of their trees would remain. At that thought Hockman picked out another half-dozen oranges and, after a moment of discussion, paid the wizened old fruit vendor half his asking price.

Two young soldiers joined him at the booth. A short man wearing the stripes of a corporal grinned. "It took me two months to figure out you don't pay what they ask. Not like a shop in Liverpool!" he exclaimed.

"Jerusalem has no equal," Hockman responded in flawless English, "either in the quality of oranges or the number of bargains struck in a day." He smiled and bowed slightly as the soldier proceeded to haggle noisily with the merchant. Oranges. The British were mad for oranges.

Hockman sometimes thought that orange marmalade was the sole reason England clung so tenaciously to Palestine.

It made little difference what their purpose was, however. Dr.
Hockman was dedicated to setting a different course for Palestine. For
two years he had been pursuing a goal, and now it was about to become
a reality.

By the clearest of German logic, the Führer had chosen Hockman to
guide the Muslim religious leadership of Jerusalem. As a Nazi archaeolo-
gist, Hockman, like Hitler and Himmler, believed without question that
the Aryan race was the original race created by God. All other peoples
and tribes were the result of inbreeding between man and the sub-
human creatures who occupied the world in the distant past.

The race of Jews, and those of darker color, were marked as
Untermenschen, "subhumans," destined for service as slave labor to the
Aryan race until they were no longer of use. Hitler himself would decide
when these races were no longer of use, and even now he was planning
an alternate solution for that time.

For the present, however, the Untermenschen Jews were performing
the greatest of services for the Third Reich. They were the issue upon
which the passions of men could come together in a mutual goal. In every
land on earth the hearts of men had united in their hatred of the Jews.

This same hatred had built Hitler's personal army of Brownshirts,
and then the SS. This hatred had been fundamental in the collapse of
Austria and the darkness that presently consumed the land in violence.
And now, in the autumn of 1938, it had rolled up and over the mountains of the Sudetenland and left Czechoslovakia broken and without
defense.

All these things the Führer had predicted. He was the prophet and
high priest of the Aryan race. Hockman made the writings of the Führer
his own bible. He lived to serve the prophecies. There was much, *much*
yet to fulfill, and so he had been selected to come to Jerusalem where
other disciples of Hitler's hatred had reasons of their own to see the Jews
destroyed and the British government driven from Palestine.

Today that purpose drew him from the vaulted souks of the Old City
and propelled him with single-minded intensity down the street toward
the gate of Bab el-Silsileh. The name meant "Street of the Chain." One
legend told that a chain had ascended into heaven from the site of the
Dome of the Rock where the street ended. Yet another legend spoke of a
Crusader king from Austria who had been hanged there by a chain. The
second tale made more sense to Hockman. If legends about Jerusalem
taught anything, it was that this was a city of darkness and intrigue and
slaughter. Nothing had changed. Nothing at all.

Spice merchants, weary of waiting for customers who would not come, closed the iron grills of their tiny shops. The scent of peppercorns and cinnamon sticks and precious saffron mingled with the cool air. Hockman inhaled, remembering that great wars had been fought over such items as pepper and cinnamon. Religion had been used as an excuse to stir up the ignorant masses of Europe, but the real reason for quests and crusades had been economics—to capture the trade routes.

Hitler himself had discussed this fact with Hockman over a late supper in Berchtesgaden. *"You see, Doktor Hockman,"* Hitler had said, fixing his blue eyes on him and leaning forward, *"this is the lesson I have learned from history. Men will do for religion what they would not do for mere economics! Clothe one's purpose in the robes of a religious cause, and they will gladly die for you. Ah—"* he had shaken his finger and chuckled—*"but tell them they are dying for the sake of cinnamon and peppercorns, and they will turn and kill you instead!"*

For this very reason the Führer had first sent his greetings and sympathy to Haj Amin el Husseini, the Muslim Grand Mufti of Jerusalem. Haj Amin had the piercing blue eyes of his distant Crusader forebears, and he possessed a hatred for the Jews that was as great as that of Hitler himself. Blue eyes and hatred of Jews was quite enough for the Führer to decide that Haj Amin must become an ally of the Reich. From that first meeting had come a promise of financial support for armed attacks against the Jewish settlers and the British armed forces. For two years men from the small terrorist bands recruited by Haj Amin had been trained in Germany by SS officers. The results had been splendid, just as they had been in Austria, Czechoslovakia, and Spain.

Hitler was certain that the English would soon throw up their hands in despair and turn all of Palestine over to Haj Amin el Husseini. He would become king and do as Hitler wished with the Jews. Hitler would keep Haj Amin on his throne for as long as it suited the Reich, and then . . . there were other plans in the works for Palestine. They did not include Untermenschen Arabs or puppet thrones.

For the moment, however, Haj Amin was most useful. He had recruited a band of five thousand guerrillas from Syria and Iraq and Lebanon—paid mercenaries who were also promised that the cause they fought for was a holy one. Drive the infidels from the holy places! *Jihad!* Holy War! And if you should die in such a cause? *Allah in his mercy will instantly welcome you to Paradise!* This was the promise of the Grand Mufti, as his men were paid with German money and armed with German-made weapons for the fight.

These holy strugglers fought against the British. They killed Jews. They assassinated members of the Palestinian Arab community who opposed the madness of this cause. Over five thousand Arab Palestians had died for speaking out against the tactics of Haj Amin or for working with the Zionists. Those labeled as "friend of the Jews" were marked for death.

Under the tutelage of his friend and mentor, Hitler, Haj Amin had placed his own followers in positions of leadership throughout Palestine. From the lowliest clerk to the muhqtar of a large village, all were indebted to Haj Amin. As it had been in Germany, so it was now in the British Mandate of Palestine. When Haj Amin called for a general strike, no Arab dared to work on pain of death. When he shouted for vengeance and called for demonstrations in the villages and towns, it was as he willed.

The blueprint of conquest was the same here as it had been up to this moment in Europe. And that blueprint was being carried to the study of Haj Amin in Hockman's scuffed leather briefcase.

Beneath the vaults Hockman walked, past the orange Mameluke buildings that bordered the Western Wall road. Always ahead of him was the great compound of the Dome of the Rock, where the Temple of the Jews had once stood. Halfway down the vaulted section, two Jews entered a small doorway on the right. Above the doorway was a Star of David in the grillwork of the arch.

Hockman moved to the left, as though the very air would be poisoned by their breath. This was one of the Jewish soup kitchens that remained open in spite of its nearness to the Muslim Quarter. He mentally marked it as a possible target for the coming activities. The southern exposure of the soup kitchen overlooked the Wailing Wall, and there was talk that the Jews wished to make the building a shortcut to the Jewish holy site that lay in the center of the Muslim Quarter. Yes. The Führer would approve. They would make even daily prayer difficult for the Jews.

It was all so amusing, Hockman thought as the scent of cabbage soup and the sound of Jewish voices mingled to assault his senses. The Jews of Germany longed for nothing so much as they longed for Palestine! "Next year in Jerusalem!" they cried. America would not have them. That hope had died with the sinking of the coffin ship *Darien*. And so it had to be Palestine. So much the better. Round them up in one desolate corner of the world and eliminate them there by stirring up the passions of the Arabs. The Muslim fanatics would save the Reich the trouble.

As was fitting the Grand Mufti of Jerusalem, Haj Amin lived in the most important building on the street. A few drops of rain splashed Hockman's cheek as he entered the small square at the end of the lane. Suddenly he was no longer alone. Ten Arabs huddled beneath the high arched portal of Tannkiziyya, the residence of the Mufti. They had come, no doubt, as petitioners for one favor or another. Haj Amin would see them in due time. If he granted their favors, he would expect them, sooner or later, to return his favor with something much greater.

At the sight of Hockman, two tall black Sudanese bodyguards shoved the petitioners out of the shelter of the portals and barked orders that the doctor must be let through immediately.

Men stepped aside and watched him with a mixture of fear and awe. The question was evident in their dark eyes: *Who could this man be who gains such immediate access to the Mufti?*

Many watched him enter the house of Haj Amin. They whispered their knowledge of his importance to one another, but no one seemed to know what his audience was all about. And certainly no one would inform the British. If he was ever questioned by the British authorities, Haj Amin had agreed to say that the meetings had been to discuss the possibility of research in the Muslim-held area of the Dome of the Rock.

Another black bodyguard bowed in deep salaam as Hockman entered the foyer.

"He is expecting you," said the man in Arabic.

Dr. Hockman replied curtly, "Good. The message I bring is most urgent. I have not had tea this afternoon."

The servant bowed again and then knocked on a massive carved door. The indolent voice of Haj Amin answered through the wood. "Enter."

The door was opened to reveal the diminuitive red-haired figure of the Grand Mufti. He was staring out the window as the rain began to pelt the glass. He did not look up but waved a hand for Hockman to seat himself in one of the two massive leather chairs before the desk. "Doktor Hockman," the voice intoned disinterestedly, "my men saw you enter Jaffa Gate. I expected you some time ago. There is no need for you to purchase oranges like a peasant. Such action delays you. Which delays me."

This Arab intelligence network was as effective as the Gestapo. Hockman tried to guess which of the new faces he had seen on the street might have passed the word along that he was coming.

"I rather enjoy bargaining in the souks," he said lightly as he sat down.

Haj Amin spoke in perfect German, learned from the Germans who had held sway in Palestine in the Ottoman-Turkish Empire before it had been lost to Britain in 1917. "As I said, such delays also affect my schedule." He turned to face Hockman. His blue eyes seemed faded, and he tugged his thin red beard as he sat down in a chair behind his desk.

"Then I offer my humble apology, Your Excellency."

Haj Amin waved an effeminate hand in disregard. "I have been waiting. My friend the Führer has kept me waiting while he bargains in the souks of the world and walks away with everything for nothing. I have waited patiently for some word . . . for more than words. And now I grow impatient as Jews still manage to straggle into Palestine from Europe. What word have you brought me from the Führer?" He raised an eyebrow expectantly.

Hockman smiled. He picked up the briefcase from beside his chair. Placing it on his lap, he held it for a moment.

Haj Amin leaned forward, his gaze on the latch.

"Here is the reply from the Führer, Your Excellency." With a flourish, Hockman opened the case and took out a manila file folder, which he placed on the desk. Then, still smiling, he removed bound stacks of bills. "Eight thousand. Nine thousand. Ten thousand pounds. It is enough to equip and train a thousand additional mercenaries." He paused. "The Führer himself is selecting a group leader for the task of training and leading your men."

Haj Amin silently contemplated the figures on the page Hockman slid across the desk. "This is a fraction of what we need to accomplish our goal. There are British officials to bribe. Equipment and food must be provided."

"Just as the British provided all that to the Bedouin tribes who fought against us and the Turks in the last war?" Hockman laughed at the thought. The British had provided these Arab bands with military leadership under Lawrence and then had given them the weapons that the Arabs now turned back into the face of Britain. "Hitler will not be so foolish as the English have been with you, Haj Amin. You cannot imagine that he would give you everything all at once? Hardly. One favor deserves another." He motioned toward the file. "Read it. The Führer has done you a favor, and now he expects one from you in return. After that, of course, there will always be enough to meet the needs at hand."

Haj Amin lifted his eyes from the stack of bills and the lists of German-made arms and ammunition. He frowned as he picked up the folder. So here he was. Trapped in the same way he trapped the peasants who came to petition him. He did not like it.

2

The Meeting

Eli Sachar sat with his back against the rounded dome of the rooftop. He pretended to watch the haze-shrouded sun as it dropped like a coin into some giant slot beyond Jerusalem.

The trapdoor from the apartment opened, and Eli's mother called up. "What are you doing, Eli? Come wash for dinner."

She did not really want to know what he was doing, so the question was followed by a command.

He answered the question but refused the command. "I am praying, Mama. I am fasting tonight."

This was followed by a long pause. "*Oy! Oy!* Fast and pray! Pray and fast! You will be a skinny rabbi, Eli Sachar!"

"The Torah sustains me, Mama," he said, giving an answer that satisfied her, even though it left a gaping hole in his own soul.

In one more year Eli would be a rabbi, graduated from the Yeshiva with honors. It was a dream his parents had carried all the days of his life. But the Torah did not sustain him. His heart was hungry, his mind ravenous. His Jewish soul was torn in two as he listened to the cry of the Muslim muezzin.

The plaintive call to evening prayer echoed over all Jerusalem. It was so common that Jews and Christians paid no attention when the Muslims stopped to bow and pray toward Mecca. The sound of the muezzin was like birds in the trees. It was not meant to awaken the conscience of those who were not Muslims. Eli had lived his lifetime honoring the song. But now it had come to pierce his heart each time he heard it.

The trapdoor banged shut. Eli was alone again with his thoughts and with the melody from the minaret. He closed his eyes and let himself imagine. *She will hear it now as she passes by her window. She will stop and look out and think of me. She will know that I am listening, that I am thinking of her. And then she will bow. She will pray. She will ask Allah if someday we might be together just as I ask.*

Emotion flooded him as he pictured the willowy form and dark shining eyes of Victoria Hassan. This was his nourishment: The thought of her as she had smiled at him and told him that her heart would meet his at the call to evening prayer! And yet this nourishment made him more hungry.

"Victoria!" he whispered. Longing for her surged up and made it hard for him to breathe. "Victoria! My love!" And yet, how could this be? How could Eli Sachar be in love with an Arab? with a girl he had grown up with? Just like the cry of the muezzin, he had never really noticed her beauty. He had grown up playing on these rooftops with her brother Ibrahim. Arab and Jew, the two boys had barely noticed the gap between them. But always Eli had known that the sister of Ibrahim was as far beyond his reach as the moon. It was forbidden. Muslim woman. Jewish man. It could never be. *Never!*

And yet here he was, waiting on the roof as he had promised. Waiting for Ibrahim to come for him again and lead him to her. That which was most forbidden had now become that which Eli desired more than anything else in his life. His body ached with wanting her. His mind reeled with the forbidden possibilities.

The voice of the muezzin died away, leaving a thousand echoes to swirl around Eli. Darkness came too slowly over Jerusalem. Silence crept in, startled by the occasional clang of a shop grate or the barking of a dog. The air became cool, but Eli was sweating in his white shirt and black trousers. His sandy brown hair was damp with perspiration. He clenched and unclenched his fists as he stared out at the broadening swirl of stars above him. "Forgive me, O Eternal! I love her! More than the Law. More than my life! More than—"

"More than your Arab brother, Ibrahim?" The voice of Ibrahim Hassan laughed from behind him.

Eli leaped to his feet. "I did not hear you!"

"You never were as good as I in hide-and-seek."

"You're late."

"I am *early*, Eli."

"It feels late."

"They tell me that is as it should be when a man is in love."

"Then it feels *very* late!"

"*That* is why I allow you to see her, my Jewish brother. Such awareness of time is not the way an Arab man looks at his woman." He stepped across the division between the close-packed housetops. "My sweet little sister deserves better in her life."

Like a drowning man in need of breath, Eli needed Victoria. "Where is she?"

Ibrahim smiled and his white teeth glinted. It was good that the brother of his heart loved the sister of his blood. Somehow even that which was forbidden must work out sooner or later.

Ibrahim stepped back across the roof and easily jumped over a three-foot crevice that dropped forty feet to the stones below. Eli followed without speaking. The two young men moved effortlessly across this rooftop terrain that had once been their childhood playground. Over the vaulted souks. Above the Christian Quarter. Over the shops and homes of the shoemakers and tinsmiths and spice merchants. Finally they crossed an unmarked boundary into the Muslim Quarter.

Even in the gloom of night Eli could see the outline of the Old City wall. Ahead and to the right was the rooftop of Tankiziyya, where the Muslim Grand Mufti lived. A presence of evil hovered above that place, but Eli was not afraid. He was with Ibrahim, so there was no reason to fear. Beyond the Mufti's residence was the great rounded mass of the Temple Mount and the Dome of the Rock. All this seemed so peaceful in the darkness and starlight of Jerusalem. Christian, Jew, Arab—all rested quietly beneath the roofs, which looked like a field of round caps scattered on the ground. Unless a man knew the borders that marked each religious group, it would be impossible to tell where Jew ended and Arab began. But the chasms were real. Invisible barriers were the most difficult walls to surmount.

"She is there." Ibrahim pointed to the high walls of the stone house belonging to a wealthy spice merchant. "You must climb the courtyard wall. Be careful; there are bits of glass embedded in the top of the wall. She stays there tonight with a friend who also works as a secretary for the British."

Eli studied the stones of the garden wall. Suddenly he was reminded of the gulf between his love for Victoria and the reality of his life as a Jewish rabbinical student. For one instant he almost turned back, but his doubt was smaller by far than his love for her.

"How will I find her?" he asked, choosing a place beside a tall carob tree where he might cross over.

"Inside the courtyard there is a room with a small balcony beside an apricot tree. She will not expect you so soon. You must wait until you are certain she is alone."

Eli nodded. "It feels so late," he said again.

Ibrahim laughed. "I will wait here for you." Then his voice became solemn. "I trust you with the honor of my sister. Words cannot harm her."

"Of course." Eli was wounded by Ibrahim's hint that nothing immoral must pass between Victoria and him. "By my life, Ibrahim . . . I would not."

"Yes. I believe you. You are a better man than I." He slapped him on the back and sent him the last fifty feet alone.

Eli reached for the thick limb of the carob tree and swung out, linking his legs around the branch. He knew this place. Twelve years ago he and Ibrahim had climbed this very wall to steal oranges. They had been caught and taken home in disgrace. That was the last time Eli had stolen anything. It was also the last time he had trespassed into an Arab courtyard.

The leather of his shoes slipped on the slick bark. The drop to the cobblestones was twenty-five feet. Cautiously he made his way through the tangle of branches. He wondered if Ibrahim remembered the last time they were here together and if the memory made him smile. Eli remembered well the bits of glass in the top of the wall. When he was ten, the barrier had not seemed as formidable as it did now.

And we climbed down through the branches of an orange tree on the other side.

Reaching the wall, Eli could easily see the dark balcony with the tree beside it. He was disappointed that she was not there waiting for him. He searched the garden for a place to hide until the appointed time. *How long it seems! But how much better to wait here where I can breathe the air she breathes. So close!*

He tore his trouser leg on the glass as he searched for a sturdy old branch of the orange tree. It was heavy with nearly ripe fruit, but tonight Eli had sweeter things in mind. He groped his way through the tangle of waxy green leaves and sharp stems, then dropped the last eight feet to the ground. *Can she sense that I am here?* He sat down beneath the orange tree, his eyes never leaving the balcony window. Like a watchman waiting for dawn, he waited for her. The anticipation of seeing her again made him feel a little drunk. He forgot he was a Jew. Forgot she was an Arab. He was simply Eli, and she was Victoria.

Nearly an hour passed before there was light in the window. He leaned forward, ready to call to her, and then he remembered Ibrahim's sharp warning. He must wait until he was sure. If he was caught here, they would do much more to him than send him home in disgrace.

A shadow, a delicate shadow, moved back and forth before the light. The sight of it made Eli's heart beat faster. He wanted to toss a pebble or run across the courtyard and stand beneath her balcony and call her name. But he dared not move until he was certain.

The French doors opened slowly. Victoria stood for a minute, framed in the doorway, silhouetted by the light. Her dark hair was loose and tumbled down over her shoulders. She wore a long white cotton shift that moved slightly in the soft autumn breeze and seemed to caress her body. *Have I ever seen beauty before tonight?* Eli ached at the sight of her. Still, he dared not move. Perhaps her friend was in the room behind her.

She leaned her cheek against the frame and gazed out on the dark and desolate garden. Her eyes mirrored sadness, longing.

Ah, she feels the pain of it too.

She sighed. It was not the wind in the leaves. He heard it. He *felt* it. Her face seemed to speak, although she said nothing after the sigh. Was she alone? Eli started forward only one step and then he heard her voice—gentle, a whisper, filled with hope.

"Who has made this rule? Is this the way it must be in Jerusalem? The English gentlemen are always off to this café or that with Arab girls. Why must it be so *hard* for us?"

Eli sank back to his place beneath the tree. She was speaking her heart to someone—to her friend, perhaps? She stepped out onto the balcony. The breeze made the cotton shift cling to her and ruffled her hair.

If only I could be the wind. To caress her so . . . Eli drew a long breath. *Be patient, Eli. Do not be a fool, or she will be the last thing of beauty your eyes will ever see.*

She leaned against the railing. Her eyes still searched the garden. Was she alone? Did she speak to herself? Eli had to be sure.

Again she whispered, "Are not all women built the same by Allah? Breasts for nursing children? A body for the pleasure of a man? I see no difference between me and the English girls or the Jewish girls—"

Eli stood suddenly and called, "Except you are more beautiful!"

Victoria gasped. She looked around fearfully. "Shhhhh! You will be heard!"

"I could not help it." He stumbled from the overgrown path.

"Shhhhh!" she said again. "They will kill you if they catch you!" She leaned far over the banister.

"And I will die if I do not speak to you now."

"But if you die, then I will die, dear Eli . . . *please!*"

"If we both die, then perhaps the Eternal will have mercy on us and let us have some small corner of Paradise where there are no garden walls to climb. Where I can love you." He moved to the trunk of the apricot tree and whispered as he climbed up toward her. "And where everyone has forgotten the names of Arab and Jew."

She glanced nervously around. "Ibrahim has brought you too early."

"It felt very late." The climb up was easy. Her face, sweet and perfect, was framed through the branches. He reached out, and she reached down. Their fingertips touched.

"Then tell me what time you would have it be, Eli. The hour strikes when our fingers touch. It would be merciful if we could die together." Her voice was a whisper—soft, like the breeze.

He was near enough to lean over the balcony. She wrapped her arms around his neck and kissed him eagerly. "We must stop the clock. Let the night stay forever, and I will perch here in this apricot tree to taste the sweetness of your lips."

Her hair brushed his face. Her breath was like flowers. With every kiss he inched nearer along the branch until the balcony was an easy step. He started to climb over, forgetting his promise to Ibrahim. Suddenly Victoria pushed him away and stepped back out of his reach. Breathless, but in control, she smoothed her hair and managed a smile. Her teeth were as perfect and white as the cotton shift. He reached for her in a gesture that begged for mercy.

She took yet another step back. Her hand rose to touch her collar as if she might quiet the racing of her heart. "You will think I have . . . that I have given you my heart too fast, Eli," she breathed.

He still reached out for her, but he did not step onto the balcony. "Come. Put your hand on my heart and feel how fast it beats for you."

She did not move toward him. She knew the danger, felt the power that might sweep them both away. "My heart answers yours, but from a distance. Please. Let our hearts beat slower so we can decide what must be done so that our hearts are not broken."

"To look at you and not hold you . . . that breaks my heart."

"A lifetime of holding me will mend it again, Eli. I . . . cannot . . . give you satisfaction tonight."

"Then satisfy me with this promise, my love. Victoria, come away with me. Be my wife. Come unto my people, and I swear to you by the stars . . ."

"Romeo!" She laughed. "You fit the part well, my Romeo. And I, your Juliet, await you on the balcony."

She drew close to him as she spoke. She reached out and put a finger to his lips. "Do not swear by the stars. They are so cold, and their brightness fades with morning. So might your love—"

"Never!" He embraced her again, kissing her face and her throat until once more she pushed away from him.

"And . . . if your people will not accept an Arab as the wife of a learned rabbi?" Fear shone in her eyes.

"But you will no longer be an Arab, don't you see? It will not matter. I will teach you what you do not know. I will teach you . . . everything . . . you need to make me a good wife."

She closed her eyes as the meaning of his words sank in. To go to him would mean denial of her people and her own faith. And yet how could she live without him? When her heart beat slower she would think. Not now. Not tonight in the dark with only a step between her and surrender.

"A good wife is a woman of self-control. So my mother has taught me. And someday I hope to teach my daughters the same." She managed a smile and blew a kiss good night to him.

"But when?" Pain welled up in his eyes and crept into his voice.

"I will find a way. I will send Ibrahim for you." She placed her hand on the door latch as if it might hold her back from him. "And now . . . good night, sweet Eli. We have so much to think about. So many things. We cannot be like other couples in love. Be careful on your way back to the Jewish Quarter."

"Send for me soon. The nights are a torment to me without you," he pleaded.

"Then sleep well tonight, Eli. You take my heart with you."

With those words she slipped into her room and closed the door behind her. For a fraction of an instant, Eli considered following. But only for an instant.

He shinnied down the apricot tree and crept back across the garden. He heard the urgent whisper of Ibrahim as he climbed back up the orange tree. "Pssssst! Hurry, you idiot! The moon is rising! You will be seen!"

"It is worth it for even a moment more with her."

Ibrahim grabbed his friend by the shirt and tugged him upward the last few inches over the wall. "You will not think anything is worth it if we are caught! You are late!" He scowled.

"It feels early," Eli said.

"I was watching from the wall. It is a good thing you did not go any further, or I would have killed you myself!"

"Then did you hear?"

"I heard nothing but the endless smacking of lips." Ibrahim was half angry.

"I asked Victoria to marry me."

The anger melted. Ibrahim stopped beneath the carob tree and embraced him with a laugh. "Brother! I knew it must be! Always my heart has known it was so! My father will have a place for you. Employment. We will work side by side."

"I asked her to come with me to the Jewish Quarter. I had no thought of leaving my people. My family. My training."

The words stung Ibrahim. Then he shook it off. "Ah, you will come to your senses. You cannot live without Victoria. I am certain of it."

Eli did not reply. A heaviness filled him again. He pointed toward the light of the rising moon. "We must hurry. They will kill me if they find me in the Muslim Quarter."

At the sound of footsteps on his roof, Rabbi Shlomo Lebowitz turned his eyes to the ceiling and whispered, "An angel you have sent to this old man tonight, Lord?"

He waited as the footsteps scurried from south to north, scrambling on to yet another room. The old rabbi shrugged. "So. Maybe not an angel. Or maybe an angel who landed on the wrong roof." He sniffed slightly in disappointment. He would have liked an angelic visit tonight to brighten the cloud of loneliness that had enveloped him. "You couldn't stay here a while? Keep an old rabbi company, Lord?"

He lowered his eyes to the photographs laid out on his bed like the cards in a game of solitaire. The silent faces of his family smiled up at him. "Tonight, my angels, I am thinking of you once again." He lifted each photograph to the light of his kerosene lamp. He recited each name like a hallowed prayer.

"Etta." He gazed lovingly at the face of his daughter. "Listen to the wind tonight. Your papa sends you blessings." He closed his eyes and held the picture against his heart as he recited a prayer for little Etta as if she were still a child and not grown up with a family of her own.

It was only a photograph, to be sure, but her clear eyes radiated warmth and happiness into his tiny apartment. A kiss, and then he replaced Etta on the quilt and picked up the wedding picture of Etta and Aaron. How young they were, and how very much in love they had been that evening in Jerusalem when they had stood beneath the canopy!

"A long time ago," the old man mused. His wife, Etta's mother, had been alive to rejoice on that day. They had not known then how little time she had left on this earth. "My Rachel." Rabbi Lebowitz caressed the name as he spoke it. "Perhaps you in heaven are nearer to Etta and Aaron and the children than I am here in Jerusalem, *nu*?" He sighed. "Can you travel anytime you like to Warsaw, Rachel? Have you leaned over the cradle of the little girl they named for you? Have you watched her grow into a beauty like her mother? Yes? *Oy!* How I envy you that. You have seen the grandsons? You have heard their voices and watched them wrestle on the floor while Aaron laughs above them?" Tears came to his eyes. He pictured his wife there with them all. They were all together while he remained here in Jerusalem. Here in the shadow of Solomon's Wall.

He paused and listened, wishing that the footsteps would return. Or wishing that he too could leave his frail body and fly up to catch a wind to Warsaw.

"Can you hear me, my love?" He spoke louder and the loneliness threatened to choke him. "You must help me. Please, you must help me bring Etta and Aaron and the little ones here to Jerusalem! Whisper to them, my angel! Tell them Grandfather longs to hold them once more." He lowered his head. "Before I am gone. Ahhhhh. Lord? Are You listening also? Then just a small request, *nu?* My family, You see. Bring them here from Warsaw."

3

Watchmen on the Walls

Tonight it was as it had always been. There were watchmen on the walls of Zion.

British soldiers, rifles slung over their shoulders, patrolled the ramparts of the citadel. From the Tower of David, eyes scanned the light and shadow of the city for some sign of unnatural movement in the streets.

October 1938 in Jerusalem represented only a few more nights among three thousand years. Again, as long ago, watchmen stood lonely vigil against the Unnamed Darkness that desired to possess Zion above any other city on earth.

Two thousand years before, the Darkness had whispered from the pinnacle of a crenelated tower: *"All this I will give you if you bow down and worship me!"*

Before that time and since, the kings and princes of this world had coveted Jerusalem from far away. They had listened to the whisper. They had believed the lie, and they had bowed down and worshiped the Darkness.

The ramparts of Jerusalem had fallen again and again throughout the centuries until now; these watchmen paced their stations on a wall rebuilt countless times. The stones were hewn by a hundred different generations of stonecutters.

From Assyria and Babylon and Rome, generals and kings had encircled the wall and heeded the whisper of Darkness: *"All this I will give you if you bow down and worship me."*

From the north, Christian knights and pilgrims had come to slaughter and rape and profane the name of the One they claimed to follow. *"Bow down! Bow down and worship me and Jerusalem will be yours!"*

The Turks had joined the butchery for seven hundred years. *"Bow down and worship me!"*

The kaiser of Germany had entered through the gates on a white steed. *"All this I will give you if you will . . ."*

Centuries of time had blown over these walls of Zion, turning watchmen and kings alike to dust. *"All this I will give you,"* the Darkness had promised. The dust remained and the stones remained, and tonight there were British watchmen on the walls.

Jerusalem, City of the Covenant, was a desolate reminder of a battle more ancient than the ramparts where these shadows now paced.

Within and above and below these stones, the Prince of Darkness and the King of Light still clashed. And the watchmen on the ramparts heard the whispers: *"Bow down! Bow down and worship me!"*

Tonight the voice of Darkness called out to the people in a new way. Over the wireless radio the president of the Arab Council in Cairo announced resolutions that amounted to a call to war in the British Mandate of Palestine:

> *"We demand the immediate ceasing of all Jewish immigration! We pronounce the Balfour Declaration to the Jewish people as null and void in the eyes of all Muslims!"*

Captain Samuel Orde picked up his Bible from beside the radio and left the small stone room that served as his office in the city wall.

> *"We pledge resistance to the British Palestinian Partition scheme by all means available to Arabs!"*

Orde took his jacket from the hook beside the door and locked the massive wooden door behind him.

> *"We demand a general amnesty of all Arab political prisoners and to those living in exile!"*

"Where you goin', Captain?" asked Wendell Terry from behind the duty desk.

"Up on the wall. Take a look around."

"The natives are restless after the broadcast, eh, Captain?"

*"We further state that these resolutions constitute the only solution
to the . . ."*

"Restless?" Orde's face was grim as he took a rifle from the rack.
"Prime Minister Chamberlain has given them lessons on how to get
whatever they want from the English, Terry. Point a gun. Throw a bomb
or two. Blame it on the other chap and then make a threat. That's all it
takes. Look what Hitler's got." His words were bitter. "Yes. Chamberlain
has given the Arabs lessons."

Terry blinked at him in amazement. The captain had never been so
blunt about His Majesty's government before. The young soldier pulled
his earlobe nervously. "Yes, sir, Cap'n Orde. Except this ain't Czechoslovakia."

Orde pocketed his Bible and pushed the door open, looking to the
right and left inside the dark area that led to the steps of the wall. His
men were at their stations. He could make each one of them out even in
the dim light. He inhaled slowly, drinking in the cool night air of Jerusalem. No scent of gunpowder. Not yet anyway. He looked back over his
shoulder at Terry. "Not Czechoslovakia, eh?" He grinned. "You would
be surprised how close it is."

He slipped out and stood beneath the star-filled sky. Crickets still
chirped in the tall grass on the other side of the wall. Back home in England the crickets would all be silent this time of year. October. It would
be cold at home. Here in Jerusalem Orde did not need the coat he
brought along as a cushion to sit on along the walkway.

Orde hailed each of his men as he climbed the steps. He climbed to
the top of the wall, not so much to watch as to pray. The world had
turned upside down. Once again prophets were being stoned because
the truth was too uncomfortable to hear. *"Meshugge,"* the Old City Jews
would say. Crazy.

"Halt! Who goes there?"

"Captain Orde." Orde emerged onto the wall and stepped past the
young guard who searched the rooftops for some sign of unusual movement. "Anything?" Orde asked.

"Quiet night, Cap'n. They've all gone to bed with their camels." The
words were brave, but the voice trembled.

Orde did not want to add to the nervous boy's tension, but he knew.
If ever there was a night for trouble, this was the night.

"I'm glad. That's fine. Two more hours and you're off, eh?" Orde had
come up to chat with the boy nearly every night since he and Palmer had
been ambushed in Ramle. Palmer had not made it. Wilson had been
saved by the sheer luck of a passing half-track. Guard duty on the wall

seemed to be the easiest position for the lad to handle since then. No patrols. No emergency calls. Just the wall. The stars. And sleeping Jerusalem.

Orde hoped that it would remain so tonight.

"Sir? I read that verse you told me about the other night. I memorized it, like you said," the boy blurted out, grateful that his captain stood the watch with him again. "You want me to—"

"Let's hear it." Orde crossed his arms and looked out over the blue light of the Jerusalem houses. His eyes never stopped searching.

Wilson stood beside him. He also scanned the shadows and light for movement. "*'My mouth shall praise Thee with joyful lips: When I remember Thee upon my bed, and meditate on Thee in the night watches. Because Thou hast been my help.'*"

Orde nodded broadly. "Memorized the Bible so I could quote it during the watches when I was in India. Kept me from being so afraid."

"You? Afraid?" Wilson laughed.

In that instant a single shot rang out from the roof of the Petra Hotel. Orde saw the flash from the corner of his eye, but it was too late. Wilson was flung forward as the bullet slammed into his back. Orde called out the warning to the other troops stationed in the citadel and along both sides of the wall. The popcorn rattle of returning gunfire drowned out his voice as he shouted, "Petra! Petra Hotel!"

Bullets began to slam the stations from other areas of the Old City as well. Where had they come from?

Orde dragged the wounded boy toward the steps. He called for help from Johnson as a bullet struck the stone above his head, splintering the chips across his face. The rattle of British gunfire by far overpowered the Arab attackers. Minutes passed: one, two, then three. As Orde and Johnson reached the safety of the enclosure with Wilson, the gunfire ceased altogether. Only echoes and silence and the labored breathing of the boy remained.

Yes, Orde was afraid. Tonight he was afraid for himself, for this bleeding soldier, and for what surely must come to Jerusalem once again as the Darkness whispered in the hearts of men.

There could be no question any longer that the German High Command would follow Hitler. The Czech-Sudetenland was secure. German tanks were poised at the very edge of the border as they awaited the next command.

The Führer paced before his generals as he spoke. Eyes flicked from him to the large painting hanging on the wall behind him. It was a bizarre image, new to the staff room, although everyone had heard that it had been stored somewhere in the Chancellery. After his victory of will over the English prime minister, the Führer had chosen to hang the painting in the open.

Disembodied spirits swirled with wailing demons around the likeness of Wotan, the German god of Creation and Destruction. The painting had been created by the artist Franz von Stuck in the year 1889, but the face of the glowering god was nevertheless the face of Hitler. Strangely, it was the same pose he had used on posters and handbills distributed to the German people.

"Frightening," Canaris whispered to Halder.

Hitler stopped his speech about the Slavic pygmies. He stared directly at Canaris. Like a schoolmaster who has been interrupted, the Führer demanded an explanation of the whisper.

Canaris was not intimidated. He returned the Führer's fierce gaze with steady blue eyes. "I was just remarking how much like the god Wotan you are, mein Führer." Although the words half gagged him, Canaris managed to smile with his flattery. Such ability had saved him more than once when dealing with Hitler.

"Painted the year of the Führer's birth," the obese Field Marshal Hermann Göring remarked, as if everyone in the room did not already know of the eerie coincidence.

Himmler, whose Gestapo rivaled Canaris's Abwehr, smiled and inclined his head as he spoke. "Remarkable. No coincidence, mein Führer."

There were men in the staff room who might have privately argued that point with Himmler in an earlier day. But the power of Adolf Hitler had somehow proved that his rule over the German people was indeed godlike.

Admiral Canaris managed to maintain his look of contentment although a sense of darkness pressed around him. He thought of Thomas von Kleistmann and hoped the Abwehr would find him first. Or that Thomas would have the good sense to kill himself before the Gestapo caught up with him. They had ways of making a man beg to tell everything. And Thomas knew enough to hang half the generals in this room.

Hitler's voice raised and lowered in a monologue. "Of course, President Beneš has not given us everything we requested. The extradition of certain criminals, for instance." A flicker of anger crossed his face. "The Jew Theo Lindheim is now in England with Beneš. No doubt he will continue to do all he can do for our defeat." He raised a finger to make a point. "You see what I have been saying! How true it is! Even one Jew can ruin everything! It is no doubt that Theo Lindheim is the cause of Thomas von Kleistmann's ruin."

Himmler spoke again. "We shall know soon enough. Commander Vargen has traced von Kleistmann to Holland. Amsterdam."

"A country of Jew-lovers," Hitler scoffed. "We could easily rid our-selves of Lindheim, but it is best if we use legal means if possible. We must be above suspicion in the eyes of the world. We must do everything *legally.*" The Führer smiled, and the men laughed obligingly, as was ex-pected. "Of course, it is possible to do *anything* legally."

More laughter. Yes. He had proven *that* in Czechoslovakia. There would be no stopping him now. Laws would topple to be remade for him. The German god had come to stand before them, to point the way, to laugh with them and berate them as a father might berate errant chil-dren. He would also forgive their former doubts because now they be-longed to him entirely.

"You also have Abwehr agents involved in the von Kleistmann mat-ter, Admiral Canaris?" Hitler asked.

"Also in Amsterdam." Canaris did not tell Hitler that his men had or-ders to shoot Thomas on sight. There must be no opportunity for even a hint of the conspiracy to escape his lips.

"Yes. On the job." Hitler stood in silence for a moment. Behind him the face of Wotan glared in evil menace from the canvas. "We have men enough to watch them all. It is wise, however, in the case of Theo Lindheim and the daughter who was so involved with the illegal immi-grants. . . . We may wait until they are no longer in England, unless op-portunity arises. The British have a sense of propriety about these things. They are upset by blood. The French do not mind blood as long as it is not related to them."

More laughter. The mighty French Army was looking smaller each day.

"Only Germans seem to be able to tolerate the sight of blood." Hitler turned and gestured toward the red sulfuric vapors that rose within the painting. "For creation of the pure race, there must be blood spilled." He snapped his fingers and a map lowered, covering the portrait of Wotan.

Canaris sighed inwardly with relief.

The map was arranged showing the new boundaries of the Reich. Just beyond the red boundaries was a second, yellow line, which encom-passed all of Czechoslovakia, Poland, and part of Russia.

"There, you see. Soon those lines will also be red." Hitler moved his hand down toward Palestine and the oil-rich Middle East. "Watch Palestine, gentlemen. You will observe that it is also outlined in yellow. What we do in Europe will be mirrored there. My plan is very clear." He lifted his hand in a fist, then raised his index finger and his little finger. "Two claws on the same beast. Poland and Palestine. I will work them in the same way."

Hitler picked up a leather-bound folder and flipped it open.

Scanning the pages, he smiled. "The Polish government has issued an edict regarding Jewish passport holders who are out of the country. Within two weeks all passports must be stamped with an additional seal or they become invalid. This will make those persons stateless, which means that Poland will not have to allow their Jews back into the country." He scanned the folder again. "This edict will leave the Reich with twelve thousand Polish-born Jews still living here within our borders. This we cannot tolerate!" He slammed his fist down on the table as though someone were arguing. "We will not keep their Polish Jews within the Reich! Such an edict is an affront to Germany and the German people!" Suddenly the voice dropped low again. "We can use such an affront quite effectively to move us toward our goal. It seems a small thing, this matter of passports. But we will use it, and when it is finished, we will march into Warsaw just as we will soon overtake the remainder of Czechoslovakia."

Admiral Canaris listened wearily. Britain had proved how little it cared about the plans of Adolf Hitler. There would be no more approaches to their secret service. Thomas von Kleistmann was a doomed man because they had not listened. His old friend Theo Lindheim was doomed. Ah well. They were small matters compared to what the god Wotan now planned for Europe.

Perched on the window seat, Elisa hugged her knees and gazed out over the dark houses of Red Lion Square in London. Murphy lay sound asleep in the huge Victorian bed he called "the Parade Ground."

Elisa pulled back the curtain a bit farther so the soft light from the streetlamp fell on his face. Such a wonderful face, even with his mouth open and the shadow of a beard on his cheek. He was handsome even with his hair tousled and his arm reaching for her. From his deepest slumber he called her name and patted the empty mattress while she looked on with tender amusement.

There was a sense of magic about this old house. Anna and Theo had found it for them while they had been in America. According to tradition, Charles Dickens had once lived here. It was a lovely place to raise two little boys like Charles and Louis, Anna had reasoned, and so the house was purchased complete with two rooms of furnishings as a belated wedding gift for Murphy and Elisa.

They had lived in the house for only a short time, but already it felt like home. There was an old-fashioned dreaminess about Red Lion Square—stately houses and ancient trees, even a fifteenth-century church!

The fact that Charles Dickens had once written in these rooms had awakened a sense of awe in Murphy. He touched the banisters and the doorknobs with reverence. He promised Charles and Louis that when they learned English properly, he would read them *Great Expectations* and *Oliver Twist*. At Christmas they would burn a yule log in the enormous fireplace and read *A Christmas Carol* together in the very house where it had been written.

Anna had beamed when her son-in-law had stooped to kiss her cheek and told her, "You did not find us a house; you have given us England!"

"Hard to believe this is the very heart of London," Theo had remarked. "And only a seven-minute walk from here to Covent Garden for Elisa!"

It was, indeed, just a short walk to Elisa's new position with the London Philharmonic Orchestra. Two minutes farther, in Bloomsbury, was the house where Theo and Anna lived with Dieter and Wilhelm. Murphy's offices as head of Trump European News Services (TENS) were only a short commute to Fleet Street.

Elisa could not imagine any place more perfect. At last, it seemed, through months of heartache, they had come to a place of tranquility.

She quietly hummed a bar from the Bach piece, "What God Has Done Is Rightly Done!" At the sound of her voice Murphy stirred and patted the mattress again. She loved the fact that he looked for her in his sleep, and she was amazed at the ease with which they had settled in. Husband. Wife. The two boys who would soon be legally adopted as their own. It all seemed perfect. And to top off their joy, the surgery to correct Charles' cleft palate had been successful. Soon the identifying mark of his physical deformity, which had put him in the Untermenschen category in the Nazi philosophy, would be barely noticeable. The boy who could not utter words before was now talking! A great miracle, indeed.

The first floor of the house had been used for storage by the former tenant. Elisa had already decided that she would convert it into a studio where she would give violin lessons when she was not playing for Sir Thomas Beecham and the Philharmonic. Her first two pupils would be Charles and Louis, who still favored the cello but agreed to try the violin and the piano since Aunt Leah had gone to Palestine.

Lovely old Georgian paneling extended up the staircase to the rooms above. The woodwork, painted a mellow ivory, gave the house a feeling of brightness. On the second floor, a short hall led from the foyer to a large airy room with three windows facing the square. Here, where the light of morning flooded in to warm the rich oak-planked floors, she

and Murphy shared their morning coffee. He spoke of all the things he
had in mind for the news service; she told him about the reported quirks
of her new conductor and the dozen musicians she had known in Germany and Austria who now played for him.

And when Murphy left for work with his briefcase tucked under his
arm, she lingered over her coffee and imagined evenings of chamber
music in this room with old friends and happy memories.

Next to this room was a smaller room with low heavy rafters that reminded her of the ceilings of the Wattenbarger farmhouse. For some reason the room gave her a sense of sadness; she willingly turned it over to
Murphy for a study. Three days earlier she and Anna had found a wonderful old rolltop desk for him. It had to be hoisted up through the window and now was against the wall opposite the fireplace. *"Like Dickens,"*
she had told him as he explored the maze of cubbyholes and drawers.
Too large to move twice, the desk was proof of Murphy's determination
to remain in England for a long time.

The desk was Murphy's toy. Charles and Louis, on the other hand, had
filled their room with crates and boxes of toys that Mr. Trump had purchased for them at Macy's in New York and then shipped to England.
Train sets and ranks of tin soldiers cluttered the floor until Elisa had rolled
her eyes in despair at the thought of ever sweeping the planks. The newspaper magnate had left no shelf at Macy's untouched. Baseball gloves and
bats like the one Babe Ruth used cluttered one corner. Murphy promised
his chief that he would see to it the boys knew how to swing a bat American style, in spite of the fact they lived in London. Mr. Trump had also
provided the funds to hire a special American tutor for Charles and Louis,
and a speech therapist from Boston who happened to be doing doctoral
work in London. It would not be long before Murphy would be able to
make good on his pledge to read the works of Dickens to the boys.

Up one more flight of stairs was the bedroom where Elisa and
Murphy slept. It was a large room, paneled in the same Georgian style as
the rest of the house. There was room enough for the four-poster "Parade Ground" and an overstuffed sofa in front of an oak-manteled fireplace. Double French doors opened onto a roof garden, where the view
was the entire panorama of London, including the spires of St. Paul's Cathedral. It was too cold to sit outside for very long, but Elisa could easily
imagine what the world would look like when spring came again to Red
Lion Square. Beautiful. Perfect. She could not let herself dwell on all the
tragic reasons why they had come here. She would not let herself con-
template for long the suffering of those who had been betrayed by
peaceful England. For a time, anyway, she longed to rest her heart and
mind. She longed to pretend that everything was just as it seemed to be.

Murphy was being merciful to her. She knew he did not tell her all the things that flooded the wire service. And she did not ask. She did not read his dispatches or open the newspaper. She kept her schedule for British Broadcasting Corporation broadcasts close at hand. Music was all she longed for. When Murphy needed to hear the news, he retreated into his study and closed the heavy walnut door behind him. There were some things her heart could not bear to know. Not now. Not yet. Not while she carried Murphy's child within her.

Elisa turned her eyes back out onto the dreamy old square. Her breath was a vapor on the windowpane as she whispered her thanks. "What You have done is rightly done."

4

One Alone Survived

For Shimon Feldstein, sleep brought no rest or peace. It had been the same each night as they sailed around the Greek islands. The room he shared with Leah on the luxury liner was a suite, but it made no difference that they were surrounded by soft-spoken stewards in white coats. In the daylight hours, Shimon could look around the cruise ship and reason that this was a lifetime away from the cramped, rusty freighter that had carried him from Germany. Each morning in a new, sun-washed port of call, he would look out across the waters and imagine the *Darien*. He would see again the bright, upturned faces of five little girls as they brought him paper lilies and told him stories from the day's Torah-school lesson.

When breakfast was served in the liner's dining room, he could manage to shake off those images. Through hours of wandering the lanes of some small Greek island with Leah, he could replace those dear, lost faces with her face, her smile.

But when the SS *Hildebrand* lifted its anchor to sail on, when the darkness descended and Shimon lay down to sleep, it all came back with crushing grief and horror.

Throbbing engines boomed out the too-familiar rhythm he had known for months aboard the *Darien*. Sometimes the cadence blended into dreams of a symphony he had performed in Vienna. Sometimes the thrumming heartbeat of the great ship intruded on his dreams as the slap of Nazi jackboots on the cobblestones beneath their apartment window, or a giant hammer clanging against glowing metal in the steel mill of Hamburg. In the end, the dream was always the same for Shimon. . . . .

The roar of thunder as lightning split the wind.
Green water above the mast of the Darien. *The groaning of metal as the hand of the deep twisted the freighter like a toy ship.*
The tiny white coffin of Ada-Marie Holbein bobbing to the surface.
The lapping of waves.
His own gasping breath.
A disembodied voice calling out to God for help.
And the silence.

The silence finally awakened him. The engines of the liner slowed and stopped. Chains rattled; the anchor slid beneath the water of yet another Mediterranean port. And Shimon Feldstein sat up in his sweat-soaked berth and gasped from the terror of the nightmare that had all been true. No figment of his imagination. *All of it. True!*

As Leah slept beside him unaware, Shimon climbed from the bed and groped his way toward the morning light streaming through the porthole. He leaned his cheek against the cool glass and breathed deeply as he tried to shake himself free from the images. He forced himself to focus on the stone houses that clung to the slopes of this rocky Greek island. In the half-light they seemed to be a soft pastel blue in color. In the daylight they would be white. On the pebble-strewn beach a fisherman gathered his nets.

Is he the only living being in the silent village? No. He is not like me. There are others sleeping in the blue houses. He is not the only one.

Each morning Shimon eased himself back to sanity in this way. But the question never left him. Why had he alone—of all those onboard the *Darien*—survived?

The London residence of Theo and Anna Lindheim was a tall, narrow brownstone, identical to every other house on their street.

It was tiny indeed, compared with the great Berlin house on Wilhelmstrasse that Hitler had just ordered destroyed. It was even smaller than the Mala Strana house in Prague.

Anna had chosen it for its brightness and for its close proximity to the house of Elisa and Murphy. *"Just a short walk, and we can have tea together. Around the corner from Covent Garden!"* she had said. *"No room for even a baby grand piano? Ah, well, I can still play Chopin and Schubert on an upright!"*

A nice little upright had been found in a dusty secondhand shop down the street. Anna had entertained the shopkeeper and six awed customers by playing the yellowed ivory keys as if they were attached to a concert grand. After a moving performance of Chopin's *Nocturnes*, Anna was able to say, truthfully, that she had purchased the instrument "for a song." The price included delivery up a flight of narrow stairs.

Theo was content with a massive walnut desk that filled half the floor space of a tiny room he called "the study." The room was a far cry from the enormous library of first-edition volumes he had enjoyed in Germany's better days. Opposite his desk were two nearly empty bookshelves.

Theo had talked of visits to London's bookshops in order to gradually fill those shelves. But now there was no time for a leisurely stroll through the booksellers' stalls of St. Paul's. It might be months before Theo could consider reading a book for pleasure.

He had all the reading material one man could handle. Theo raised his eyes over his glasses and shook his head in wonder at the overflowing mailbags that flanked his desk. The British postman had estimated that nearly two thousand letters addressed to Theo had come in the last two weeks. As many as fifty a day were still pouring in—letters from Berlin and Hamburg and Munich, letters from Vienna and Salzburg, postmarks from the mutilated Republic of Czechoslovakia and from faraway Warsaw:

> *Dear Herr Lindheim, as a young man I worked for the great Lindheim's Department Store in Berlin. . . .*

> *Dear Herr Lindheim, we saw your photograph with much amazement here in Germany. It was thought that you were dead. . . .*

> *Dear . . . since my mother was a longtime employee, we were hoping you could . . .*

> *The consulate decrees that we must have a sponsor before we can have a visa. . . .*

> *By a miracle we saw your photograph, and once again we have hope that you might help us. Our father worked in the haberdasher department from 1925 until . . .*

> *It is with much hope that we write you . . .*

Two thousand letters. All different, yet all the same. Desperate. Hopeful. Terrified. The letters asked Theo for help in acquiring a sponsor so that immigration might be allowed.

Ironically, the Nazi press was responsible for the flood of communication Theo faced. A photograph showing Theo with former Czech President Beneš as they had arrived in England had rated only a back-page

space in the London *Times*. The Nazis, however, had splashed the
"traitor-Jew" Lindheim's face across the front page of every official
propaganda sheet in the Reich.

Along with Theo's photograph with Beneš, *Der Stürmer* devoted an
entire page to a violent attack on the Lindheims. The story described
how the famous Berlin department store had grown from a little peddler's shop through typical Jewish trickery and fraud. Theo was described as a "Jewish extortioner" who "exploited his Gentile employees
and seduced young Aryan salesgirls." A picture of the famous store
facade was shown with its Closing Sales signs in the windows. "This is
how the Jew sucks profits from the Aryan public," the caption cried. Beneath that, the address of the British consulate was given so that letters
might be written to extradite this Jewish criminal back to the justice of
the Reich from where he lived regally in London on the stolen money of
the German workers he had exploited!

The response to the Nazi request for justice had been overwhelming.
The letters had come by the tens and by the hundreds to the British consulate. But along with Nazi indignation, two thousand pleas for help had
also managed to reach Theo Lindheim in this little house in London:

> *Herr Lindheim . . . Perhaps you will not remember me. I have
> managed to escape Berlin and now I am in Warsaw. Life is very
> difficult. . . .*

> *We fear for our lives here in Hamburg. Each day it grows more
> violent. . . .*

> *They broke my mother's nose in the market. . . .*

> *My father and brother have been arrested. . . .*

> *If only you could send a letter on our behalf. . . .*

> *We pray that we might go to Palestine. Not to be a burden but only
> to . . .*

> *Might you use your connections to help me, Herr Lindheim? Once
> I worked in the shoe department and if you remember . . .*

The German Reich had not expected such a response. The British
consulate forwarded the mail faithfully to Theo even as it considered the
fierceness of Nazi wrath against him in the other letters that flooded in.

Theo Lindheim had never been a man to straddle a fence. Now, it seemed, that attribute carried over into public attitudes about him as well. Theo was a much-hated man in Germany. He was also a man much loved and trusted. Whatever was England supposed to do with such an enigma?

Theo Lindheim worked far into the night. A pool of light from his desk lamp encircled piles of correspondence, newspaper clippings, and Theo's open Bible.

Anna did not knock as she entered her husband's study with a tray of cookies and a kettle of steaming tea. "Almost finished, Theo?" she asked quietly, mindful that their sons slept in the next room.

He shook his head slowly, then removed his reading glasses and rubbed his tired eyes. "Not finished. Probably will never finish." He spoke in short choppy sentences as if the effort of speaking was too great at such an hour. "It will not end, Anna. We are at war. At war, you see." He laid his hand over the Bible.

Anna placed the tray on a coffee table laden with books and files of correspondence. The rim of light touched the letter from America that Elisa herself had delivered to Theo. The letter was from Trudence Rosenfelt. Bubbe. Anna picked it up and began to read softly.

> *I am an old woman. I have no delusions that my life will go on forever. Indeed, I pray that when my usefulness is at an end, my life will also come to an end. That moment has not yet come to relieve me of the grief I feel over the loss of my dear ones. And so I continue to work, to live, so that their precious lives might also have meaning. So that their deaths might somehow awaken the consciences of good people in every nation. For this reason I ask for your help. . . .*

Anna lowered the page. Her eyes met Theo's.

He spread his hands in a gesture of helplessness. "They are only numbers. Meaningless numbers among the millions, Anna. And the nations say there are too many to help. So it seems they are expendable." He winced. "But each life is precious. As precious and beautiful as the family that old woman lost. Ah, Anna, what can we do?"

He held up yet another letter. This one bore the official seal of the British colonial office. Within its neatly typed lines was the request—the *order*—that Theo and Anna Lindheim, as guests of the British government, restrain themselves from any activities on behalf of illegal immigrants.

"They have tied our hands," Theo concluded. Ignoring this "request" would no doubt result in their expulsion from Great Britain, possibly even a deportation to Germany. "We have Wilhelm and Dieter to think about. Our own family. We cannot share this burden with Elisa. Not now. She deserves some time of happiness before . . ." His voice faded. He wanted to say *"before war comes,"* but he did not. "She needs this time," he finished simply.

Anna poured two cups of tea. Her eyes were full of sympathy for Theo's feeling of helplessness. Had she not felt the same impotence in Prague? Had God not given her a vision, a way to reach out in the midst of such darkness?

"Theo—" she managed a sad smile—"those people, the numbers you speak of, they are each precious in the sight of God. The very hairs of our heads are numbered—so it is written. We must only be willing to dedicate our hands to the service of God's love. Then He will assign our tasks to us. We must not be overwhelmed by the vastness of the problem, sweet husband."

A touch of sugar. A drop of cream. Theo sipped his tea and considered the truth of Anna's words for a long time. This was the Covenant. *God would not refuse the prayer of a willing heart!* Theo had learned this much in the hell of Dachau, where men became numbers—still loved by God, yet mere numbers to the Nazis.

"I alone survived that place," Theo whispered. Anna understood his words. "Like Bubbe Rosenfelt, I alone survived. There must be some reason. Some reason why I am here to sip tea with you in London, Anna, while the rest of our world suffers so needlessly."

"The Lord will untie your hands, Theo, when your hands are ready. Rested. Strong again. Until then we will watch and pray together that we will make a difference even to one among the millions."

Ernst vom Rath felt the presence of danger at his back as he boarded the Paris subway nearest the German Embassy in Paris. He tried not to peer over his shoulder. What would he see, anyway? The faces of a thousand weary Parisians traveling home after work. If he was being followed by Gestapo—and he was almost certain of the fact—his pursuer would wear the face of a Frenchman. Frayed coat. Black beret. Shoes run down at the heels. Everyone on the crowded train felt like the enemy. Ernst disciplined himself not to look, not to guess who it might be.

He held the leather strap as the buzzer shrilled its warning. Doors slid shut with a loud crash. Wheels clacked against the tracks, and lights in the tunnel passed with a strobe effect over the faces of the commuters.

Ernst did not even know where he was going. Had he even bothered to consult the marquee? He had not thought beyond leaving the embassy building for a few hours, escaping the tortured reminders of how

Thomas had killed Georg Wand. Ernst was just as guilty as Thomas. They had whispered their treason together before the votive candles of Notre Dame. They had gazed out over Paris from the observation platform of the Eiffel Tower. They had not spoken of Paris, however. Their thoughts had been directed to Berlin. Their hopes had taken the shape of plans for an end of the Nazi stranglehold over their people and their land.

A voice crackled over the speaker. "Metro L'Opera." Doors popped and slid open even before the train came to a full stop. Ernst pushed through the crowd and stepped from the train. He had no reason for disembarking here. He felt himself flush with the memory that here, at the opera, Thomas had killed Georg Wand. *Why have I come here?* He backed up a step as crowds surged around him. He turned as if to reboard. Too late! The doors slammed in his face. He spun around again and followed the hundreds up the steep stairs to the diminishing light of dusk and the bustle of the broad avenue that faced the ornate opera building.

Vom Rath mopped his brow. Here in the chilly autumn evening there was no physical reason for the beads of perspiration on his brow. He stopped at a newsstand and pretended to peruse the racks of postcards. Pretended that he was not drawn with morbid fascination to the place where Thomas had killed Georg Wand.

"You would like a picture postcard, monsieur?" asked an aging, stoop-shouldered vendor as Ernst passed his fingers absently over a card bearing the image of the Eiffel Tower. *We stood just here, Thomas and I. We talked of hope for Germany without Hitler. He told me about the girl he had loved.*

"Monsieur?" the vendor asked again. "Three for the price of two."

Ernst dug in his pocket, paid the man, and slipped the postcards into his coat. He raised his eyes to the building where the greatest musicians of Europe played, regardless of their race. And he remembered the reason Thomas had killed Georg Wand. He raised his chin slightly as the cold breeze stung his cheeks. Taking a place at a dusty outdoor table in a nearly deserted café, Ernst pulled out his pen and began to write. He prayed that if he must also die, death would come quickly, that he would not have a chance to betray anyone.

A postcard to mother. One to my sister. They must know that I love them. That I think of them.

The last postcard he addressed to another opera house—in London.

"Friday again, Rebbe Lebowitz," Hannah Cohen hailed the old rabbi as he hurried past the steps of Tipat Chalev. "Any word about your daughter, Etta, in Warsaw? You are a grandfather again yet?" Hannah swept the steps, although there was no sign of even a speck of dust.

The old man shrugged. "The child will be two months old and reciting Torah before I hear any word," he replied with a grimace. "Still—" he held up his weekly offering to the mailbox—"you see I have a letter to mail, *nu*? Every week it is the same—I beg them to come home to Jerusalem, and they send me clippings about how terrible it is here!"

"Things are better in Warsaw, I ask you?" Hannah leaned on her broom as Rabbi Lebowitz paused.

"At least here it is not so cold in the autumn."

"Give me a nice Muslim neighbor any day. Compared to those Catholic anti-Semites in Warsaw the Muslims are saints!" The old woman raised her eyes toward heaven, as if she could visualize Muslim saints flying above her. Then her expression changed from benevolence to one of disapproval. "*Oy! Gottenyu!* Rebbe Lebowitz," she cried and pointed the broom skyward. "They're burning rubber tires *again*!"

The old man's gaze followed the upraised broom to where a dense cloud of black smoke billowed up from Allenby Square. "So much for Muslim saints." He scratched his head and grimaced down at his envelope. "The mailing will have to wait, I suppose, until the British soldiers put the fire out. But then again, it's only a little smoke. Better to mail it."

"*Phui!* Such a stink! *Oy gevalt!* Why don't these Arabs burn something else beside old tires for a change?" She waved her hand in front of her nose and then rushed into Tipat Chalev to slam down the windows.

The old man stared up at the first cloud of smoke and then back to where another and yet another cloud rose up to blacken the bright morning above the city. He clucked his tongue in disappointment and coughed at the stench that now pervaded everything.

He resented this. He resented this more than the closing of Arab shops in the marketplace. More than Muslim chants from the Haram. These stinking black clouds would soil the wash on every clothesline, make every bite of food unpalatable, spread a film of coarse black residue on every roof and step and stick of furniture in Jerusalem.

Will these Arab children never run out of old tires to burn? the rabbi wondered.

Hannah poked her head out of the door. Black ash was falling. "All over my steps!" she cried. And then, "You had better not mail your letter today, Rebbe Lebowitz. Looks like the biggest fire is just in Allenby Square."

The old man waved away her warning with a gnarled hand. These tire burnings presented little chance of danger. With such a stink in the air, even the most militant Arab also was forced to retreat indoors to wait until the fires died.

Rabbi Lebowitz covered his head and face with his coat and trudged on as shop grates slammed around him and furious Armenian shop-keepers rescued their displays of merchandise from the street.

Every native of Jerusalem knew that this murky display was for the benefit of the pristine English lords who traveled to Palestine with their notebooks open. Of everything they would see, nothing would make an impression on them as profound as these heaping mounds of burning rubber. Smoke and fire. This was the image they would take home with them to England.

Such foolishness, Lord. True? Of course true. The rabbi shook his head.

Just so no one missed the point, flaming tire bonfires would also blacken the skies of other cities in Palestine. Haifa, Jaffa—anywhere there were English eyes to see and English noses to smell.

Rabbi Lebowitz ducked down a side street that led to the Armenian Patriarchate Road. He walked close to the facades of the buildings as the smoke darkened the sun. The street was nearly deserted. British soldiers in gas masks, resembling giant insects, stood watch from the stone walls. Swathed in smoke and shifting degrees of darkness, they seemed like strange, unearthly creatures, the stuff that nightmares and visions are made of.

5

The Hiding Place

Today the Grand Mufti spoke to his flock with the help of a loudspeaker. Rabbi Lebowitz could hear his voice as it floated over the walls that surrounded the Dome of the Rock. As Haj Amin called for rebellion and commanded hatred, his voice stirred the passions of ten thousand Muslims more than any other voice had done since the time of Saladin.

The roar of cheering worshipers erupted at the end of a sentence. Haj Amin Husseini was certainly one example of English foolishness. The British government had put him firmly in place as Grand Mufti, and since that day there had been no real peace in Jerusalem.

Another roar rose up. The faithful liked whatever Haj Amin told them. It was hard to make out the words exactly. The voice crackled amid static from the PA system powered by British electricity.

The old man shrugged and walked quickly through the winding streets. Everywhere Jewish shopkeepers had stepped from their stalls to stand in small groups and strain their ears to hear what Haj Amin was up to now. No one seemed to notice the rabbi as he made his way past familiar faces of friends and neighbors. He knew that Haj Amin would continue to shout his Friday sermon for at least another hour. That was certainly time enough for him to get to the post office in Allenby Square and back. It was the best time for him to leave the Quarter, he reasoned. After all, the Arab populace was crammed into the Haram instead of out on the streets.

Muslim voices rolled like a wave over the entire Old City. To his right and left along Rehov Habad, the stalls of Jewish and Armenian merchants began to close. Beneath the domed roof of the souk, men and women stared up at the vaulted ceiling as if it might fall on them. The religious rallies of Haj Amin always had that effect on Christians, Armenians, and Jews alike. It was hard to say what might follow these fanatic tirades. The last twelve years had borne witness to what the twisted hatred of one man in power could accomplish.

"Rebbe Lebowitz!" shouted Memel the basket maker. "Where are you going?" He had his entire display moved indoors and was just locking the metal grate.

"To the post office to mail a letter to Etta and the children!" the rabbi answered without slowing.

"Better wait! You can't hear that crazy man? He is in a very bad mood today!"

"It is Friday," he explained. There was no need for further explanation. Everyone knew that on Friday Rabbi Lebowitz mailed a letter to his daughter in Warsaw. It was the last thing he did before Shabbat services began—his way of sending a blessing to his only child and the grandchildren.

"*Shabbat shalom*," Memel called nervously. The words meant "Sabbath peace," but from the sound of things there would be little peace this Sabbath.

"*Shabbat shalom!*" The rabbi returned the greeting, which was lost beneath a resounding cry of "*Allah Akhbar!* God is great! God is great!"

He quickened his pace. The back of his neck prickled with an uneasy sense of what could happen in Jerusalem after such a sermon. The graveyards were full of reminders of what had happened before. He fingered the letter in his pocket. Nothing would happen. The Muslims always ended their Fridays with this tumult of shouts and chants. Why should today be different? This was the safest time for a Jew to walk out of Jaffa Gate. The safest time. When all of them were—

"And Allah has promised the faithful that the time is near when the Holy City will no longer be occupied by infidels! The end is near for them!" Suddenly the words sounded clearly along the Street of the Chain. Had someone turned a speaker this direction from the wall of the mosque? Did the Mufti mean for everyone in the Old City to hear these threatening words?

Not one shop remained open. The Suq el-Bazaar was shuttered tight. David Street was empty except for two Copt priests hurrying away in their flowing black robes. The towers on either side of Jaffa Gate were lined with British soldiers who looked pensively toward the shiny Dome of the Rock.

Omar Square, usually a picture postcard of activity, was deserted. The old man stopped and gazed toward the New City beyond the gate. It was only a short walk to Allenby Square from here, but his uneasiness escalated into a fresh and wild sense of fear. A soldier cupped his hand and shouted down, "Old man! What are you doing? Get indoors!"

Foolish. He saw how foolish he had been. He should have turned around the first time he heard the roaring passion of Haj Amin's followers! Things were not as they had been—they were getting worse every day, every minute! He should have known. Armenians do not shut their shops for no reason. How many times had the people of the Old City witnessed violence erupting like a storm? It had come without warning. Was this such a day?

"Old man!" shouted the soldier in Yiddish. "Get to your house!"

The rabbi's eyes widened as the rattle of gunfire sounded from behind. The dam had broken. A sea of violence swept toward him. Shouts and screams drowned out the warning of the soldier. The crackling sound of bullets aimed at nothing, yet meant to kill everything!

Rabbi Lebowitz turned to see where he might run. Everywhere the shops were shut. It was half a block to the closest side street. He could not run back now. Instead he ran forward toward Jaffa Gate. He glanced up toward the soldier who had shouted, but the man had disappeared.

"*Allah Akhbar!* For Allah and the prophet!" voices called out.

The rabbi ran as fast as he could. He hugged the face of the shops, searching for some opening, praying for some crevice to hide in until the storm swept past. He was old. He *felt* old. As never before, he felt years hanging on his legs, holding him back from the road of the Armenians.

Breath came hard, yet he managed to breathe the name of God. He cried for help! English guns took aim over the heads of the mob. Fire and smoke burst from their rifles. Shrieks of alarm wailed at his back. Had any Arab rioters fallen in that volley?

Bullets whined above the old man's head, and he dashed toward the corner where he imagined safety to be. There was lead in his shoes. The nightmare of a body that would not respond became reality. He stumbled and fell, tearing his trousers and bloodying his knees.

Get up, old man, or you will die!

And then he was on his feet, half running, half crawling toward the corner. A slim dark crack was visible between two shops. With his last ounce of strength, the rabbi clutched the edge of the hard stone and pulled himself forward into the tiny space.

Within seconds the mob swarmed past. Women, their hair loose and wild, shrieked with the same venom as the men. Those docile followers who had entered the holy gates of the Dome of the Rock this morning now tore their clothes, hurled stones, and shot their British-made rifles into the air and through the windows of the shops and houses.

In the shadow of his hiding place, Rabbi Lebowitz clutched at the pain in his chest. He fought to breathe and used his breath to pray that no Muslim would discover him while they shouted, "Death to Jews! Death to Zionists! Death to the British oppressors!"

He could not guess how many thousands surged by. How many passed through Jaffa Gate and Damascus Gate into the New City? He did not look at their faces anymore. But there was one thing he noticed, one sign that marked the depth of their frenzy—the rioters were all *barefoot*! Not one had stopped to put on shoes before the hysteria had pushed them into the streets. Bare feet. Empty shoes and empty prayer rugs on the stones of the Temple Mount.

The last of the rioters straggled past. Old men and old women. Their faces reflected the same bitter hatred as the young who had gone before them. And then there was silence. Stifling heat. The hum of flies and the distant crackle of gunfire.

Rabbi Lebowitz dared not move from his hiding place.

The Promised Land. Holy Land. Zion. All these phrases that had once seemed so near to the heart of Leah Feldstein did not reflect the truth of those first moments when dreams, at last, became reality.

From the harbor, the flat, drab skyline of Tel Aviv was a shabby comparison to the Ringstrasse of Vienna. The sun beat down unmercifully on the heads of passengers onboard the SS *Hildebrand* as they hung against the rails to absorb first impressions of their new homeland.

At the far end of the docks the rusting hulk of a cattle boat was moored beside a small British gunboat. British soldiers roamed the decks in search of hidden refugees.

"Tried to get past the British navy," observed a passenger who stood next to Leah. "Poor fools. What do they think will become of them now?"

Leah turned her eyes away from the captured vessel. She tried to smile at the pitiful collection of buildings lining the docks. This was Zion. The Jewish homeland. She should feel joy, but she could not. She felt nothing but a dull ache for Shimon as he stared at the cattle boat and remembered another ship, other pilgrims.

Shimon's arm was still immobilized in a plaster cast. Sweat trickled down between the cast and his skin. It was so hot, even in October, when the trees of the Vienna woods would be turning a thousand shades of red and gold. They had talked about the heat of Zion, discussed the aridness of the land and the malarial swamps of Galilee. Yes, they had dreamed of the glorious sunlight on this land when the rain had kept them indoors with their fiddles and pots of hot coffee. Yes, they had dreamed. But they could not have imagined what it was *really* like.

"Well, here we are, Shimon!" Leah tried to sound cheerful, but the brightness of her voice quavered slightly. When Shimon glanced at her, she knew he was aware of what she was really thinking.

Tugboats nudged the ship against the dock. Thick ropes were thrown down to men who shouted and cursed in a strange language. All along the waterfront were stacks of crates and swarms of flies and dogs and beggars and urchins and donkeys and muck.

"You are not really going to do it, are you?" Shimon asked grimly.

"Do what?"

"You said that as soon as you stepped on the soil of Palestine, you would kneel and kiss the earth."

Leah shook her head slowly. No. That was one vow she would not keep. In the photographs there had been no flies, rotting fish guts, camel droppings. The photographs had been clean and perfect. They had not revealed the heat that now beat against their backs like hammers. They had not smelled. Black-and-white photos had been studied with the same adoration one studies paintings by Monet or Renoir. Now that the waterfront was a fact before their eyes, Leah could see that nearly everything was still black and white and varying shades of gray. The sky was blue, of course, and the water was blue. She had guessed that, but she had never dreamed that Tel Aviv could be so entirely drab.

A long metal shed stretched along the wharf. A white sign with blue lettering spelled *H. M. CUSTOMS AND IMMIGRATION*. This was written first in English, then in the fluid script of Arabic, then in the blocky alphabet of Hebrew. Six British officials stood outside the building and watched the docking of the *Hildebrand* from beneath their shadowed visors. They, too, seemed to be a part of the sameness of the scene—all dressed in khaki, all with the same tight disgust on their faces, waiting for this latest load of European Jews to pass beneath the tin roof of His Majesty's customs house before they emerged into the life of Zionist Palestine. Like a troop of warriors they waited, daring anyone to try to get past their stations with forged papers or smuggled weapons or some undeclared taxable item.

The last matter was really of little concern lately. With the passage of time and the tightening of Reich regulations, the Jews had come through the shed with less and less. Still, there were always a few who thought they could sneak by.

Bullhorns shouted directions in a dozen languages. All luggage was piled into one net on the deck of the ship and then lowered like a catch of fresh herring onto the dock.

Leah had been forced to argue hotly that her cello could not be treated so casually. This discussion took place with a fellow who had never heard of Bach, never seen a cello. What did he care?

Tearful appeals were made to the captain, who was mercifully sober for the second time on the journey. Yes, he would radio the customs authorities. The instrument—what was it again?—could be hand-carried off the ship, but must be immediately handed over to a British official for inspection.

A splintered wooden gangplank crashed into place, and the final crossing into the Promised Land took place single file and very cautiously. There were actually some displays of emotion when Jewish soles touched hallowed ground. One Orthodox-looking fellow from Latvia actually did drop to his knees and kiss the ground, such as it was. Leah clung tightly to the cello and to Shimon's big hand. She tried not to step in anything unpleasant. She tried not to think of Vienna—its beauty and elegance. Of course, there was no more Vienna. Vienna had died, almost taking her and Shimon with it. No, Leah would not let herself think back and remember the golden days. She must turn her eyes to the land of their future and their hope.

Her chin quivered slightly. Why hadn't Moses wandered farther north? It seemed that a forty-year odyssey could have brought the children of Israel someplace more picturesque—like Italy, or the southern coast of France.

FORM LINES HERE! This sign was written in several languages besides Hebrew and Arabic and English. These British fellows were catching on—most of the people in their lines read languages like German and Polish and Czech . . . especially Czech, these days.

A grim-faced customs agent marched up to where Leah and Shimon stood. He scowled and postured as he looked at the cello case.

"Who said you could carry that off the ship?" he demanded, extending his hand to take it from her. "Against regulations!"

"Very valuable instrument," Leah sputtered. "Centuries old. *Please* be careful."

The man muttered, "Regulations!" and turned his back on her.

With a little cry, Leah put her hand against her aching head. "Whatever did Moses see in this place? I *ask* you!" Her indignation caused slight smiles on faces around her. All except for one sad-eyed little man who was sweating profusely in his European-made wool suit. He tapped her lightly on the shoulder and pointed a hundred yards down the waterfront, where several hundred illegal refugees from the captured cattle boat were caged behind a wire fence. They were guarded by soldiers with guns. Men. Women. Children. Ragged, haunted-looking people like the ones Leah had seen at every turn in Europe, like those who had perished aboard the *Darien.*

Shimon drew his breath in sharply at the sight of them. Crates of oranges were stacked just beyond their reach outside the fence. Only the flies of Palestine passed freely through the wire.

"At least they are alive," Shimon managed.

Suddenly Leah felt ashamed. Why was her heart not thankful that they had arrived here with legal documents when there were so very many who tried to come but were kept out? How could she forget so soon after Austria? after all that Shimon had told her?

The people behind the wire began to sing a mournful dirge. *"Vi aheen zoll ich gain?* Wherever shall I go?" This was the anthem of the coffin ships. Shimon had once sung this song with those who had not found any harbor in this life. He stopped in the slowly moving line and watched and listened. So many longed for this place. How many would not make it? How many would do anything to stand in this line and brush away the flies and bless the heat of the sun?

Leah tugged his sleeve. "Come along, Shimon. Come, love. We cannot help them now, but we can live for them, *nu?* Come along, Shimon."

Inside the immigration shed Leah found a bench and sat beside Shimon as they waited for their names to be called. Shimon sat, silent and preoccupied, as she took out her pen and began to write the letter she had promised Elisa.

> *Dearest Elisa,*
> *I did not kiss the ground of Palestine, but I am glad we are here all the same. . . .*

Outside on the Tel Aviv dock, six distinguished-looking Englishmen chatted among themselves as their luggage was unloaded from a British naval launch. Diesel fumes rose from the sputtering engine, adding another element of unpleasantness to their first stifling moment in the Promised Land.

Captain Samuel Orde looked on as lordly glances were cast in the direction of the caged refugees.

"What are the Jews singing about?" asked one of the men with a hint of irritation.

Orde had heard the song before. "They are asking where they will go," he explained, concealing his own emotion at the sad refrain.

"Where they should go?" a member of the group bellowed. The disdain on his face was evident. "What business is it of His Majesty's government *where* they go? That's the trouble with these Jewish beggars. They expect us to provide for them after they've got themselves into a corner."

"Quite right," agreed a second member of this latest British venture, the Woodhead Royal Commission of Inquiry. He mopped his brow and then adjusted the brim of his Panama hat lower against the sun. "Things have changed in Palestine over the last year—and not for the better; that is obvious. We'll have to review this partition and immigration question very carefully again."

Captain Orde tugged the brim of his own cap lower so these eminent British politicians would not read the anger in his eyes. He held his tongue as he had a thousand times before. *Woodhead,* he thought. *An appropriate name for this group. When they see thousands of acres of Zionist citrus orchards destroyed by Arab marauders, I suppose they'll ask what appeasement they might make for the Arabs to settle down.* Spain was in the midst of a civil war, after all, so the British Mandate of Palestine had become the chief source of oranges. Now that was being interrupted. What would hasten the return of order? *Cut Jewish immigration?* Orde thought bitterly. *Limit the land sales to Jewish settlers? Give the Arab leadership what they want? Forget about the 1917 British promise of a Jewish homeland?*

The Jewish refugees inside the cage let their dark eyes linger on the group of officials. Hostile glances were returned by the British in reply to such impudence. Did these Jews dare to sing their little song to the government of England?

"There are procedures for immigration," remarked yet another commission member. His aristocratic face was unmoved. "If *they* want to get into the British Mandate, *they* should have followed the procedures." The man eyed Orde. "Isn't that right, Captain Orde?"

Orde hesitated, resisting the impulse to shove the entire lot of these haughty gentlemen into the water. "Hitler at their backs with clubs . . ." His voice cracked. He was having difficulty finding words. "What choice have they?"

The man in the Panama hat interrupted. He was irritated. "None of our business," he sniffed, turning his back on the captain.

"Feldstein! Leah and Shimon Feldstein!" The harsh voice of the British immigrations officer echoed through the enormous tin building.

The sound of her own name and the din of a thousand voices startled Leah. Shimon nudged her slightly, urging her back to reality.

She nodded and tucked her pen back into the thin writing case. She would finish the letter later. There was so much she wanted to share with

Elisa. Paper would not hold the myriad thoughts and emotions that assaulted her every passing moment.

The long lines of immigrants at the ten desks had diminished. One by one the holders of legal documents were passing from one side of the shed to the other, where representatives of the Jewish Agency gathered them into groups for transportation to tent cities where they would be initiated into the life of a Zionist in Palestine.

"Feldstein!" the Englishman roared impatiently.

"Hurry, Leah." Shimon was nervous. He had not recovered from the thought that these British immigration fellows had the authority to throw them behind wire for deportation. Such power *must not* be kept waiting!

"Yes. Shimon and Leah Feldstein." Shimon presented passports with visas to the tight-lipped officer who barely glanced up as he checked the official seals against the names on his clipboard.

"You have family in Jerusalem," he said flatly.

"My great-aunt," Shimon answered softly.

"All the same, with the Arab demonstrations, you are required to stay at one of the refugee centers." He shrugged and stamped the papers.

Shimon and Leah exchanged looks of relief at the thump of the rubber stamp on their documents. So. It was official. They could pass through to the other side of the desk. Only two desks to the right, a young couple with two children had been escorted into a private office. Such a procedure did not bode well for the little family.

"How long will we be delayed from entering Jerusalem?" Shimon asked, almost bowing. Beads of perspiration stood out on his forehead.

"Out of my hands." The officer slapped the documents into Shimon's palm. "Up to the colonial office. They'll decide when it's safe enough. Quite common, these delays. A little welcome from the Arabs for the Woodhead Commission from England."

"That is all?" Leah laughed. How very different this was, compared to the brutality they had witnessed toward illegal immigrants. Once again her heart measured out the vastness of their good fortune. The contrast was amazing. How could they mind a slight delay?

Luggage, including Leah's precious cello, was stacked in giant piles in the center of the concrete floor. Each item was marked with blue chalk to indicate that it had passed inspection for contraband.

Leah stood in front of the jumbled heap as she searched for her cello case. They had already informed her that all luggage would be hauled separately to the induction center, but she could hardly imagine traveling without her instrument.

Holding Shimon's uninjured hand, she slowly circled the pyramid until at last she spotted the case near the top.

Only then could she turn her attention toward the groups of immigrants gathered beneath signs that named their countries of origin: *GERMANY. AUSTRIA. HUNGARY. POLAND. FRANCE. ENGLAND.*

A babble of European languages filled the room. A thousand questions were being hurled at the Jewish Agency representatives all at the same moment. Answers to panicked voices were always calm, always polite—always meant to quell the fears of those who had come from the verdant beauty of Europe to this forbidding place.

"Tents! *Nu!* We are going to live in tents?"

"Will the tents have floors?"

"Can I stay with my husband?"

"Do we stay together by families?"

"You mean we have left Warsaw to come live in *tents*? *Oy!*"

Within each language group, smaller cliques of Orthodox Jews stood beside angry young students who were eager and ready to take their places in the wilderness settlements. All had reasons why they should not be confined to the indoctrination center. The Hasidim were eager to pray in Jerusalem. The socialists had already studied farming and the principles of Zionism.

How brave these Jewish Agency representatives are to come here and take on such a group of disillusioned pilgrims, Leah thought as she and Shimon made their way through the confusion.

Shimon squeezed her hand. He had seen this before. Onboard the *Darien,* he had learned that the title *Jew* had a thousand variations and nuances. Onboard the *Darien* they had somehow ironed out their differences. They had become one working unit that had lived together in relative peace and had finally died together. It would be so for these would-be Zionists. It *must* be so if they were to survive!

Leah had never imagined so many different kinds of Chosen People all trying to be heard at the same moment. *Moses had it easy compared to this,* she thought, making a mental note that she must write Elisa about the odd assortment of people who all called themselves Jews.

As if he had read her thoughts, Shimon leaned down and whispered in Leah's ear, "Like an orchestra tuning up. That is all. You will see, Leah. We will all find the same note eventually."

6

Watchdogs

Only the occasional crack of rifle fire broke the utter stillness of the Jerusalem streets. Wedged tightly into his refuge, Rabbi Lebowitz wondered how it was possible that a city the size of Jerusalem could be so silent, as if a giant hand had reached down to scoop up every living creature. Only he remained, and ten feet farther back in the spacer, a calico cat nursed five kittens.

The old man was grateful for the mother cat, who seemed unperturbed by his presence or the events unfolding beyond this shelter. When the rattle of guns erupted and his heart began to pound like a hammer, he looked at the cat. The cat looked back and blinked pleasantly at the intruder.

Three kittens were gray. One was calico, a duplicate of the mother, and one kitten was purest white with wide blue eyes. Certainly this was an ecumenical group; all shared equally in the bounty of the mother cat. They tumbled blissfully over one another and occasionally toddled forward in a coy attack on the rabbi's cuffs.

A burst of machine-gun fire rattled in the street. The rabbi gasped and instinctively covered his head as a bullet whistled by the opening. There was not enough room for him to crouch down between the buildings. He could only stand and lean against the cool hewn stone of the souvenir-shop wall. His legs and back ached in this position, but there was no help for that. He felt lucky to be alive.

The kittens purred and meowed. They arched their backs and hopped about in mock warfare. The old man watched them. Amazingly he was able to smile. *Who would believe this?* he wondered. *An old man caught between two buildings in the middle of a cross fire, and I can smile!* If he lived through this day he must make a prayer of blessing for the cats of Jerusalem who kept him from going crazy!

Machine guns again. Closer. A block away. A scream of someone who must be dying. English? Arab? Jew? Is it someone like me who only wants to go home?

The old man blinked and forced himself to look at the kittens. The white wide-eyed piece of fluff moved cautiously toward the big strange thing that shivered at the door of their den. Paws danced sideways toward him, then stopped and backed and started forward again more slowly. The kittens had seen thousands of human feet pass by, but none had ever stopped and stayed so long!

"Come, little one," the old man whispered as he extended a foot toward it. His own whisper sounded too loud. More bullets whistled by. He had not heard the report of a gun, but the bullets seemed to be flying up the street all the same. He dared not stretch his head out for even a quick look.

The white kitten was attacked from the rear by a gray brother, and the two tumbled over and over in a playful battle.

Rabbi Lebowitz heard the engines of a vehicle—the grinding of gears just beyond Jaffa Gate. His heart lifted. *British! It must be British soldiers!*

Did he dare run to them? He imagined himself slipping from the hiding place and crouching to run toward the British vehicle. Across Omar Square? Every gun must be trained on the square. Snipers would have their rifles aimed at Jaffa Gate, where he must pass.

The end of the imagined sprint to the English side of the lines left the old man certain that he would be dead before he took two steps from this place.

Sweat dripped from his gray hair. He was thirsty. His tongue felt swollen and parched like leather. The kittens nursed happily again as the old man watched. It would be a long time until he could drink again, if ever, God willing. Maybe tonight he could sneak out and somehow make it through the Armenian Quarter that bordered his own neighborhood. Maybe.

The engine of the vehicle roared away down Jaffa Road. The city fell silent again. Not even the birds dared to sing. The pigeons roosting on the spires of the minarets and the domes of churches and synagogues alike remained in their nests as if to see which of their hosts would be victorious. The bells of the great churches did not ring out the hours.

There was only one certain sign that time passed. Afternoon shadows lengthened across the cobblestone of Omar Square like the finger of a sundial. The old man guessed that it was nearly four o'clock. The others would be frantic with worry, and somehow this knowledge was a comfort to Rabbi Shlomo Lebowitz.

God had sent the kittens to help him get through the ordeal. He would personally see to it that this mother cat was fed scraps every day . . . that is, if he could only get back to Tipat Chalev alive!

More gunfire rattled clearly from the rooftops not a block away, answered from David's Tower. Another scream . . .

The old man groaned and closed his eyes. Death was a near and tangible presence. Eighteen inches from him, the street was alive with fresh volleys!

He whispered the Shema: "Hear, O Israel! The Lord our God is one Lord!" This he said for the sake of the dying even though he could not know if they were Christian or Muslim or Jew. Death was turning its hollow black eyes slowly around Omar Square to see whom it might devour. The old man's breath was shallow as he felt Death probe this small space between the souvenir shop and tourist information building. *Yes!* Death had noticed that someone might be hiding there! Had it seen the old rabbi?

He trembled. He turned his head away and again watched the frolicking little family. He forced himself to study the colors and markings. White paws on the littlest gray kitten. White snip on the nose of another. The last strutting, brazen gray kitten was without even a dash of white. The little calico was shy and sweet. She nestled beneath the chin of her mother while the white kitten batted at the mother cat's tail.

I thank You, O Eternal, for kittens and cats! The rabbi's prayer was silent. He did not want to tempt the ominous Darkness that strolled the streets. It might hear and stop to look.

The London morning was scented with the imminent rain, damp wool coats, and the diesel fumes of the unwieldy double-decker buses that roared past.

Elisa inhaled deeply. It seemed like months since she had felt such freedom. *To work again! To play in an orchestra conducted by the great Sir Thomas Beecham!* How Elisa had admired the man at the Bayreuth festivals as he had conducted the works of Wagner! He was, like Toscanini, one of the maestros of Europe who was beyond politics, but not beyond honor. Elisa heard that he had made room for at least thirty Jewish musicians who had been expelled from Germany's orchestras over the last four years. Elisa was number thirty-one.

A raindrop landed on her cheek and then another and another. So many tears had been shed, but the London rain was washing those memories away.

She put up her umbrella, but only for the sake of the precious Guarnerius violin. She did not mind the downpour that followed a few seconds later. No morning had ever seemed as perfect as this one.

The Friday of Elisa's rehearsal had been a day to look forward to for Charles and Louis. Theo had promised he and Anna would take them to the zoo.

But the London rain poured down, sending lions and tigers scurrying to the shelter of their caves. American grizzly bears shook themselves and peered out at the empty bars where normally thousands of specta-tors stood. This was a day when all sensible creatures remained indoors.

"I'd rather be drinking a cup of tea before a fire," Anna said as Theo took Charles and Louis by the hand and dashed through the puddled sidewalk to the subway station.

"I should have known when my leg began to complain last night." Theo paid the fare as Anna shook the water from their umbrella. "Ah, well. We will be the only tourists in London today! Probably the only ones in the entire British Museum."

This thought was exciting to the boys, who had heard tales of trea-sures from Egyptian pyramids and golden coffins with mummies inside. For such a sight they would gladly forego seeing dripping elephants and slimy reptiles.

Bubbe Rosenfelt had taken Charles to three museums in New York. None of them had mummies, so this excursion might surpass any other for the two Kronenberger boys. Louis had never been to a museum; he could not imagine the vastness with which the British Museum was de-scribed by Theo. And when he first laid eyes on the huge building with its Ionic portico, he could not imagine that *all this* had been built just for a place to store old mummies.

Only a handful of die-hard tourists stood at the ticket kiosk. All were older people, Charles observed—American, mostly. He could tell by their comparatively stylish clothes and conversations in the peculiar dia-lect that Murphy used. There were no children. English children were all in school today. Perhaps there would be tours of schoolchildren later, but such a possibility made Charles hope that the rain would never stop. He still did not enjoy the thought of meeting other children.

The marbled entrance of the British Museum went up and up. The rain from the boys' slickers made puddles on the floor while they craned their necks backward.

Theo studied the map in search of the Egyptian antiquities sections. "Books and manuscripts to the right. Roman sculptures to the left. Upper floor . . . medieval . . . glass and ceramics . . . ha! North wing!" he cried and set off across the foyer with his peculiar limp, looking like a wounded explorer.

They followed arrows and signs up the broad staircases, through rooms with ancient bronze statues and golden masks, past shining armor and cases displaying weapons that might well have killed Spanish conquistadors in an Aztec temple. Onward marched the four solitary tourists, onward toward the Egyptian antiquities department.

It was Charles who first noticed they were not alone. In each room, along each corridor, another tourist followed at a discreet distance. When Theo paused to read and explain a sign, the small man in the English tweed jacket and trousers also paused, leaned forward to examine something, cast a look toward the little group, then resumed walking when Theo progressed to another display.

Perhaps it was a lifetime of being followed, stared at, and pursued that made Charles finally tug at Theo's sleeve and nod toward the man. Theo was also attuned to being tailed. But here in London? He had hoped it would not be the case.

From ceramics to prints, from Etruscan artifacts to Phoenician antiquities, the little man did not deviate from their path. He did not attempt to conceal the fact that he was tailing them. If anything, his routine— pause, look, glance sideways, and walk on—was so obvious that at last Theo exchanged unhappy looks with Anna, turned, and walked directly toward the man.

The little man smiled as Theo spoke to him in an impatient whisper. The man inclined his head slightly and looked toward Anna and the boys, who stared back openly. His smile broadened. He nodded as if to greet them. He gestured with an open hand toward the entrance to the extensive collection of mummies. Theo bowed slightly as if to thank him and then returned to their little party.

"Well?" Anna asked softly.

"Polite people, these English," Theo answered.

"Well?" she asked again, this time in French so the boys would not understand Theo's reply.

He answered in French. "Yes. We are being followed. Watched. This fellow makes it sound as if it is all for my own good."

"Perhaps it is. The Nazis have not stopped raving about you, Theo. Perhaps it is not a bad thing to have the British government take an interest."

Theo took her hand. He nudged Charles gently and encouraged them to run ahead into the hall where the mummies were displayed. Then he led her back alone to where the Englishman had remained at a discreet distance.

"Mr. Beckham," Theo said, not unkindly, "please explain to my wife the purpose of your assignment."

Mr. Beckham was as pleasant as a shopkeeper—polite, soft-spoken, and straightforward. "Your connections with the immigration of Jewish illegals is quite well known. You are guests in our country. My superiors hope you will be respectful of our laws. It would be a pity if you were approached by some underground organization and because of a misunderstanding violated our laws. I am simply a reminder to you, as I understand it. You are a public figure, after all, Mr. Lindheim."

Theo smiled, but it was thin-lipped. "So you see, Anna, the government of Great Britain has set a watchdog over us. Not a snarling mastiff like the Gestapo in Germany, but rather a terrier who will bark if someone undesirable comes to the door."

The voices of Charles and Louis echoed excitement from the north gallery. Anna glanced nervously toward the entrance. "Have we not all been through *enough*, Mr. Beckham?"

Beckham was sympathetic. "I have my assignment, Mrs. Lindheim."

"Then must you be *so obvious*? These children . . . might we at least have the illusion of freedom?"

Mr. Beckham nodded his long, thin head. "Certainly. It is enough that you know we are watching. Henceforth you may have your illusions, and we will remain . . . invisible." He backed up a step. "It is enough that you know. Good day, Mr. Lindheim. Mrs. Lindheim."

With that, he turned and walked briskly across the floor. His heels clicked and clacked, receding down a corridor until they diminished to nothing and Theo and Anna were alone. At least, they *seemed* alone.

Anna looked up at Theo. "Why does this not make me feel better?"

The playful banter of members of the London Philharmonic Orchestra was a tonic for Elisa. She was the new kid on the block, as Murphy said, but the block was filled with the familiar faces of old friends who had played with her in Austria and even faraway Berlin.

Backstage conversations were in English now instead of German, but the subjects seemed remarkably unchanged from the carefree days of Vienna. Names of conductors like Toscanini and Fuchwanger were mentioned, along with the discussion of the music festivals that would continue to be held in Austria in spite of the Nazi takeover. It was still undecided if the London orchestra would be traveling to the Reich for the Wagner festival or the Mozart festival. Thought of such a journey back into the land of their persecution made many of the newest members of the London Philharmonic nervous in spite of the assurances of Sir Thomas Beecham, the London conductor.

This very issue clouded Elisa's first days with Sir Thomas and the orchestra. Now that she carried Murphy's child, she had more to think about than just her own safety. And she had to consider Charles and Louis as well. She did not feel free to perform in Germany for the same people who had persecuted even these little ones.

For this reason, Elisa had made an appointment to speak with the great conductor this morning. The eyes of Frieda Hillman, Beecham's Jewish secretary, were full of understanding as Elisa explained her concerns as unemotionally as possible.

Frieda, a heavyset woman with a doctoral degree in music, had come to London from the Berlin orchestra of Maestro Fuchwanger after the Nazi purges of 1935. Her obviously Semitic features had made it impossible for the brilliant and capable woman to show her face around the Berlin concert hall even though she arranged all the daily details of the orchestra. She had remained poised on the brink of the Nazi inferno in Berlin until Sir Thomas had asked her to join his staff. Her mother still remained in Germany as a hostage to guarantee that Frieda would not speak ill of her former persecutors. Many like Frieda carried such a burden with them. And yet their faces did not reflect openly the pain that must certainly be felt privately.

As Frieda led Elisa through the backstage maze of the Royal Opera House, she introduced every stagehand and technician on a first-name basis. Elisa's mind was reeling as Frieda spliced in questions about Anna and Theo, both of whom she had known well in Berlin. Elisa answered in rapid fire between introductions and the hail of business questions being shot at Frieda from the right and left.

The return to such wonderful chaos was like a warm bath on a frosty day for Elisa. How long had it been since she had hurried through the corridors of a concert hall? How long since those blissful days in Vienna when she had looked through such innocent eyes at a condemned world?

"Sir Thomas may seem gruff at times, but you will see . . . in spite of the bark, there are no teeth in the bite!" Frieda had been around long enough to adapt English clichés to her own style.

The two women paused before the impressive mahogany door marked with a brass nameplate: *Sir Thomas Beecham.* Frieda patted Elisa. The message was obvious: Elisa must not be nervous in the presence of this man. Then Frieda knocked.

"It is open," came the mellow voice of the conductor.

Frieda opened the door then stepped aside, allowing Elisa to enter the office first. Sir Thomas was lounging on an overstuffed sofa. Music scores were spread on a low table before him. He puffed on a cigarette in a long ivory cigarette holder. Barely glancing at Elisa from beneath his bushy eyebrows, he waved a hand for her to be seated.

In spite of Frieda's assurances, Elisa's calmness evaporated. Sir Thomas with his precisely groomed goatee was an imposing figure in his silk smoking jacket.

"Elisa Murphy, Sir Thomas," Frieda volunteered. She was still standing, uncertain if she should remain for the talk.

"The new first violinist," he said gruffly, like a general discussing a private. "Your concerts with the BBC were quite nice. But what is this nonsense that you may not be able to travel with my orchestra to Bayreuth? to Salzburg?" Then he glared at Frieda. "Sit down," he commanded. "I may need you to explain a thing or two."

Elisa hesitated. As Sir Thomas turned his piercing eyes on her, she swallowed hard. He had a way of making her feel like a music student again. "My family . . . ," she began. "We are quite . . . out of favor with the Nazis."

Sir Thomas cleared his throat impatiently. "Just as it should be. If that were not the case, you would still be there instead of here. Correct?"

"Yes . . . I . . . as a matter of principle . . . cannot imagine playing there again. For the Nazis."

"As a matter of principle, you *must* consider it. They have managed to disrupt the life of one of Germany's most promising young violinists. But you must not allow them to imagine that they have destroyed your career with their silly racial nonsense." He looked to Frieda. "Tell her, Frieda!"

"Last year I traveled to Bayreuth. When I was with the Berlin Orchestra, I could not have done so. But the Nazis did not act as though my presence there was anything unusual because I am under the protection of Sir Thomas, you see."

The great conductor's chin lifted regally. "You see?"

Elisa decided she needed to add another dimension to the story. "Well . . . I traveled to Germany from Vienna . . . before the Anschluss. I . . . worked to aid refugees to escape without the knowledge of the Reich."

"Good heavens! Do you think we have not?" Sir Thomas brushed away her objections. "Take a look at the faces in this orchestra, Elisa." His voice became more gentle. "You have been through an ordeal. But *here* we think of *music*! We perform where we are called to perform. We are above politics in many ways, although our perfection as musicians may make a political statement. They are fools, these Nazis, with their lunacy about German culture and this and that."

He puffed on his cigarette as he chose his words carefully. "I attended the 1936 Olympics in Berlin. It gave me great pleasure to see the black American Jesse Owens demolish the Aryan supermen on the track." He smiled smugly. "It also gives me great pleasure to outperform Hitler's purebred albino musicians. The Nazis have banished the very best musicians in Europe. And *I have inherited them*! That includes you, Elisa. I would have hired your friend Leah Feldstein and her husband in a moment as well, but alas! They are in Palestine." He shrugged. "At any rate, I wired the High Commissioner that they were coming. He will see to it they perform there as well."

Elisa drew a deep breath. Sir Thomas was telling her that she had no choice but to travel with the orchestra even into Germany if it was arranged. The thought made her feel sick. "I . . . there is something else . . . I am expecting a child."

Sir Thomas drew himself upright, surprised. "Congratulations." Then he brushed over the news as though it had nothing to do with the subject at hand. "Such things seldom affect the quality of one's music. We encourage families to teach their children to play well—providing me with another generation of musicians, as it were."

"Sir Thomas, I . . . fear for my safety in Germany." She tried to emphasize the danger.

He was gentle again, remarkably so. "I can understand that. Frieda and a dozen others have felt the same. But they have learned—and so must you—that while you are a member of my orchestra, no one would dare to harm or threaten you, my dear. To do so would cause an incident of world proportions." He sat back. He was finished. Clapping his hands, he dismissed them. "You will learn to trust. And now . . . to work!"

7

No Sabbath Peace

There had been no sound within the walls of Old City Jerusalem for two hours. The gunfire had ceased, and the only audible noise now was the purring of cats and the old rabbi's own labored breath.

Soon the evening would come and it would be Shabbat. He wondered if there would be services tonight. Who would lead the congregation in prayers for peace?

Every muscle in his body ached, and he could find no position that offered relief. He fingered the envelope in his pocket. The weekly letter to Etta and Aaron and the children. In it he had told them how peaceful things had been the last few weeks. Once again he had begged them to return to Jerusalem after the baby was born. There was room here. And how the old man longed to see his grandchildren!

Rabbi Lebowitz determined that he would not mail the letter. How could he ask Etta and Aaron to bring the children here when a new wave of violence had erupted? No, he would not ask Etta and Aaron again. They had almost come back once before, but that had been before the riots had squeezed off Jewish immigration to a trickle. Life was good for them in Poland, Etta wrote. Certainly anything was better than this. Three million Jews together in Poland were certainly safer than this rag-tag little remnant who clung to the scarred earth of Zion and scratched out a living in the hills of Galilee.

"*Oy!*" Rabbi Lebowitz moaned in spite of his pledge to keep silent. Thirst had become almost unbearable. Were the battles over in the Old City now? Did the lengthy silence mean an end to the clash between the Arab rebels and the British?

The thought tempted him to step from the hiding place, but he did not. Soon it would be evening, and he could walk home under cover of darkness. As the congregation prayed in the synagogue, he would come through the doors and proclaim that the Eternal had been merciful.

Such a thought this was! It almost made him smile to imagine such a thing, but his lips were so dry that they cracked when his mouth turned up. He would save his smiles until he was safe at home with a cool glass of water drawn from the cistern.

Creeping shadows offered the only movement in the square. The sun dipped lower in the sky beyond Jaffa Gate. The old man shifted his weight from one foot to another. He wondered if he would be able to make his body move when he left the shelter. Certainly he would make an easy target if there were snipers still in the minarets or on the roof-tops. But perhaps they had all gotten weary and gone home.

How easy it would be to step out into the square right now. Why would anyone wish to shoot an old man? Did he have a gun or a uniform? Only one letter. They should kill him for that?

He inched nearer the opening. It would be so easy. Such a relief.

As he moved, the mother cat stood.

"So you have had enough too, little Mama-leh?"

The cat purred and walked easily toward the aching legs of the rabbi. The kittens laid back their ears and remained behind in their nest of rags. The mother cat brushed against the old man's legs and then moved with calm elegance toward the opening.

He decided he would follow the cat. Both of them had had enough of this nonsense for one day.

"After you, cat." The rabbi was careful not to step on the little calico just ahead of him. The cat was unconcerned. This was not her war after all. Her tail was erect, like a flag of neutrality. She meowed and stepped from between the two buildings onto the cobbles of Omar Square.

From both directions a dozen guns erupted! The old man stifled a cry as he fell back and bullets tore through the calico cat and shattered the stones where he had stood a moment before!

The only sign of life on the street had been shot to pieces. The kittens blinked in bewilderment. Where had their mother gone?

The rabbi moaned softly into his hands. Death was very near. *Very near!* Shabbat was coming to Jerusalem, but there would be no Shabbat peace tonight.

Rabbi Lebowitz wondered if Death would be placated by something as innocent and unconcerned as the calico cat. Or must it also reach in and take him as well?

The trees of the English countryside had shed their leaves, leaving tattered, barren branches to point at a somber sky. While Prime Minister Chamberlain congratulated himself and hailed the betrayal of Czechoslovakia as "peace in our time," the realists knew that hoping for peace now with Germany was like hoping the trees would bloom in December.

Among those realists was Winston Churchill. At his side stood men like Anthony Eden and Duff Cooper, who had resigned their cabinet positions rather than support the fiasco that Prime Minister Chamberlain was bringing upon a slumbering England. Publicly these men had stood against the cheering members of Parliament and declared that the Munich Agreement was a fraud, a sham. A delusion that was, in fact, the worst defeat ever suffered by England. Churchill had endured the boos and catcalls of his fellow MPs when he took the floor of Parliament and spoke the truth:

> *"I will begin by saying the most unpopular and unwelcome thing, what everybody would like to ignore . . . we have sustained a total and unmitigated defeat."*

His voice had been nearly drowned out by angry shouts. Indeed the truth was most unpopular in England during the days following Munich.

That being the case in England, it was also true in faraway America. One of the exceptions was Trump Publishing, whose publisher insisted that the truth would be printed. The first cabled orders this morning from Mr. Trump to his editor-in-chief of Trump European News Services had been a confirmation of Murphy's instincts.

> MURPHY RE: TROUBLE IN HOLY LAND STOP GET YOUR TAIL TO CHARTWELL FOR IMMEDIATE INTERVIEW WITH CHURCHILL STOP GOT TO GET CHAMBERLAIN AND HIS UMBRELLA OFF AMERICAN FRONT PAGES STOP SIGNED TRUMP

This was an assignment Murphy welcomed. While other newsmen with Hearst, INS, McCormick, and Craine publications were being forced to print the fairy tale of appeasement politics, Murphy was already driving the narrow rutted lanes toward the Churchill estate.

Through the barren trees he could see the steep gables of the ancient brick country house. The lush green ivy of summer had also deserted Churchill, leaving the facade of the house naked and forlorn. *Gloomy* was the word for Chartwell these days. Murphy had heard that the master of the house was also gloomy. He had reason to be.

Gravel crunched beneath the tires as Murphy stopped in front of the house. Someone pulled back a curtain, then let it fall. The pudgy, somber-faced housekeeper Murphy had met last summer opened the door. In a whisper, she asked for his hat and coat. She led him quietly from the foyer to the closed door of Churchill's study. Murphy could smell the reek of cigar smoke through the panel. The maid looked almost fearful as she raised her fist to knock. The master was obviously in a black mood!

The soft tapping was followed by a bellow from within. "Who the devil is it now?"

Murphy answered for himself. "Murphy."

The door flew open. Churchill stood in his dressing gown, glaring at Murphy. "You mean they haven't tarred and feathered you yet?" He took Murphy by the arm, pulled him in, and slammed the door in the housekeeper's face.

The room was hazy with smoke from the myriad cigars Churchill had fired in his battle against depression. The strain of knowing the truth and losing to lies showed on the face of the old prophet-politician. He jerked his head at a chair piled with newspapers.

Murphy took this as a signal to sit. He moved the papers and obeyed. He did not open the conversation. After all, what was there to say? *You're really looking bad. Hitler got away with everything in spite of you, didn't he?*

Churchill stood facing the window.

A gray and dreary day, somber and funereal like the cemetery scene in Our Town, Murphy thought. He cleared his throat lest Churchill forget he was in the room. Apparently the great statesman had forgotten about the interview.

Churchill growled, "I know you're there."

"Is this a bad time?"

"There are no good times left, I fear. If you wish to interview me while I am a member of Parliament, you will have to do so now."

"You are . . . resigning your seat?"

"I heard this morning there is an organized opposition within my own constituency; it has come to this for me at last."

If there were no good times to interview Churchill, Murphy could not imagine that he could have picked any time worse than this! For his outspoken stand against Munich, Winston Churchill was being punished by the Conservative party machine. The affairs of Palestine would be far from Churchill's mind.

Murphy stumbled over words. "But you . . . you are one of the few who *sees*!"

Churchill exhaled. He turned away from the window, and in the dim light Murphy could see that the man had not shaved today. "Matters in my own constituency have come to such a pass that I have made it clear—" he raised his cigar for emphasis—"if a resolution of censure is carried out against me, I shall immediately resign my seat and fight a by-election!" He shook his head and sank down in an overstuffed chair. "And yet I would give everything . . . *everything* . . . if only I could believe that this terrible folly in Munich could truly bring peace."

"Would it be better . . . the interview . . . another day?"

Churchill almost smiled. "There is nothing I may say that will bring down additional brimstone on my head, Murphy. Indeed, if I am silent now, of all times, I might burst, and what a mess that would be to clean up, eh? Of course, it might give the Nazis another reason to celebrate." He flicked ashes from the arm of his chair. "At least I am not paying for my opinion with my life, as some brave Germans may well be doing right now."

"You know of German opposition to what has just happened?" Murphy leaned forward.

"Not everyone in Germany is mad, although those who are not mad may soon be dead. Hitler has managed through us—through the prime minister of Great Britain—to crush all opposition against him in Germany. Who would dare oppose him now? He has taken the Rhineland without a shot. Rebuilt his armies without a protest. Marched into Austria . . . and now carved up Czechoslovakia like a roast duck." There was deep bitterness in Churchill's voice. "And all of this with the blessings of our government and that of France. Hitler pointed a gun at our heads and demanded one pound. When that was given, two pounds were demanded. Finally the dictator consented to take one pound, seventeen shillings and sixpence, and the rest in our promises of goodwill for the future."

He laughed a short, bitter laugh. "Left to themselves and told they would get no help from the Central Powers, the Czechs and President Beneš would have been able to make better terms than they have got after all this! Now we have lost the support of thirty-five Czech army divisions. All has come to nothing with the stroke of a pen. What remains of Czechoslovakia will be swallowed up soon enough. There is hardly a way this fiasco could be worse for us. . . ."

"And for the refugees?" Murphy led him slightly as he took notes.

"Refugees." Churchill puffed his cigar. "They continue to shipwreck on the shoals of politics. The best interest of nations is not the best interest of individual human life, I'm afraid."

"You have heard about the violence in Palestine?"

Churchill shook his massive head in disgust. He had heard. "Chaim Weizmann called me just after you, wanting some reassurance of my support for a Jewish national home. What use is my support at this hour? I am the pariah of Parliament. I stand by my commitment to the Zionists. I stand by the promise given to world Jewry for a national home in Palestine. This seems to me a matter of honor. But what value have we put on honor these days?" The great man closed his eyes in a private grief. "And what value have we put on human life?"

Silence. Churchill looked as if he had seen some terrible vision.

Murphy cleared his throat. "You believe Britain will yield to the demands of the Arab Council?"

"The Arab Council simply mimics the words of Adolf Hitler. Britain has not failed to yield to his demands yet."

"Palestine will be closed to Jewish immigration." Murphy spoke these words as if the announcement had already come from the colonial office. He felt queasy at the realization. He had seen the crowds gathered outside the embassies of Prague—and that had been before the Munich Agreement. How desperate were those thousands now?

Churchill nodded. "The same claw that cut the heart from Czechoslovakia now digs into Palestine. The same." He sighed. "I cannot imagine what is to become of all those people trapped in the middle. Chased out of the Reich. Kept out of Palestine for the sake of appeasing a hoodlum."

Murphy jotted a few lines, then looked inquiringly at Churchill. "You know, I can quote you . . . or you can write it yourself. A column for an American chain of newspapers?"

At this cautious suggestion the old lion eyed Murphy with a new interest. He rubbed a hand over his stubbled chin. "My mother was American, you know. You may call my agent, Murphy."

With this last comment, Murphy knew that, literary agent notwithstanding, he had somehow struck a very unexpected bargain with Winston Churchill. The old lion had begun his public career as a journalist in the Boer Wars of Africa. Writing political commentary for the land of his mother's birth seemed a natural extension of his talents as orator and writer.

Churchill lifted his chin slightly. "In spite of my current unpopularity, Murphy, I am convinced that history will one day be kind to me." He chuckled. "Because I intend to write it myself."

So the matter was settled. Churchill called Murphy to the window and pointed to where a large, swarthy gardener labored pruning rosebushes. "Since I am unpopular now, however," Churchill continued, "I have engaged a bodyguard."

"Unnecessary, I hope." Murphy studied the man who snipped at brown branches even while he gazed toward Churchill and Murphy.

"That is my hope as well—" Churchill paused—"but even so, for the sake of my health and that of my family I keep this muscular insurance policy nearby at all times." He cocked an eyebrow at Murphy. "You would be wise to do the same."

A chill of fear prickled the hair on Murphy's neck. He scrutinized the bodyguard and then Churchill to see if the statesman was serious. There was no amusement in Churchill's eyes. "Is there . . . some reason . . ." Murphy's voice faltered.

"Over the past months, I had some contact with a certain young German officer. I received a wire from him in code that he was coming to England seeking political asylum. The day of his scheduled arrival came and went, and he did not come. I fear the worst."

"But what has that got to do with me? with us?"

"The officer in question is an old friend of Elisa's . . . Thomas von Kleistmann."

For weeks Thomas von Kleistmann had been dodging his Gestapo pursuers, and now it had come to this.

Behind him the shrill whistle of the train screamed in alarm as he ran through the crowds on the dock. A hundred yards away was the ship that he had prayed would carry him to England. To safety. To his right, three men pushed through porters and passengers moving slowly toward the gangplank of the Channel ferry. To the left, just ahead, three more Gestapo agents moved to intercept him.

The ship's horn bellowed. Thomas pressed on. He shoved a woman from his path. She shouted an indignant protest at him. The Gestapo agents moved without taking their eyes from Thomas, who stood a head taller than nearly everyone in the crowd.

It was cold in the morning air, but perspiration mingled with the mist on Thomas's forehead. Twice he had managed to evade Leo Vargen, the SS commander in charge of his capture. Perhaps he would be lucky a third time. Anything else would mean a certain and terrible end.

The line of passengers moved slowly past the customs clerk. Thomas managed to pull out his passport and visa. False documents, of course. He glanced to his left. Vargen and his men were making steady and rapid progress. There would be no time to show papers to anyone. He crammed them back in his pocket and stopped.

His pursuers straightened and shouted an alarm as he turned to push back the way he had come. Escape by ship was hopeless now. Hopeless.

He would have to make it to the warehouses. Hide in the labyrinth of crates and cargo boxes until it was safe to come out. He could not be taken—he knew too much. Too many names, dates, plans. Elisa's face swam before his eyes, then the image of Ernst vom Rath, Admiral Canaris, and the others. The Gestapo could make a man betray everyone and everything! No, he must not fall into their hands!

"Get out of the way!"

Hearing the angry voice of Vargen, Thomas pushed and struck at those who blocked his path.

The engine of a train hissed as passengers departing the quay boarded for Amsterdam.

Thomas fought the panic that threatened to rob him of his ability to think. Green train cars blocked the path of his escape to the warehouse complex. Vargen and the others made better progress than he was making. If only he were not so tall!

He peered back again at the Gestapo agents. Their faces registered determination, but they seemed to have no fear of losing their quarry. Vargen smiled. He raised his hand and pointed toward Thomas. The train screamed again as two more men stepped from the high step of a green passenger car.

Now the path was blocked three ways. He could only hope to turn back. He might make it to the ship—or perhaps dive into the water!

He spun around. And then he saw them. Unmistakable in their department-issue trench coats, two more agents waited a mere ten paces behind him, their Lugers drawn.

"France, yes. Poland? Yes, of course. Maybe even Prague." Murphy paced the length of his study and back. "But you are not going back to Berlin. Or Salzburg or Vienna!" he declared to Elisa.

"Then perhaps Sir Thomas will ask for my resignation from the orchestra," she said quietly. This was not an argument, but a regret.

"We will cross that bridge when we come to it. But you are *not* crossing the border of the German Reich! Not again, *ever*!" He exhaled loudly as if the very thought of it terrified him. "I am having difficulty even letting you out of my sight in London, let alone thinking of you going back *there*!"

"We still have months before the festivals." Her voice was soft, full of hope. Was it still possible that Hitler could be taken from power between now and then? Hadn't Thomas believed? "But of course . . . you are right, Murphy. I won't risk anything. Not myself . . ."

"For my sake, Elisa. For my peace of mind."

"And for the sake of our little one."

"Within a few months all Europe may be at war. I don't want to frighten you, but festivals at Bayreuth won't mean much compared to that. And if things happen as some are saying . . ." He did not discuss Churchill's prophecy. "Then I am sending you and the boys and the baby back to the States to sit this one out. You understand me?"

She shook her head. "Tell me I cannot perform in Salzburg or Bayreuth, but do not make me leave you, Murphy. Not ever." Tears swam in her eyes. The day had begun so perfectly. Why must this shadow hover over them still?

She put up her arms to him and he knelt beside her, laying his head in her lap. "Maybe I'll go home with you. Write a sports column. Brooklyn Dodgers. Yankees . . ."

She stroked his hair and knew with certainty that such a life could never be for them. "Are we supposed to fiddle, Murphy, while the whole world burns down around us?" Both of them knew it would be impossible. "If darkness defeats us by simply wearing us out, then where is there any hope for the light?"

"Listen." Murphy raised his head. "Right now I just want you to be okay. Promise me that for a while, anyway, you will just fiddle, huh? Sir Thomas is right about that much at least. Just play your Guarnerius and let that baby have a little peace and quiet in there. There isn't anything you can do now that will stop whatever is coming. You have done your bit. Lay low. Take it easy for a while? Promise me, Elisa—"

"An easy promise to make," she whispered, "as long as you do not bring me the front page, Murphy!" She said the words with a sad smile, but both of them knew they were true.

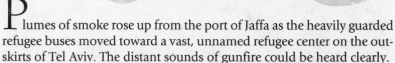

Plumes of smoke rose up from the port of Jaffa as the heavily guarded refugee buses moved toward a vast, unnamed refugee center on the outskirts of Tel Aviv. The distant sounds of gunfire could be heard clearly.

Shimon squeezed Leah's hand as he stared bleakly out the window of the bus. "They have not told us everything, these Englishmen."

"Only disturbances," Leah murmured, arguing inwardly with the same awareness that Shimon felt. Things were indeed much more serious than the authorities were letting on. A demonstration to show the English politicians the extent of Arab dissatisfaction.

"If it sounds like war, and looks like war—" Shimon raised his chin and sniffed the faint scent of gunpowder on the air—"and smells like war . . ."

Ahead lay an immense city of tents, surrounded by tall barbed-wire fences.

"This must be home," remarked a young man bitterly.

"At least it is not Dachau! I have seen that place!" Shimon blurted out defensively. "Here the guards have their eyes turned out. Their guns away from us. The wire is to protect us, not keep us prisoner."

"Wire is wire," argued the young man angrily. "Guards are guards."

"You would not think so if you had been to Dachau," Shimon muttered.

Only Leah heard him. Somehow his words lessened her renewed disappointment with the Promised Land. Drab green army tents on a barren plain. This was not going to be a pleasant campout in a lovely Alpine setting. When members of the halutz had described *hardship* at the Zionist meetings, Leah had imagined *adventure. How did I ever manage to confuse the two?* she wondered.

The caravan slowed. Armed escorts sped past on their motorcycles. Inside the compound, additional British soldiers peered out from behind sandbags.

Leah craned her neck to look back where the plume of smoke thickened and broadened. A distant explosion sent up yet another billowing black cloud.

"They've hit the fuel depot!" shouted a British soldier, and all heads pivoted to watch.

Only Shimon could imagine what such an inferno was like at close range.

"What is happening?" shouted a woman out the window. "Is it war?"

The soldier throttled back and glared resentfully at the frightened faces on the bus. "Not a war. Just a little welcoming demonstration in your honor. In honor of the Jewish refugees, see?"

Without waiting for reply, he revved his motor and sped off.

Those who understood English interpreted for those who did not. A heavy silence lay over the men and women onboard. So. The English soldiers were being forced to fight because of this Jewish dream of a homeland. Good boys from Brighton and Blackpool were going to die today because an English politician named Balfour said that there would be a homeland for the Jews. Arabs attacked because these buses were filled with people who hoped the promise was true. The accusation in the young soldier's words was unmistakable.

Suddenly Shimon clapped his hands together and cleared his throat. "Yes! I knew there had to be some connection between me and all this messy business! Everywhere I go, things start blowing up!"

An uneasy laughter followed his remark.

"So it's *you!*" bellowed a man who had been a lawyer in Weimar. "All the time I thought it was me! Every place I went in Germany windows got smashed. Stones thrown! You must have been close by!"

The laughter came with an easy relief as others joined in the game. "It was Shimon Feldstein all the time!"

"That was my business!" Shimon half stood for a bow. He raised his cast above his head. "What do you expect from a man who plays kettledrums for a living?"

One by one the convoy of buses passed through the heavy gates into the compound. Seventh in the long line, the bus that carried Shimon and Leah was filled with laughter and jokes by the time it entered. Even the bitter young Zionist who had protested against the barbed wire joined in.

The five kittens huddled together miserably in the gathering gloom. Wide eyes blinked up at the rabbi from a patchwork ball of fur.

He knew how foolish he was to worry about the kittens when his own life hung by a thread. Still, he could not help it. *If the mother cat had not stepped out, I would have done so, and it would be me in pieces now instead of her! Oy! And now they will starve while I go home, God willing, and try to forget about this day! Or they will be eaten by dogs or trampled underfoot. And all because God did not want me shot! Oy! God, you could not have sent out a tomcat to get shot instead? It had to be a mother?*

The Eternal, blessed be His name, had left the old man with no choice. When night came—and that would be soon—he would slip out from this place and take the kittens with him. *If* he could catch them. And, when he got home, he would say kaddish for the mama cat who saved him from certain death.

He clucked his tongue. Little ears perked up in curiosity. The kittens were several feet away. In the narrow crevice he could not stoop to pick them up. This operation must be coordinated carefully with the coming of night.

Two stars appeared in the darkening sky. There was little time. The Arabs would feel freer to wander the streets under cover of night. They would shoot whomever they found. They would search the cracks for stray Jews and stray cats, and they would shoot. Rabbi Lebowitz had no doubt of that.

He clucked his tongue again in hopes that the kittens would wander toward him. No luck. He could not tell where one kitten began and another ended.

He wagged his toe at the ball of fluff. It seemed to roll backward, farther from reach. He meowed, without effect. He did not meow like a mother cat and deserved no respect or attention.

Troubled, the old man stared at them. They stared back. Resigning himself to the fact that he was an old meshuggener after all, and that they would have to be left to their fate, he remembered that a failed mitzvah is still honored by the Eternal. He had tried. The kittens would not be saved.

As the minutes ticked by, the old man clucked and meowed again. Futile. Soon the night would fall. Darkness would come to Jerusalem, and then the violence would be renewed. If he ran fast enough, he could make it to the Armenian Quarter, and from there to the Jewish Quarter a hundred yards down the street. *If. If. If . . .*

If these old legs can move, after such a day. And if the Arabs do not shoot me from behind and the British from the front. And if the Armenians will let me through the barricade! Oy! You have enough to trouble you!

Still, that furry heap against the wall plagued him—innocent creatures who could not fathom the fact that they were going to die or the reason for it.

Wedged into the tight space, he struggled to remove his coat—one arm scraping against the wall, then the other. The kittens jumped and climbed over one another in fear.

He looked up at the sky and asked the Eternal to be patient with such a foolish old man. Slowly he dangled the sleeve of the coat down along his leg. He wriggled it up and down, like bait on the end of a fishing line.

Ears perked up again. Here was something of interest, much like the tail of mama cat. The tough little gray swaggered out of the heap first. He paused. He crouched. He pounced toward the elusive sleeve.

The rabbi rolled his eyes upward and thanked the Eternal. The white kitten bounced up, arching its back in warning of battle. The two remaining grays followed in a charge as the white leaped to snag the fabric with sharp little claws. He hung there for a moment. The old man pulled him up and unhooked the claws, then slid him into the roomy pocket of his baggy trousers. *Yes!*

Down went the sleeve again, and up came the blustery little gray. He scratched and hissed unhappily as the rabbi dropped him in on top of the white.

Darkness descended. The old man waved the sleeve while the two captives in his pocket fought. The tiny calico did not move forward to join in the game. At last little paws scampered over the rabbi's aching feet. Another attack on the fabric netted the second gray.

Shouts began to ring out across the domed rooftops of the Old City. "Hey, Jews! You think you will live through this night?"

The old man was uncertain. Perhaps they would find his body in the morning and stop to wonder why the old rabbi's pockets were full of kittens.

He dared to speak. "Come on, little one! I will take you to Tipat Chalev for a drop of milk, *nu?*"

The last gray kitten snagged claws and fangs on the fabric. The rabbi swung him up and dropped him into the other pocket. That left the last calico. The sweet one. The shy one.

There was no time. Back toward the Haram, a single shot was fired— a call to arms for the bandits in the Old City.

Rabbi Lebowitz drew a deep breath. He could wait no longer. "Sorry, little one," he whispered as he slid out of his hiding place and plastered himself against the wall. "May the Eternal keep you safe in His pocket."

More shots. The old man could plainly see the fire leap from the guns. Five shots. Five different guns on the roofs of the Old City. They fired up into the air. Flashes momentarily illuminated the ghostly forms of men in Arab dress.

He hesitated, thinking which would be the safest path. He had thought of it a thousand times throughout the day, but confronted with the need to run, he could not remember *where* to run! His heart pounded as it had during the riot. His breath grew short, as if he had already run ten miles. But he had only taken one step!

The kittens wrestled in the deep pockets. Little needle-sharp claws penetrated the fabric and stuck his thighs as if to wake him up from a stupor.

Angry Arab voices advanced. The old man looked toward the square. Two blocks, and then the Armenian Quarter! Yes—now he remembered!

He tried to find breath. And then, from the hiding place came a tiny voice. The old man peered down. A small shadow moved. *Be patient with me, God! The calico!*

He stooped and gathered the little one up, and then he ran, kittens bouncing against him. He held the calico in his right hand and dragged himself forward along the stone facades with his left.

Gunfire cracked like a whip. He had not run like this since he had been a young man. Uneven stones jarred his old bones. Kittens clawed him through his pockets. The calico dug into his arm until he bled.

At last the outline of the jagged wall loomed up. Would British soldiers mistake him for the enemy? No time to think! Under his breath, he muttered the name of his daughter. "Etta! Etta!" It was Shabbat in Poland. Peaceful Shabbat. Etta must never come back to Jerusalem, never come home to this!

The corner was a few yards from him. *Merciful God!* The eyes of Death turned toward him.

"Someone is moving down there!"

"Shoot! Shoot him!"

More gunfire rang out behind. He did not stop. He did not turn to look.

"Shoot! He is getting away!" Boots ran toward him from the Armenian barricade.

"Don't shoot! I am a rabbi! *Gevalt!* Don't shoot!"

The floors of the tents were wooden slats, salvaged from packing crates discarded by the British military.

The entire camp was asleep now. Or at least the confusion had died down into a stupor of exhaustion. A dim light still burned in the cubicle next to that of Leah and Shimon. Beyond the thin canvas partition, a family of six from Württemberg occupied two small spaces. The children slept more soundly than the parents, who groaned like the springs on their bunks.

From the top bunk of their allotted space, Leah studied the letters of shipping labels that remained on the slat floor.

B-L-A . . . perhaps the word had been *blankets*? Blankets for the British soldiers? Or maybe *black boots*? On the slat at the head of the bunks the initials *H.M.* were stenciled in red paint. That must stand for *His Majesty*. The floor was courtesy of His Majesty King George of England. She wondered if the English king in his palace could imagine that the discarded rubbish of the government in Palestine would be put to such good use by the Jewish Agency on behalf of the new immigrants. And if it was discovered that the Jewish Agency had created floors out of His Majesty's wooden slats, would the English demand the crates be returned?

Shimon slept soundly in the bunk beneath her. He had hardly touched his supper after reading the sheet of precautions that had come with the issued bed linens:

Caution: All linens should be checked nightly before retiring.

"Checked for what?" he had asked a man who looked as if he might know.

"Scorpions. And bedbugs. They come up through the slats and climb the legs of the bunks. You will notice that each leg is set in a tin can half filled with water. When the creatures climb up the side of the can they fall in and drown. You will be saved by this device mostly. Except for the ones that come up the inside of the canvas and drop down from above."

This had been meant to comfort, somehow, but it had left Leah sleepless and searching the cracks between the planks. Tonight she was more terrified of things than she was of the Arabs who seemed to be tearing up all of Palestine at once.

Caution: Upon rising, be certain to check boots and all articles of clothing before wearing.

What sort of place is this? she asked herself again. Why had the Zionist lecturers not spoken about bedbugs and scorpions and . . .

Caution: Use of washing facilities should be restricted to daylight hours whenever possible.

The same fellow who had told them about bedbugs explained how snakes like to curl up beneath the washbasins. It was not so bad this time of year, but one could not be too cautious. And now with the Arabs on the rampage, it was not at all safe to leave shelter after dark.

With trembling hand, Leah had added this information to the letter addressed to Number 36 Red Lion Square in London. She told Elisa that such things did not distract from the joy of being here in the Holy Land. But Elisa knew her well enough to know the truth. She would close her eyes and picture Leah lying sleepless and terrified in a sandy tent, while Arab bands slaughtered whoever crossed their paths and scorpions tried to find ways around the tin cans on the legs of the bed.

"Oh, Lord," Leah whispered, "at last I am here, and I am afraid. This does not feel like home. No place feels like home."

Shimon's sleepy voice drifted up. "If we were not so desperate we would let the Arabs have it, eh?"

"You're awake?"

"I keep imagining little things trying to get into bed with me."

"Me too."

"Then why don't you come down and get into bed with me?" He was laughing at her, but she didn't care.

"We will break the bed."

"We will frighten away the enemy. Two of us together. Come down, will you? I need something sweet and soft tonight."

"Oh, Shimon," she chided him, but before the words passed her lips she was climbing down to slip between the sheets. The lower bunk complained loudly and sagged down another three inches. Leah snuggled close to Shimon. With her head against his chest, her arms and legs tangled with his, somehow she felt much safer.

"There now." He stroked her hair and held up his cast. "If anything tries to get you, I will squish it with my plaster arm!"

"Much better." She sighed. "Much more . . . comfortable . . . down . . ." Her voice trailed away as sleep at last came to her.

Shimon lay awake beside her for a long time before his own troubled thoughts finally let him sleep.

It was Shabbat night at Tipat Chalev. They had hardly noticed that Rabbi Lebowitz had been gone all day. No one was worried much. No one asked where he had been or if he was stuck in a crack between two buildings. And they were not happy about the kittens either. He had broken a Shabbat commandment by carrying them.

Hannah Cohen faced off with Rabbi Lebowitz on the back step of Tipat Chalev as the orphan kittens scampered over his scuffed shoes. "Kittens make cats!" said Hannah. "And cats make other kittens! And kittens make other cats!"

"And all of them kill Old City mice and rats!" the old man argued.

"Not in the kitchen of Tipat Chalev, they don't!"

"Not in the *kitchen*! Here in the *alleyway*!"

"We do not wish to listen to the endless bawling of a chorus of cats!" Hannah stamped her foot, and kittens jumped straight up and took refuge to peer out from behind the legs of their protector rabbi.

"The mother of these five kittens saved my life! And so I made a vow—"

"Not in my kitchen!"

"So! I *told* you, already! Not in the kitchen . . . in the alley. Maybe in the basement! They will kill the rats, and now, as head of the charitable distribution of food in the Jewish Quarter of the Old City—"

"No females!" Hannah shouted. "*Oy!* Sort them out! No females!"

At the sound of shouting, six round, wide-eyed faces peered into the kitchen. Hannah Cohen and Rabbi Lebowitz were arguing about kittens, which was unusual. The children whispered to themselves in amazement as the learned rabbi picked up each kitten in turn, lifted its tail, and scrutinized each backside as if he were searching for a message. "There!" he cried, thrusting the gray into the arms of Hannah. "A boy!" Then again, "A boy! A boy! A boy!" The calico was the last to be examined. He picked it up. The kitten meowed sweetly and batted his beard. The old man scowled at Hannah Cohen angrily and then slipped the calico into his pocket. "This one will be mine. She almost got me killed saving her, and so I am responsible for her now, *nu?*"

Four kittens purred in the arms of Hannah Cohen. She looked away haughtily and then peered down at them. Her expression changed briefly to one of pleasure, but she caught herself quickly. "All right, then! They will grow up to be big man cats and they will fight all day, and you will be sorry." The kittens purred louder. "What will we name them?" Her voice was alarmingly gentle.

The rabbi reached out to scratch the chin of the white kitten. "I thought . . . Genesis. Exodus. Leviticus. Numbers." He smiled and lifted up the calico. "And this will be Psalms."

"Just keep her away from my boys." Hannah's eyes narrowed in threat. "That is all we need around here! More cats!"

9

Sabbath Travel

It was Saturday in Catholic Warsaw.

A low-flying biplane rattled noisily over the roofs of the city. To the south and east and west a forest of redbrick chimneys belched smoke and soot into the cold autumn air. These were the Catholic chimneys of Warsaw. During the cold Polish winters this dark mist rose from Catholic hearths seven days a week without stopping. Like the incense of Mass or the light of votive candles before a saint, the smoke was a sign that clearly showed which chimney belonged to a Catholic.

It was Sabbath in Jewish Warsaw.

In the northeast quarter of the city, ten thousand redbrick chimneys pointed heavenward. Not even one wisp of smoke drifted up from Jewish hearths. On this holy day of rest, work was forbidden for the Chosen. Adding even a handful of coal to the fire was considered labor; the grates had been stoked with fuel in the last moments before the evening star signaled the beginning of the Sabbath. Hour by hour the coal had been consumed as the soft chants of prayer and blessing had risen up.

> "Lights are shining, hymns outpouring,
> Welcome, holy day of rest!
> Now the soul, unfettered soaring.
> Hold with God communion blest."

The fervor of Sabbath greetings warmed the homes in Jewish Warsaw even as coals glowed and cooled and finally tumbled to ash.

Those who bargained and bartered and shoveled coal in Catholic

Warsaw viewed the cold Sabbath chimneys of their neighbors with suspicion, even hatred. The peddler would not stop to sell where such a chimney stood. The milkman made his route blocks around the smokeless chimneys, lest his milk sour on the stoop of a customer who would not carry it indoors. A shrug and a shake of the head were the Polish answer to the clear blue sky above Jewish Warsaw. *Strange creatures, these Jews!*

From the high viewpoint of a clattering biplane, Warsaw was easily divided. And from this perspective, the sight of one lone plume of smoke rising from the Jewish district caused the pilot to turn his head and look again.

The thick double chimney of the corner of Muranow Square and Nalewki Street spewed a column of gray into the air. This three-story house was not the house of a Catholic in the midst of the Jewish residential district. It was too near the rounded dome of the synagogue—almost within the shadow of the great iron Star of David. It was a large house, square like a box, with three windows on each floor facing the square below. The brick construction had been faced over with stucco and painted pale yellow. The cornice work was cast with scrolls of leaves and flowers. This house on Muranow Square was the house of a well-to-do Jew. *Perhaps*, the pilot thought, *the owner hired a Gentile to build his Sabbath fire for him. A Shabbes goy, as Jews call their Gentile help.*

Just then the stately mahogany door burst open and a young woman ran down the steps—dark hair, bouncing curls, dark blue dress with a dropped waist, high-button shoes. Even from this distance he could see that this must be the daughter of a wealthy Jew. A pretty thing. Perhaps she was in her early teens. She did not look up at the biplane as children usually did. Instead she stopped at the bottom of the steps and turned her face upward toward the second story, where the window swung back and a bearded Jewish man leaned out to shout instructions. His words were indistinguishable, drowned by the roar of the engine. But something was up. The man was in his shirtsleeves—open collar, suspenders off. His face seemed pale, almost angry behind the thick black beard. The girl nodded and, with a fearful look, began to run across Muranow Square, past the sleeping facades of Pokorna Street, where the traffic gradually thickened and Jewish Warsaw melted into the bustle of Catholic Warsaw.

The pilot caught one final glimpse of the girl before her figure became only one among ten thousand in the streets. Then other children looked up and pointed at the biplane. They shouted and chased its shadow. The pilot dipped his wings in salute and laughed and forgot all about the one chimney in the Jewish district that smoked even on the Sabbath.

The chill wind cut through the fabric of the young woman's blue Sabbath dress. She had forgotten all about her coat when her father had sent her on this urgent errand. In spite of the wind, the note in her hand was damp from perspiration. Her fair skin was even paler than usual from the exertion of running.

Ahead, the rail tracks ended at the Umschlagplatz. Great locomotives puffed and hissed, impatient to be gone from Warsaw. The girl was only halfway to the doctor's house. Her lungs burned and her legs ached. For an instant she considered slowing to a walk. *Why did Papa not send David? He is younger, yes, but he runs faster than I.* She stumbled and almost fell at the feet of a group of broad-faced Polish railway workers. A man in a black wool cap reached out to break her fall.

"Careful, pretty one! Hurry too much, and you will miss your train because your head will be broken!"

She tried to thank him. There was no time to explain that she was not running to catch a train at the Umschlagplatz. She had no breath to explain. Willing her legs to move, she broke away and called an apology over her shoulder.

Her Polish was tinged with a heavy accent, causing the workers to joke that they had caught a little Jew running on the Sabbath. They would watch and see if the Jewish God would hurl a bolt of lightning down on the Umschlagplatz when He noticed the violation!

Such a joke brought a round of laughter that gave the girl a new strength born of fear. She would not speak to one of *them* again. It was forbidden by Papa to speak to the goyim. *They* were dangerous; she knew that. She had not meant to speak. Had not meant to stumble. Had not meant to be caught by one of *them*!

A strange sense of guilt dogged her. She forgot her lungs, forgot her aching legs. Before her was the picture of Mama's strained face and the soft apology she had whispered to Papa. "So sorry, Aaron. I had not meant to begin this on Sabbath."

Papa had touched her forehead as another pain came. "I tried to call Doktor Letzno. They have cut the phone wires again. I will send a note to fetch him."

Mama had blinked back tears and bitten her lip as she nodded. "Yes. Doktor Letzno."

The girl clutched the note tightly. She was afraid she might drop it, and it would be trampled beneath the shoes of Saturday Warsaw. Grandmothers pulling their apple-cheeked grandsons to the barbershop. Cliques of young women gathered outside the theaters. Couples crowd-

ing into the cafés for long talks over coffee and fresh pastry. Shopwindows displaying the latest Paris fashions. Brightly colored dresses
and pert little hats and silk stockings with high heels . . .

This was a foreign world to the girl. Only blocks away from her home
on Muranow, within sight of the cupola of the synagogue, the world
seemed to mock the peaceful Sabbath. Did they not know of the commandment? The girl had never been beyond the borders of her own neighborhood on Sabbath. She had not realized, could not imagine, how they
spent the holy day. She felt ill. Was it from running so far, or from passing
through the streets where certainly every one of the 613 commandments
were being broken all at the same moment—and on the Sabbath?

In her mind she recited the prayer for Sabbath evening as Papa had
taught her. It did little to comfort her. Ahead was the street sign: *Dzika
Street.* Her heart lifted. Only five more blocks to the home of Dr. Letzno!

The doctor was a friend of the family, a Jew who had also once lived
near Muranow Square. He had grown up there within the safety and security of that society, yet when he had reached manhood he had gone
out to study at the University in Prague. He had become a physician—
quite renowned, Papa said. When he returned to Poland, he moved into
the world of Saturday Warsaw. It was difficult to tell that he was not one
of *them.* On Dzika Street he spoke Polish without a trace of Yiddish accent. Only when he returned to Muranow did he use such words as
Gottenyu and oy! He seemed a Jew again, even though he did not wear a
yarmulke or worship any longer at shul. Papa loved Dr. Letzno—loved
him like a brother. Papa forgave Dr. Letzno for moving away from
Muranow Square and turning his back on his heritage.

But at this moment, the girl could *not* forgive the doctor for living a
world away in Saturday Warsaw. Because he had turned away, now she
must run coatless through the streets of the Catholic Poles! She must violate the Sabbath and dodge the children playing hopscotch and the
women hefting their groceries and the men smoking on the street corners.

"Is someone chasing you?"

"Where is such a little beauty running without her coat?"

She did not answer. She would not. Her accent would be taunted, her
identity revealed.

Only one block more. The beautiful house of Dr. Eduard Letzno
loomed ahead. Shining automobiles were parked along the curb of the
towering three-story structure. It was built much like the houses at home
on the square, but although this house had two chimneys, both of
which emitted smoke today, everyone knew that Dr. Letzno had not
moved away to find a better house.

A tall wrought-iron fence surrounded the house—not a fence to keep people out, but only an ornament. The girl stumbled again and reached out to grab the bars of the fence for support until she could find her breath again. Papa's note was crumpled in her hand. She exhaled with a little cry of pain when each breath did not fill her tortured lungs.

Inside the grand house, a string quartet played. She could hear the music and see a crowd of people in the parlor. Pulling herself hand-over-hand along the fence, she stumbled toward the front steps. There was a party inside. The house was full of Saturday people, and Dr. Letzno was their host. She would be brave. She would not cry as she faced them.

The stairs reared back, daring her to climb. Clutching the wide banister, she struggled toward the massive front door until at last she leaned against the wood and reached up to grasp the brass knocker. She let the metal slam down and then slam down again. The music continued. She could hear laughter and voices through the door, then footsteps and the rattle of a hand on the doorknob. The door was opened in sudden and violent welcome. They had not expected a girl to tumble panting into the foyer.

The delicate white hand raised the crumpled note to a black-coated butler. "For . . . Doktor . . . Letzno! Please . . . urgent!"

"My God, how far have you run? And without your coat on such a day! Herr Doktor! Doktor Letzno!"

Her task completed, the girl buried her face in her hands and sobbed in spite of her vow not to. There were rapid footsteps. The music did not stop, but the laughter died away.

"Who . . . well! It is Rachel Lubetkin! *Rachel!* Without your coat! You ran? Why did your father not telephone?"

Rachel could not speak. She could not tell the doctor that they had cut the telephone lines into the old Jewish section of Warsaw. Perhaps even one of those who sipped champagne in this very house had done the mischief!

The doctor put his arms around her and helped her across the black-and-white tiled floor. He guided her into a paneled room with green velvet curtains and walls of books, placed her on a leather sofa, and poured a glass of water, which he held to her lips. "Easy, now . . . you are blue with cold."

"Please . . . it is Mama . . . she is . . ."

Dr. Letzno tore open the envelope and read the message in a glance. He chuckled to himself. "Some kinds of labor will not wait, Rachel—not even until Sabbath is over."

Sabbath came to every town in Germany, but this night there was no Sabbath rest. The streets of every city teemed with people shouting, "Send the Jews to Palestine!"

In Berlin, in Leipzig, in Cologne, it was the same: "Send the Jews to Palestine!"

In Hamburg and Hanover and Essen people raised their fists and roared: "Send the Jews to Palestine!"

In Dusseldorf and Bremen and Munich the fires of a million torches lit angry faces: "Send the Jews to Palestine."

Tonight the Jews who had come to Germany from Poland a lifetime ago were rounded up and placed under guard in police stations and concert houses and abandoned buildings. Twelve thousand men, women, and children huddled beneath the weight of those shouts: "Send the Jews to Palestine!"

In every Jewish mind was the thought—the hope—that they might by some miracle be sent to Palestine! *Jerusalem!* Zion—a homeland where they might live in air not so thick with hatred!

But it was not Palestine that the Nazis had in mind for these twelve thousand. The British would not allow more Jews into that land for fear of Arab reprisals. And so, magically, the raging mobs changed their cry to, "Send the Jews back to Poland!"

Every Jew arrested in Germany that night had some former connection to Poland. The Führer, led by the will of his people, decided that indeed these Jews *would* be returned to Poland!

The Gestapo agents began to scream, "Sign here! You are being deported!"

Those who protested that they had brought nothing with them for a cold autumn journey were told, "You had nothing with you when you came to Germany, and you will take nothing out!"

All over Germany that night, groups of twenty were led from their places of confinement. Men. Old men. Women. Old women. All sizes of children. They were led through the streets, through mobs who spit and threw paper sacks of excrement onto these twelve thousand. "Send the Jews to Poland!" Dozens of locomotives leading hundreds of cattle cars were jammed full of Jews who longed for Palestine.

Trains clattered along the tracks of Germany throughout that long and terrible night. The German people left the streets of their cities and went home to sleep a deep and satisfying sleep. Germany was safe from these twelve thousand Jews at last!

Lazer Grynspan was having trouble breathing. His wife, Rifka, and daughter, Berta, leaned heavily against him. Others in their cattle car leaned against them until Lazer was crushed against the wooden slats. He drew his breath in short, shallow jerks. It was just enough to keep him alive.

Throughout the night he thanked God that his son, Herschel, was in Paris. How wise they had been to send him to Paris, where he was safe and free! Lazer asked himself why they had not done the same for Berta. Why had they not moved faster so they would not have been trapped in the Nazi cauldron?

Lazer had a hundred reasons why, but now those reasons seemed small and foolish. He could not so much as draw a breath to whisper a prayer, but he prayed all the same. Again and again he thought of Herschel. He thought of Theo Lindheim, who had barely managed to escape. He wondered where those Jews who had left Germany of their own will had gone. Theo, Anna, Elisa, and the two sons—they had money. That is why *they* could go. Lazer was only a poor tailor, and now he was leaving Germany anyway. Strange how Nazi hatred had leaned down to look at someone as small as a tailor. Why should the Germans care if a Jew stitched their buttons and hemmed their cuffs?

The clack of the train wheels lulled many into a stupor that was not true sleep but semiconsciousness. People had long since stopped weeping. There was no strength for that. This nightmare had begun Thursday night, and it was almost Saturday morning! There were only strength to breathe and energy to pray for help—as long as the prayers were silent.

Now the morning sun hovered just below the German horizon. Leaves on the trees were red and gold, and the sky took on the hues of burnished copper rimmed with pink and blue.

Lazer Grynspan peered through the slats of the cattle car and knew the real reason he had not left Germany before. Was there any land on earth so beautiful? Any other time he might have said that the beauty of Germany took his breath away, but this morning it was the barbarity of the German people that left him breathless.

Outside in a wide green field a farmer led his herd of milk cows to pasture. Did he know what cargo rode behind the slats of the cattle car that passed him now? The farmer did not look up. Peaceful morning. Beautiful morning. Lazer hoped the farmer did not know.

It was almost six in the morning. The tick of the wheels began to slow. Someone moaned, then someone else, and suddenly the entire train began to moan as the brakes squealed a protest.

A green sign with white lettering said *Neu Bentschen*. Lazer knew this place. It was the German border station on the frontier between Germany and Poland. Lazer had crossed into Germany through this very station in 1911. His wife had been a beautiful bride then. They had fled Polish Russia as a wave of violence against Jews had engulfed the land. Thousands of Jews had died that year beneath the clubs of the

Ukrainians and Russians and Persians. Lazer and Rifka had imagined they would be safe in Germany. Such a civilized land. They could raise their children in peace if they fled to Germany. It had *felt* true in 1911!

As if Rifka read her husband's mind, she moaned and managed to straighten her neck. "Here we are . . . again," she croaked. There was no humor in her voice. They were returning to a land of anti-Semitism. Brutality toward Jews. Centuries of pogroms.

But perhaps it is better than Germany, Lazer dared to think as the train finally jerked and shuddered and slid into place beside another train.

The groans of the passengers continued, punctuated by shouts of German SS who waited at the station. Metal rattled. Bolts and chains crashed back. The doors were opened to the shouts of, "Out! Out, you filthy swine!"

For a moment no one moved. Inside the cattle cars the bodies had been molded into one mass of human flesh that must break apart carefully, lest parts of it collapse and be trampled.

Rubber truncheons landed on the legs of those who moved too slowly. The sun burst up as long shadows reached across the border into Poland.

10

Night Sounds

Herschel Grynspan was only seventeen years old. Somehow he knew he would not live to see his eighteenth birthday.

It was raining in Paris. Not a hard rain, not the sort of downpour that washes away the dust and leaves the air clean and transparent. This rain was a gray drizzle, obscuring the view from Herschel's attic window and mingling with the smoke from the chimneys to coat everything with a dirty, wet film.

At least the attic air was cool now. Herschel had hidden here for five months since Le Morthomme had stepped between his gun and Thomas von Kleistmann. As the old bookseller had crumpled to the ground, Herschel had run back along the narrow lanes of the Left Bank until he had come to the home of Hans Schumann. Hans had secreted him in the attic and here Herschel had remained through the Paris spring, the stifling humidity of summer, and into autumn.

Hans had brought him food each day and news of each succeeding Nazi outrage. Hans provided him with German newspapers that carried the latest speeches by the Führer. Hans kept his spirits up. He promised that the hour would come when Herschel would fulfill his vow to teach the Nazis a lesson.

When Herschel had openly spoken of suicide, Hans had taken Grynspan's gun away and reminded him that there was only one way left for a Jew to die—*for the cause*!

So it was that on this drizzly day, Hans carried a radio up the steep steps to the attic. A long cord trailed behind and music played as Hans emerged, smiling, through the trapdoor.

"Herschel!" the swarthy young man hailed the captive. "See what I have brought for you!"

Herschel could not manage a smile of gratitude. "Not a visa to Palestine."

Hans looked hurt. He held up the blaring box. "A radio. Music and news for you so you will not have to wait for me to come before you know what is happening in the world!" He set the radio on an upturned crate.

"I would rather have a visa to Palestine." Herschel hated his own ingratitude, but he could not help it. Although he owed everything to Hans, he still felt like a prisoner.

"We are trying. Such things take time. Perhaps they are still looking for the one who killed the old bookseller. Perhaps you would be arrested before you had a chance to improve your aim and kill a Nazi, Herschel." The hurt look was replaced by determination as Hans fiddled with the tuning dial.

"If I were in Palestine, I would not have to kill a Nazi." Herschel lay back on his groaning metal cot. *Why am I not more grateful for the radio?* he wondered.

"In Palestine you could kill Arabs and English—" He stopped midsentence as the dulcet tones of a French broadcaster came through the speaker.

> *"Following the action, the German minister of propaganda issued a statement assuring the world that those Jews deported from the Reich all held Polish passports. . . ."*

Herschel's breath caught in his chest. He sat bolt upright and leaned forward with both hands raised to silence any words from Hans. "My family!" he whispered. "They hold Polish passports!"

> *"Nearly twelve thousand Jews of Polish origin have been rounded up throughout the Reich, and as the German people demanded their immediate expulsion, they are being shipped by train toward the frontier between Germany and Poland. . . ."*

Hans looked first at the radio and then at Herschel. He clucked his tongue in sympathy and shook his head. "Been going on since Thursday, I hear. No doubt your family is among them."

Herschel cried out, "Papa . . . my mother and sister!" He cradled his head in his hands as Hans punctuated the reports of violence with the certainty that Herschel's parents must be among the thousands of victims.

"I thought you would want to hear." Hans frowned. "Something to keep up your resolve, eh, Herschel? A man must be brave in times like these. I was afraid you might be slipping. But you were born for braver things." Hans shrugged and adjusted the tuner to eliminate the faint crackle in the reception as the broadcast shifted to live coverage of the chanting Germans in Munich.

"*Jews to Poland! No more Jewish swine in Germany! Jews to Poland!*"

Night fell over Warsaw with brittle coldness. Sabbath was ended, and once again smoke from the Jewish section of Warsaw mingled with the smoke from Catholic chimneys.

Aaron Lubetkin sat at his massive desk and tried to concentrate on passages of the Mishnah. A green-globed desk lamp cast a ring of light on stacks of books and papers, but increasingly, Aaron found his eyes wandering to the lighted hallway and the banister of the stairs that led up to the bedroom.

The children had long since been put to bed by Frau Rosen. Rachel had not stopped shivering until she soaked in a warm bath. Aaron felt badly that he had sent his daughter on her errand without so much as a thin sweater. Etta would not be happy if she knew. She would have sharp words for him if she ever found out.

The house had been silent since Dr. Eduard Letzno had arrived with his black bag in one hand and Rachel at his side. Etta was always silent at times like this. She did not cry out as some women did in childbirth. Her labor had begun nearly four weeks early. Eduard's face betrayed the seriousness of premature delivery. Etta understood the danger, and she did not wish to frighten Rachel with a display. After all, perhaps one day Rachel would give them grandchildren, and it would not be good to fill her young mind with a terror of childbirth.

Etta was able to think of such things even when the contractions were four minutes apart.

Practical, beautiful Etta.

The thought of her made Aaron's throat tight with emotion. How could he live without her if something went wrong? He wiped his eyes with the back of his hand. He had not turned a page in his book for nearly three hours. After Dr. Letzno had come and expelled him from the room, he had gone through the motions of normalcy with the children; then he had retreated here, just beneath the room where Etta labored.

The floorboards creaked above his head—Eduard's footsteps. The encouraging voice of Frau Rosen penetrated the study, then the voice of

Eduard: "That's it, Etta!" Muffled, but understandable. "Once again!" Still no sound from Etta.

Aaron stared up at the ceiling as if his gaze could pierce the rafters that separated him from her agony. His own breath was heavy with the exertion of his thoughts. "That's it, Etta," he whispered. "That's it, darling."

Suddenly her silence was broken with one explosive cry. "*Aaron!*"

Aaron felt the blood drain from his face. He jumped from his chair; it toppled backward, spilling a stack of books onto the floor. Taking the stairs two at a time, he reached the landing within seconds. He threw open the bedroom door, then stopped.

Etta lay on the bed, draped in a sheet and quilt. Her hands grasped cords tied to the bedposts. Her head was thrown back, and her teeth gritted with the strain of her effort. Mrs. Rosen supported her shoulders. The doctor was reaching out to guide a tiny, crumpled form from her womb.

No one noticed Aaron as he stood panting and ashen in the doorway.

"Once again, Etta! He's almost—"

"She called me," Aaron blurted out.

"Close the door, Aaron." The doctor's words were clipped, preoccupied.

Aaron continued to gaze wide-eyed at Etta. Damp hair clung to her face. Her eyes were squeezed tight. Aaron breathed with her. He clenched his fists and moaned softly. Tears stung his eyes. He had never seen her like this, never witnessed—

"Close the door, Rebbe Lubetkin!" Frau Rosen barked her command. "The draft."

Aaron swallowed hard and obeyed. Etta did not look at him. Her knuckles were white as she strained against the cords and sat halfway up in the bed as she bore down.

"Beautiful, Etta! Another son!" Eduard held the slippery gray child gently as he wiped away mucous and blood. "So tiny, and yet *alive!*"

"The Eternal be praised!" Frau Rosen helped lower Etta to the heap of pillows and wiped Etta's forehead with a damp cloth.

"A boy!" Etta wept happily, raising her head to look.

"Ah!" Aaron tried to speak, but the words became garbled in his throat. Etta's face swam before his eyes.

"Sit down, Aaron," Eduard commanded. "You will fall down."

Suspended upside down, the four-pound infant bleated his first angry protest against the world. Then he squalled louder and spread his fingers at the end of flailing arms as his father sank to the floor at the bedside.

ᐧᗉᐧ

The gentle touch of Elisa's hands pulled Murphy from his sleep. It did not matter; he had been dreaming of her anyway. He answered her urgent kisses with a slow and drowsy response, and when at last she fell asleep in his arms, he lay wide awake for an hour still dreaming of her.

Downstairs the mantel clock chimed two o'clock. She stirred and moved closer to him. Her skin smelled like a flower garden. Her breath smelled like toothpaste. Murphy had come to love those scents, come to look forward to sliding between the sheets and inhaling her. Just the thought of it made him want her again. He wished she would wake up and lift her face to him and say his name in that funny way of hers, "*Murrrf . . .*" Nobody but Elisa called him that. And she only called him that when she whispered his name between kisses.

Somewhere on a distant London street a siren wailed. It seemed impossible to Murphy that anything unpleasant could be happening tonight when his own world seemed so perfect. The thought made him frown. Of course, it was his job to report the news of this terribly imperfect world. But for now, he wanted to protect Elisa from it. She seemed fragile since the *Darien* had sunk. She left the room when the BBC announced the latest. She did not ask him what news had flashed across the wires. It was just as well. She had done her part. Nobody deserved a rest more than Elisa, except maybe Anna and Theo.

He smiled at the irony of that. Already Anna and Theo had joined Bubbe Rosenfelt in her work with the F.A.T.E. group. Murphy had sent the story to TENS himself.

> *Theo Lindheim, former department-store owner in Berlin, escaped Dachau to head the Fair Anglo Treatment of Emigres. The organization seeks to aid thousands of homeless as well as establish fair laws for those attempting to flee the tyranny of Hitler's Germany.*

Some people never stopped. Murphy had married into just such a family. And were it not for the fact that a new little Murphy was on the way, Elisa would have also jumped right back into the thick of it.

Murphy slid his hand over her abdomen. Not even a bulge yet, but he smiled all the same. *Thank you, little guy. Now maybe we can stop long enough to listen to the music.*

All Murphy wanted to do was protect her, hold her, keep her safe. The doctor figured the baby would come along nine months to the day after their second wedding at the cottage in New Forest. The legal wedding. Short version. Murphy chuckled out loud in spite of himself.

"What, Murrrf?" Elisa asked dreamily.

"Just thinking about the night in New Forest. Snow White's Cottage—remember?"

"Hmmmm?"

"What a night."

"A good thing I made you marry me," she said.

Murphy breathed in the scent of toothpaste. He raised up on his elbow and bent to kiss her.

She smiled through his kiss and said his name.

He pressed his cheek against hers. "You think we'll ever sleep the whole night through again?"

"I hope not."

He caught the flash of her smile in the darkness. He was glad she was awake. "Tell me what you want," he asked.

She thought for a moment. "It doesn't matter. As long as it's healthy."

The moment was perfect. Delicious.

And then the phone rang. Once. Twice. Three times.

Murphy had come to hate telephones. He groaned and reached across her to the night table, finally yanking the receiver off the table and pulling it toward him while Elisa muffled a giggle.

It was Harvey Terrill from the office. His voice sounded unhappy and desperate even before he managed to explain the reason for the call. Elisa moved away from Murphy. She turned over as if to cover her ears lest anything reach her. When at last Murphy replaced the receiver and switched on the light, she was looking at him with eyes filled with memory.

He shrugged and sat up. "Sorry. This is worse than being married to a doctor." He tried to smile, but somehow he could not find the lightness even for that.

"Germany?" she asked, running her hands through her hair.

He attempted to pass it off. "Nazi demonstration. You know how that goes."

She nodded slowly. Yes. She knew.

The burled-walnut grandfather clock at the foot of the stairs chimed. Etta rested peacefully with the new baby in a cradle beside her.

Aaron took two glasses and a bottle of cognac from the cupboard behind his desk. Dr. Eduard Letzno sat down heavily in the wingback chair across from his boyhood friend. He leaned his head against the brown leather and sighed.

Aaron glanced up as he poured. His friend was wearing suit trousers and a white shirt open at the collar. His stethoscope dangled from his neck like a tie. His thick brown hair was tousled, as it had been after a hard game of stickball when they were children. Eduard had grown up, but he had aged very little—except for his gray eyes. His eyes somehow looked ancient and weary.

"You have been working too hard, my friend." The glasses clinked as Aaron passed one to Eduard.

"You fathers are all the same." Eduard sipped and grimaced. "You think delivering babies is work. All we doctors do is wait and act as if the process could not happen without us." He raised his glass in a tired toast. "But don't tell anyone."

"*L'Chaim,*" Aaron returned the toast.

"*L'Chaim,*" Eduard replied. "To life. A new little Lubetkin. An arrow in the quiver of Aaron and Etta Lubetkin." He drank and this time did not grimace.

Aaron sprawled in the chair across from Eduard. *I do not look like a rabbi should look,* he mused. *Sitting in my study with a clean-shaven fellow who looks as much like a Gentile as any Catholic.* "Thank you for coming," he said, feeling a bit guilty that he had thought such things about Eduard. "Rachel told me you were having some sort of party."

Eduard sniffed and stared into his cognac. "Raising money. You know. For the Zionist settlement in Palestine. Just what we must not speak of among the Jews of this neighborhood, yes? 'There can be no homeland without Messiah,' they will say. And then they will throw me out on my ear."

"Well, it is just you and me, Eduard. I will not throw you out." Aaron tried to joke. "Until you present your bill."

"You are certainly the only one of my old friends who welcomes me. The apikoros. The apostate. The traitor Zionist who no longer believes in your Jewish God."

The last was spoken with such bitterness that Aaron dared not reply. All of what Eduard said was true, down to the word *apostate*. A thousand times Aaron had asked how it happened. And why? As boys they had shared the same bench at Torah school. They had discussed the Baal Shem Tov with the same enthusiasm. But Aaron had gone to study in Jerusalem and Eduard to the University in Prague. When Aaron at last returned to Poland, Eduard had changed.

There was pain in this change, for both men.

"Perhaps one day you will find yourself again. And find the One who makes a Jew a Jew. In the meantime, you are Doktor Eduard Letzno. You deliver the children of your friend the rabbi."

Eduard did not smile. He swirled his cognac. "And is my friend the rabbi leaving Warsaw? leaving Poland, as I have hoped?"

Aaron tugged his beard thoughtfully. This was a matter they had discussed with unfailing regularity. "You were at Evian. I only listened to the nations of the world as they denied us. You were there, Eduard. So tell me . . ." He asked the question in Yiddish: *"Vi aheen zoll ich gain?* Wherever shall I go?"

Eduard leaned forward. His gray eyes smoldered with intensity. *"Palestine!* Zion! There is still time, Aaron! Take Etta and the children to her father in Jerusalem."

Aaron smiled sadly. "We have thought much about it. Jerusalem, where the Jews of the Old City live on the charity of the Jews of Warsaw. If all of us leave for Jerusalem, then who will be left to send money to Jerusalem?"

"Have you still not seen it, Aaron? The ground is burning beneath our feet! The one thing Poland has in common with Germany is a hatred of Jews."

"We are three million Jews here in Poland. Three million and one, as of tonight. What can they do to us? We have been here for centuries, and we will be here centuries from now. Etta and I have talked. Things will get better. People are civilized now. What can they do to us here in Poland?"

Eduard Letzno fiddled with the end of his stethoscope. "You know what they did to the Jews of Austria, and what is being done in Czechoslovakia since the Germans entered the Sudetenland."

"This is Warsaw. The Germans are not here."

"Yet."

"They will not come here." Aaron raised his chin as if he were trying to comfort a frightened child. He had been frightened himself. But now he was confident. There would be no war. Hitler said that the Sudetenland was his last territorial claim in Europe. "There are more of us *here* than anywhere in the world. Safety in numbers, Eduard."

"I pray you will leave this place before it is too late."

"How can I set any hope in Palestine when every day the Arabs are blowing up the Zionists? There is as much violence in Jerusalem as there is in Vienna. We have the letters to prove it, letters from Etta's father. Do you think I would take my children to such a place?" Aaron exhaled loudly. It was too late for such talk. "New York, America. That is where I wanted to go. I *tried*! You know I did. And now they have closed those doors. Quotas filled for two years."

"Then get your name on the list for the day *after* those two years are up, Aaron! Get out of Warsaw. Those two years must pass, and who knows what is ahead for us."

"And what about you? Where are you going?"

"Palestine. Next week."

Aaron placed his glass on the blotter. "So soon?"

"Palestine is in desperate need of doctors. I have an assignment with the Jewish Agency for work in a clinic in Jerusalem."

"Can you not stay long enough—" Concern showed in Aaron's eyes. "The child is so small and fragile."

Eduard hesitated. "There is another matter." He swirled the cognac in his glass. "I have been questioned by the police here in Warsaw."

"Questioned?"

"It seems Poland is also listening to the broadcasts of Herr Hitler, Aaron. All Jews are subversives, he says. Bent on the overthrow of every government and the domination of the world." There was bitter amusement in his eyes. "My Zionist connections are suspect, of course." He frowned. "I have been . . . requested by the Poles . . . to leave."

"But you are no threat!" Aaron argued for Eduard as if the argument would make a difference. "Not a Communist."

Eduard stood and stepped to the window. He drew back the heavy brocade drapery and scanned the square beyond as he spoke. "Russia is at the back of Poland. The Nazis stand at the front door. Hitler raves that the Russians will overrun Poland to attack Germany. He says that the Bolshevik Jews who live within Poland are even now preparing the way for Russia. Do you think this government is not listening? looking for subversives who might be playing out this scenario?"

"But you, Eduard! You are a humanitarian, not a politician!"

Eduard looked out the window. "Humanitarians are the enemies of politicians, Aaron. Have you not learned that here in Warsaw?" He turned from probing the dark street. There was a strange smile on his face, as though he saw Death and yet was not afraid. "Come here."

Aaron joined him at the window. He did not want to know what Eduard knew. Did not wish to see the apparition Eduard must somehow see in the streets of the Warsaw ghetto. And yet he searched the dark square, the empty cobbles of Muranow Square. There was no one there. "What is it?" he whispered.

"Across the square on the corner you will see his cigarette," Eduard answered hollowly, confident in his knowledge.

Aaron turned his eyes toward the corner of the street that led to the Umschlagplatz, the train station. The distant whistle of a train penetrated the glass. And then the small orange glow of a match flashed for an instant, illuminating a man. "You are being watched."

Eduard let the curtain fall. He nodded. "We are all being watched, Aaron. The eyes of Darkness have turned east. Again they linger on us."

He sat down slowly while Aaron remained beside the window, stunned.

"Then you must leave for Palestine. But I am no Zionist. I am a rabbi only."

There was silence in the room except for the ticking of the clock. Again the train whistle pierced the night. *A call to leave Warsaw?* Aaron wondered. *A warning to those who sleep peacefully through this night?*

Eduard averted his eyes from the shadow that crossed Aaron's face. He frowned and sipped his cognac thoughtfully. "Sit down, Aaron. Sit. I will stay in Warsaw until after the baby is circumcised. Perhaps by then you will be convinced—"

A sharp knock interrupted them. Eduard raised his finger as if to hold his place. The knock sounded again, this time more urgently.

"Herr Doktor Letzno," the housekeeper's voice penetrated the door. "A gentleman has come looking for you. The Nazis, Herr Doktor! They have deported twelve thousand Jews from the Reich!"

11

God Is an Optimist

It was two kilometers from the German border station of Neu Bentschen to the Polish crossing. Most of the twelve thousand Jews under guard at the place had not eaten since Thursday.

Lazer felt weak, as if his legs would not carry him. He was not as old as some of the deportees; he could only guess how they must feel after such a journey.

On one end of the platform a young man was being beaten by two SS officers as a group of soldiers laughed and looked on. There were many Nazi Blackshirts strutting up and down the long lines of prisoners. Lazer wondered why so many soldiers had been called to drive the Jews out of Germany.

Everyone had been searched—men, women; it made no difference that there were no female guards to search the women. These SS soldiers enjoyed their work. To humiliate a Jewess was to make their comrades roll with laughter. They would carry stories of this day back to the barracks, and they would laugh again and again.

It began to rain, a hard, ruthless downpour. Lazer removed his torn jacket in an attempt to shelter Rifka and Berta. Others who stood waiting along the tracks also tried to shield themselves from the drenching rain. There were no umbrellas. No offer of shelter was made by the Nazis. Some mothers with small children begged to be allowed to get back into the cattle cars just for a while. Permission was refused. The doors slid closed to punctuate the German hope that even very small Jews would perish from pneumonia.

"Sensible of the gods to drown these vermin," scoffed the SS commander beneath his hooded black rain slicker.

Lazer thought how much these SS men resembled executioners in their wet-weather gear. All of them were strong and tall. They had been chosen for their physical prowess. Ah yes, Germany was a land of beauty until a man looked into the hard, cold eyes of one of these magnificent beasts. Lips twisted in cruel enjoyment of the misery of twelve thousand. Such power there was in making these rotten Jews stand for hours in the rain!

Young Berta's eyes were filled with a haunting fear that added centuries to her fifteen years. She had seen such brutality before, but now it was directed at her!

Lazer wrapped his arm around his daughter's shoulders and pulled her close against him. She was shivering with the cold and with the spectacle.

"I am thirsty, Papa," she said.

Lazer held his hand out and caught the rain. He held the cupped hand to her lips, and she drank. She smiled.

"Better?" he asked.

"I did not want to drink water that has touched this German soil," she said. "It is good that we have rain."

That was Berta. Always she looked for the best. The rain had become a fountain from which she could drink. "We will arrive in Poland free from German dust," Rifka added through chattering teeth. "A blessing, this rain. It washes us clean from the past." Her words were brave for the sake of their daughter, but Lazer could clearly see the pain in his wife's eyes. *Where will we go? What will become of us?*

A little before noon the soldiers came with the dogs. They stood beneath the roof of the platform and looked out at their conquered thousands. Black-muzzled German shepherds sat serene and proud beside their handlers. Beautiful, perfectly disciplined animals, these German dogs. Five hundred SS against twelve thousand Jews. It was more than enough.

By noon the dogs were hungry. The colonel beneath the black slicker shouted his command: "Only two kilometers across the frontier to Poland. Let's see how fast these Jewish pigs can run!"

Suddenly, as if they understood the colonel's words, the dogs leaped to their feet, snarling. They strained against their short leather leads, lunging again and again toward the long line of Jews.

Guards began to shout, "Run! Run! Run!"

The SS moved from beneath the shelter of the station and laid their truncheons on the backs of their quarry. Jewish blood mingled with the rain until the road was dark red.

Lazer grasped Rifka's hand and Berta's hand. He began to run blindly as the screaming, panicked mass pressed around them. Hands reached out toward Poland, as if the reaching could bring the border closer.

The soldiers and dogs followed. They flanked the Jews, herding them like cattle. Whips raised and crashed down on the heads of anyone in the way. It did not matter how fast they ran; it was not fast enough. Mothers and fathers carried shrieking children, but the blows fell on them as readily as they landed on the young men of the group.

The dogs' teeth tore open the legs of men and women alike. That blood mingled in rivers on the road.

Everywhere people fell into the mud and were beaten for their failure. Others who tried to help them up were also beaten for their efforts. "Run faster, Papa!" Berta shouted as a snarling Blackshirt slashed at a woman beside him.

Lazer willed himself to go forward. Rifka tugged his arm. Two kilometers to the Polish border! How his lungs ached!

"Run, run, you filthy Jewish pigs! Out of Germany, and don't come back!"

Lazer stumbled and fell in the mud. An old man fell on top of him and took the brunt of blows that came down with the rain. Rifka screamed. Berta wept and begged the German to stop. When the old man's arms went limp, the soldier lost interest and turned to yet another victim.

Lazer pushed the dead body from him and struggled to stand. Berta clutched his hand and pulled him. "Get up, Papa! Hurry! Get up! Run, or they will kill us too!"

The Polish border was in sight when the Nazis began to fire on stragglers. "Women first!" shouted a bloodied man. "Women through the checkpoint first! Women and children."

Lazer pushed Rifka and Berta away from him. Berta reached out for her father, but he denied her stark terror and urged the two women forward as gunfire crackled over their heads.

On the Polish side of the line, border guards stood gaping at the terrified mass.

"Open the gates! Open the gates!" The shouts were indeed in Polish, but how could the guards check so many at once?

From behind, the gunfire continued, the smell of gunpowder an acrid contrast to the rain. In the front women were pressed painfully against the wire of the gates as those in the rear surged forward.

"Open the gates! *Please!* We will be crushed, and our children with us!"

Lazer lost sight of Berta and Rifka. He prayed that he would not lose his footing. To fall meant certain death. *How many have been trampled?* he wondered. *What would the Germans do with the Jewish dead who lined the road these last two kilometers?*

"Open the gates!" he heard himself cry. "We are Polish! We are *Polish!* Can't you hear? That is why they beat us! *We are Polish!*"

There was a space of only twelve feet between the Western Wall and the shabby houses of the Moroccan neighborhood. The houses of the Muslims of Morocco always stood at the backs of praying Jews like Rabbi Lebowitz. Some of the Chosen were ill at ease as they prayed before these stones. After all, more than one rabbi had been killed as he raised his hands to the holy wall and lifted prayers to heaven.

But Rabbi Lebowitz was not nervous. He had decided long ago that there was no better way for a Jew to die than in the posture of fervent prayer.

For this reason, he breathed easily as he lifted his prayer shawl over his head and let the soft wind rustle the pages of his siddur. Before these individual stones of the holy wall, the old rabbi lifted his heart to the Lord of heaven.

Today the narrow space before the Wailing Wall was almost empty. There were a few worshippers who, like Rabbi Lebowitz, had come with their petitions written out to slide between the chinks in the wall. Some sat on a wooden bench to pray. Others leaned against the cool of the stones that were tarnished from the hands of two thousand years of loving touches. A soft wind whispered down the alleyway to twirl the fringes of prayer shawls and tug at aged beards. On such a day the old man lifted his eyes to the crisp blue slit of the sky and imagined the winds were stirred by the wings of the angels who hovered above this place. Ah, there were always angels here; everyone knew that. It was said that this part of the wall had been built by the beggars of Solomon's time, and that on the day of the Temple's destruction the angels had linked their wings around the wall and the command had been given: *This, the work of the poor, shall never be destroyed!*

The Shekinah glory of God remained here, and at certain times the very stones wept for the destruction of the Temple.

Was there a better place, then, for Rabbi Shlomo Lebowitz to bring his request before the Lord? Was not this sheer face of hewn rock the one place on earth where a chink remained open to the throne room of the Almighty?

Into that small opening, the old man urged his request. Perhaps the wings of the angels fluttered when they heard it. Perhaps their stirring carried the prayer of the old man near to the ear of the Almighty. Perhaps they smiled at such an old fool who came every day, rain or shine, with the same prayer on his lips.

More plaintive than the call of the ram's horn seemed the words of this prayer: "With Your mighty hand, reach down and carry Your children home to this place, this small piece of earth. For the sake of Your name, for the sake of Your promise, call out to the north and bring them home that the kingdom of Your Messiah may be established, and His throne forever in Jerusalem!"

Could the Lord ignore such a prayer? And always there was a small postscript to this faithful request: "And while You are at it, Lord, if You don't mind too much, bring Etta and Aaron home along with the rest of Your scattered children, *nu?* No matter what You may have heard me think, this is still our home. Just between You and this old rabbi, such a small thing. And I would be eternally grateful for the favor."

By the time the Western Union messenger raised his hand to knock on the door of Rabbi Shlomo Lebowitz, a small crowd had gathered around to hear the bad news. Telegrams did not come to the residents of Old City Jerusalem unless someone had died. Everyone knew that last night as Arab rebels attacked outposts in Palestine, the Nazis had rioted in the Reich and expelled twelve thousand Jews to Poland. No doubt there had been many deaths during that brutal pogrom.

Rabbi Lebowitz wiped his hands on a dish towel and opened the door. He looked first at the grim-faced young Arab messenger, who propped his bicycle against the wall and then doffed his Western Union cap as he presented the telegram.

From the small group of onlookers, Eli Sachar called, "Sit down, Rebbe! *Sit down* before you read it!"

The ladies auxiliary of Tipat Chalev all chimed in with agreement. Young boys from Torah school urged their venerated rabbi to sit. "*Sit! Nu?*"

The rabbi took the yellow envelope and paid the Arab messenger a shilling. Then he left the door to his tiny flat open and motioned for his friends and neighbors to join him inside.

A man did not wish to open a telegram alone, after all.

He muttered a prayer as he sat slowly at the table. His friends stood around him. His students. His neighbors. They whispered, "Who could it be?"

"Maybe Etta?"

"Maybe it did not go well for her. She *was expecting.*"

The phrase *was expecting* was certainly ominous. It had the sound of words that are said over the departed: "She *was* a good person. She *was* liked by everyone. She *was* expecting. . . ."

"Maybe it isn't her. It could also be his brother in Chicago, America, *nu?*"

Rabbi Lebowitz had thought of nothing else since news had come of the violence on the German border last night. Could there be any connection between that and this terrible yellow envelope?

"Be brave, Rebbe Lebowitz."

"Remember, the Lord giveth and the Lord taketh away."

The old man nodded. His eyebrows knit together in a solid black line as he opened the envelope. Carefully he unfolded the paper. The address read *Warsaw, Poland.*

"Warsaw," he said.

A shocked sigh passed through the room. So it had to be *her. His only daughter!*

He opened the next fold and began to read. His head moved back and forth. He opened his moth and cried, *"Oy! Etta! Etta!"*

Sad shakes of each head. So it was *her!* "When did it happen, Rebbe Lebowitz?" Hannah Cohen moved through the crowd.

"Oy! The Eternal . . . be *praised!* It is a baby boy! They will call him Yacov!"

Good news in a telegram was hard to understand. Did this mean that Etta had died, but the baby had lived? Half a blessing. Or had Etta lived and the baby also? If this was so, then why send a telegram and give everyone a heart attack?

"Is Etta . . . ?" Hannah broached the subject.

"Fine! *Fine!"* Rabbi Lebowitz wiped away tears of joy. "They sent the wire so I should not worry with all that is going on. My son-in-law has gone to aid the Jewish refugees at the border. They ask that we might help with a relief fund of some sort. *Oy!"* He raised his eyes to heaven. "They are all *fine!* We have a new little Lubetkin! A new grandson! He is named Yacov! In the midst of such a terrible night for Jews, still . . . God proves He is an optimist, *nu?* He sends another Jewish baby into the world!"

The damp stone walls of the little apartment now echoed with applause and cries of *"Mazel tov!"* So. At least there was some good news from God this morning for Jews, *nu?*

What had begun as a morning filled with fear and foreboding was transformed into a day of energetic joy. News of the baby passed from mouth to mouth. Word of the request from Warsaw for help in aiding the refugees gave everyone a new purpose—money to collect from those few who had it, socks to knit, clothing to collect and mend and package. The Jews of Jerusalem were poor, but they were not so poor that they could not help their unfortunate brothers and sisters in the border camps of Poland.

The telegram was posted on the wall of Tipat Chalev for everyone to see. Beneath it was a list of items needed for the refugees. And scrawled across the yellow paper were the rabbi's words: *GOD IS AN OPTIMIST!*

Everyone understood the meaning.

12

"And Yet I Must Believe"

Somehow the numbers of people deported from Germany had not been translated into the reality of human misery that now unfolded before Rabbi Aaron Lubetkin.

Twelve thousand huddled together in the abandoned stables. The sky spit rain until the earth was a quagmire and each footprint filled with water. No hats. No blankets. No food. Only twelve thousand shivering people. Haunted eyes. Bloodied faces. Tears hidden by the rain that seeped through the broken shingles on the roof.

"So many!" Aaron managed a whisper as he and Eduard entered the largest of three stables. Family groups had claimed stalls as dwelling places. Never mind that everything they owned had been confiscated.

Eduard's face was flushed with rage at the sight of such needless suffering.

From within the unlit stalls, no one looked up at the two men framed in the entrance to the stables. Aaron and Eduard were just two more bodies among the thousands.

"Where do we begin?" Aaron asked.

An answer was not required; a plaintive voice called out from a stall where the door hung askew on its hinges. A woman called in anguish, "Herr Doktor? Are you a doktor, there? You with the bag! *Bitte! Please!* It is my husband, Lazer! *Mein Gott!* He is . . . *please!*"

In three steps Eduard entered the stall with Aaron at his heels. A small, thin man lay unconscious on the damp dirt floor. A woman and girl of fifteen or sixteen huddled over him. The unconscious man was almost a luminous white, and Aaron thought for a moment that it was too late for him. Eduard took off his overcoat and threw it over the man as he grabbed the limp wrist and felt for a faint pulse.

The woman was weeping. The girl seemed dulled with the shock of what had come upon them.

"He is alive," Eduard said. He began to ask the sobbing woman questions. "When did you last eat?"

"Days ago. They came for us at suppertime. Berta and I had at least a bite . . . but not Lazer."

"Was he beaten?" Eduard probed the man's abdomen.

"Crushed. The train. Cattle cars. And then at the border, he fell. Someone kicked him, and . . ."

Aaron studied the girl, the daughter of the fallen man. She was pretty, her features finely chiseled and her brown eyes large and round. But her face showed no expression at the words of her mother. She squatted in the dirt near her father's feet and simply stared with glazed eyes at the green paint that flaked from the boards of the stall.

Aaron said the girl's name. "Berta."

The mother did not notice as she talked on about their ordeal. The eyes of the young girl did not flicker recognition at her name.

Again Aaron said the name. "Berta? You are safe now. Safe in Poland."

Still no sign of comprehension. Eduard looked up from the father toward the girl. "Your father will recover," he said without hesitation. "He is exhausted. Do you hear me, girl? He is sleeping. Soon there will be food."

At last the young woman blinked. Her faded eyes focused, then moved to the face of her father and then to the black bag that marked Eduard as a doctor. The girl began to weep silently. She reached out to touch her mother, who enfolded her in her arms and wept with her.

Eduard stood slowly. "Keep him warm," he instructed, leaving his own coat over the frail body of Lazer Grynspan as fulfillment of that instruction. "Berta, when the trucks come with food, you must be the one to stand in line, yes?"

The young woman nodded. Tears still streamed down her cheeks. "Yes," she sobbed. "When . . . food . . . comes . . ."

Mercifully the rain had stopped by the time the bread trucks arrived at all the stables where the refugees had taken shelter.

The lines consisted of thousands like Berta Grynspan who waited for a ration on behalf of thousands more inside the stables.

Rabbi Aaron Lubetkin and Dr. Eduard Letzno had spent eighteen unbroken hours among the refugees before volunteers came to take their places—groups of ten at first, then hundreds. Blankets and clothing were distributed with the food. Enormous kettles of soup simmered over open fires in the stable courtyard.

Miraculously there had been only seven deaths throughout that long first day. Most of the victims were old—unable to survive the ordeal of the journey and the cold and hunger and grief. One little boy had died only seconds before Eduard entered the stalls. He had fallen and been trampled. There had been little chance of survival under the best of conditions, but here, it had been hopeless.

Aaron did his best to comfort the family, who were among the Catholics in the group. They asked for a priest to attend them in their grief, so Aaron had sent for one to come from the village six miles to the east. Some hours later he had passed the stall and paused to listen to the words of the Polish priest: "You are welcome in my parish . . . gather up your things."

"We have nothing."

The priest wrapped the dead child in his cloak and stood. "Come with me."

Aaron turned away and fought to control his own emotion at the sight of the black-garbed man leading his tiny flock out of the suffering. The lifeless form of the child made certain that the family took all their suffering along with them. There would be no joy in the warmth of a fire or in clean beds to sleep in. They had lost a son.

Aaron felt a light tapping on his back. He looked down to see the still-grieved face of young Berta Grynspan gazing up at him. "How is your father?" he asked.

"Better. Sitting up. He ate some soup and bread." She extended an envelope to him. "The nurse found me some paper, Rabbi Lubetkin. I have written a letter to my brother. His name is Herschel. He is in Paris. Safe in Paris. But he will be frantic with worry. Would you—" she looked hopefully at the envelope—"I have no stamp, you see, and . . ."

Aaron took the letter from her. He slipped it into his pocket. "You have given a return address? Where he may write?"

Berta nodded. "The authorities say we will be here for some time." She pointed as yet another truck caravan brought supplies into the compound. "At least we will be fed. Someone said they will bring stoves and coal to heat the buildings with. At least we have a roof." The young woman uttered these words with a tone of such hopelessness that Aaron found it difficult to respond.

He tried to smile. "Perhaps it will not be long and you will be in real houses, eh?" He patted the pocket that held the letter. "Your brother will be relieved that you are all right."

Berta shrugged and stared down the long row of stalls. "Paris," she mumbled. "Maybe we will . . ." Her voice trailed off, and she walked away from the rabbi without saying good-bye.

It was a short walk from the headquarters of the Gestapo on Albertstrasse to the Chancellery building where Adolf Hitler awaited word from Commander Leo Vargen.

The Führer had his suspicions about the possible involvement of certain military leaders in a conspiracy against the Nazi government. With the capture and interrogation of Thomas von Kleistmann, no doubt those suspicions would be resolved.

Beneath his arm, Commander Vargen carried a leather file case containing all the information gleaned from the records and from von Kleistmann himself over the past few days.

Vargen looked up at the great eagle of the Third Reich that spread its granite wings over the entrance to the marble reception hall. The heels of SS guards clicked as he entered. Inside the doors a hundred black-uniformed SS men stood at rigid attention the entire length of the vast hall. Their clean, proud reflections shone on the polished black marble floor.

The hall was said to be longer than that of the Palace of Versailles. The Führer himself had ordered its huge dimensions so that foreign representatives and heads of state might be intimidated by the glory of the Reich. The floors were waxed until they were slick, so that, according to the Führer's reasoning, foreigners were forced to watch their step lest they fall before the leader of the German people.

Vargen did not doubt these little stories that contained evidence of the Führer's wit. Adolf Hitler left nothing to chance, not even the choice of floor wax for the Chancellery. Leo Vargen knew that he also must watch his step in the presence of the great man.

Bronze double doors swung back, revealing a sitting room with an enormous fireplace. The mantel was crowned with an eagle clutching a swastika in its claws. The Führer stood with his back to the roaring blaze. As Vargen entered and saluted, it seemed to him as if Hitler had just emerged from the fire. *Was this appearance also thought out beforehand?*

To his right, Gestapo Chief Heinrich Himmler sat in a comfortable overstuffed chair. When Vargen hesitated a moment too long, Himmler motioned impatiently for him to come into the circle of sofas and chairs in front of the fire.

"Well? What news do you have for us from von Kleistmann?"

Himmler asked. The Führer did not speak. He did not turn his gaze on Vargen.

Vargen held out the leather case. He clicked his heels and bowed slightly. Still the Führer did not seem to notice him. "We captured him quite easily as he attempted to board ship in Holland."

"That ship was bound for?" Himmler asked.

"England."

At the word *England*, the face of the Führer darkened. His eyes narrowed as if this confirmed his suspicions. Yet still he did not speak.

"And who did von Kleistmann name as his conspirators?" Himmler leafed through the pages without reading them.

Vargen felt his face grow red with embarrassment. "He . . . admits to nothing . . . no one else involved, he said."

"You believe him?" A peculiar smile played on Himmler's lips.

"I cannot see that a man could lie under such . . . circumstances." Vargen shrugged. He had tried everything. What else was there to do short of killing von Kleistmann?

Himmler studied the photograph of Thomas. "A handsome man, was he not? Strong."

"It is his strength that keeps him silent . . . that is, if there is any more to tell."

The Führer's face was unmoved, dark and angry. He wanted answers from the traitorous young Abwehr officer, not examples of Aryan endurance!

"Exactly what does he admit to?"

"Nothing," Vargen said.

"Not even the murder of Georg Wand?" Himmler leaned forward.

"Not even that. He says he had a personal hatred for Wand. A distaste for worms such as Wand who soiled the German people. And he admits to secretly disliking . . . our party."

Hitler's face contorted. "Traitor!" he cried. "*That is enough!* He admits his guilt! Have I not said that he who is not for me is against me? *There!* We have a verdict on this arrogant aristocrat! And mark my words! He is not alone in his conspiracy! I want *names!*"

Both Himmler and Vargen drew back at the outburst. Vargen stuttered a reply, an apology that he had been unable to extract the desired information from von Kleistmann.

"But . . . what if he *is* alone? What if there are no others, mein Führer?" Himmler managed to ask.

"Are you saying he is *innocent*?" Hitler shrieked. "Innocent? Then do what is always done with the innocent! *Crucify him!*"

Vargen and Himmler exchanged looks. Could the Führer mean such a thing?

"Crucify him!" Hitler screamed again. "He would destroy me! Did he think I would not see? *Crucify him!*"

Vargen swallowed hard. "Yes, mein Führer. But . . . if he still does not speak?"

"*He is against me!*" A black lock of hair had fallen across Hitler's eye, completing the picture of madness. "He has slept with a Jewish whore! That is *enough! Kill him!*" Hitler took a step toward Vargen. For an instant it seemed as if Hitler might strike, then abruptly he turned on his heel and faced the fire.

Awkward minutes of silence ticked by. Vargen dared not move. Himmler dared not speak. The Führer was once again deep in thought. It was often like this. Great passion, then silence as the mind of Germany's leader moved on to other matters.

Vargen was sweating. He mopped his bald head and waited until the Führer's inspired thoughts would take the form of words. Logs crackled in the heat of the flames.

At last the Führer spoke again. "Palestine." He turned and faced the two men. He was smiling as if the rage over Thomas von Kleistmann had been a dream. He rose up slightly on his toes and beamed. "Yes. Palestine!"

He gestured for Vargen to be seated, and he also took a chair across from Himmler. Pleasant. Charming. An answer had come to him, and now he would share it.

Vargen was only barely able to make the jump from von Kleistmann to Palestine. Himmler, on the other hand, shifted gears smoothly.

"So, mein Führer." Himmler smiled and polished his glasses. "An answer has come to you at last?"

"It took the presence of Commander Vargen for me to see clearly." Hitler was almost jovial now. He turned to Vargen, who was still perspiring, still inwardly contemplating the rage of this now reasonable man.

"Me?" Vargen ventured.

Hitler fixed his piercing blue eyes on Vargen. "You served with the Turks during the Great War against the English, did you not?"

"Yes." Vargen still failed to see where this was leading.

"Then you know how essential the territory of Palestine is to our aims, especially now."

Vargen nodded as though he understood, but he did not. "Of course."

Hitler slapped his knee. "The Arabs do us the greatest service in their rebellion against England and the Zionists. You see? There are nearly twenty thousand British troops in Palestine trying to keep the peace. *Twenty thousand!* More men deployed there than anywhere else in the

British Empire. More in Palestine than are pledged to support France when war comes."

Not *if,* but *when* . . .

"How might Commander Vargen be of service, mein Führer?" Himmler asked earnestly.

"We have been training the Mufti's men here in Germany for some time. I propose that Commander Vargen return to Palestine, where once he knew defeat at the hands of the English! Yes! That he train the men on location. Fight and train in Palestine and Jerusalem beneath the noses of the English while we continue to fortify our western defenses."

Vargen could not think of a more distasteful task. Perhaps this was some sort of banishment from Germany since he had failed to crack through the wall of von Kleistmann's silence. He had no choice but to accept the assignment. "An honor."

"You must engage the British, you see. Keep them tied up. Occupied by their own problems." Hitler stared thoughtfully at the ceiling. "I will send orders by courier this afternoon. We have an agent in Jerusalem now who has contact with the Mufti. It will be all arranged." He waved a hand absently. "First you may finish this unpleasantness with Thomas von Kleistmann, of course." He smiled again, as if he were discussing a favor, a gift.

Vargen was taken completely off guard. He had no chance to express opposition to duty in Palestine. Perhaps this had all been planned, like the wax on the polished floors of the Chancellery, to keep him off balance.

Himmler picked up Hitler's enthusiasm. "Of course, all of this will also serve to demonstrate the hypocrisy of the Western nations in dealing with the Jewish problem, *ja?*"

Hitler appraised Vargen. "If the matter is handled well, then yes. We will see that even a self-righteous race of governesses like the English will be part of the final solution to the Jewish question." The gaze lingered on Vargen like that of a snake on a bird. Then the smile reappeared. "There are great cosmic forces behind all this, Commander Vargen. Do you believe that?"

Vargen had never thought of any force greater than the man seated before him. "If that is so, then you are their prophet."

This answer pleased Hitler. "Ah. So some say." He relaxed again. "And now I will share a secret with you, Commander. Men like us are chosen to serve. We must be willing to serve in this battle . . ." He lifted his hands and eyes upward. "There are spiritual forces at work here, Commander Vargen. We are their tools. Their weapons. Like the Crusaders of old you will return to Jerusalem, and there you will fight against the Jews until our side is victorious."

There was no escaping the news; horror and dismay were evident on the faces of the orchestra members. This morning the halls buzzed with the word of the brutal deportations of Polish Jews from Germany.

For Elisa, the mention of cattle cars heading east to the Polish border was a stark reminder of an old nightmare. Some among the orchestra members knew people in Germany who had come from Poland. Names and faces came to mind. Questions were unspoken and unanswerable. Elisa thought of the old tailor Grynspan and wondered if he was with the thousands in the cattle cars.

The orchestra played badly throughout the morning rehearsal. Horns came in late. First violins were hesitant and preoccupied. Woodwinds squawked like an amateur orchestra until Sir Thomas bellowed and barked and at last threw his baton to the stage in frustration.

"All right, children! And what can we do to change the headlines in this morning's *Times*?" he asked his silent and shamed musicians. "Do you think it will help those people if we play like the Ladies Home Auxiliary Band?" Without explanation Sir Thomas turned his steely gaze on Elisa, as though she had personally caused the disruption. She felt herself color as other members of the orchestra glanced nervously in her direction. "Any suggestions?" He seemed to direct the question to her.

Elisa stared self-consciously at the fine old instrument in her hands. She was fiddling while the world beyond was burning.

She closed her eyes and prayed for an answer. Some small thing. Something to give her prayers hands to work with. An instrument to play for the sake of mercy in an unmerciful world.

"A benefit performance!" she blurted. Her own words surprised her. She blinked in amazement that she had dared to reply.

Sir Thomas drew back as if her words had struck him. He frowned and continued to glare at Elisa. Finally his eyes shifted to the baton on the boards of the stage. He pointed at it and addressed the gray-haired concertmaster. "If you would be so kind . . ."

The concertmaster retrieved the baton and bowed slightly as he presented it to the maestro. Sir Thomas whirled the stick in his fingers. "A benefit," he remarked at last. "Yes. An excellent suggestion." He almost smiled at Elisa. "And now may I have your attention, ladies and gentlemen. We will begin again at the eighth bar, please."

It seemed natural that Theo, as head of the F.A.T.E. organization in England, would be chosen by Sir Thomas Beecham to travel to Poland with funds collected by the orchestra for the Jewish deportees. The request gave Theo hope that not everyone in England was asleep.

Theo's limp took on a purposeful and resolute strength as he made his way to the British colonial office. He intended to travel to Poland to see to the condition of the Jews recently deported from Germany and discuss their options.

The clerk in the visa office—a tall, thin man—so resembled a stork that Theo half expected him to be standing on one leg over a nest behind his counter. The fellow peered down his long nose at Theo's papers. His eyebrows arched as if in permanent surprise and disdain. "Mr. Lindheim." He sniffed. "If you leave for Poland, of course, His Majesty's government can make no guarantee for your safety, nor can we guarantee your readmittance to England."

Theo stared at the clerk in disbelief. He was being told that he and Anna were veritable prisoners on the little isle of Great Britain. To travel elsewhere might mean the revocation of their residence papers. Could it be that their hands were still cruelly tied by the British bureaucracy when they wanted so desperately to help?

"Is there no appeal?" Theo asked wearily.

"Your residence papers were issued under certain conditions, Mr. Lindheim. We simply follow the regulations as stated. And you did sign the forms. You agreed to the terms. Travel outside Great Britain is limited." The man began a countdown of the conditions of Theo's residence appeal.

Theo cut him short. With a curt nod, a thank you, and a good day, he left the office and limped, less resolutely, out the door.

What was the use of pretending any longer? The Reich had marked Theo as a criminal and a traitor in Germany. His extradition had been sought while he was in Prague. England had accepted him conditionally—the condition being that he do nothing that might offend Germany while he was in England. This meant that his physical presence among those spurned and persecuted by the Nazi Reich might well be misunderstood by the Führer and used as anti-British propaganda.

Anna met him as he descended the steps of Whitehall. The look on his face told her everything. She took his arm as he jammed his fedora down on his head and tugged angrily at the brim. "In a word," he said gruffly, "I am an offense to the Reich. And we must not offend the Führer by assisting those whom the Führer has singled out to destroy."

"They will not let you travel to Poland to the refugee camp." This was not a question, but a statement.

"My hands are tied."

"Your heart is willing, Theo," Anna chided her husband gently, "and so God has some other task for your hands." She intertwined her fingers with his and squeezed his hand in encouragement. "He will show you, my darling. And if you stop and think for only a moment, you will remember that you also believe this."

Theo stopped walking. He scanned the vast city of London, where he was now a prisoner of the politics of appeasement. He shook his head, then lowered his eyes in acknowledgment of Anna's words. In that moment he again accepted God's sovereignty in his life—and hers. The anger melted from his heart and his face. "How hard it is for an old warrior not to want to fight the battle in his own strength," he said. "The doors slam shut. And yet I must believe."

13

Wise as Serpents

Murphy scanned Trump's latest wire from New York. In America, news of the deportations had gone unnoticed by the vast majority of the public. The horrible reality of the latest Nazi persecutions had been obscured by, of all things, the Halloween radio broadcast of Orson Welles' *War of the Worlds*. Thousands had actually believed that aliens were invading the nation and the world with the intent of destroying human life. American roads had been jammed with fleeing automobiles. Men and women had committed suicide in the belief that the performance was real. In the face of this, the fate of a few thousand Jews deported to Poland from the Reich was relegated to the back page of every newspaper except those of Trump Publications.

Murphy studied the reports of the American panic with the feeling that perhaps Orson Welles had not been far off in his make-believe story. Perhaps there was some sort of unseen power attacking the world with the intent of destroying human souls. Somehow reports of Nazi brutality fit very easily into such a plot line.

The thought made him shudder, and with that came the realization that even as the British threatened Jewish immigration to Palestine, Hitler was turning up the flame to a white-hot intensity.

Trump in New York, along with Bubbe Rosenfelt and thirty Christian and Jewish leaders, was bombarding Congress and President Roosevelt with requests that he personally intercede with the British government on behalf of the British pledge for a Jewish homeland.

At the same time, Theo and Anna had continued with Britain's Zionist leaders to fight against what was whispered to be inevitable in the face of Arab protests in Palestine.

Murphy's repeated phone calls to the British colonial secretary in hopes of getting the straight scoop on the matter had been curtly refused. What business was it of the United States if Britain did close off Jewish immigration to appease the Arab Council? he was told. Had not America closed her doors to the Jewish paupers as well?

The failure of each nation had in turn become an excuse to other nations for more failure. Today's editorial in the *Manchester Guardian* expressed world sentiment about the homeless refugees who now huddled in stables at Poland's border:

> *Can Germany expect the rest of the world to receive and settle thousands of paupers in the next few years? This is carrying international cooperation to the limits of lunacy!*

Thus the matter finally became clear as Murphy pointed out the column to Theo over lunch. This was not an issue of what was morally right. It was not a matter of saving lives. It was a matter of *money*.

If England's rulers were suspicious of Theo, there were many other men who were not. This afternoon half a dozen of those men gathered in Theo's little study to plan what must be done since the utter failure of the Evian Conference. Surely *something* must be done, after all. Were the persecuted thousands of the Reich expected to be offered up as a sacrifice to apathy? The possibility seemed unthinkable to these few.

Dr. Chaim Weizmann lit his pipe and considered the flame of his match. "Perhaps we have been wrong in appealing to human decency then, Theo?" he asked.

Theo nodded slowly. He gazed sadly at the lined face of the great British scientist who had played such a vital part in Britain's first promises of a Jewish homeland. "The Nazis have proved that appeals to humanity fall on deaf ears. The failure of Evian confirms that this is true for others besides the Nazis."

"So what do you propose?" Weizmann asked, shaking out the match.

"The refugee problem is an economic problem to the leaders of world governments." Theo let out his breath slowly. He had read and reread the transcripts of Evian. Money. Cold, hard cash was always a central issue. "Germany intends that every Jew within its borders be driven out. Not one nation has disputed that intent seriously. And not one nation is willing to accept paupers as immigrants." Theo spread his hands. "So here is the dilemma: The Reich will not allow Jews to leave with any money. Nations will not take in those who are penniless."

Heads nodded in agreement. "There is not money enough that we

can raise to solve the problem," said Weizmann as a wreath of smoke encircled his head.

Theo smiled. "I was a businessman in Germany. I know what turns
the hearts of these men. And also the key that will open the doors of the
Reich and the doors of other nations to refugees."

"Please," Weizmann urged him on.

"If the Reich will allow its Jewish population to leave with, say, one-
third of their assets, this would satisfy the countries who refuse to take
paupers."

"And how do we convince Hitler and Himmler and Goebbels of the
value of such a scheme?" Weizmann expressed the question in every
man's mind.

"If we manage to lift the boycott on German exports, if the nations of
the West pledge to purchase large quantities of German exports . . . you
see? This would then be a matter of simple economics."

"Ah." Weizmann frowned at the simplicity of the idea. "The Nazis
have attempted to sell Jewish hostages without success. The only profit
they have found is in looting Jewish homes and businesses. But . . . if we
can make it more profitable for the Reich to allow the refugees to leave
with even a fraction of savings in exchange for larger purchases of German goods . . ."

"Then we manage to appeal to the *bank account* rather than the decency of Hitler's Reich. There is no other way."

The men in the room exchanged startled glances. Why had they not
thought of such a plan before Evian? And where would they begin, now
that doors seemed to be closing around the world?

Theo also had the answer to that question. "Perhaps it would be sensible to propose a meeting with the British foreign secretary. And another with the colonial secretary?" He again directed his proposal to
Weizmann. "You know them both well."

Weizmann nodded. It would take a businessman to match wits with
the Nazis, all right. "What is the saying?" Weizmann pondered a moment. "We must be wise as serpents and as gentle as doves."

So. Just like that, the Old City was open for business again. Had anyone
been shot on the wall? You could not tell it from the way the merchants
argued over the prices of fresh vegetables in the souks. Back to normal,
they said this morning among the minyan of Rabbi Shlomo Lebowitz.

"Maybe the English have given the screaming Arab child his lollipop
under the table, *nu?*" Something had quieted the racket, at any rate.

Rabbi Lebowitz carefully penned a note to the Eternal and headed through the narrow lanes of the Old City toward the ancient stones of the Western Wall. Once there, prayer shawl over his head, he raised his hands in blessing to God and placed the folded slip of paper into a crack between the stones. The prayer of eighteen blessings rose in a whisper before the Eternal, who hears the hearts and secret desires of the righteous. "And grant, O Eternal, that I may live to see my grandson here in the land of Zion. That we may worship You together in this place where our fathers worshipped You in days of old. A blessing upon Yacov, son of the Covenant."

The black smoke of Muslim bonfires was replaced this morning by a cool breeze and rain clouds that promised some relief to all of Palestine.

Still in Shimon's arms, Leah was awakened by a crisp knocking against the wooden tent frame. A cheery British voice called out their names. "Shimon and Leah Feldstein in here, are they?"

Shimon wrapped a rough army-issued blanket around himself and pulled back the tent flap a fraction. A smiling British officer with a broad handlebar mustache touched the brim of his hat in greeting. "Mr. Feldstein?"

"I am Shimon Feldstein."

"Yes. They told me you were here. You have friends in high places, eh?" He presented Shimon with a folded yellow slip of paper. "From the British high commissioner himself. Permission for you and your wife to continue ahead to Jerusalem without the usual stay here in the camp."

Shimon studied the message. "But the demonstrations . . ."

"Nothing more than demonstrations." The cheerful officer shrugged. "No danger. A few burning tires is all. Little show from the Muslims for the benefit of the Woodhead Commission. Quite effective. I heard they were trembling in their shoes. Thought the ground was exploding around them."

The fellow peered around Shimon to where Leah gazed back with sleepy curiosity. "Mrs. Feldstein," he said. "Leah Feldstein." He touched his cap again nervously. "I heard you perform once in London. Several years ago. Stunning." He motioned toward the slip of paper in Shimon's hands. "The high commissioner heard you had arrived. He is quite hopeful you might perform for the troops in Jerusalem. A bit of civilization from Europe, as it were. There is an important British committee visiting from London. It would be . . . *helpful* . . . for their impression of the Mandate."

"Perform?" Leah and Shimon exchanged looks. "Where? When?"

"Tonight. The mess hall at Allenby barracks in Jerusalem. Members of the Jewish Agency would also be invited. Your recordings are quite popular with the high commissioner, I understand. After yesterday's demonstration, a little music to calm the savage beasts, eh?"

"And then?" Shimon asked wonderingly. They had never dreamed they would be allowed into Jerusalem so soon.

"Well, then I suppose you may go where you like. You have relatives in the Old City, we were told."

"One relative. A great-aunt. I have never met her," Shimon explained. "But we have corresponded. Our things were shipped to her address in Jerusalem."

"Well, then." The officer seemed quite pleased. "It is all settled. Tonight you sleep in Jerusalem. Your bus leaves in twenty-five minutes."

With the promise he would phone the high commissioner with the good news, the officer hurried off across the tent-studded compound.

Haj Amin gestured with a sweep of his hand at the twelve sullen Arab warriors who now gathered to meet with Dr. Hockman. Beneath their keffiyehs, black eyes burned, impatient for news from the Führer of Germany.

Hockman had memorized each name, each country of origin. Most of those within the crowded room were not from Palestine. They had been sent from neighboring Arab states to express complete Arab solidarity in the fight against the hated British and the Jews.

Hockman knew that Adolf Hitler was admired and now emulated by many of those in Muslim leadership. After all, the Führer had managed to defeat the decadent Western powers on the issue of Czechoslovakia without even a shot being fired. Britain's leadership cowered before Hitler's demands, and increasingly the Czech industrial territory was being devoured by the Reich. Every demand was being met. Every expectation was being exceeded. Hitler had only to speak and Britain and France obeyed, even at the expense of their allies. Perhaps it would be the same in Palestine. Even here the Führer would prevail!

Hockman opened his mouth to speak. "What you have seen in Czechoslovakia will also be accomplished here, my friends. Our armies marched over the Czech fortifications, and all the enemies of the Reich fled to Prague in hopes of shelter." He smiled at the irony of anyone running to Prague for safety. "The Führer has demanded that those enemies be returned to the Reich for proper punishment. Thousands are already on their way to German prisons for the punishment they deserve. The Czechs now tremble at the Führer's words, just as England and France trembled. Nothing is refused."

A surly, grim-faced young man from Iraq lifted his chin defiantly. "Why does the Führer let the Jews go? Why does he let them come here to Palestine? Why does he simply not settle the Jewish problem on German soil instead of letting them go free for the nations of Islam to deal with?"

Heads nodded to this troublesome point. Haj Amin raised a hand to silence the muttering. "Have you forgotten?" he asked with a righteous smile. "Our holy prophet Mohammed tells us that when the Jews of the world are gathered east of the river, we will destroy them there. These refugees, these Jews, show us that this day is coming soon. The German Führer is the hand of Allah, as the prophet foretold. He drives the Jews toward destruction."

Hockman smiled as well. "The Führer wishes you all to know that he has chosen a messenger of that destruction to come here to Jerusalem soon. Very soon you will meet him face-to-face, and he will teach you what you need to know to make the words of the prophet come true."

A soft autumn mist drifted across the face of the Mount of Olives. Gray wisps snagged on the onion-domed spires of the Russian convent that bordered the Garden of Gethsemane.

Samuel Orde slowly climbed the narrow path that wound upward toward the ancient olive trees. He came here often—to pray, to think, to find some shred of hope in the fury that was wrapped around Jerusalem as the mist swirled among the olive trees.

This morning Orde's heart was heavy. He knew the purpose of the Woodhead Commission's visit to Palestine. The words and faces of these English aristocrats betrayed their intentions even before the inquiry had begun. And Orde had been commanded to keep his personal beliefs in check, or else.

He raised his eyes as a white-robed shadow moved beneath the branch of a gnarled olive tree. Stopping, he waited as the figure knelt on the hard ground—not to pray, but to pull weeds.

He smiled as he watched her. The Mother Superior of the Russian convent pulled weeds with the same concentration as she might have exhibited saying her rosary.

Glancing up at him, the old woman smiled and waved, her fist full of grass. "Good morning, Samuel."

"Morning prayers again, Mother?"

"A task that reminds me of the shortness of this life." The old woman placed the weeds in a heap beside her and gestured for him to sit down. "We are like the new grass of the morning," she said quietly.

"'In the morning it flourisheth . . . in the evening it is cut down and withereth.'" The old woman raised an eyebrow and considered the troubled expression of her companion.

"A depressing thought, Mother," he said glumly.

"On the contrary, Samuel." She brushed the soil from her hands and sat back on her heels. "It is a thought of great comfort for those who love God and do His will. Life is short. Our trials in this life will pass quickly. *'Teach us to number our days, that we may apply our hearts unto wisdom.'"*

"Psalm 90, verse 12," Orde responded, but his voice was not light as he spoke. He looked away from the old woman's sparkling eyes. She was the daughter of a Russian aristocrat in Moscow. Once, before the revolution, she had been young and beautiful and courted by many men. But she had never been happy until she came to Jerusalem as a penniless refugee. She had lost everything she had loved, but here, she had found true life.

"You are troubled today, my friend." The old woman patted his hand.

He nodded slowly, grateful she was here for him to share his thoughts. "Things are . . ." He faltered, wondering how much he could say. "I am afraid a great injustice is about to be done."

She raised her chin slightly. "I am certain you are right."

"And I am unable to speak up. To do anything about it."

"Ah." She nodded. She was remembering *something* . . . something very far away, and yet still very fresh and near to her. "Perhaps you do not yet see how you may help, Samuel. It is not always clear until the Lord puts it right in front of you."

"These are great matters. Dealing with many innocent lives." He spoke carefully, reasoning his way through the frustration he felt. "Men from England who will decide . . ."

"I have read about their arrival. About the matters of the refugees." She picked up a spindly weed and sighed. "These great men. They forget that they are grass, do they not, Samuel? I pray their decisions are wise. Merciful. Because great men are also grass." She tossed away the stem and sat in silence for a moment, then closed her eyes and whispered, *"'But You, O Lord, sit enthroned forever. You will arise and have compassion on Zion, for it is time to show favor to her; the appointed time has come. The nations will fear the name of the Lord. The Lord will rebuild Zion and appear in His glory.'"* A soft smile crept across her lips. She opened her eyes. "It is written, Samuel. Do not be afraid. Men are unjust. But God is still God."

That was all true, yet Orde could not rid himself of this sense of hopelessness, helplessness in the face of such twisted political power. He did not want to wait until the Lord Himself returned to this peaceful mount in order for things to be put right! He longed for a righteous world *now!*

Orde looked around at the garden where Jesus had prayed until drops of holy blood had dripped onto the ground—this ground, where the weeds grew and an aged nun knelt to pray while she worked in peace. He felt a twinge of resentment that the old woman could manage to lump the wicked and the innocent into the same pile and say that God alone would sort them out.

"I do not doubt God's future justice, Mother," he said with a frown. "I only wish it would come now. Today."

She returned to her work, gathering another handful of weeds from between the thick roots of a tree. "We mortals have a small and troubled view of time. If the wicked could have one glimpse of their eternal future, perhaps they would repent." She shrugged. "And if the righteous could have one glimpse of their eternity with God, they would no longer fear what evil men might do to them in this life. No. I think we might pity the wicked man for the price he will pay for his sin."

The old woman dumped another handful of grass onto the pile and then began to hum softly to herself. It was usually this way. She was right in what she said, yet Orde found very little comfort in that truth. He longed to *do* something! *Anything* to help ease the suffering of Jerusalem! But all he could do now was pray.

14

Gentle as Doves

Great heaps of luggage were piled on the roof of the Jerusalem bus. Ashen-faced, Leah gasped as her precious cello was tossed from one man to another and then up to the very top of the pile. She watched with horror as the case was wedged between two large wooden crates of chickens bound for the poultry market of Old City Jerusalem.

"Be *careful* with it," Leah called up to the scruffy young man threading rope through luggage handles and wood slats until everything on top of the bus was connected.

Shimon squeezed Leah's hand. "I would bribe him so the cello could ride inside with us, but we may need our last few shillings for lunch."

Leah pressed her lips together in disgust. She peered up at the threatening sky. "Welcome to the Promised Land," she said dryly. "Come perform for us in Jerusalem if your cello is not ruined in a rainstorm or pierced by a stray bullet." She closed her eyes and sighed. "My whole life is up there tied onto a chicken crate."

Shimon's brow furrowed as he studied the bus tickets. He handed them to Leah and kissed her cheek. "Not your whole life, darling. Not yet." Then he began to climb up the metal rungs fastened to the back of the bus.

"Shimon! What are you doing!" She knew what he was doing. He was going to ride on top with the luggage while Vitorio rode inside in his precious seat. No one could protest the cello case if it had a proper ticket just like every other passenger. "Shimon! Come down!" she cried, her heart beating fast at the thought of Shimon riding up the pass of Bab el Wad in such an exposed place as sullen Arab eyes watched him and Arab fingers stroked hair triggers.

Shimon did not listen. He untied Vitorio and passed it down ever so gently to a luggage handler who shrugged at this *meshugge* fellow and handed the instrument to Leah. "Vitorio is our ticket to Jerusalem," Shimon said stubbornly as he took a seat beside the chicken crate. "If it rains, I will dry out. Me and the chickens, *nu*? Get on the bus!" he demanded.

"But they might shoot you!" Leah protested as the other passengers gaped out the bus windows.

"Pray they do not," he instructed, turning his eyes forward and lifting his chin. "Or the world will lose a great percussionist, and you will lose a great lover."

At these words, the men on the bus cheered out the window for Shimon. The engine coughed and sputtered to life. And it began to rain. Just a few drops, but definitely rain.

Leah looked at the cello, then up at Shimon.

"Get on the bus!" he ordered, covering his plaster cast with the corner of a wicker basket.

More raindrops. It had been so clear and hot yesterday. Why had it chosen this moment to rain?

The bus driver shouted at her. "Are you coming, lady?"

Shimon gave her a gentle look. *Go on. I will be fine. We have no choice.* "I will be the first to see Zion," he called. "The earthly Zion, of course." He motioned her away.

She backed toward the bus door. Clutching the cello, she reluctantly climbed the steps. The other passengers cheered as she and the cello took their seats.

Rain suddenly burst from the clouds, falling on the bus like the pounding of drums.

Ram Kadar inhaled deeply the smoke of the water pipe. His words came forth with the smoke on his breath. "I am speaking of your sister. Of Victoria." He smiled and inclined his head. A black keffiyeh framed his darkly handsome face.

Ibrahim wiped his mouth nervously. He felt the curious eyes of his half brothers on him. For Victoria to marry a man like Kadar would be a great honor. It would also guarantee the safety and position of the family of Hassan within the Mufti's council.

"She is . . . not ready for marriage." Ibrahim smiled and lifted the cup of thick Turkish coffee to his lips.

"She is too old not to be married." Kadar shrugged off the answer. "My own mother had three children by the time she was Victoria's age."

"Times are different now." Ibrahim shrugged. "You know, since the Mandate. She has her job."

"A job that will be helpful to our cause." Kadar narrowed his eyes. "She will obey a husband. She will help us once she is in my bed. Beneath my protection."

His words brought laughter from the six men in the back room of the coffeehouse. Every man but Ibrahim.

"My father is in Iran on business," Ibrahim persisted, attempting to put off the discussion. "It is my father who will have the final word in such a matter as her marriage."

"I am not asking permission." Kadar seemed amused. "Marriage is a business proposition. I am prepared to pay well. I can promise your father all the things and more that would give Victoria a satisfactory life. I ask only that you support me in this. Stand with me as I make my proposition. This will strengthen my stand with him. *Insh' Allah!* May Allah will it!"

Ibrahim nodded with the single jerk of his head. "I must think. She is a jewel in the crown of the prophet, and . . . I must think."

Kadar leaned forward. There was a hint of impatience in his dark, brooding eyes. He pulled the tasseled hem of his keffiyeh over his shoulder. "What is there to think about? She is a woman of marriageable age. I am a suitor who meets the requirements of the Koran. I can pay the price your father asks." The smile reappeared and he considered Ibrahim carefully. "Unless you know of another suitor. But my offer will still surpass that of any other man in Jerusalem."

"A generous offer. I . . . my sister is . . . she thinks like the English. She thinks of things like . . . love." Ibrahim was embarrassed to admit such a thing in the company of men.

"Is that all?" Kadar glanced around the circle of men. "A much easier matter to deal with than her price. A problem I intend to solve on the night of our wedding, Ibrahim." He laughed. Genuine relief radiated from his eyes. "I will make her beg for me to keep her beneath my protection." He lifted the hem of his black robe as if it were a blanket to spread over her. No one missed his meaning. More laughter rippled through the circle. Checkered keffiyehs bobbed with approval of Kadar's words and wisdom about women.

"Perhaps my father will let her make her own choice."

The laughter died. "Then he will be thinking too much like the English himself, and no doubt Haj Amin will wish to instruct him on what the Koran says about women." This last sounded suspiciously like a threat. The family of Hassan lived on the very edge of approval. To fall off that precarious edge at this time could mean a swift death with a dagger between the ribs.

"I did not mean to offend, Ram Kadar. Allah knows . . ." Ibrahim spread his hands in innocence. He was not handling this problem well. He was angry that Eli was taking so much time in his decision to cross the Street of the Chain. If he and Victoria were married, if Eli were already a follower of the prophet, this discussion would be settled.

Kadar nodded slowly, deliberately. He was set on his goal. He had seen the face of Victoria Hassan and liked what he saw. She was single. She was of a social class equal to Kadar's. Seldom had there been so much talk about such a simple matter as the marriage of a girl to a man like Kadar! He could afford more than one wife. He was a wealthy man in his own right, but he remained unmarried. He wanted Victoria as his first wife; then he would have others. He would marry her as soon as the contract was negotiated and signed. Kadar had consulted Ibrahim only to gain some idea of what to anticipate from Victoria's father. He had not expected talk of love at such a time.

"Give your sister my regards." He touched fingers to forehead. "Tell her I have seen her. That I consider her . . . a worthy woman."

Ibrahim acknowledged the request. He would tell Victoria. *Yes!* He would tell her that there was no more time to play games in the matter of Eli's conversion! Even now, things had become too dangerous for secret rendezvous. "It will be as you ask, my friend."

"My *brother*," Kadar said, leaning back and resting his hand on the gleaming silver hilt of his dagger. In his mind it was settled. Victoria Hassan would be his wife. The thought pleased him. The image of her face and body pleased him also—perhaps even to the degree the English might call love. But this last was not a matter he would speak of openly. When the business arrangement was complete and the wedding finished, then he would show her without words how he perceived her. That would be enough.

From his bedroom window, Eli could easily see the Dome of the Rock. He could also see the corner of the home where Victoria and Ibrahim lived with their parents and three younger brothers.

Every day that week Eli had run home from Yeshiva and bounded up the steep steps to the apartment above the Cohens' grocery store.

"What is wrong with him?" his brother Moshe would ask when Eli charged through the front room with hardly a greeting.

His mother would shrug and roll her eyes. "Too much fasting." She would tap her temple. "It affects the mind, *nu*? I'm telling you. I will talk to the rabbi about him!"

But it was not fasting that affected Eli. Each afternoon he sat at the window and waited. At 5:35 Victoria would return from her secretarial job. She would pass within his vision for the barest instant as she rounded the corner on the Street of the Chain. He would see her in her English-cut suit as she hurried home after a busy day of typing reports for the English government now housed at the King David Hotel.

Eli lived each hour looking forward to that fraction of a second when he would glimpse Victoria. It had been seven long nights since he had held her. His heart had not stopped racing since that night. Victoria had not sent for him as she had promised. She walked quickly past the corner and cast a look over her shoulder toward Eli's house. Then she walked on without a break in stride.

The frustration of it nearly drove him mad. He could not study. He growled irritably whenever Moshe tried to talk to him about things happening at Hebrew University. He ignored his mother's pleas to *eat, eat, eat!*

Why had Victoria not sent word? Yes, things were tense in the Old City just now, but the only tension Eli felt was from not speaking with her. Not touching her. Did she not understand what he was feeling? Had she decided against his proposal of marriage? Perhaps the call of the muezzin each day had drawn her away from his love, after all.

This morning Eli rose early. He sat at his window in hopes of catching a glimpse of her as she left for work. Moshe, twenty-three years old, was determined to figure out the mystery of his brother's behavior. He lay quietly on the bed, studying Eli's back. Perhaps Moshe would miss the bus to Hebrew University, but after a week of Eli's strange actions, Moshe was willing to miss his class on Canaanite pottery.

Eli squinted and looked at his watch. The bus would be leaving from Jaffa Gate in ten minutes. She would walk past the corner . . . *right now!*

His sense of timing was impeccable. Dressed in a powder blue dress, Victoria walked by. Not breaking stride, she looked up toward the Sachar apartment. Her hair was piled onto her head and glistened like the black wing of a raven.

At the sight of her, he whispered her name. "Victoria!" It was only a whisper, but he sensed his mistake. *Too late to call it back!* He stiffened, feeling the eyes of Moshe on him. He turned slowly to see his brother grinning from his pillow.

"So that's it!" Moshe crowed, raising up on one elbow. "My brother the rabbi is in love! So *that's* it!" Dark brown eyes radiated a delicious glee. "Ha! All this praying and fasting up on the roof. Have you got a telescope up there to watch her?"

Eli's face hardened. He decided to deny it. "I am sure I don't know what you are talking about."

"You said her name!"

"You were dreaming."

"No! You were dreaming. Of Victoria Hassan, no less. There is only one girl I know in the Old City with a British name, and that girl does not go to synagogue!" Moshe was enjoying himself.

Eli wanted to strike him. Moshe was mocking him as if this did not matter. She was not just any girl! "You are *meshugge*! Crazy!"

"I am not the crazy one, dear brother! I am not the one running home each day and rising up in the morning for one peek at a girl! Especially not an Arab girl!"

"Shut up!" Eli warned. He stood slowly and pretended to rummage through his chest of drawers.

"Although I must admit you have good taste. Even at the university I have not come across anything as gorgeous as Victoria Hassan." Moshe would not be silenced.

"You talk like a goy!" Eli said angrily as he still attempted to disarm Moshe.

"Yes? Well, that is what happens when a good little Orthodox boy grows up and goes to the university, *nu*? We should all become rabbis just like you, eh, Eli? Stick to all the old ways. Do not consider looking at a woman unless she is a Jewess who also grew up in the Old City."

"You are mocking."

Moshe laughed sarcastically and climbed from the bed. "No. I am not the one in love with an Arab. I am not the one who mocks."

Moshe was still grinning when Eli's fist struck him square in the face. He had not expected the blow. Eli had not expected it either. Moshe flew back onto the bed and lay there with a startled look on his face. He rubbed his chin as he eyed his brother with a new concern.

Eli stood sweating in his underwear. Bare feet. He blinked and looked at his fist as though the thing had a mind of its own. "I . . . I . . . I am . . . I," he stammered, not knowing what to say.

"I am sorry," Moshe said at last. "I did not know." He sat up. "This is . . . you really are . . . serious."

Eli cried out. He ran his hands through his hair and sank down on the bed opposite Moshe. He cradled his head in his hands and moaned. "May the Eternal forgive me. May He . . . I love her. *Oy!* Moshe. I . . . I . . . I . . ."

There was a silence. Misery. Unquenchable fire inside Eli.

"How long?" Moshe spoke gently now. He was convinced of his brother's agony. This was not a light fantasy, and the implications were terrible to consider.

"Six months. No. Seven. I had not seen her in a while. Then I saw her in the souk. Buying vegetables. Cabbages. *Oy!* So beautiful."

Moshe refrained from the urge to joke about such a less-than-romantic meeting. "Yes. Victoria is beautiful."

"You noticed."

"Uh-hmmm. You have good taste, Brother." He reached over and pounded Eli's shoulder, hoping to lighten this moment of discovery.

Eli would not be lifted up. "I tried not to notice."

Moshe believed that. Eli was the type of man who would try very hard not to notice. "Does she feel the same?"

"Yes. I mean . . . *yes!*"

"You see her?"

"Yes."

"Often?"

"I have . . . we have met once a week. Sometimes more."

This news startled Moshe. "Where? Does Ibrahim know?"

"It was he who helped me. You know . . . he is still like a brother to me in spite of . . ."

"In spite of the fact that his brothers are all supporters of the Mufti. And now anti-Semites, I hear."

"That has nothing to do with Ibrahim. Or Victoria," Eli defended.

"It will have something to do with you if you are caught with their sister! You *know* all this!" Now it was Moshe who was gripped with fear. "They are friends with assassins, Eli. In a moment they could have you killed and then melt away. No one would know why. Just another Jewish Yeshiva student murdered in the Old City."

"We are careful." Eli rubbed his hand over his sandy-colored beard.

"How can you be careful? I could pass for an Arab, but *you*! Look at you. Practically a goy! Almost a Gentile with your light hair." He frowned and shuddered as he pictured Eli walking through the Arab Quarter on his way to a secret meeting with the sister of young Arab thugs. "Where do you meet her?"

"Different places." He sighed. "Ibrahim is always with us. He knows how we love each other."

There was almost an accusation in Eli's words. After all, this had been going on for six months and Eli had not told Moshe about it. Only Ibrahim.

"So what now?" Moshe asked, looking toward the window.

"I asked her to marry me."

"You . . . what?"

"To convert. She could do it."

Moshe stood and went to the window. He looked out at the corner where Victoria passed each day. She was an Arab. She would never convert. To do so would mean the end of her relationship with her family.

Possibly the assassin's knife might be unsheathed for her pretty throat as well. Muslim fanaticism had risen to a fevered pitch recently. Such things were becoming more frequent.

"And when you asked her to convert to Judaism, what did she say?"

"That we needed to think. A little distance." Eli looked up. His eyes were tortured, pleading for help. "I have to see her. You could . . . Moshe, would you carry a message to her for me? She is in the office of transportation. First floor in the British wing of the King David Hotel." All these words came in a rush. Of course Moshe could more easily go into the hotel and drop by the desk of an Arab woman on some pretext. Moshe was clean shaven. He wore the clothes of the present day, instead of the garb of an Orthodox Jewish rabbinical student.

Moshe gazed into the haunted eyes of his brother, then out to the corner again. He was definitely going to miss his class this morning. The hotel was only a short way out of his way, however.

"Sure. Yes. I will take her a note."

This first rain of the season moved like a gray curtain preceding the bus up the pass of Bab el Wad. A deluge to compare with the days of Noah, it drove the Jihad warriors indoors lest their weapons rust. It came in waves from the skies above Jerusalem. Drops chased drops until torrents rushed in the usually barren ravines and scrambled over ancient rocks.

Inside the bus, the Jerusalem travelers rejoiced. The first rain had been late this year and so the season of revolt and violence had gone on longer than usual. The cisterns of Jerusalem were nearly empty and now they would again be full. There would be celebration in the Jewish section of the city tonight.

"Your husband has brought the rain, madame," laughed a beady-eyed little man across the aisle from Leah. He sliced a hunk of salami and offered it to her in a gesture of goodwill.

She shook her head and mouthed the words *no thank you.* How heartless and unfeeling all these laughing people seemed!

"You should be grateful! Not even the devil himself would stay out in this! Not even for such a fine big target as your husband makes!"

This was supposed to make her feel better?

"He may be wet, but he will be alive!" cheered the man with the salami. "Yesterday I would not have said so. Yesterday they were sniping at buses all along the pass."

Leah's eyes widened as she looked out the window at the steep, rocky slopes. In places the road seemed to double back on itself. The water had no chance to rest, no rocks or plants to cling to. No wonder half of Palestine had been malarial swamps before the Zionists came. They had drained the swamps, but what could they ever do to the barren hillsides?

This was misery. What sort of homeland was this, anyway? What kind of bus company that made a woman choose between her cello and her husband?

Leah took out her pen and notepaper and began to write as the reek of greasy salami assailed her nostrils and the lurching bus made her stomach rebel.

> Dear Elisa,
>
> Maybe I am not so glad to be here, after all. If ever on this earth there was a place more desolate, more forsaken by God than Palestine, I cannot imagine it! Why, I ask myself, why would anyone want to come to such a place? The English have England. The Muslims have most of the Middle East. And so that leaves us. Raised in the shadow of the glorious Alps and the green farmland of Austria. Oh, Elisa! If there was any place else on earth but this place . . .

Her pen trembled as she wrote. The bus lurched around a particularly sharp corner, and Leah's stomach finally rebelled. "Stop the bus!" she shouted. "I am ill!"

The driver smirked. Nothing doing. "Open a window."

Retching out the window of a moving bus in a rainstorm, Leah got her first glimpse of Jerusalem. A jumble of white stone houses set among the white stones of a boulder-strewn hill. A few buildings of size and substance were in the panorama, but Jerusalem was far from glorious. Ah yes, there was the Dome of the Rock. The Muslim shrine in all the postcards. Nobody had mentioned that the man in charge of that place wanted every Jew in Palestine dead. Somehow that thought detracted from the first thrill of seeing a postcard picture come to life.

Leah let the rain wash over her face and hair while passengers in the seats behind her complained that she should finish her business and close the window.

She ignored their indignant jibes and breathed deeply of air without the scent of garlic and greasy salami. Maybe Shimon had not had such a bad trip after all. She called up to him, "Shimon! Are you all right? Shimon!"

Either he had fallen off or he did not hear her. If he had fallen off, the driver would not have stopped the bus, Leah was convinced. Such a place this was! And such people!

She and Shimon had been idealistic fools. It had taken her less than twenty-four hours in the Holy Land to figure that out.

She wiped her face and opened her mouth to catch a few raindrops before she ducked back into the stuffy bus. She closed the window halfway and let her fingers dangle out through the opening.

The bus moved past a few low houses, and the salami man asked, "So. Your first trip to Jerusalem, eh? How do you like it so far?"

Leah simply smiled a reply. She had left her opinion of Palestine beside the road a mile or so back.

The Old City of Jerusalem bristled with expectation of the arrival of the Woodhead Royal Commission of Inquiry. Samuel Orde inspected the ranks of his soldiers. Bayonets were fixed. Gas masks hung within easy reach. Heads were helmeted against a stray stone or roof tile. Faces were grim and ready.

This morning's march would cover every backstreet and alleyway within the circle of the city wall. It was meant to be a display of British might. Arab, Jew, and Christian were meant to tremble at the sight of such force. At the sound of tramping boots and bagpipes, they would stop their work for a moment and consider that such a show demanded that every citizen of the city remain on his best behavior.

From the citadel the men marched to stand in impressive columns in the very center of Omar Square. The voices of red-faced sergeants accompanied the precise crashing of boots against the stones. The company divided into four groups of soldiers, who then swiveled to face in four different directions. At the command of Captain Orde the skirl of bagpipes commenced anew and the soldiers tramped off to scour the Old City for any sign of threat.

Today, Captain Orde served double duty. He was not only the protector of the members of the Woodhead Committee, he was also, regretfully, their tour director.

"No one knows the place like you do, Orde!" his commanding officer had shouted. "You and your articles for the *Geographic*! By thunder, Sir John Woodhead has asked for you by name! Keep your Zionist nonsense to yourself, or you'll find yourself back in England guarding coastal defenses!" A finger in Orde's face had emphasized this last point. Then the instructions had continued: "No repeating of biblical verses unless they have a direct bearing on some historical point of interest. No comments about the biblical prophecies regarding the return of the Messiah and the Jewish people to the land of Israel. No religious drivel. No comments that might influence the commission on behalf of the Jewish population over the Muslims. Fairness and impartiality must be observed by you at all times—or else!"

The *or else* had put Captain Orde in a particularly nasty mood. His men whispered among themselves. Their normally personable and gentle captain was looking for heads to roll. A half-shined shoe was reason for confinement to quarters. A misplaced gas mask was offense enough for a stay in the brig.

Wide-eyed, the Old City residents gathered before their shops and stalls in the souks to watch the mighty display of precision. Here was the law of the land in evidence for any who might doubt its weakness. The display was comforting for many, frightening for some, enraging for a handful.

The visit of the English lords of the commission was supposed to be impromptu, an example of daily life in the Old City—how the Jews and the Muslims mixed freely in the souks with all the Christian sects that warred against one another in a different kind of battle. But not one footstep went unplanned for these honored gentlemen. Not one word unrehearsed.

In the Arab Quarter, schoolchildren who usually begged from the English for a living put on their finest clothes. In the Armenian Quarter, the bearded patriarch wore his ceremonial best. In the Christian Quarter, Greeks and Copts and Ethiopians and Catholics glared at one another from across invisible boundaries in the various shrines. They silently competed for the greatest glory of each of their sects before the lofty Englishmen.

In the ragged Jewish Quarter, the steps of synagogues and apartments were swept. The shelves of shops were put in order. The dung of sheep on the way to slaughter was cleaned from the streets. Chicken crates were moved out of sight into an alley behind the kosher butcher shop. Yeshiva students cleaned the windows of Nissan Bek, while ancient rabbis prayed for a favorable impression and admonished the schoolchildren of the significance of this visit.

15

Great Performances

The little kitten Psalms was such a comfort to Rabbi Lebowitz. She had lost any vestige of her original timidity, and now she claimed his one-room flat as her own.

The old man, mindful of the four boy cats at Tipat Chalev, carried her in his pocket to a vacant lot where she tended to her basic needs twice a day. The rest of the time she strutted languidly about the room, staking claims on the table and the bed. At night she slept on the old man's chest just beneath his beard, where she purred happily until he fell asleep.

He filled his most recent letter to Etta and the children with all the news about the little creature—about her brothers, who now followed Hannah Cohen everywhere as if she were a mother cat. He told how Hannah Cohen seemed to act as if *she* had rescued them from a pack of wolves. Ah, well. They would maybe grow up to kill rats. In the meantime, they had their own special plates, a warm bed in the basement, and another beneath the steps in the alley.

My little Psalms sends greetings to the children, wrote the old rabbi. *Since Hannah has stolen her brothers, she hopes she will soon have children from Warsaw to come play with her here in Jerusalem!*

"Today is an important day," Rabbi Shlomo Lebowitz addressed the serious group of five-year-old boys in the classroom where Eli taught at the Torah school.

Eli looked first at the sturdy old man with his lined face and gnarled hands, then at the collection of miniature Orthodox students with their black coats and earlocks and yarmulkes perched on shorn heads. The old man shook a finger at them in warning. "Today the English gentlemen are coming with Captain Samuel Orde from the British Army. They are coming to see if Jewish boys are *good* boys and if more Jewish children should be allowed to come to Palestine!" There was a long pause. Rabbi Lebowitz let the weight of responsibility rest heavily on the shoulders of Eli's pupils. The entire fate of Jewish immigration depended on their behavior during the visit from the Englishmen!

A small hand moved tentatively into the air. The rabbi jabbed a finger toward it in response. The tiny brown-eyed child stood beside his desk to speak. "And if we are not good, will the Englishmen not let your daughter and grandchildren come here? Mama says that you want them to come very badly."

The old man glanced toward Eli. Perhaps it was wise to make this a personal issue. "This is correct, Yosef. If you chatter or squirm, or misbehave, the Englishmen will notice. They will say, 'Well, we want no more of that in Palestine!' Then they will send me a letter saying that my own grandchildren cannot come to Jerusalem. And there are many thousands more just like my own family who will wish to come, but will not be allowed."

This was effective. Yosef took his seat. Brows furrowed in consternation at the thought of one errant spitball on the back of an English head. The consequences were great and terrible!

Rabbi Lebowitz turned the classroom back over to Eli. Eli walked to the lectern. Today was indeed an important day in the Old City Jewish Quarter, but he could think of nothing but the fact that it had been over a week since he had seen Victoria. This was going to be the longest day of his life. *Carry on,* he told himself as he thanked Rabbi Lebowitz.

"And so, students, you can see that each of us is a representative of *all* our people, *nu?*"

Little heads bobbed in silent agreement.

Eli continued. "Perhaps some of you have family in Germany or elsewhere who want very badly to come here, just as Rabbi Lebowitz wishes his grandchildren to join him."

Again, nods of assent. Rabbi Lebowitz seemed pleased. He crossed his arms in satisfaction and stepped back against the chalkboard. This classroom would behave well for Captain Orde and his group of politicians. They would go home to England and tell their committees how polite Jewish children are in Jerusalem, that such politeness should be considered when they decide how many more should be allowed through the Mandate.

Eli consulted the clock. His morning teaching assignment would end in thirty minutes. The English commission was scheduled to pass through in five minutes. After that, he would have to dismiss his pupils and return to his own studies.

He turned toward the rabbi, who was smiling pleasantly through his beard. "Would you care to remain with our classroom while the Englishmen are here? Then you can see for yourself that my students will be the best behaved of anyone in the Torah school."

"It will be a pleasure."

The old man took a seat at a desk near the back of the crowded room. Eyes glanced furtively in his direction. Determination was on every young face. They would not let him down or disgrace all Jewish children by their behavior.

Eli resumed instruction of the Hebrew alphabet. Rote memorization was the method of teaching. When he had been given this assignment as part of his training as a rabbi, Eli had hated the monotony of it. Now it was a relief. While his mouth taught the alphabet, his mind could wander easily to Victoria.

The British delegation arrived. Even though the school had been planning for this visit for weeks, all the teachers were warned that everything must appear normal.

Rabbi Lebowitz went smiling to the doorway. The suntanned face of Captain Samuel Orde appeared. Behind him came six men in British suits, varying in age from forty to sixty. They peered around the room as if they were looking for a speck of dust or a desk out of line with the others.

"This," Rabbi Lebowitz said with pride, "is our class of five-year-olds." He extended a hand toward Eli. "Eli Sachar is their teacher. He himself was once a student in this very classroom, and now he studies to become a rabbi."

Eli stepped forward. He extended his hand and smiled. What a nuisance this was, performing for a collection of English bigwigs when he could have been daydreaming about Victoria! "How do you do?" He applied his most perfect accent and was immediately assaulted with half a dozen how-do-you-dos in reply.

Rabbi Lebowitz motioned for the men to come farther into the room. The boys looked like little clay figures. They sat rigidly with their hands clasped on their desk. It was almost their time to perform!

"Our children learn several languages," Rabbi Lebowitz said. "Including English, of course."

Eli raised his hand like a conductor. Little mouths opened to draw breath. Out came the much rehearsed words that must appear unrehearsed and spontaneous: "How do you do-o-o!" The class recited this in unison. It was perfect. There was not a single straggler in the lot. Eli nodded his approval, and a little boy sighed with relief. They had not failed their people!

And then it was over. En masse, the Woodhead Committee turned and proceeded to the next classroom, where the same little drama was repeated.

Rabbi Lebowitz seemed pleased. He smiled. "Very good! And tonight at dinner you will have a special treat for dessert! Hannah and Shoshanna have made cookies for you in honor of what good boys you are!"

A delighted *a-h-h-h-h* followed him from the room.

This was good. Now the old man would go back to the soup kitchen where he supervised charity meals. The boys would recite the alphabet and think of cookies. Eli would drill them and dream of Victoria.

Against Theo's better judgment, he accompanied Dr. Chaim Weizmann to the offices of the British colonial secretary, Malcolm MacDonald. Since the afternoon at the British Museum, Theo had regretted his request that the officer who tailed him remain out of sight. The illusion of freedom was always tainted with the awareness that somewhere on the street a man named Beckham watched his every move.

Today, with a sort of bitter amusement, Theo considered that agent Beckham was probably walking into his own headquarters.

Weizmann and Theo were five minutes early. Secretary MacDonald kept them waiting for ten minutes later than their scheduled appointment. When they entered his large, opulent office, he was warm and friendly to Weizmann and yet cool to Theo Lindheim. No doubt he had read the Nazi accounts of Theo's "crimes" in Germany.

Half an hour passed as Weizmann patiently explained Theo's plan to the colonial secretary. He concluded with a wave of his hand. "I am a scientist and a humanitarian. Born and raised in England. I thought it best if you have any questions that you would be able to address them to a former businessman from Germany." He gestured toward Theo, who had not offered to speak during the entire meeting.

MacDonald appraised him with an indifferent gaze. "So, Doktor Weizmann." He refused to address Theo. "You propose that we increase our purchase of German goods in exchange for German Jews released from the Reich with some assets. I fail to see how this benefits Great Britain." He smiled a quick, unfriendly smile.

Weizmann did not reply. He looked at Theo for a response. For a moment an uneasy silence hung in the room. Weizmann cleared his throat expectantly and at last Theo spoke.

"It would seem," Theo said deliberately, "that the successful placement of German Jews among the Western democracies should be a major goal of this government."

"Oh?" MacDonald was almost rude in his strained propriety. "And why would you think that?"

Theo shifted in his chair. "Palestine is currently the only haven for Jewish refugees, is it not?"

"Both legal and illegal, Herr Lindheim. We have heard that you know well enough about the illegal sort."

Theo ignored the jibe. He would not defend himself or his actions in financing underground immigration from the Reich. That was not the issue here. "It would be better . . . for England . . . for everyone if all immigrants were legal. If other nations were willing to cooperate in a trade agreement with Germany, as Doktor Weizmann has explained, then perhaps there would no longer be such a flood of those attempting to flee to Palestine. Perhaps the pressure would be taken off the British Mandate."

The pure logic of Theo's explanation took the colonial secretary by surprise. He frowned, then opened his mouth in some attempt to argue, but he could not find an argument. "All very well and good, Herr Lindheim." He sniffed. "But will the German Chancellor go for the idea?"

Theo smiled knowingly. "I would ask your British ambassador. Mr. Henderson, is it?"

"Henderson. Berlin. Yes."

"I would suggest that Hermann Göring be approached with this idea first. He is, after all, in charge of the plan to improve the German economy."

"Göring. The fat one?"

"Yes. That is Hermann Göring. The one with all the medals," Theo prompted. "We were pilots together in the last war. Hermann Göring has always been a man with his mind on money. He agrees with the Führer about German Jewry mostly because he sees Jewish wealth as something he would like to have in his own account. He is a practical man."

Theo's bluntness surprised MacDonald. "He was a friend of yours, you say?"

"Of a sort. After he had me thrown into Dachau, I heard my paintings were on the walls of his home. He also confiscated my library of rare books in the name of the Reich. I am certain he enjoys the volumes almost as much as I did when they were mine."

MacDonald smoothed his eyebrows as he considered the practicality of Theo Lindheim's statements and insight. It was no wonder the Nazis wanted the man bound hand and foot and extradited back to Germany in a brown paper wrapper!

A cautious respect filled MacDonald's eyes now as he offered his hand to Theo and then to Weizmann with the assurance that he would bring up the matter in tomorrow's cabinet meeting. He inclined his head slightly and said in a lofty attempt at pleasantness, "It was quite . . . interesting to meet you after all this time. Perhaps we shall talk again."

Victoria raised her eyes from her typewriter as Parker, the British supervisor, entered the office and called for attention from the two dozen typists.

Frail and nervous on the best of days, today Mr. Parker mopped his brow and grimaced behind his round spectacles as he waved a piece of paper over the heads of his all-Arab staff.

"Attention, girls!" he cried a second time when Tasha had not stopped her furious typing. "An important assignment has come our way."

There was silence in the room. Victoria was grateful for the break. She looked past the harried supervisor to where the rain tapped against the window.

The high, effeminate voice of Mr. Parker began again. "For reasons known only to God and the British Mandate, an assignment has been passed down the chain to me. Unfortunately I have no one else to pass it to." His statement was thick with irritation. Parker, as the lowest man on the British administration's roster of command, was often handed the unwanted chores.

"The high commissioner has arranged some sort of concert for tonight. Not that I am invited," he added under his breath. "Someone needs to meet this musician at Egged Terminal. This musician is, I am told, from Germany or Austria or some such non-English-speaking place. I haven't the foggiest idea about the language of the Huns past *Guten Tag*—" He shoved his glasses up on the bridge of his long nose. "Pray God," he said dramatically, "that someone among you has a rudimental grasp of that language?"

Victoria and Tasha exchanged looks. Had Allah ever made a bigger fool than their supervisor? Victoria shook her head imperceptibly and smiled as she raised her hand. German was one of several languages spoken by her father in his business as purveyor of Persian and Oriental carpets. An easy language. Much like English. Victoria understood and spoke it quite easily.

Mr. Parker slapped his chest in relief and rolled his eyes like a pilgrim overcome with ecstasy. His red polka-dot bow tie trembled under his bobbing Adam's apple. "Miss Hassan! Thank God! Divide your file between Miss Habashi and Miss Aman and come along quickly then! We just have time to motor to the terminal before they arrive."

Victoria grinned happily as she deposited her day's stack of transcription onto the desks of her glowering coworkers. "You just did not volunteer fast enough," she whispered to Tasha in Arabic.

The rain had become a cloudburst by the time Moshe ducked beneath the awning of the King David Hotel where the administration office of the British Mandate was housed.

Following the example of the English hotel patrons around him, he greeted the doorman with a cheery greeting: "Quite a storm, eh wot?"

Shaking the water from his slicker, he entered the lobby of the King David Hotel as if he belonged there. The plush red Oriental carpets were damp from the feet of British officers and faithful British civil servants and the Arab staff who served them. Today there were more uniforms than usual in the lobby, owing to the visit of the Royal British Commission of Inquiry headed by Sir John Woodhead. Everyone in Jerusalem knew of the important visitors from London, and so it seemed that the British high commissioner was taking extra precautions against any sort of potential dangers.

There were guards at the doors of the elevators. Guards at the foot of the grand staircase. Guards beside the men's room. Guards flanking the doors of the administrative wing of the hotel where Victoria labored over the endless paperwork required to run such an operation as the British mandatory government in Palestine. Eli had told Moshe that Victoria typed requisitions for everything from tea and cigarettes to toilet paper. *How small are the cogs of great government.*

The question was, how could Moshe, who was not in any way related to this grand operation, slip by the guards and reach Victoria? Even the most proper-looking Englishmen were being halted at the portals and checked for identification, as if a company of eunuchs had been set in place to guard the harem of secretaries.

Moshe evaluated his rumpled khaki clothes—perfectly acceptable among the archaeologists of Britain who came to the digs of Palestine. But dripping on the red carpets of the lobby, he looked like a potsherd among Royal Worchester china.

He gazed up nonchalantly at the gilded ceiling. He looked down at the potted plants, then searched for an empty chair where he might consider the problem. *Too late!* He had been spotted by an elevator eunuch. The fellow strolled purposefully toward Moshe, who glanced at his watch and tried to look impatient.

"Looking for someone?" asked the guard.

"Waiting." Moshe displayed his most precise mastery of Oxford English. "For Professor Hrachabad. Professor of ancient Syrian ethnology, you know. We have a meeting scheduled, and he is quite late. Quite."

The guard looked doubtful, even though Moshe spoke the King's English better than Sir John Woodhead.

"Professor . . ."

"Hrachabad." Moshe scoured the lobby in search of the imaginary professor as the soldier peered doubtfully at him.

And then, miracle of miracles, Victoria Hassan emerged from the administrative offices at the side of a man who could quite easily be a professor of Syrian ethnology! "There he is now!" Moshe strode happily toward Victoria, who eyed him with a combination of muted astonishment and fear.

Moshe took no chances. He hailed the fellow in the polka-dot tie in the Arabic street language of the Old City. Pumping the confused man's hand, he did not look at Victoria as he smiled and chatted to the non-comprehending Mr. Parker.

"Eli is frantic with worry," Moshe said with a broad smile.

"I daresay!" Mr. Parker was flustered. "Can't understand a word. Do I know you?"

Moshe continued in Arabic. "Eli languishes and must meet with you before his heart breaks with the pain of his love. I am sent as a messenger."

"Please!" Mr. Parker remained blinking in confusion as Moshe pumped his hand. "Miss Hassan, can you understand this blighter?"

"Indeed," Victoria nodded graciously, then through gritted teeth she smiled and answered in Arabic as well. "You are insane to come here."

Mr. Parker managed to free himself from Moshe's handshake. "Whatever does he want? Doesn't he speak English?"

"He wants an address," Victoria replied, calmly pulling pen and paper from her handbag and scribbling a note. After a minute she handed the note to Moshe with a slight bow. "Tell Eli I love him," she whispered softly in her own tongue. Then with the grace of a duchess she swept past him and out through the doors of the lobby entrance.

Victoria recognized the musician by the cello that rested on the floor of the Egged bus station beside a large wet man with a broken arm.

Both Leah and Shimon Feldstein appeared to be wet—he more so than she, however. There was not one dry inch on the body of the big man.

"Good heavens," muttered Parker as he spotted them across the lobby. "They must have run behind the bus all the way from Tel Aviv."

The couple looked quite miserable and lost. The wide brown eyes of the cellist held an almost childlike expression of worry, like a little girl lost in the souks of the Old City.

"Leah Feldstein?" Victoria called. She walked toward the musicians and saw Leah's lost expression change to one of immediate relief.

"Tell her I said good day," mouthed Parker, exaggerating each word. "*Guten Tag!*" he said loudly as he extended his hand.

Leah accepted the handshake doubtfully; then as the strange little man likewise took Shimon's good hand, she said in German, "Should we tell him we speak English? His German is remarkably bad!"

Victoria laughed at the comment, immediately deciding she liked Leah Feldstein. She replied in German, "My name is Victoria Hassan. I have been brought along as your interpreter."

"Your accent is much better." Leah was smiling warmly as she glanced up at Shimon. "What do you say, Shimon? Shall we keep it among us three?"

Parker's mouth enunciated broadly as he relayed his message through Victoria to the musicians. "Tell them we wel-come them in the name of His Maj-es-ty's Man-da-tory Gov-ern-ment!"

"Is he just learning to speak English also?" Shimon quipped.

"Just barely," Victoria replied. "And tonight you are performing for the British Army, yes?"

"For free bus tickets to Jerusalem for me and my cello," Leah said. "Shimon was forced to ride on the top of the bus with the chickens, which may have been a blessing compared to what I rode with inside."

Victoria shook her head in sympathy. "I hear they hire these bus drivers at an insane asylum in Hebron. They stop for no one."

"I have heard that as well." Leah laughed. "And now, where are you taking us?"

As Mr. Parker continued to relay messages through Victoria, the car arrived at the King David Hotel. Arrangements had been made for Leah and Shimon to stay here the first night, if they wished, as guests of the government. If not, a taxi would take them anywhere they wished to go after the performance this evening.

Leah squeezed Shimon's hand as the doorman walked from beneath the awning of the King David to open their door. The gracious stones of the hotel seemed to Leah to mirror some of the elegance they had left behind in Europe. One night in such a place! The thought of it comforted her.

"Last night we slept in a packing crate," she said to Victoria. "Just tell me there are no scorpions or snakes here."

"None that I have seen," said the dark-eyed beauty with a laugh. "Except the two-legged kind."

"And is there hot water with which I might thaw out my husband?"

"That will take an hour at least," Shimon quipped through chattering teeth.

Victoria nodded. "And European-made tubs are big enough even for a man his size. And it is free. If you like, I will help you find your way to your great-aunt's flat in the Old City tomorrow."

"Consider the request made," Shimon said.

This Victoria relayed to the blissfully ignorant Mr. Parker. Ah yes, he supposed he could spare Victoria for half a day tomorrow. The government would expect such a courtesy, no doubt.

Thus, the matter was settled. Leah and Shimon were shown their suite by the white-gloved bellhop who led them though the lobby and past the stiff-backed guards flanking the orange brass elevator doors. For just a moment, Leah felt as Jerusalem was not the end of the world, after all. Strange that her first friendly conversation had been with an Arab woman. It was not at all what Leah had expected.

16

A Land of Milk and Honey

Now I know how Joshua and Caleb felt when they came across the Jordan to spy!" Moshe grinned down at Eli as he presented the note from Victoria.

Eli held the folded slip of paper as if it contained news of life or a sentence of death for him. He did not open it. "Is she . . . all right?"

"She is a land of milk and honey, brother!" Moshe sat down on the ledge of the roof and crossed his arms with self-satisfaction. The mission into enemy territory had been a complete success. "So? Why don't you open it?"

Eli did not want to open such a personal note in front of Moshe. What if Victoria had rejected his love? Then it occurred to him that Moshe had probably read the note. He probably knew its contents backward and forward. *Why did she not seal it in an envelope?* He looked at Moshe, then asked, "Did you read it?" He knew the answer by the Cheshire-cat smile on Moshe's face.

"I had to know what it said." Moshe touched the bruise on his chin as the memory of Eli's fist came to mind. "What if the wind had torn it from my hand? It would have blown away and then you would not have known." He saluted. "Sergeant Joshua reporting as ordered, sir!"

Perhaps Moshe was smiling because the affair was finally over. Perhaps . . .

The trapdoor raised slightly and the irritated voice of Ida Sachar called up, "Eli? Have you seen Moshe?"

"He is here with me, Mama." Eli tucked the paper behind him.

Silence. "What are you boys doing up here?"

Moshe answered, "Praying and fasting, Mama."

"*Oy! Oy!*" She poked her head up and looked as if she could not believe her ears. She shook her finger at Moshe. "You could use a little praying, Moshe Sachar! You teach him, Eli. He is practically one of the goyim with all this archaeology nonsense!" She narrowed her eyes threateningly. "But if I hear another word about fasting tonight!" She shook a fist, then growled, "We *eat* in ten minutes!" She disappeared like a squirrel down a hole and let the door slam shut.

Eli sat rigid, his smile frozen, his eyes wide with false nonchalance. This was the sort of look his mother would have recognized as caught-in-the-act innocence if she had stopped long enough to notice. Neither brother breathed as the sound of her footsteps died away.

Seconds ticked by. At last Eli wiped his brow and, with a shaking hand, pulled out the crumpled note.

"So read it, already!" Moshe whispered. Mama had frightened the cocky smirk from his face.

With a jerky nod, Eli opened the paper and scanned the neatly written note. "She wrote in English!" he protested, thrusting the paper into Moshe's hands.

"She knows Mama and Papa do not read English all that well." The grin returned.

"Neither do I," Eli protested. "Speaking is one thing. 'Hallo, old chap! Cheery-bye! Can you show me the way to the W.C.?' These Englishmen. Nonsense! Read the note!"

"I knew you would need me, dear brother."

"Just read!" Eli said this too loud and instantly ducked at the thought of his impatient voice carrying through the window to Mama's ear. Or down to the street to a customer at Cohens'. "But read quietly," he whispered.

Moshe cleared his throat and in a whisper he translated into Arabic what Victoria had written.

> *"Dearest Love,*
> *Not a moment passes without thoughts of you . . ."*

Moshe paused and glanced up. He expected a blush of embarrassment on Eli's face. Instead, Eli had melted like a lump of butter in the sun, his eyes dreamy. Truly he was *meshugge* for this girl!

Eli sighed happily as he digested the first sweet words. He rolled his hand as a sign for Moshe that he was ready for the next delicious bite.

> *"There are reasons I could not send for you or meet with you. The torment is terrible without you. Please, please, my dearest heart, say*

you will meet me at one o'clock on Friday in the chapel of Christ Church. I will be there waiting for you! I am your beloved. V."

Moshe handed the note back to Eli who scanned it over again. Had Moshe translated correctly? *Meet her in the chapel of a Christian church?*

"Why Christ Church?" Eli pondered out loud. "She a Muslim and me a Jew. And she wants to meet in Christ Church?"

"She is smart," Moshe interjected. "Friday is the Muslim holy day. Her brothers will all be gathered in the courtyard of the mosque to hear the Mufti's sermon. Muslim shops will be closed. None of her people will be around to recognize her."

Eli raised his eyebrows slightly at the sensible plan. "And none of my people would set foot in Christ Church. Yes. She has been thinking."

Moshe reached out and tapped the round black yarmulke on Eli's head. "You will have to take that off. No one wears a hat in these goyim houses of worship. And you should wear my clothes. Comb your hair back. They will think you are an Englishman, Eli."

"Yes, and our people will be preparing for Shabbat. Everyone will be busy. Friday is a good day. The best day. I am not sure why we did not think of it before."

"There is less chance you will be killed in a Christian church than sneaking around after dark in the Muslim Quarter." Moshe was still smiling, but there was relief in his words. "Although there is less chance that you will kiss her with much satisfaction in the pew at Christ Church with the rector looking on, *nu*?"

Eli nodded. That much was inconvenient, to be sure. But seeing her again, just sitting beside her, seemed as urgent to him now as breathing. "I will be content," he said, counting off the days and the hours until Friday. "One o'clock at Christ Church." The thought would sustain him.

Below them, a shrill voice penetrated the trapdoor. "Enough prayers, already! Eli and Moshe, come eat! And wash your hands well after being up there with the pigeons!"

News of Roosevelt's latest appeal on behalf of a Jewish homeland had just clattered off the London wires. Murphy scanned it briefly. He was certain that the American response to the Woodhead Commission's purpose in Palestine would evoke a spate of indignant replies on British editorial pages in the morning. After all, the young soldier killed on the wall of Jerusalem had not been American, but English. It was not an American family who was receiving home the body of their son, but an English mother!

Beyond the glass cubicle of Murphy's office, the typewriters of a dozen reporters pecked out the latest news from around the continent of Europe. The arrival of the body of this soldier killed on the Old City wall had sparked a greater response than the brutality against twelve thousand Jews in Germany.

The phone on his desk rang insistently, pulling him from his bitter reverie. He picked up the receiver, uncertain of the voice on the other end of the line.

"Mr. Murphy? John Murphy?" asked the precise English accent of a man.

"Speaking."

"You are the husband of Elisa Murphy?"

The question made Murphy stir in a moment of dread. "Yes. What is it?"

There was a moment of uneasy silence on the other end of the line. "This is Sir Thomas Beecham," the conductor began. "I assure you that I am not normally in the habit of reading other people's mail, but the secretary brought me something quite disturbing a few moments ago."

Now Murphy's stomach churned. "Okay, concerning Elisa?"

"A card addressed to her from Paris. I did not want to alarm her or frighten her considering her . . . delicate condition. But the message is one word. Written in German. It says, simply, *Gefahr*. You understand German, Mr. Murphy?"

Murphy nodded before he repeated the word in English. "Danger."

It was the look in Murphy's eyes that frightened Elisa most. She cradled her violin in her arms and glanced first at Murphy, then back to the towering hulk of a man who stood grinning down at her.

"Freddie has worked at the loading dock of the *Times* for years." Murphy thumped the giant on his back. Freddie tipped his ragged tweed cap and continued to smile benignly. His face was pleasant but deeply lined, and his nose took a slight bend to the right. His chin jutted forward as if daring some invisible adversary to take a poke. Large ears protruded on either side of the lumpy face. The ears were the most interesting aspect of Freddie's physical appearance. They seemed to have been inflated like helium balloons. Normal folds and indentations were the very image of cauliflowers.

"Freddie was once one of the greatest Rugby players in Great Britain." Murphy thumped the giant again and then tugged on his own earlobe as if to explain the man's battered appearance.

Elisa smiled politely. She had not yet guessed the reason Murphy had brought this kind ox home. At six feet five and three hundred pounds, Fred Frutschy was a man to reckon with; that much was undeniable. But why?

Freddie shuffled his feet slightly. He doffed his cap, revealing a nearly bald head. He smiled broadly, displaying a gap where his four front teeth should have been. "Missus Murphy," he said in a gentle voice, the voice of a man much smaller, "real pleased to meet you, missus."

"You are working for Trump News now?" Elisa tried to guess why the dockworker from the London *Times* now stood wringing his cap in her front room.

Murphy and Freddie exchanged glances. Murphy cleared his throat and raised his chin authoritatively. "Elisa," he began, faltered, and began again. "Freddie is working for me . . . for *us*."

Freddie was nodding enthusiastically and looking eagerly at his new boss to explain his position as an employee.

"How . . . very nice." Elisa was confused. There were no stacks of newspapers to load like at the news service. Janitor? Messenger?

"Bodyguard." Murphy dropped the title like a boulder in a clear pond.

Elisa worked her mouth open and closed. Open again. "But *why*? Mr. Tedrick said there was . . . *no threat!*"

"You don't trust that government goon, and neither do I." Murphy frowned. He thumped Freddie for the third time, as if demonstrating the muscle of a fine horse. "Nobody's gonna get past Freddie here. Not Tedrick, or Tedrick's men, or . . . *anyone*."

Elisa found herself nodding. Yes. The very fact that Murphy could think there was need for a bodyguard made her tremble inside.

"We got me a uniform, missus." Freddie's head bobbed vigorously.

"Uniform?" Elisa squeaked.

"Chauffeur." Murphy was more confident, relieved that she had not protested.

"But we don't have an auto," she protested.

Murphy jerked a thumb toward the front window. He stepped aside as she went to look. A gleaming black car was parked at the curb. It seemed to stretch the width of the house. "A 1932 Duesenberg," Murphy said sheepishly. "I got a deal on it."

"Used to drive a taxi, missus," Freddie volunteered. "An' I can carry packages for you." He waved a big paw toward her violin case. "I likes children. Me an' the missus have seven of our own. Mostly grown now. An' twenty-two grandchildren, too."

"He says he'll teach Charles and Louis to play rugby." Murphy exhaled with loud relief. Elisa accepted this rather large addition to their household with astonishment, but little evidence of resentment.

Elisa glanced at the man's ears. She inwardly winced and gently suggested, "Perhaps you could start them with soccer?"

"Ah, 'tis a woman's game compared to rugby." Freddie's lumpy face scowled. "But as you wish, missus."

Murphy mouthed the words *thank you* to Elisa. She shook her head slightly in disbelief. A car. A chauffeur. And a bodyguard who could carry packages and teach the boys to play rugby.

"All this," she said, "and a performance tonight." She extended her hand to Freddie. He shook it heartily, then tugged the violin from her arms.

"I'll carry this, missus." Then he screwed up his face in an expression that displayed deep pondering. "Of course, first I'll have to put on me uniform. Them tall black boots." He thrust the violin case back into her arms and bowed slightly at the waist before he turned and clumped down the stairs to the Duesenberg.

As Leah considered what to wear and what to play and what to say to several thousand British soldiers and the Woodhead Commission at tonight's performance, Shimon penned a note to his great-aunt, announcing that they had at last arrived in Jerusalem and would come to the Old City tomorrow. At the suggestion of Victoria he sent the note by way of a hotel errand boy with the instructions that if he returned with a note from the old woman, he would receive another shilling for his efforts.

Thirty minutes before the scheduled departure to the Allenby barracks, the messenger returned to the hotel room. Shimon opened the door to a boy who stood wringing his hands and panting as if he had run all the way without stopping. The look on his face betrayed that something was definitely wrong.

"I am sorry, mister. I am very sorry, but I could not give your letter to your aunt in the Old City!"

"Why not?"

"I knocked and knocked on the door, mister. I knocked until the lady in the flat downstairs yelled at me that I should quit knocking." The boy's hands were trembling as he pulled out the original note.

"But did she say where my great-aunt was?"

"Yes, mister." Curly hair bobbed as the boy nodded. He looked as if he might cry. "That woman, she says the old lady was eighty-seven and nobody was surprised except now maybe you. They sent a letter to Vienna, where the boxes came from."

"Where is she? Is she ill?"

"No. She is dead this one month past, mister. She left you with four months lease on her flat but not a farthing besides, and you can get the key from the woman in the flat downstairs."

Shimon's lips formed a round, soundless *oh* of surprise. "Ah. I was not expecting. She was very old." He winced and opened and closed his note to her.

"I am sorry, mister," croaked the boy. "But . . . I came back with a message and . . . so . . . my other shilling?"

Shimon blinked uncomprehendingly at the boy for a moment. Dressed in her black concert dress, Leah reached around Shimon and paid the nearly frantic boy, dismissing him with a curt nod as he thanked her and thanked her again. She shut the door and pulled Shimon to the bed. "Sit down, darling."

He nodded blankly and obeyed. "I did not know her. I . . . I am sorry." He put his hand to his forehead. "I am made of stone. Of stone. All I can think is that she left us with four months free rent on her flat. And . . . I am relieved."

Leah sat down beside him. She put her arm around his broad shoulders and leaned her head against his. She sighed. "Why are you relieved, darling?"

Shimon looked wonderingly at Leah. "I wrote her and told her that you and I . . . that we are *Christians*." He whispered the word and looked over his shoulder as if someone might hear. "I thought perhaps the news killed her. That she opened the letter and died of a heart attack. But then I counted. She could not have gotten my letter before she . . . died! She would have left the lease to someone else."

"Wrong, Shimon." Leah grimaced. "I wrote her the news from Paris. Before I knew you were safe, I told her I believed God would deliver you. That we would be here together in Jerusalem, and that I had found the Messiah of Israel."

"And she still left us the apartment?"

Leah nodded and patted his leg. "You should say kaddish for her, Shimon. She would have liked that."

17

In Concert

Victoria held two handwritten invitations from Leah Feldstein to the performance tonight at Allenby barracks. *"A way of saying thank you in advance for helping us our first day here,"* Leah had murmured.

Two passes. Not just one. Any one of the girls in the secretarial pool would have given a week's wages for the chance to attend the concert. Every important official in the government would be among the audience.

Victoria felt rich. She would not give the extra pass to Mr. Parker, nor to a friend among the secretaries. She looked out across the lobby of the King David Hotel and thought of the brave and foolish Moshe Sachar meeting her this morning. Eli must be desperate!

She smiled and called to a passing messenger. She hastily scribbled a note and slipped the pass into a white envelope with Eli's address on it.

"A shilling if you are back within thirty minutes," she promised the boy. "I will wait here in the lobby for you."

The delicious scents of fresh-baked bread and chicken soup with dumplings filled the house. "And apple strudel for dessert," Ida Sachar said, opening the door. The breathless young Armenian boy on the step wore the uniform of a page from the King David Hotel. He bowed briefly and presented the note. He did not withdraw his hand, as it was customary for a tip to be given at both ends of the line.

"She wishes me to wait for a reply," said the boy.

Ida's eyes widened. The message was to Eli. And it was from a *she*? "Eli! Eli! Eli! A message for you from a *she* at the King David Hotel!"

Eli and Moshe descended the stairs together. Both looked strangely pale, but calm. Ida knew this look. Guilt. The guilt of boys who have been into the cookie jar. The guilt of boys who knew whose ball went through Mrs. Schlemeker's window but would not tell.

"A message for you, Eli, and *she* wants a reply, whoever *she* is." Ida tapped her foot and watched as Eli opened the note. He frowned, and then his eyebrows practically raised up over his head. Something was up. Moshe clearly knew about it, too. Ah, well. It was time for Eli to notice girls maybe. As long as *she* was a nice Jewish girl from a good family!

"So?" Ida asked.

"It is not signed." Eli handed his mother the strange invitation.

Ida's eyebrows went up and down. "Tonight. A personal invitation from—*oy!* Is this the wife of old Idela Feldstein's grandnephew? The one she was talking about? The cellist. *Oy!* Hulda said she thought a messenger had gone to the flat. And now my Eli is invited to the . . ." She paused, puzzled. "Why? How does she know *you*?"

Moshe spoke up. "I think he should go, Mama. Maybe the British drew names or something. Yeshiva students. To . . . uh . . . to represent every aspect of Jewish life in the Old City and New." He scratched his chin. "I bet that is it!" He clapped Eli on the back. "Lucky fellow. He should go. It is an honor."

Ida forgot about the guilty look. An honor? Of all the Yeshiva students, her Eli was chosen? *And the bigwigs from England will be there and also those from the Jewish Agency!* "Yes! He should go." She tipped the messenger. "Yes! Tell them my Eli will attend! Hurry now!" she instructed her son. "You have just time for supper before you go."

From over her music stand, Elisa could see the huge frame of Freddie Frutschy watching the performance from the wings of the stage. Properly dressed in a dark gray uniform and tall, shining black boots, he was an enlarged version of the chauffeurs of the British lords and ladies who had flocked to this evening's performance of Mendelssohn's *Scottish Symphony*.

Unknown to her, Murphy had placed a telephone call to Sir Thomas Beecham, conductor of the London Philharmonic Orchestra. Murphy had managed to prepare the maestro for the fact that the orchestra's newest violinist would be watched over by a toothless giant in a chauffeur's uniform.

Knowing of the cryptic warning and a fraction of Elisa's history, first in Vienna and then in the saving of the former president of Czechoslovakia, Sir Thomas was not the least bit surprised. "Splendid idea," he had declared, as if he had thought of it himself.

And so tonight Murphy once again watched Elisa play from row ten, aisle seat in the Royal Opera House in Covent Garden, just as he had in better days in Vienna. Louis and Charles sat quietly beside him. After the first number, Louis poked Charles and whispered, "I wish Leah was here playing Vitorio." Charles did not answer, but kept his eyes straight ahead. A single tear rolled down his cheek; he brushed it aside fiercely and fixed his gaze on Elisa.

All the while, vigilant Freddie Frutschy stood just offstage and tapped the shiny toe of his enormous new boot to the rhythm of music he had never heard before. *A wonder and a marvel!*

His lumpy face revealed his determination that no one would get within ten feet of the beautiful young Mrs. Murphy! She smiled at him and nodded slightly when he put his huge hands together to applaud with the same enthusiasm as Murphy and the boys.

When the audience rose to its feet and shouted "Bravo!" Freddie seconded the shout and tossed his cap into the air. Such a job sure beat tossing stacks of the *Times* into the back of a delivery truck.

The mess hall of the Allenby barracks in Jerusalem had no real stage. Sheets of wood were laid across supports, providing a platform three feet above the concrete floor. Three thousand British soldiers talked and laughed with the steady uproar that always preceded concerts everywhere. Above their heads, the rain drummed on the corrugated tin roof, adding to the noise.

Members of the Woodhead Commission were seated in a section of folding chairs reserved for British officers and the British high commissioner. These civilians were dressed in black dinner jackets as they would have been for a concert in London's Royal Opera House.

The sight of them, and that thought, made Leah suddenly homesick for Elisa. She held tightly to Shimon's hand. "Close your eyes and listen, Shimon," she said. "Where are we?"

Eyes closed, they stood very close to each other and remembered.

Once again the audience of the Musikverein waited in red velvet seats. Behind the closed curtain, Leah and Shimon took their places. Rudy Dorbransky swung the bow of his fiddle like a sword as he strutted onto the stage. Elisa . . . dear Elisa, laughed and rolled her eyes as an unspoken message passed between her and Leah. The orchestra tuned up with a cacophony of noise that blended into the clamor of expectant voices in the audience. And then, as the oboe sounded the A, Rudy found the note and everyone suddenly came to attention.

Vienna. The Musikverein. What days those had been! How far they had come to reach this night!

At the sound of thunderous applause, Leah opened her eyes. Stacks of long dining tables lined the walls of the room. Chairs were folded and stacked in rows along the back wall, where an opening showed huge black stoves and racks of tin plates.

Leah looked up at Shimon. His eyes were still closed. *Yes. He sees it. He is there. Vienna.* She squeezed his hand as the British high commissioner climbed onto the makeshift stage and nervously grasped the neck of a microphone. The clamor fell silent except for the still-drumming raindrops on the roof.

The distinguished Englishman spoke, retelling the story of Leah and Shimon's flight from Germany. He had heard the story, he said, in a wire sent from Sir Thomas Beecham, conductor of the London Philharmonic Orchestra. How fortunate Palestine was to have stolen Leah Feldstein from the great orchestras of Europe.

Leah was not listening to the man's empty flattery. He could not know the pain and struggles and endless miracles that had brought Leah and Shimon to this place. For the first time since their arrival, Leah knew somehow that they had come home. She knew that the elegant British official on the stage and the thousands of men crowded on the floor would someday leave Jerusalem, but Leah and Shimon would not leave. They would stand on the shores of a Jewish homeland and wave good-bye to the men who made it so difficult to come here, to the men who welcomed her onto the stage. She prayed silently, asking God to shine through her first performance tonight.

". . . and so we wish to greet virtuoso cellist Leah Feldstein. We welcome her now to the British Mandate of Palestine and to Jerusalem."

Shimon helped her up to the platform. Victoria stepped forward and handed her the cello. The applause and the rain were one continuous roar.

Victoria watched as Leah crossed the crude stage. Someone had rigged a spotlight and it shone on the bobbed hair of the petite musician. Her hands and face were a bright, animated contrast to the black of her long concert dress. The deep red wood of her instrument seemed alive, radiating with an existence all its own. The wood caught the light and sent it out, then turned in her hands to capture the light again. There was applause and more applause as she bowed slightly, turning toward David Ben-Gurion and Golda Meir and a dozen other proud Jewish faces among the members of the Jewish Agency. And then a slight bow to those men who had come to Palestine as judges—the Woodhead Commission.

This is not a beautiful woman, as men define beauty, Victoria thought as she watched Leah capture the audience with a smile. *But there is an elegance, a poise and confidence about her that is deeply beautiful.*

Victoria glanced up at the face of Shimon. He was smiling and weeping at the same time. He was so proud and so in love. The look in his eyes made Victoria search the crowd again for Eli. He was somewhere among these cheering men. *Somewhere.* She scanned the rows. Column on column of English faces. Uniforms and civil servants. Very few women among them. She still had not found Eli when the cheering faded to expectancy.

Leah stepped up to the microphone. The drumming of the rain competed with her first words, and then, suddenly, even the rain fell silent as she spoke. "I have played in all the great concert halls of Europe. But this is my first performance in a mess hall."

Much laughter. She smiled. Waited for silence again.

"This is also my first performance in my new, yet very old, homeland. And for the first time in my life—" she glanced at Shimon—"in *our* lives, we feel that we are finally home indeed." She paused.

Victoria saw the emotion behind her words, and yet Leah was in control.

"There is a saying in the Talmud: if a jug falls upon a stone, woe to the jug. And if a stone falls upon a jug, woe to the jug also."

A small wave of laughter erupted before Leah continued. "It has been this way for the People of the Book for two thousand years. We have fallen on the stones. The stones of every nation and people have fallen on us. And yet, here is a miracle far greater than any I can think of . . . still we remain. And still we are here. As the prophets have foretold, we return now to Zion from the four corners of the world. And when we are returned, so will our Messiah also return, as it is written: '*To Jerusalem Thy city, return with compassion, and dwell within it as Thou promised: Rebuild it soon in our days—an everlasting structure.*'"

The silence was thick in the hall. This message had not been expected! And then Victoria saw Eli. He stood across from her, half obscured by a stack of tables. His eyes were bright, on fire, as he listened to Leah Feldstein.

"The one you call Jesus, the one we call Messiah—He will return when the People of the Book come home to Zion! That is written. It is promised. And that is the reason the Darkness fights so hard to keep us out of this, our homeland! And that is why behind us the whole world burns and rages to destroy us!"

She looked directly at the stony faces of those honored gentlemen from London. "It is a miracle, you see, that even one of us has survived to come home. It is proof that God exists and that He does not lie! He has not forgotten His Covenant with Israel. Though men may forget, God has not forgotten us."

She lowered her head for a moment, and Victoria thought perhaps she was praying. The words had stirred something inside Victoria. Leah had somehow interpreted a mystery for her tonight while she awakened a thousand questions. *Who is Light, and who is Darkness?*

Leah Feldstein spoke no more with her lips. She backed up and took the chair set in place for her. The men and women were silent. The rains were silent. And Leah Feldstein said again in music what her heart had told them all a moment before.

Dressed in his black suit, Eli felt strangely out of place among the press of British uniforms that surrounded him. He pushed his way slowly through the throng, ignoring the comments that followed him.

"What's the Yid doin' here? Thought this was just for us."

"This is Jerusalem, after all. He must know somebody."

Eli knew Victoria. And for that reason he had come to the concert. He could see the head of Shimon Feldstein over the crowd. Victoria had stood near the big man throughout the performance. Would she still be there? He prayed as he moved closer. Through a small crack in the dam of admirers, he glimpsed the upturned face of Leah Feldstein as she smiled and chatted with David Ben-Gurion. And there, just beyond them, was Victoria in conversation with an elegantly dressed woman. The wife of an Englishman, no doubt. Victoria was smiling, too. Eli stopped just to watch her. He had never seen her in such a setting—so beautiful, so light and at ease. Life should always be this way for her.

And then she glanced toward him. She had not been looking for him, but her eyes caught his and held him there. The Englishwoman continued to speak, "How wonderful! How wonderful the music was! Oh, my . . . she should be playing in London! And you know her . . . you are her interpreter! Oh, my dear!"

Victoria was not listening any longer, although her head nodded in feigned attention as she touched Eli with a look.

He did not come closer. In this crowd it would not be wise. To hold her in his mind was enough. She smiled at the Englishwoman and then turned toward Eli. The smile was for him.

He mouthed the words *Christ Church*, then nodded. Her smile broadened before someone stepped between them, and the connection was lost.

CRU

Herschel Grynspan heard his friend, Hans Schumann, ascending the steep stairway to the attic room. When he opened the door, he carried a basket of bread and two different kinds of cheese, as well as a bar of Dutch chocolate.

Herschel sat up on his cot and wordlessly watched Hans. The radio played sad French love songs as the rain drummed on the roofs of Paris overhead.

"As I promised," Hans said happily. "I have been to the home of your uncle."

Even this news did not cheer Herschel. "And?"

"He is well. He sends his greetings. He also sends this." He tossed an envelope to Herschel. It tumbled onto the floorboards faceup. Herschel leaned forward and stared at the Polish stamp and postmark. The name *Berta Grynspan* was on the return address. "They are—" Herschel swallowed hard and fought to regain his breath—"in Poland." He picked up the envelope. It had been opened. Herschel looked sharply at Hans. "What does it say?"

Hans shrugged. "I did not read it. Your uncle . . ."

As if the paper were holy, Herschel pulled it gingerly from the torn envelope. He looked up at the high window and the gray patch of sky beyond. He tried to imagine himself in Poland, with his parents and his sister. Tears of longing stung his eyes as he began to read silently:

> *Dear Herschel,*
>
> *By now you must have heard what happened—we have been deported back to Poland. Papa was hurt, and I have been so frightened! On Thursday evening, rumors were circulating that Polish Jews in our city were being expelled, but none of us believed it. At nine o'clock that evening a policeman came to our house to tell us to report to the police station with our passports. When we got to the station, practically the whole neighborhood was already there. Almost immediately we were all taken to the town hall. No one told us what was happening, but we realized this was going to be the end. They shoved an expulsion order into our hands, saying that we had to leave Germany before October 29. We were not allowed to go home, so we have nothing—not a penny. Could you send something to us?*
>
> *Love from us all,*
>
> *Berta*

Herschel could feel his olive skin blanching as Hans watched him. "What is it?" Hans urged. "Are they all right?"

"They . . . want me to send them . . . something. I have nothing to send!" Herschel lay down on his bed and stared at the dark rafters of the attic. "What can I do? Oh, Hans! How can I help them? . . . I cannot. I cannot!"

The hands of Ernst vom Rath trembled only slightly as he held the tip of his cigarette to the flame of the match. He should not have been smoking, he knew, but something about these Gestapo men reawakened the old urge . . . *the need* . . . for tobacco.

He inhaled, then tried to gaze steadily into the face of the Gestapo agent who had called him to Berlin from Paris for the express purpose of investigating the death of agent Georg Wand.

". . . a tragic loss to the force. Georg was quite effective. Too effective, some said." The man rubbed his bald head and smiled gently. "Perhaps it was his effectiveness that got him killed, eh?"

Ernst shrugged. He flicked the ash of his cigarette with practiced nonchalance. "This business of espionage is far beyond me, Herr Vargen." Did his nervousness show? Inside, he seethed with anger toward Thomas von Kleistmann. Why had Thomas not been content to slip away in the night? Why had he killed Georg Wand and left Ernst alone to answer these questions?

"Espionage, beyond you?" Leo Vargen laced the question with amusement. He studied Ernst, as if waiting for him to react. Was he frightened? Did he have something to hide?

"In the embassy we call it by another name. *Politics.*" Ernst played the game well.

Vargen did not accept the lightness of his tone. "But you and Thomas von Kleistmann were friends."

"Acquaintances. Two single German men in the Paris Embassy. We had an occasional drink."

"How is it that you did not know he was against the Führer?" Vargen bore down.

"He never told me." Ernst shrugged.

Incredulous, Vargen's eyes widened in disbelief. "Are you saying that he never expressed his feelings about our Führer and the goals of the Reich?"

"Why should he tell me? Would you tell someone if you were a traitor, Herr Vargen?" Ernst inhaled again. The cigarette helped. He was doing well.

Vargen tried a different approach to the inner workings of the young aristocratic diplomat. "Who do you think might have let him out of his quarters that night? Who among the embassy staff?"

"Thomas had a way with women. Have you interrogated the French maid?"

"She was not working that night."

Ernst smiled a knowing smile. "What has that got to do with it?"

Vargen would not be pulled from the scent. "We are almost certain that a member of the German staff unlocked the door."

Ernst no longer trembled. "I still say that the guard did not lock it in the first place. Those of us who remained in the dining room would have noticed if anyone had sneaked up to let him out." Ernst played the role of one who was also curious about the miraculous escape of Thomas. He was almost enjoying himself now. *Almost.*

"Friedrich Wanger expressed the thought that you might have let the prisoner go free." A direct assault.

Ernst deflected the blow with a laugh. "The French maid is still a better guess than that!" He leaned forward. "Believe me, Herr Vargen, had I known what von Kleistmann was up to, I would have killed him myself."

Vargen's eyebrows raised in a sort of satisfaction. "Ah. Yes." He rubbed his bald pate again and took a step toward the door. "Come on, then," he said lightly.

Was the interview over? Ernst rose from his chair and followed. He snubbed out his cigarette in the ashtray as Vargen crossed the foyer and jerked his head toward the stairs that led to the basement offices and storerooms below the Ministry of Information.

Ernst grinned quizzically as the two men descended the steps in silence. Vargen closed the door firmly behind them and walked quickly down a long corridor with unoccupied rooms on either side.

"You espionage types," Ernst quipped, wishing he had another cigarette. "I did not even know there was such a maze down here. What is—"

Vargen was smiling broadly now, enjoying his own game. His look stopped Ernst midsentence. The weight of foreboding washed over him. Vargen unlocked a steel door and opened it slowly before he switched on the light.

The scene before him made Ernst gasp and choke back the bile that rose in his throat. The room was spattered with blood. On the concrete floor, the body of a man lay stretched out on two wooden planks fastened together like a cross. Railroad spikes protruded from his hands and feet. The face was battered beyond recognition, but Ernst knew instantly who it was.

"Thomas—?" He felt the chamber spin around him.

Vargen had an almost cheerful look. He kicked the steel door shut, and Thomas turned his head toward the two men. *He is still alive!*

"We caught him in Holland. Boarding a ship to England. Thought he would escape, no doubt. Traitor. Convicted, sentenced, and duly executed."

Ernst felt his stomach churn. He could not lean against the wall. The blood . . . he must not faint. What had Thomas told them? He must not have told them everything. How could a man endure this and not beg to tell all?

Ernst looked in horror at the smiling face of the Gestapo executioner. "Then why have you not . . . *executed* him? For the mercy of God, why *this*?"

"You politicians." Vargen laughed. "You like things clean." He shrugged. He walked over to Thomas and placed the toe of his boot on the head of the spike in his hand. "He is not dead because he has not told us what we want to know."

Thomas coughed, cried out in agony. "Nothing . . . to . . . tell. God! Let me die."

Ernst turned away and retched on the floor. "Kill him," he breathed. "Please. Get it over with. *Kill him!*"

Ernst did not look at Thomas, but everywhere he looked was proof of his friend's courage.

Vargen pulled his Luger from its holster and extended it to Ernst. "But Herr vom Rath, you said you would have killed him yourself . . ." Vargen shook his head in amusement. These diplomats could talk, but when it came to the actual matter of one's duty, they were less capable than a woman. "Well?"

Ernst stared at the pistol. Thomas groaned. "I cannot—" Ernst gasped—"cannot kill . . ."

"Ah, well." Vargen was still smiling. "He will die eventually anyway." He started to put away the gun. "Perhaps before I leave for Palestine tomorrow, or after you return to Paris?"

"Please!" Thomas moaned. "For God's sake . . ."

Ernst snatched the weapon from the hand of the Gestapo agent. Sweat poured from his brow, nearly blinding him. He took a step toward Thomas. His hands trembled until he feared that he would drop the gun.

Thomas gazed at him pleadingly, forgiving him for what he must now do.

Vargen looked on with the satisfaction of the master of the hunt. He was always pleased to blood a young hound for the sake of the Reich.

He continued to smile even as the shots rang out. Four of them. One after another.

18

Beg, Buy, or Steal

Göring studied the proposal presented by the British ambassador. He immediately called the Chancellery to speak with Hitler. Now he was sorry he had done so.

Hitler's invitation to Hermann Göring to join him at the Chancellery for an evening meal was more an order than a request.

Göring hung up the telephone and scowled at his servant. "So. I am to have dinner at the chancellor's Merry Restaurant," he quipped dryly. "To tell you the truth, the food there is too rotten for my taste. And then, those party dullards from Munich! Unbearable!" Göring patted the broad expanse of his belly. "Tell the cook to have my meal prepared beforehand. I will eat here before I go to dinner at the Chancellery."

After a dinner of veal topped with asparagus and washed down with a fine white wine, Göring felt that perhaps he could face the Führer's simple vegetarian fare and mineral water.

The Führer said nothing of his purpose to Göring as he led an entourage of thirty guests into the large dining room, forty feet square. In the center was a large round table ringed by fifteen simple chairs with dark red leather seats. Here the most honored guests were seated with Hitler. There was a small table in each of the four corners of the room for the less important sycophants and toadies of the Führer's intimate group.

Göring faced three glass doors that led out into the garden. Trees were leafless and desolate in the autumn twilight of Berlin. In spite of Hitler's great diplomatic triumphs over Great Britain and France in Munich, he was as moody as the weather these days.

"I did not listen to my Voice," he was telling his astrologer, who sat to his left. "You see, we might have had all of Czechoslovakia if only I had heeded the whisper of the Voice. Instead, I listened to statesmen and generals." He inclined his head to Göring, for Göring had not been among the army staff who had urged the Führer to overcaution in the matter of Czechoslovakia.

The astrologer, a thin, pale man with a fringe of gray hair like a laurel crown around his head, seemed quite sympathetic. "It is not too late for that, perhaps, mein Führer. We will consult the charts in the matter of what remains of Czechoslovakia. Call in your medium, and we will pursue the question."

Hitler raised a finger. "But not tonight." Again he looked at Göring. "I have pressing business after dinner."

Göring pretended to eat the same poor meal that Hitler ate—meatless, tasteless dishes with cabbage soup. This sort of simplicity gained Hitler respect among the folk of the Reich. Plain china plates. Plain, smoothly plastered walls painted ivory. The seeming austerity of Hitler's Merry Restaurant, as he called his dining room, was an example of his own modesty.

Within this setting, the gaudy uniform of Göring seemed more tasteless than the vegetarian main dish. Hitler, however, did not resent Göring's outlandish uniform or ostentatious lifestyle. When the meal was finished Göring alone accompanied the Führer through yet another set of glass doors, through a salon, and back into a living room that was about a thousand square feet in area. In this room nothing about the furnishings was austere. A fireplace illuminated the beamed ceiling with dancing shadows. Wood wainscoting circled the room occupied by leather furniture and marble tables.

The medals across the broad expanse of Reichsführer Hermann Göring's uniform glistened when he walked into the Führer's private quarters at the Chancellery. His flabby cheeks were red with the rouge he applied to his waxy skin. His face was ecstatic with the news he brought to Hitler today—almost as bright as Hitler's look was dark.

"We have had an interesting question posed to us from British Ambassador Henderson, mein Führer," Göring began.

Hitler glared at him. "Well?"

"It involves a sale of sorts of the Jews . . . modified slightly from what we discussed earlier. It may well be a benefit to the Reich economy."

Hitler nodded. "I am aware of this plan. Composed by Theo Lindheim in London and presented to the British government by the Jew-warmonger Weizmann."

Göring was startled by this detail. He had not known. He had heard only that the plan had been discussed by Chamberlain's cabinet as a humanitarian possibility for relief of the Jewish problem. "Theo? *Lindheim?*"

"Close your mouth, Hermann!" Hitler snapped. "The man was always clever. You cannot expect him to be otherwise until he is dead." Hitler gazed thoughtfully at the eagle on the mantel of his fireplace. "But that is only a matter of time."

Göring became apologetic. How could he have thought the plan to export German products in exchange for Jewish lives was a good one? How could he have been so foolish to assume that this plan might work? His face was flushed in earnest by the time he finished.

"It is a good idea," Hitler replied. "If Satan himself appears at my bed with a plan to benefit the German people, I listen. Perhaps as we turn up the flame on the Jews, we should also reconsider how we might profit from their pain and cause the other nations of the world to suffer as well." He stood and warmed his hands by the fire. "Tell Foreign Secretary von Ribbentrop to refuse all approaches of the British in this matter. And then you negotiate privately with them, Hermann. Your own little arrangement, as it were. We cannot allow the English to think that they have any power over us in the matter of trade or our treatment of Jews, can we? *No!* And so I delegate this to you!"

The lamps of Hermann Göring's vast Karinhall estate were all dimmed, except for the one that burned on his desk.

His field marshal's uniform was slung carelessly over the back of an oversized leather armchair. Like the uniform and the mansion, the furnishings had been specially constructed so that the bulk of Göring could sit anywhere comfortably.

Tonight he worked on some solution to this Jewish economic problem, as Hitler had instructed him. As supreme head of the Ministry of Economy and commissioner of the Four-Year Plan for making Germany independent from other countries, the Jewish element suddenly added another dimension to the unsteady situation. Simply confiscating the personal belongings and assets of the Jews had not paid off over the years, as he had originally expected. The Reichsbank had benefited in only a small way compared to the loss of trade experienced from foreign boycotts of German goods.

How strange it seemed that it was Theo Lindheim who had conceived the plan—Theo, who had lost everything he had in Germany, and then had almost lost his life in the bargain.

Göring lifted his massive head from the pool of light and stared at the wall of bookshelves that held the rare books once owned by Theo.

Göring had saved them from the Nazi book burnings, not because he was as well-read as Theo, but because they had value. Economic value. One day, when this fanatical reaction against literature had burned itself out, no doubt Theo's first editions would be worth even more. This was also the case with the Lindheim collection of Monet paintings that now graced the bedroom of Göring's wife. *"Decadent art,"* the Führer called it. But Göring himself had chosen it; it would certainly appreciate in value when things settled down again in Germany.

He yawned and rubbed the back of his neck with weariness. A slight smile crossed his lips. He owed a lot to Theo Lindheim. Books. Art. A few pieces of Louis XIV furniture and . . . the piano in the ballroom. The Jew had been an excellent judge of value. A shrewd and clever businessman indeed. Göring almost liked him. At least he respected him for his financial judgments and his ability as a pilot.

Göring groaned slightly as he lifted his bulk from the desk chair and walked in his stocking feet toward the green leather sofa where he collapsed. His blue eyes were red-rimmed with exhaustion. He stared at the books, then glanced at the light that glinted on the medals of his uniform. He remembered the words of his Führer and whispered a dark prayer in hopes of an answer to this economic problem—an answer that would give him praise from his master and another Reich medal. "Satan himself . . . by my bed," he murmured. His words drifted off and his heavy eyelids closed of their own will.

The vision came clearly to Hermann Göring. Outside in the starlit night he could hear the hounds of Germany baying in the depths of the great forest. The hunt was on. . . .

He opened his eyes, and sound and color swirled into the room. He had seen these colors somewhere—somewhere. Trying to focus his eyes, he looked toward his uniform. It was splattered with the red blood of a stag. Behind it he saw the shrouded image of the painting of the German god Wotan that hung in Hitler's quarters. The colors emanated; the howl of the hounds sounded from this canvas, from within its brushstrokes. The eyes of Wotan were the eyes of Adolf Hitler. Göring tried to comment on the remarkable likeness, the beauty of the color and the excitement of the sounds of the hunt, but his voice failed him.

The lips of the image moved. The painting spoke. "Hermann . . ." The eyes of the German god turned to him. He was ashamed he was not wearing his uniform. But then he remembered the blood. "Hermann," the voice called again, and Göring was filled with amazement—the voice of the god was that of the Führer!

He opened his mouth. His voice returned to answer the apparition as yet

another burst of red pulsed from the undulating canvas. "Yes! Mein Führer!"
Göring sat up, leaving his sleeping form on the sofa. He turned to see the fat,
middle-aged man and then looked at himself. Slim. Young again. He wore the
green uniform of a Jäger, a huntsman. He smiled, and the eyes of the god
seemed pleased.

"Go to the window," the god ordered.

Göring obeyed. Outside on the lawn a bonfire of pine branches burned
brightly. A row of dead stags lay on the grass nearby. A man dressed in the
green of the head forester stepped from the shadows into the light of the bonfire.
He held up a slip of paper and began to read the names of the hunters and the
names of the fallen.

"Shot through the heart by Field Marshal Hermann Göring . . . Theo
Lindheim." The man swept a hand toward the stag, but the animal had taken
on a different form. Before the startled eyes of Göring, the stag transformed into
the body of Theo Lindheim. There was only a moment to marvel as the death of
the stag was sounded on the horns of invisible Jägers. With a sweep of the hand,
the forester caught the flame of the fire and threw it onto the dead body. The
brightness of that fire outshone all others. Göring looked down at his chest; the
medals on his uniform sparkled like new jewels in the light.

He clapped his hands together in delight and turned to show the god what
he had done. The colors swirled around him, embracing him with warmth.
"Well done," the Führer said.

Göring raised his hand to salute. His mouth formed the words *Heil Hit-*
ler! and in that instant he was once again on the sofa, once more trapped
inside the heavy body of the middle-aged field marshal.

Hermann Göring opened his eyes, expecting to see the painting. It
was gone. The colors were gone. The face of the German god was not
there. No light shone in through the window.

Göring sat up. There was no blood on his uniform. His medals were
still metal. The air was not filled with the sound of horns or baying
hounds. Yet one thing seemed clear in his mind: the broken body of
Theo Lindheim consumed with the flame of the bonfire.

True to her promise, Victoria Hassan was waiting in the lobby of the
King David Hotel when Leah and Shimon stepped off the elevator at
8 AM. According to her instructions, they left their luggage in the room to
be retrieved later in the day by the porter. The cello was locked in the hotel vault with the assurance that even if the place was blown up, the instrument would be safe from harm.

This was to be a trip of exploration—which buses to take where, how much to pay for what. Never, never must Leah look directly into the eyes of a man in the Old City! Nor should she smile or giggle or allow too-familiar conversation. A stern look and a sharp tongue were the safest policy when shopping the Old City souks. That is, of course, unless Shimon was also along. Then Leah could be pleasant and no one would dare bother her.

Leah felt a sense of magic as the bus arrived just outside Jaffa Gate. The towering walls reflected the morning light in a hundred variegated shades of pink and rust and cream.

Everywhere children, with feet bare and clothes ragged even in the cooling of autumn, seemed to be waiting for the arrival of the tourists. The children were beggars by profession, Victoria explained. They were astute businesspeople and could spot a kind face like that of Shimon before the bus even stopped. "You will have to look angry and tell them you are German. Then they will leave you alone."

This proved impossible for Shimon as dirty hands reached up to him, and so Victoria clapped her hands at the troop and told them this fellow was a very mean German whom they must not trouble. In an instant they were gone, crowding around a less wary British pilgrim who stood in the center of the mob looking very unhappy.

Victoria leaned in close. "The children are fed, you know. You must not worry. There are soup kitchens and medical clinics now." She pointed to the bell tower of the church just beyond the square. "Christ Church," she said simply, as if that explained everything.

During the next two hours, Victoria walked between them, showing them her city as only a native could. "Here you may buy orange juice. *Mitz tapuzim.* The vendor will squeeze it before your eyes. It is wise to bring your own cup. And there you may find boiled eggs and *ka'ak,* like a roll. Ask for *za'atar,* which is a salt and cumin mixture. A very cheap breakfast, and you will be respected in the Old City for knowing what to ask for!" She nudged them. "You have not had breakfast. I had mine already this morning. Go on . . . this is a good time to learn!"

Munching the *ka'ak,* which tasted suspiciously like a bagel, Leah and Shimon followed her through the teeming souk of el-Dabbagha, past the Church of the Holy Sepulchre and through the Triple Bazaar, where everything needed for existence in the Old City was sold.

Within the crowded souks and vaulted bazaars of the Old City, a flood of humanity threatened to overflow the narrow boundaries of shops and stalls. Like rivulets, the tiny alleyways emptied their human current into side streets, which then poured men of every nation into the teeming bay of the marketplace.

Wide-eyed, Leah clung to Victoria's hand in front and Shimon's hand behind as they wove through the traffic like little ships maneuvering through a great port. She bumped into a Copt priest. Jumping back with an apology, she stepped on the toes of a giant Armenian priest, who glared at her from beneath the pointed hood of his cowl. Arab porters groaned beneath the burdens on their backs, like the little donkeys who seemed to carry their own weight of the merchandise that filled the shops. Rolled carpets extended fore and aft of one heavily laden animal. Sheepskins were piled high atop another. Bolts of bright cloth were stacked onto the back of one donkey, who seemed to disappear beneath the load.

Within the open booths that lined each street, Muslim merchants sold Christian crucifixes alongside Jewish menorahs. There were whole streets crammed with brass candlesticks and urns and ashtrays. Other streets had olivewood carvings packed on every shelf, and each member of the Holy Family was said to be carved in genuine olivewood from the Garden of Gethsemane. Leah made a mental note that they must visit Gethsemane to see if there were any olive trees remaining after such a harvest of timber!

There were Bibles for every language and every sect. Leah considered this merchandise to be the one great treasure in the Old City souks. Stacked up like all the other wares and hawked and bargained over like so much cabbage, the Bibles, nonetheless, contained precious treasures between the carved mother-of-pearl covers.

As Victoria looked on with benevolent patience, Leah purchased a Bible printed in the beautiful fluid script of Arabic. She bargained for it herself, without the assistance of Victoria, and when she asked Victoria's opinion of how she had done, their lovely guide informed her that she had paid twice too much, but she would learn.

Leah slipped the purchase into her pocket and determined that she would give it to Victoria as a thank-you on another day—perhaps when Victoria was not thinking of the price Leah had paid.

The beggars were everywhere, the spidery-legged children whom Victoria promised were actually well fed. Large, liquid brown eyes stared up at them. Hands reached out to these wealthy-looking European "tourists," and all the while Victoria warned that Leah must not pay attention to them, must not give them anything.

"Please, lady! Hey, lady! Something. Just a little change!"

At last, Leah removed her newly purchased Bible from her pocket and placed it into the hand of a ragged little boy whose right arm was just a stub protruding from his torn shirt. He looked up at her as if she were crazy. A Christian Bible? He could not eat it. He could not read it. The souks were overflowing with such merchandise.

Leah took his dirty face in her hands. His dark eyes considered her with puzzlement. "It is the prettiest one," she said, sorry now that she had nothing else to give him. "You can sell it after you read it if you like."

"I cannot read, lady."

"Then sell it today, and remember the Word of God has fed you. I wish I had something else for you."

The boy's face brightened. Yes, he would sell the Bible. Eventually someone would buy it from him, and he would earn in one moment what it took an entire day to make in begging.

"Thank you, lady!" he cried as he ran off to join his sobered friends. Their looks at Leah betrayed their new conviction that maybe she was not so rich, after all.

Victoria looked at her disapprovingly. "Why did you do that? His father probably sells Bibles in the souks."

Shimon squeezed her hand and winked with relief. He had been wanting to do something like that all morning long.

"I will buy another Bible sometime and will not pay twice the price," Leah said brightly. "And I will pray that he sells it for twice what I paid for it."

Victoria walked on. "Be careful. He might sell it back to you!"

Leah knew she looked foolish in Victoria's eyes, but it didn't matter. The truth was evident within the walls of the Old City that poverty and want pervaded Jerusalem. This place, which drew the hearts and love of people from all nations, was also harsh and brutal to her own citizens. Even the faces of the children seemed old, hungry, and desperate.

Leah studied the undulating human current and suddenly knew why Jesus had wept over Jerusalem. She watched the little beggar run up to an English soldier and hold up the Bible for sale. The soldier brushed the boy aside, and for a moment Leah thought she might weep as well. She silently prayed that one day she and Shimon might be able to offer these little ones bread in the name of the Lord, and that then the children might beg for the bread of God's Word. She looked up into Shimon's pained face. He felt it too. They could not speak of it in front of Victoria, who seemed not to see, but Leah loved Shimon for the wordless depth of his compassion. Their souls and the desires of their hearts were one.

She tugged on Shimon's arm and he bent for her to whisper, "I love you."

He smiled and nodded as they pressed on after Victoria.

"Now will we go to the Jewish Quarter?" Leah asked, her head spinning from the sights and smells of the Old City Christian Quarter.

Victoria's smile faded. "I cannot take you there. I am an Arab. A Muslim. The Christian Quarter is a sort of neutral ground for us these days. I can walk with you here. Show you the shops, greet the merchants. But a Muslim woman cannot go into the Jewish Quarter, and you will not be safe in my neighborhood at any time either." She frowned. "Not in these times."

Shimon and Leah exchanged glances. They had just lost their guide, it seemed. And the rules of the Old City still seemed obscure to both of them. They had seen every Christian vegetable merchant and every shoe-maker's store with the help of Victoria's mastery of Arabic. But now they were to be cut adrift in the land of beggars and unscrupulous merchants who expected that anyone sensible should know how to dicker over prices. The unwary, on the other hand, deserved to be cheated.

"Well, then—" Leah extended her hand in farewell—"does this mean I cannot invite you home for tea?"

"It means I will take you to Christ Church, and Reverend Robbins will guide you the rest of the journey home." Her eyes were apologetic. "And I will meet you for tea sometime outside these walls. Perhaps at the King David."

"Tomorrow, if you like." Leah tried to press a coin into her hand. "When I fetch my cello? Four o'clock?"

Victoria recoiled from the attempted payment. The concert last night had been payment enough and then some. "A cup of tea with you would be an honor. But tomorrow is Friday—our day of worship. Next Tues-day, perhaps?" The young woman looked momentarily distant and thoughtful. "I spoke with Reverend Robbins about you last night. You are expected."

Leah sensed that she had somehow insulted Victoria in a way she could not understand. Victoria's warm personality cooled noticeably as she cut across Omar Square and led the way down the Armenian Patri-archate Road toward Christ Church. Her conversation was less than friendly, almost terse.

She entered the iron gates of Christ Church like one who had been there before. Greeting the British pastor with a proper yet preoccupied hello, she did not meet his gaze when she introduced her charges and passed them into his care. And when conversation turned to the concert of the night before, Victoria slipped away without another word.

19

Strangers in Paradise

There were beggars here, too, in the Jewish Quarter of the Old City. But the beggars were not children. Here and there, old men sat shaded by an alcove as they put their cups out in hope of reward from Leah and Shimon. "A blessing for a coin," called one feeble old man from his street corner.

Children ran everywhere, playing in the lanes. Yarmulkes perched atop shaved heads, and earlocks bobbed as they called out to one another in Yiddish. These children had shoes, at least.

Leah craned her neck up to the arch of the Great Hurva Synagogue. Although the residences of the Jewish Quarter were mostly poor and shabby, the synagogues were mighty reflections of the synagogues of Europe. The cupola of this temple had been donated by the emperor Franz Josef of Austria. Two blocks beyond, an entire complex had been built with money donated by the Jewish citizens of Warsaw. Indeed, Leah thought as she laid eyes on her new neighborhood for the first time, the faces that peered out at them from the shops and houses were faces she had seen a thousand times before. In Vienna. In Prague. In Warsaw. Some fragment of the broken Jewish homeland had always remained here in Jerusalem in the shadow of the Western Wall.

The lack of even the barest luxuries within the tiny shoe-box apartments did not seem to be a matter of personal concern. As long as their houses of worship reflected the glory of God and Zion, then what did it matter if water must be fetched from a cistern? Who was concerned if the toilets were down the stairs and to the right behind the building? Tenacious poverty was a way of life.

Knowledge of the Torah was the only wealth here. The young faces of children and the ancient faces of the learned rabbis who taught them . . . this beauty Leah saw as they entered the Quarter.

Most streets were unpaved. Squealing with delight, ten young boys dashed through the puddles, then stopped to stare at Shimon and Leah as they trailed after the resolute Reverend Robbins. Dressed in their New York clothing, the couple looked as if they had dropped in from another century.

Childish whispers followed them. Their high, urgent voices found Leah's ears and made her smile at the excitement their arrival seemed to be causing. Wide Orthodox eyes followed their progress down the street toward Tipat Chalev, and then the tide of children turned to follow after at a safe distance. There had been rumors that the great-nephew of the recently deceased Idela Feldstein would be coming to claim his inheritance—such as it was. Perhaps he would sublet the flat and then leave. The thought was intriguing. Two members of the black-coated coterie peeled off to find their mothers.

"They do not look like us."

"Are they goyim, you think? Maybe Mrs. Feldstein's great-nephew from Europe is one of them! *Oy!* You think they'll stay here?"

"Mama says people in Europe do not even keep a kosher kitchen, let alone believe in the Eternal! Look at the big man. A goy, surely. He does not even have a beard!"

At this, Shimon self-consciously put a hand to his cheek. He wished he had not shaved. Leah eyed him in mock dismay. He would have to grow it back, and she liked his kisses so much better without the whiskers.

Two mothers, guided by the hands of their determined children, emerged from a side street. Heads were covered in scarves. Their dresses were as plain and drab as the coats of their tiny future rabbis. Shimon tugged his sleeve in a signal that none of the clothes Elisa and Leah had purchased at Macy's were made for the streets of the Jewish Quarter.

"We might as well leave our bags at the King David," Leah said quietly to Shimon as she smiled and nodded back at the unsmiling eyes and suspicious faces that studied her openly.

"*Shiksa,*" hissed one woman to another. "*Shaygets.*"

"If Idela Feldstein were alive to see this, it would kill her!"

"A goy for a great-nephew! *Oy gevalt!*"

"Such nerve. They bring their priest with them."

"Maybe they will sublet Idela's flat, *nu?* Poor Hayim and Judith are living with her parents. Maybe these goyim relations of Idela Feldstein's will sublet the flat to them, *nu?* Go get the rabbi. He can ask them. They probably do not even speak mama-loshen, the mother tongue."

Reverend Robbins turned one last corner and then stopped before a white house that stood like an upturned rectangle listing slightly to the left. He smiled good-naturedly. "This is it."

The Orthodox chorus stood a few yards away, waiting for the reaction of these Jews who were not Jewish at all. Leah drew in a deep breath. Rickety stairs led up from a mud puddle to a door covered with peeling white paint. Two windows looked down on the unpaved lane, where the crowd grew by the minute. There were bars on the windows, giving the stark little place the feeling of a jail—a very small and impoverished jail, at that.

The pastor pushed his canvas hat back on his head a bit. He lowered his voice. "Victoria told me the address. Last night I advised her you might not want to bring your luggage until you saw it. Perhaps we should hire a porter in the souk to help you carry away the things you had sent from Vienna."

The eyes of the audience bored into Leah's back. Shimon had singled out two husky, apple-cheeked youngsters and was grinning at them—to no avail. Dark and solemn looks were returned. Shimon preferred the Arab beggars to this.

The shutters of the downstairs flat opened a bit, then flew open with a crash. A thick-featured woman of about fifty, wearing a polka-dot scarf to frame her leathery face, scowled at the newcomers. "*Oy*," she said, not quite under her breath. "If Idela were alive this would kill her." She rubbed her cheek, frowned at the crowd behind the three newcomers, and shrugged. *What can you do? He doesn't even have a beard like a man*, the shrug seemed to say. She disappeared from the window and then reappeared a second later at the door. On her arm she carried an iron ring with a single key on it.

"You must be the great-nephew of Idela Feldstein, God rest her soul."

"Omaine," said a voice behind Leah. "And may she not be spinning now."

The woman with the key pronounced her name. "I am Shoshanna Reingolt. Downstairs neighbor to Idela Feldstein for twenty years." The woman's eyes widened and then narrowed as she scanned Leah's plum-colored dress and matching shoes. "Idela told me you were coming." She shook her head as if she could not believe it. "She told me *when* you came you should have the flat. She had a little money, but that was gone with the funeral, and so . . ." She pushed past them and started up the creaking stairs.

Leah looked pleadingly at the kind Reverend Robbins, but he whispered, "You're in enough trouble already without inviting a Christian pastor up for tea. I'll wait here. Keep the party lively."

Shimon eyed the crazily leaning steps and tested the banister. It wobbled. He wondered if it would hold his weight.

"Well, come on!" snorted the unamused Shoshanna as she inserted the key and leaned against the door until it opened with a reluctant groan.

Leah and Shimon smiled in a frozen, fearful sort of way as they climbed the stairs and entered the dark and musty little space. Leah stepped in a puddle of water just inside the door. Shimon blinked as a drop hit his face. Together, in one unified motion, they looked up at a ceiling stained from water leaks.

"Well, you'll have to fix that!" snapped Shoshanna. "But there is a primus stove for cooking. A bed for sleeping." She reconsidered the last comment as she compared Shimon's size to the narrow iron cot against the wall. "You can take turns sleeping, anyway." She sniffed. "And a rocking chair." She pointed to a small wooden rocking chair beside the barred window.

Leah eyed the rocker—one small luxury in this room, which was more like a cell than an apartment. "How lovely," she remarked, noting the deep patina of the wood. "It is a very fine rocking chair."

"Yes," barked Shoshanna. "I found your great-aunt right in that very chair. Sitting frozen in death. She was staring out the window. *Oy*, what a shock! A woman of her health to die like that!"

"Ah . . ." Leah quickly looked away from the chair.

Relief! There were the shipping crates they had sent from Vienna! Some spark of elegance and beauty! The weight of disappointment was lessened a tiny bit by those friendly boxes. Elisa had helped her pack them in the days before the Nazis had come. How perfect life had been then! *Oh, God!* Leah prayed that her unhappiness did not show on her face. All her emotion and every brave word she had uttered last night now seemed to mock her.

"Well, are you staying?" demanded the woman. "Or subletting? There is a line of people who would take a nice apartment like this, you know."

Shimon stepped forward and took the key. "We are staying," he said firmly. There was no chance for Leah to protest. "At least for now." He bowed slightly at the waist. "My great-aunt wrote to me of your kindness to her." Shimon was smiling—a miraculous smile! Did he not see the hovel they had come to? No! He was winning this horrid, iron-eyed woman over with lies about how kind she had been!

Leah turned away and stared at the box containing her china. They had china plates, but there was no table to set.

"We had to sell a few things to pay her debts. The table. It was quite nice. It sold quickly."

Leah squeezed her eyes shut at the words. A bed for one. A kerosene stove and a rocker. *The very rocker . . .* she felt the room spin around her. "Shimon—" she reached out for his hand—"I . . . am . . . I feel . . ."

There was a flurry of activity around her. Shoshanna's voice expressed dismay. "*Gottenyu!* Sit down in the chair!"

"No," Leah breathed, as she groped for the bed. Helped by Shimon, she lay down on the groaning cot and closed her eyes as she fought to control a wave of nausea. The harsh voice of Shoshanna became instantly sympathetic. "I'll make tea," she promised, patting Leah's hand. "You're expecting, maybe? Such a pale little thing. I'll tell them you are staying."

Shafts of dusty light beamed down through the high windows of the Yeshiva school classroom where Eli studied with forty other students. He sat on the end of a long bench shared by a dozen young men. Books and papers were piled high on desktops. Bookshelves rose twelve feet high on every wall of the room where Rabbi Shlomo Lebowitz led the discussion, which was of great interest to each student.

"Marriage!" declared the old man as he paced across the front of the classroom. "Who has the reference that is reflected in the Jewish wedding ceremony?"

A forest of hands sprouted up. Eli did not raise his hand. The subject made him uncomfortable, unhappy.

"Yes, Yagil!" The rabbi paused as a beam of light fell on his face like a spotlight.

Yagil, with his stooped shoulders and eyes that looked in different directions through thick spectacles, seemed the least likely to speak of marriage, but he rose to his feet. His smile blinked on and off through his straggly beard. He began to quote the law. " '*No man without a wife. Neither a woman without a husband. Nor both of them without God.*' Genesis Rabbah 8:9." He was pleased with himself. He had said it correctly. Even a fellow as odd-looking as Yagil must have a wife. And somewhere there must be an odd-looking woman who would love to stand with him beneath the chuppa! Perhaps one day Yagil would be a father of a flock of little Yagils with eyes looking this way and that. As long as it was a proper Jewish ceremony!

Eli found himself feeling ill. He thought about Victoria. He knew what the Law said about marriage. This reminder frightened him for their future.

"Very good, Yagil," intoned Rabbi Lebowitz. "Now sit." Yagil obeyed, shrinking back to his position behind his books. "It is easier for us to prepare for a wedding ceremony than it is for us to prepare for marriage, *nu*?" The rabbi paused as the weight of this penetrated the minds of the students. "What is the basis for a sanctified relationship in accordance with the law of Moses?"

Again hands shot up. "Emile, please."

Emile, big and hairy, with a frame like an ox, stood and began to speak in his surprisingly high voice. "This is a union between a man and a woman where the precepts of the Lord are fulfilled and where the children will be raised in the atmosphere of religious faith. Marriage is not merely a legal bond. Or a bond for the gratification of physical desire or emotional . . ."

Eli could not hear the rest of the citation. He knew the answers. In an examination about marriage he would not miss even one. In a mixed marriage, the foundations of a Jewish marriage were absent. He knew this. The awareness of it kept him awake each night. It followed him into the Yeshiva and plagued his every waking thought. There were deeper matters that he had not even shared with Victoria when he spoke to her of marriage. He longed to be outside right now. He looked at the swirling flecks of dust in the light and wished that he could be caught up and swept out the window of the room.

The harsh voice of Rabbi Lebowitz interrupted his thoughts. "Eli! Eli Sachar! Are you dreaming?"

"Huh?"

"Would you answer the question for us?"

"Am I dreaming? I . . . uh . . ."

"No. The question regarding marriages that are forbidden to you as a cohen."

The question was like a slap in the face. The eyes of every man in the room were on him. He drew in a ragged breath. He began, "By Torah law . . ."

"Reference?"

"Leviticus 21:6-7."

"Correct. Not bad for a sleeping man. Continue."

"A cohen is forbidden to marry a divorced woman."

"Go on."

"One who is known to be promiscuous."

"Yes, yes."

"A proselyte." Eli swallowed hard.

"There! *Nu!* You see how very narrow the way must be for you!" The rabbi swept a gnarled hand over the group, but Eli felt he had pointed only at him. "You may not marry a woman who converts. And who will answer why that must be?"

Eli sank down into his seat. He did not hear the rest of the day's lesson and discussion. At the end of class, when Rabbi Lebowitz asked him if he was feeling ill, Eli answered that he had not felt well in days. This seemed to satisfy the rabbi, who wished him a speedy recovery. But Eli knew he would never recover from his heart sickness. There was no answer to this dilemma. Victoria could convert, but Eli would never be a rabbi if he married her. He would not tell her, lest she turn from him and think she did him a kindness. His heart had made his choice for him. But he simply could not think what to do next.

Victoria did not know what drew her through the gates of the Haram into the courtyard of the Dome of the Rock. She had simply come. Like a child searching for a lost toy, she had come here to the perfect octagon of the shrine. She paused in her steps and examined the turquoises, greens, and golds of the tile-encrusted facade.

Above the south entrance to the dome, *God, the Eternal* could be read in the mosaic. In the shadows beneath the arch, the words of the Prophet were gracefully inscribed: *He who clings to this life will lose the next one.*

She gazed over the vast and empty place where thousands of the faithful came each week to bow and worship toward Mecca. Strange how very empty it seemed. Devoid of the shouts and exhortations of the Mufti, devoid of the faithful followers, the place also seemed devoid of God. She did not move forward, but lingered at the gate, lost in her thoughts. This site, the jewel of Jerusalem, no longer felt like a place she belonged. She viewed it as a tourist might. A sense of amazement touched her briefly as she scanned the green and brown marble columns and mosaics surrounding the arched windows, but the reality of an eternal God seemed very remote to her. She was without fear of that fierce Eternal One. Without awe, she considered the faith she was leaving.

Perhaps she had always been irreverent and faithless. Had she ever really spoken to God when she touched her forehead to the ground in obedience? She had said words, but her heart had never uttered a single prayer to the Allah whose name was intertwined with the gold leaf and mosaic of the holy place.

She shook her head at her own coldness. She did not believe. Gold and filigreed turquoise could not impress her heart. She saw here only beauty made by man.

She leaned against a column and was startled to hear a voice behind her.

"Victoria Hassan?"

She turned to see the smiling, sun-darkened face of Ram Kadar as he entered the compound. His black robes and keffiyeh billowed in the slight breeze. He looked very much as if he might fly. His black eyes shone as he fixed them on her face, and he smiled. His teeth were white and perfect. He was a handsome man, and he knew it well.

Victoria lowered her eyes and touched her forehead in salaam. "Ram Kadar." She said his name but did not return his smile. She did not like the way he looked at her. She would not encourage him with even a hint of anything beyond simple courtesy.

"It is good to see you here. You have come to petition Allah?"

"I have come here . . . to think," she answered truthfully.

"I have come to petition." Kadar moved uncomfortably near to her. "I intend to take a wife soon."

She did not look up at him. She felt his gaze sweep over her and instantly became self-conscious in her blue cotton British dress and high-heeled shoes. "Congratulations," she muttered.

He laughed when she did not look at him. He raised his hand as if to touch her face. She flinched, and he laughed again. "Such beauty should be behind a veil. Reserved only for the pleasure of a husband, Victoria."

"A veil will not do when one is working at the Mandate offices." She turned and brushed past him.

"And such a body is made for bearing children," he called after her as she hurried out the gates and into the souks of the Old City.

Only four china dinner plates had survived the long journey from Austria to Palestine. Leah would have grieved if it had not been for the note she found tucked into the packing crate:

> *My Dearest Friend,*
> *What a joy it is for me to think that when you find this little message you will be safe in your home in Zion! And yet there is grief also that I remain here in Vienna without your face to smile at me from across the stage! My prayers go with you as I remember the words of Isaiah 52:9—"Break forth into joy, sing together, ye waste places of Jerusalem: for the Lord hath comforted his people, he hath redeemed Jerusalem."*
> *All my love,*
> *Elisa*

Inside the envelope Elisa had placed a hundred Austrian shillings. Austrian bank notes were worthless now, of course, but the note and the cash reminded Leah once again how far God had brought them to come to this moment. Instead of tears shed over eight broken dinner plates, Leah was able to smile and thank God for the four that remained.

20

Jerusalem Welcome

"And Shoshanna thinks she must be . . . *expecting* . . . such a pale little thing." Ida Sachar filled the ears of her husband and sons before she filled their plates.

"That Shoshanna! Such a yenta! She would say that Moshe was expecting if it would draw a crowd. What does she know?" Hermann Sachar chided as he spooned out potatoes onto his plate.

"So what do you think, Eli? *You* have seen her! Last night at the concert. Did she look like she *was* . . . ?" Ida pried.

Embarrassed, Eli shrugged. "She played like an angel, Mama. She wore a black dress, and I—"

"Aha! A *black dress*! Very *slimming*." Ida's eyes narrowed.

"They always wear black dresses when they play." Hermann shook his head and rolled his eyes. "These women . . . as if there was not enough to talk about!"

"Shoshanna said she looked like she stepped out of a shopwindow in Beirut, or maybe Berlin. Everything matched! They have money or else why didn't they sublet the apartment? I ask you." Ida's face betrayed a knowledge of such things.

Hermann lowered his chin and peered at his wife over the tops of his glasses. "First you say she is pregnant. Then she is rich. You also say she is a *shiksa* who certainly must not keep a kosher kitchen." He clucked his tongue. "All this and you have never laid eyes on the woman!"

"What do men know? *Oy!* Why couldn't God give me at least one daughter to talk to over the dinner table?" Ida snapped. "Pass the potatoes, Hermann. You do not understand these things."

Hermann obeyed with disgusted amusement. "Those children," he said under his breath.

"*What?*" Ida's eyes flashed. She was ready for what was known as a discussion. This was an unusually loud conversation, which increased in volume as it changed from topic to topic until no one knew where it had started.

Eli marked the opening topic in his mind. This time the discussion was beginning with Leah and Shimon Feldstein. "Tales of the Vienna Woods," so to speak. He and Moshe exchanged glances and ducked slightly as they proceeded with their meal.

"I said," Hermann repeated loudly, "Those children!"

"What children?"

"Those . . . what are their names? . . . the new ones. The rich pregnant ones."

"He is not pregnant! *She* is!"

"You yentas! How do you know such things!"

"Because we are women!"

Hermann rolled his eyes heavenward. "Thank You, God, that You made me a man."

Ida pouted. Only one phase of the discussion. Hermann pretended that it was over. Moshe and Eli knew better.

"So what about them?" Ida asked quietly, leading Hermann along.

"About who?" Hermann looked around in mock bewilderment.

Ida roared, "The Feldsteins! The children! Oy! As *you* call them!"

"Well then, Ida, I'll tell you what, since you are asking me . . . a *man* . . . for an opinion! There they are in that little place, probably because they have no place else to go. And every yenta in the Old City is gabbing about them! But do I see the meat and potatoes of the Sachar house being shared with these strangers? *Nu!* They have arrived here, and old Aunt Idela is dead."

"She is spinning in her grave at one look at those apikorosim in her flat!"

"She is too dead to spin . . . or care. But *you* are not!" His lip was very far out. He had the look of a man with a budding case of indigestion. He turned to Eli. "This Leah plays like an angel, eh? *So!* You be the angel these yentas will not be! Take the leftovers."

"What leftovers?" Ida protested.

"And tonight we can live without your mother's fine strudel!"

"What?" Hands crashed down on the table.

Hermann's chin came up in defiant response. "That is my final word, Ida," he proclaimed. "I am the papa and this is my final word. You will package the food nicely and send a kind note to these poor children. And I will be able to hold my head up in shul because"—now his fist slammed on the table—"My wife is kind to the poor and the stranger!"

His eyes protruded slightly. The lower lip extended with the chin. This meant the discussion was at an end.

It was, of course, the answer to Eli's most fervent prayer. His arms laden with food, he hurried through the dark streets of the Jewish Quarter. Shimon and Leah Feldstein's flat was in the poorest of the poor sections of the Quarter. Leah's matching dress and shoes notwithstanding, he sided with his father. They could not be very rich and wish to stay in such a place. He had been searching for some reason to visit them to mention Victoria's name. To thank them for the ticket and then to talk about Victoria. Surely they knew her well. Or at least well enough to notice what a wonderful person she was. Had she mentioned his name to them? he wondered. Were they also part of the little conspiracy?

Dodging a particularly deep puddle, Eli considered that coming from a place so decadent as Vienna, these liberated Europeans would not be at all dismayed by the fact that he and Victoria were in love.

A dim orange glow shone in the window of the Feldstein flat. The window was quite dirty, Eli noticed. It probably had not been washed in years. The contrast between that straining little light and the spotlight at Allenby barracks was startling. Eli could not imagine the woman he had listened to last night would choose to live in such a gloomy place as this.

Leaning against the wall for balance, Eli climbed the steps to the flat. It had always been a marvel to him that old Idela had managed to climb these steep steps at eighty-something. Her legs must have simply gotten into the habit.

On the stoop he waited a moment, trying to juggle his burden. Through the thin wooden door, the sound of peaceful music emanated. *Music? Here?* He knocked with his foot. The door swung back, revealing the enormous form of Shimon Feldstein. He was smiling. Strangely peaceful as if the music were coming from inside him.

"Shalom," he said.

Eli remembered his voice. "I am . . . my mother is . . . Ida Sachar . . . and I . . . she sent me here with this, in case you have not eaten."

Shimon stepped aside. The light behind him fell on Leah as she sat on an upturned packing crate. Another packing crate served as a table, complete with candlesticks and real china plates and linen napkins. A third crate was laden with food in all sorts of containers. Small tin buckets held stew. There were bowls of boiled potatoes and a bit of lamb. A phonograph stood in the corner of the clutter, playing some wonderful music. An orchestra. Violins. It was . . . so very elegant!

"Another one!" Leah said in delight. "Come in. Won't you join us? Everyone else is gone, and we have plenty."

Dumbfounded, Eli stepped past the big man. He thought about how amazed his mother would be when she found out that everyone had brought supper to the new arrivals! Could any disaster have been greater for Ida Sachar than to have been left out of doing good when everyone else did good? The thought of it made him shake his head as he placed the Sachar offering on the crate. A glance showed there was no fresh strudel among the plates. This would please his mother. *No one else brought strudel!*

"My mother sent me with some supper. And strudel. Have you had strudel yet?" Eli asked, just to make sure. His mother would ask him if he asked.

Shimon unwrapped the package and inhaled. "Not since Vienna," he replied. "And that was too long ago to remember."

Eli hesitated in his real purpose as Leah and Shimon filled his ears with the kindness of the Jewish Quarter. Eli told them his name again and watched their faces to see if there might be a flicker of recognition. There was none. This was disappointing. Shimon pulled up a crate for him to sit on as he told how Hannah Cohen had showed them how to start the primus stove. Eli mentioned that Hannah was their landlady and that she knew everything. He did not say, however, that probably every woman who came through the door had come bearing gifts and left bearing tales. *China plates! A phonograph! Candlesticks on a packing crate! Oy! But is she expecting?*

That question played over and over again in Eli's unwilling mind. He forced himself not to look at Leah for fear his eyes would lock on her stomach as he spoke. The sheer romance of this strange little dinner party made him flush slightly and think about Victoria. What would it be like to be someplace with her alone? *Candlelight. Music. Maybe his child within her?*

He should not have let his mind wander from the trivial to the magnificent. Suddenly he blurted out, "Victoria sent me a pass to your concert last night." Pain and longing were etched on his face. "I saw her. I could not speak with her in public, of course."

Shimon and Leah stared at him blankly until the full meaning of his confession sank in. Leah smiled gently, sympathetically. "Ah. You and Victoria . . . ?"

What relief it was to spill it out to these strangers. So maybe he was interrupting their romantic candlelight dinner with his tale of misery! Why should any couple be so lucky as to have candles to blow out and a bed to lie on together and no one to say they could not, when Eli and Victoria lived in such torment?

He did not tell them everything, of course. There were some things he did not admit, like how he ached at night when he thought of her.

And then he finished with a sigh. "She looked so happy last night beside you both. It is so hard. We live in two worlds. You cannot understand what it is like." He hung his head, feeling the first violent wave of embarrassment. Why had he told them this? "It must be the music," he finished lamely and stood up.

Their understanding eyes followed him. "I am going to have tea with her next Tuesday, Eli," Leah said gently. "I would be happy to give her a message if you like."

"*Oy!* You are the only one who can do it without risk." He tugged his beard in thought. "I will bring a letter on Sunday." He smiled at Shimon. "Would you like to join us for morning prayers at shul? The men are less nosy than the women; I promise."

The music had stopped by the time Eli left. He descended the stairs and looked back over his shoulder at the orange glow of the candles through the window. The music began again. It floated through the grimy glass into the cleanly washed night stars. And then, as Eli watched and envied, the light of the candles went out.

Tonight an American double feature was playing at the London Palace Theatre. *Charlie Chan in Paris* and *Song of the Thin Man*.

Charles and Louis had not stopped bouncing since Elisa had announced that she and Anna held four precious tickets for this evening's program.

Murphy read the advertisement over the dinner table.

"The world's greatest detective, Charlie Chan, spots forgery in gay Paree!" He lowered the newspaper and screwed his face up in an imitation of the Chinese sleuth. "Ah-so. What you think of that, Charles? You named Charlie too!"

Charles laughed and clapped his hands, ducking down in embarrassment at being named after a Chinese detective. "I . . . talk . . . be'er." He giggled.

"Better, better, *better*," Louis corrected, sounding each letter *T* distinctly.

Murphy continued his imitation. He peered at Charles through squinting eyes. "Charlie Chan not say *the* or *a* when he talk. Not good for boy-detective learn English from Charlie Chan."

Charles frowned and tried again. "Bet-ter. I talk bet-ter!"

Elisa nodded approval and stacked the dishes. "He figures out the mystery quicker too. Charlie Kronenberger, master private eye." She winked. "Go wash up. Comb your hair. Freddie will be here in five minutes with Mama and Papa."

As they ran happily up the stairs, Murphy took her hand. "You're more than I bargained for," he whispered. "Married a few months, and already you're a terrific mother of five-year-old boys."

"I should have listened when they told me you work fast," she teased. Then, changing the subject, "You're sure you and Papa won't come along?"

Murphy shook his head. Tonight he and Theo Lindheim would listen to Hitler's speech from Saarbrücken. Murphy had a reporter on hand in Germany to cover it live, but he wanted to hear for himself what pretense the Führer might have for serving up another portion of Europe on the Nazi platter. He did not trouble Elisa with the details.

"You and Anna have a good time. Theo and I will stay here and bemoan the condition of the world." He smiled at her, but she saw the reality behind his words. Worry flashed across her face. She did not want to know!

Dressed in matching tweed jackets and knickers, the boys clattered down the stairs. Caps in place, they seemed the very picture of English schoolboys. Charles carried a magnifying glass in his hip pocket to aid in his search for clues. He examined Louis' hand under the glass as Elisa retrieved her coat and Freddie honked the horn outside in Red Lion Square.

They flung the door open to reveal Theo with his hand raised to knock. With his steel gray hair and craggy features, Theo appeared to have completely regained his health, but his eyes still betrayed sorrow at all he had seen over the last few years. Even a smile of greeting did not hide Theo's private anguish from his daughter.

"Two old bachelors," he tried to joke as Charles and Louis led Elisa down to the waiting automobile and the enormous chauffeur.

She waved without smiling as Freddie opened the door and she slid into the backseat, where Anna was waiting. Without being told, she knew the news Theo and Murphy heard tonight could not be good. Like the two small boys, she would stare at the screen and try to figure out "whodunit" in tonight's murder mystery.

Murphy and Theo fiddled with the radio dial. There was no mystery left for them as they once again listened to the shrieking voice of German's undisputed leader.

Murphy stared at the radio perched on top of his huge desk. Behind them, a fire crackled in the hearth. Theo sat with his head back, eyes fixed on the low rafters, mouth pressed into a tight line.

Radio Cairo broadcast Hitler's Saarbrücken speech in its entirety. Still in his British uniform, Samuel Orde joined a small group of dedicated Zionists on the campus of Hebrew University, where the speech was to be analyzed and discussed.

The room held a group of twenty young men and women as well as a handful of professors and the Jewish Agency leader, David Ben-Gurion.

The British government's present policy of yielding to violence and pressure did not bode well for the Jews of Palestine—nor for the Jews of Europe who clambered at the gates of every embassy to escape the shadow of Hitler's Reich. Tonight David Ben-Gurion was more grim than usual. The time of Hitler's speech in Saarbrücken had been announced by the Arab Council in the Middle East. That proclamation alone seemed ominous for the Jewish Yishuv.

Samuel Orde had known Ben-Gurion for ten years. When suspicious glances were cast at the captain's uniform, Ben-Gurion made it clear that Orde was present as his guest, his friend, and his advisor. How would the English react to Hitler's newest attack on the Jewish settlement?

There was no confusion in Orde's mind as to his government's response to Hitler's speech.

Orde stared at the radio at the front of the classroom. David Ben-Gurion sat with his hands clasped, eyes focused on the light fixture.

Hitler began his attack on the Jewish settlement in Palestine by first attacking democracy.

> *"The statesmen who are opposed to us say they wish for peace . . . and yet they govern in countries that make it possible that these men may be removed from office. What if, in England, instead of Chamberlain, Mr. Duff Cooper or Mr. Eden or Mr. Churchill should suddenly come to power?"*

There was an ominous pause. Had the Nazi audience not heard that all three of these English statesmen had been booed from the chambers of Parliament for their strong stand against appeasement? Was it not clear that their public political careers had never been more bleak? It made no difference to Hitler or his audience. Hitler continued his attack on a personal level.

> *"We know quite well that the aim of one of these men would be to start another world war. He makes no secret of the fact. And we know further that now, as in the past, there lurks the menacing figure of that Jewish-international foe. And we know further the evil power of the international press, which lives on lies and slander."*

Ben-Gurion smiled bleakly. "Well, he has managed to condemn everyone in this room. The Jews . . . strange how this lord of Darkness ascribes us so much power when by the millions we are so powerless. Of course, I would hate it if a man like him had something good to say about me," Ben-Gurion added.

Hitler continued.

> *"These enemies oblige us to be watchful and to remember the protection of the Reich. I have, therefore, decided to continue construction of our fortifications in the West with increased energy."*

Orde exhaled loudly. "So much for 'peace in our time.'"

Ben-Gurion's lined face seemed suddenly older. "We can only hope that Chamberlain is listening. Hearing. That the English will use this *peace* as a time to rearm."

The voice of Hitler drowned out his comment.

> *"We cannot tolerate any longer the tutelage of British governesses! Inquiries of British politicians concerning Germans within the Reich are out of place! We do not concern ourselves with similar matters in England! They should concern themselves with their own affairs—for instance, with affairs in Palestine!"*

At the mention of Palestine, Ben-Gurion leaned forward. For nearly twenty minutes, Hitler raved about the unrest in the British Mandate of Palestine. He recited the minute details of every violent act against the government there. The Arab attack and murder of Orde's young sentry on the Old City wall was somehow twisted until in Hitler's mouth the English had fired upon innocent civilians in Omar Square. Upon such distortion of events the Führer based his argument that England had enough trouble of its own without concerning itself with what happened to a handful of Jews and Catholic protesters within the Reich.

> *"And if the entire Arab world in all its vast domain cannot tolerate the presence of Jews in Palestine, how then are we to tolerate them within our limited borders?"*

These words were established with thunderous applause by the Nazi audience of Saarbrücken.

Murphy and Theo exchanged glances. There was never a mystery about whom Hitler would blame for the world's problems. Murphy scribbled notes on the Führer's phrases and word choices: *"cannot tolerate . . . vast Arab domain . . . limited German borders . . ."* All of this was uttered when twelve thousand Jews had been deported to Poland without a word of protest from the League of Nations. And as for limited borders, the echo of German jackboots on the streets of Czechoslovakia had not yet died away.

"He's still raving about this living space for Germans," Murphy said under his breath.

"Such talk can mean only one thing." Theo did not finish the thought as Hitler's voice broke through the acclaim from his audience.

> *"If the English themselves cannot control the immigration of Jews to Palestine, if they turn them back and imprison them, then how can they condemn those of us who cry, 'Germany for Germans'?"*

Here the speech was interrupted by an unending chant: *"Germany for Germans! Deutschland über Alles!"*

Murphy did not doubt that in Palestine the same chant was being repeated by the Arab Council with a slight variation: *"Palestine for Arabs! Jihad! Holy war! Jews to the sea!"*

The image made him shudder. Suddenly it seemed as though the fate of the coffin ships like the *Darien* was the only alternative left for the Jews of Europe. The dark waters of the ocean would not refuse them. The yawning chasms of the deep would offer them their only peace.

Hitler let the German voices of his audience carry the rest of his message to the world.

The cheering had not stopped before the telephone rang. The gruff voice of Winston Churchill was on the other end of the line.

"We should all be quite flattered that Herr Hitler has singled us out as personal enemies," Murphy quipped. "Winston Churchill. The press. And the heritage of my father-in-law."

Churchill also sounded amused. "Interesting minds these Nazis have. Hitler asks, 'Is this the trust and friendship of our Munich Pact? If we are friends and you trust us, why must England rearm? Let me have the arms and you show the trust.'"

Murphy laughed in spite of the dark truth in Churchill's humor. Theo simply frowned and stared at the radio as if it emitted a poison gas through the speaker. "Certainly interested in British troubles in Palestine tonight, wasn't he?"

Churchill's drawl became somber. "You have a good journalist in Jerusalem, I trust? There will be a story to cover soon enough, I'll wager."

"No one yet." At the statesman's warning, Murphy thought of Leah and Shimon and shuddered at the ominous words he was hearing tonight.

Churchill exhaled in amazement. "No reporter? Why? That is Hitler's second front against the Jews. And also against British foreign policy!"

Murphy tried to explain. "Just getting started . . . haven't had a chance to . . ." He mentally thumbed through a card file of reporters who had at one time covered Middle East politics.

"There is no time to lose in this matter!" Churchill's voice carried the emphasis he might use on the floor of Parliament. "The British foreign secretary has sent his lackeys to Palestine to examine the questions of Jewish homeland and immigration for the second time in sixteen months! That can mean only one thing—they mean to disavow our promise of a Jewish national home. The Woodhead Committee will most certainly reverse every other White Paper, and this will be done at the most crucial time in the history of the Jewish people!" He coughed. "And you do not have a reporter in Jerusalem to cover the outrage? Hitler's speech tonight must be reason enough for you to acquire one before the week is out!"

Murphy had only asked Winston Churchill to write a few articles, not to run the European operation for Trump Publications. He felt embarrassed, indignant—and properly chastised by the great man. "You would not be so insistent that I hire a man for a position in Jerusalem if you did not already have one in mind, Winston."

Churchill chuckled softly. He had been found out. Indeed, he did know of a man who would serve the purpose splendidly. The fellow was not a journalist by profession, but a staunch supporter of Zionism and the Jewish national home. Better than most men, he understood the cost of current British appeasement policies and had quite a grasp of the connection between Nazi Germany and the terrorist activities in Palestine.

"He is a brilliant fellow," Churchill said. "Reminds me of me forty years ago."

"And is he modest?" Murphy asked.

"To a fault."

"I am convinced."

"I thought you would be."

"Then how do I get hold of this boy wonder?"

"I have known his family for years. The lad is currently a captain with the British military in Jerusalem. He's had several articles published in the *Geographic*. Scholarly. Historical. I don't think it will raise any eyebrows if you contact him. But he may wish to write under a pseudonym." Churchill coughed slightly. "The name is Samuel Orde. I took the liberty of ringing the *Geographic* editorial offices for his address this afternoon."

21

Hopes and Dreams

The light from Murphy's study still burned, illuminating a square of sidewalk below the Red Lion House where Freddie parked the Duesenberg.

Both Charles and Louis had fallen asleep on the drive home from the theatre. Freddie gathered them up in his massive arms to carry them up the stairs as Anna and Elisa climbed out of the backseat.

A tousled blond head resting on each shoulder, Freddie preceded the ladies with his bundles.

"Murphy can carry one, Freddie," Elisa called after him.

"Ah, missus . . . they're both of 'em not so heavy as even one bundle of the *Times*." As if to make his point, he took the steps two at a time.

Anna laughed as he reached the landing, and then the laughter died on her lips. From the shadow beside the stairs, a man emerged. His face was half-concealed beneath the brim of a hat. He blocked the way of Anna and Elisa up the steps.

First startled, then alarmed, Freddie charged back down, still lugging the boys. "Who d'ya think y'are, there?"

The stranger's hat was doffed. A polite but strained voice said, "Mrs. Lindheim?"

Anna squeezed Elisa's hand as if to reassure her. "Mr. Beckham, is it not?" Anna replied coolly.

"Mother . . . ?" Elisa backed up a step.

"'Ey there!" Freddie bellowed as the boys raised their heads.

"It is all right." Anna held up a hand to quiet Freddie.

Beckham glanced at the big man with some amusement. He bowed slightly to Anna. "I am relieved you remember me."

"The British Museum," she said. "Hardly a day has passed that I have not thought of that encounter."

"Your husband is in the house?"

"You must know where he is." Anna was not unfriendly.

"Of course." Beckham seemed almost apologetic. "I have been *requested* to have a word with him. We realize the hour is late, but—" he glanced beyond Freddie toward the top of the stairs—"perhaps we should talk inside?"

After a few minutes alone with Mr. Beckham behind the closed door of Murphy's study, Theo emerged. His face radiated peace and assurance as he embraced Anna.

"I will only be gone a short while," he whispered. "Something important has come up. Something I did not expect."

He could offer her no other explanation than that. And so, praying silently, Anna stood at the window beside her daughter and watched as Theo was led to a black government-issue sedan and driven away into the gray fog of London midnight.

Theo took his place at the long horseshoe-shaped table among thirty other men who had gathered at this emergency meeting called by the British foreign minister, Lord Halifax.

Some faces among the party Theo recognized. Lord Winterton, who had represented British interests at Evian. George Rublee, the American lawyer who had been in charge of the international refugee question since the Evian Conference. Chaim Weizmann, looking particularly aged and weary, waved and nodded tacitly at Theo. They were not seated near enough to one another to speak. Colonial Secretary Malcolm Mac-Donald glanced almost apologetically in Theo's direction. There was no mistaking the fact that Theo's plan of trade with Germany in exchange for Jewish lives and assets had gotten a favorable reply from the Nazis. If that was not the case, then why would such prominent men have bothered to come here to meet and confer in the middle of the night?

Portraits of long-dead English kings and lords gazed down regally from gilded frames on the red satin walls of the room. Illuminated by small lights, these painted onlookers had more color on their cheeks and more expression in their eyes than the living humans who met together amid the rustling of papers and clinking of water glasses.

Theo stared back into the smirking face of an amused King Charles II. Dressed in ermines and a flowing wig, the king seemed warmer on his canvas than Theo felt in the drafty room. Ah, well, these kings had lived and committed their mistakes already; now they were dust. It was some-

one else's turn to change the world or fail in the task. Tonight was a call
to action, or a call to judgment.

Lord Winterton stood and banged down the gavel as a call to order.
"Hear ye, gentlemen! Pray silence as Foreign Minister Lord Halifax ad-
dresses the meeting!"

There was a pattering of polite, if exhausted, applause from the gathering as Lord Halifax, pale and languid, stood to speak.

"Last week, we were so fortunate as to receive a suggestion for a possible solution to the economic woes brought upon the empire and the
free world by the refugee question." He paused and inclined his head toward Theo. Others also looked at Theo curiously. Halifax continued.
"The suggestion of a trade agreement with Germany that would allow
refugees to depart with a portion of their assets was presented to German
Foreign Minister von Ribbentrop." A long pause. "A representative of the
Reich, von Ribbentrop rejected the offer outright."

A murmur of surprise filled the room. Theo looked unhappily at his
clasped hands. Useless hands, tied, helpless to help others. How he had
prayed for a different response from the Germans!

Halifax continued, raising his hand to silence the questions. "Three
days later, however, our office received word that another high official in
the Nazi government may well be interested in personally negotiating
such an agreement in Berlin."

Theo exhaled loudly with relief as other members of the group first
exclaimed their pleasure audibly and then applauded the news. Here at
last was hope, some glimmer of light! There was a smile on every face
around the table now.

Halifax nodded and raised both hands. He was the only man not
smiling. Silence. "There are certain conditions for these discussions with
the Germans, however." He waited as the word *conditions* cut through
the exuberance of the group. Questions filled the minds of the men. And
dread. There were always conditions when negotiating with Nazis. The
terms were never favorable to anyone but the Nazis.

Halifax turned his eyes toward Theo. His next words were directed at
him. "Those men with whom we have had contact have indicated that
the plan must be drawn *in its entirety* for presentation at a meeting in
Berlin *next week*." He held up his hand again. This was not the only condition. "And . . . they request . . . no, *insist*, that Theo Lindheim, who is
the originator of this plan, present it himself without members of the
committee to accompany him to Berlin or to the meeting."

There was no response. Not a murmur of sound. Weizmann caught
Theo's gaze and held it in strong sympathy and a hint of fear. *Theo to re-*

turn to Berlin! Were there any in the room tonight who did not understand the significance of that Nazi demand?

Theo looked up at the smirk of King Charles. *I am dust,* the portrait
seemed to say, *and so too will you be, Theo Lindheim, if you return to Berlin.*

Halifax broke the thick silence. "Of course, it serves us no purpose to
work to complete such a plan unless that condition is met. They have
made that clear. And yet we cannot expect one man to place himself in
jeopardy when the entire scheme might be a ruse. As heads of various or-
ganizations with concern for the Jewish refugees and political refugees
of the Reich, we thought that it was imperative that we keep this channel
open with the Reich. They have given us a deadline of noon tomorrow to
respond. We should have an alternate plan to present."

Blank stares were exchanged. What could be said at this late hour?
Who had a better idea for some economic relief for the refugees and the
governments expected to take them?

For an instant Theo wondered how the Nazis knew that he had pro-
posed the original plan. How had his name been brought up in such a
delicate matter? Perhaps that was a question he would ask later. For
now, however, there was no denying that in an odd and frightening way,
his prayer had been answered—not as he expected. Not as he would
have wished or imagined.

For a moment he thought of Anna. Elisa and the boys. The baby.
Those he loved with all his heart. There was no doubt that he would lay
down his life for them, return to the hell of Dachau if it was for the sake
of their lives. But that was not required of him. They were safe. That
made this decision all the more difficult. A demand was being made on
his life for the sake of strangers, people he knew only as thousands who
shared a common heritage with him. He smiled slightly as he asked
himself, *What would the Lord do?* In that instant, he knew what was required of him.

The expressions on the faces of the canvas kings remained unchanged as Theo stood slowly at his place. The eyes of the others around
the table filled with respect, with fear. They doubted they would do the
same in Theo's place.

And so the choice was made. Only hours remained between this moment of decision and the time when Theo would have to leave for Berlin.
Hard work would fill the time.

In the dining room of the Hassan residence in Old City Jerusalem sat a dozen
men whom Victoria did not recognize. Her stepmother poured strong coffee
for them from the large brass samovar reserved only for guests.

As Victoria passed by the open archway, buzzing voices fell silent. Her stepmother paused in filling a cup. Victoria looked in at a still and sinister tableau, a council of darkness here within the walls of her own home.

Ibrahim, whose face betrayed a nervous guilt, hailed her with a smile. "It is only Victoria. Only my sister."

The urgent whispers of conversation did not resume. The eyes of these keffiyeh-clad men evaluated her in her Western clothing as though she were a piece of meat in a marketplace.

She bowed in salaam. Something flickered in the eyes of several of these guests as they let their gazes sweep across her body and then return and linger on her throat. Instinctively she put a hand to her open collar. She backed up a step and resisted the urge to turn and run.

"Victoria works as a secretary for the British government," her stepmother volunteered.

A new interest sparked in the faces of the men.

Ram Kadar nodded and flashed a smile at her. "Such beauty should not be wasted on the Englishmen, Ibrahim."

Ibrahim glanced nervously at Victoria, then replied, "Perhaps if you will instruct her, Ram Kadar. She may be beautiful, but my sister is ignorant as women often are. The Englishmen, being also ignorant, do not seem to mind."

Victoria continued to smile throughout this unflattering flattery. She kept her eyes downcast and did not dare meet the gaze of Kadar, who stared at her more intensely than the others.

"If my brothers and my mother will forgive me—" Victoria backed another step. She touched her hand to her forehead in salaam, and twelve male voices responded as she hurried up the stairs.

Victoria paused on the landing as the voices resumed. "It is only in these ways that the English will see our dissatisfaction." She recognized the voice of Kadar. "These politicians must return to England with their eyes smarting from the smoke of Palestine."

Late into the Jerusalem night, Victoria sat, unmoving, on the edge of her bed. A cold fear filled her. She had heard the whispers of her brothers before. She had not been surprised by the faces of Daud and Isaak and Ismael. But the words of Ibrahim somehow felt like a personal betrayal. *He is one of them! He is part of those who murdered the Englishmen and cheered the voice of the Arab Council in Cairo!* She had not known. She had not expected his complicity in the works of Darkness.

Victoria wished that her father would return from his buying trip in Iran. He would know what to do. He would talk sense to Ibrahim!

Never had Victoria felt so alone. Eli, though just a few blocks away, was another world from this world.

Not even Allah could help her now. It was Allah, was it not, who breathed the dark anger into the hearts of her brothers? It was for the sake of Allah that they gathered together and made their plans.

Victoria frowned. She must not speak the treason she felt in her heart against those plans. For Allah might whisper in the soul of Ibrahim Hassan: *"Your sister, Victoria, is a traitor to her people. Listen, Ibrahim! Victoria is no longer one of us."*

The entire Lubetkin household seemed preoccupied with tiny baby Yacov. Could it be that he was smiling already?

Frau Rosen declared that it was *not* a smile but a gas bubble in the infant's stomach! Aaron insisted that it was not gas but a genuine smile! Did Frau Rosen not see what innate intelligence the child had? Of course he could smile at such a tender age!

Such conversation made Etta smile. If there was one thing she could say about her beloved Aaron, it was that he believed that his children had been born with an understanding of the Law and Prophets . . . they simply had to be taught to speak and read and write before they would *know* what they *knew*!

David was fascinated by his new brother; little Samuel was hurt because he was no longer the baby. For Rachel, the arrival of little bundle Yacov was the awakening of some hope within her that one day she, too, would present a son to her future husband.

She watched her mother nurse the child and suddenly was filled with wonder at her own budding breasts. She had not thought of the changes in her body as anything but a bother until now. But there was something miraculous about the way this new and tiny life turned its face toward Mama. Something overwhelming about the look of joy and peace in Mama's eyes as she cradled the new Lubetkin.

As Samuel walked unhappily up to bed and David took one last big-brotherly look at the little one, Rachel stood in the doorway and absorbed the scene with a sense of awe. Perhaps someday she would sit where her mother sat and a man would gaze at her with the same love that Papa carried in his eyes.

"Good night, Mama," Rachel said, feeling as if she must turn her own eyes from such a private moment.

Mama glanced up with a soft, dreamy smile. Had Rachel ever known her mother to wear such tender emotion so plainly on her face? "Good night, kinderlach," she said. "Don't forget to say your prayers. Tomorrow is the bris milah of your brother. Rachel, wash your hair before bed, *nu*? David, take a bath."

These mundane instructions were issued in a tone laden with love. To-morrow baby Yacov would be circumcised. Tomorrow another son would enter the Covenant! Such an event made the washing of hair prac-tically a holy ritual—or at least that was the way Mama made it sound.

Rachel wondered if David noticed the magic that surrounded their mother and father. No. At the mention of a bath David groaned and asked if Samuel must also bathe. Still smiling, Papa looked up and told him sweetly to mind his own business. Samuel's bath was not his affair.

Had Papa ever said such a thing in *that* tone of voice? This new baby Yacov must indeed be very special. Not even a scowl of authority accom-panied Papa's words.

David shrugged and followed, grumbling, after Samuel. Rachel lin-gered a few seconds longer in the doorway, and when she left they did not notice her absence.

Like an old friend, the wishing star hung in the azure sky above Warsaw. From the window of her bedroom, Rachel watched it glisten blue and red in the reflection of the northern lights. It was a beautiful star. Her own star. Sometimes she thought it must be an angel God had placed in the sky to watch over her. Such thoughts made it impossible to be afraid of the dark.

Often she lay awake when the voices of her parents drifted up through the floor, and she imagined what it would be like when she and Reuven were married. She would share her star with him. She would point to its place in the sky and tell Reuven, "*I asked it to shine on you, too. I prayed that you would be handsome and smart and that someday you would make a good husband. And now I share my star with you.*"

She had never met Reuven, although they had been pledged to each other many years before. He was three years older than Rachel, and Papa said that he was a kind young man and that he excelled in Torah and now at the Yeshiva.

When she asked if he was handsome as well, Papa had answered that he was handsome enough to make her forget such a question.

Rachel hoped that he was as handsome as her own father. She saw the way Mama looked at Papa. Handsome! Yes, and smart. From a good family descended from Baal Shem Tov! Someday Rachel wanted to look at her betrothed with the same light in her eyes that Mama had when she looked at Papa.

Rachel gazed very hard at her wishing star. "Do you hear me, little star? Someday when Reuven and I are married, I will thank you if he is all these things and handsome too."

She squeezed her eyes shut and said a prayer for Reuven. Then when she opened them the star seemed to be blinking a happy *yes* down to her. *Someday, someday, someday!*

In another year she would meet Reuven face-to-face. She would be almost fourteen and he would be seventeen—almost a grown man. She wondered if he would see how much she loved him even now. Would he imagine that she had sat at her window and dreamed what it would be like to have him beside her?

"Can you see my star, Reuven?" she whispered quietly. "Do you sit at the window of your room and wonder about me?"

She turned to see her silhouette reflected in the mirror. Long dark hair. Creamy skin. Tall and slender, she was halfway between a girl and a woman. "By next year when you meet him," Mama had promised, "he will not look upon a child."

Rachel was impatient for that time. The days moved so very slowly. Week by week new feelings awakened in her changing body. There was so much she did not understand. So many things she wanted to ask Mama. Instead she whispered her secrets to the wishing star. She learned to cook. Learned to be the sort of woman she must be as the future wife of a future rabbi. These things she learned from Mama, as was proper.

From Papa, Rachel learned Torah. Mama had also been taught by her father. This was one of the things Papa loved about Mama. She was smart; she could talk with him. Other women cooked and cleaned and bore children, but Mama was a scholar, he said. No doubt young Reuven would appreciate such a gift in Rachel as well. This would also help her to understand the things going on inside the head of her future husband, Papa said. All the same, it would not be wise to talk about her lessons outside the family. And, Papa warned, she must never act as though she knew better than her learned husband! Knowledge was a dangerous thing in the hands of a woman who would use it to belittle her husband! The Eternal counted such misuse a grave sin! *Such a woman would be worse than a golem! A witless simpleton would be better than such a wife!*

Thus warned, Rachel applied herself to the study of the Torah with humility. *Thank You, O Eternal, that I who am only a woman . . . almost . . . may be privileged to study Thy Holy Law. May I never use it against my future husband but for his pleasure only!*

Her prayer had become a promise to God, a vow that she would be the best wife young Reuven could have. He would never regret that his father and her father had struck a bargain and signed a contract of matrimony before she had learned to speak! Her entire life and education had been shaped for the purpose of fulfilling that agreement.

There was security in tradition, even for a little girl. A man was a man. Some were better than others, but all men knew their responsibilities before God. A woman was a woman. Some were more beautiful or clever than others, but it was possible for anyone to be a good wife and mother if she learned her duties.

All these things were ingrained into Rachel's life. Even now she knew what was expected of her. She did not fear failing in those duties. But suddenly, when she dreamed of Reuven and her future, there was a deeper longing within her. She could not put a name to it. Not yet. But it frightened her.

She sighed and whispered her prayer as she did every night:

> *"Spirit and flesh are Thine,*
> *O heavenly Shepherd mine;*
> *My hopes, my thoughts, my fears, Thou seest all;*
> *Thou measurest my path, my steps dost know.*
> *When Thou upholdest, who can make me fall?"*

Rachel opened her mouth to continue her evening prayers, but tonight the wishing star seemed less remote than God. It winked and blinked at her, encouraging her to speak again.

"Little star, you are closer to heaven than I am. Please tell God that I want to be more to my husband than just a dutiful wife. Please tell Him that I wish . . . I pray . . . that one day my beloved will look at me the way Papa looks at Mama."

From the room below her, the strong, mellow voice of her father drifted up. Then Mama answered. Muffled voices. Loving words whispered with a sort of urgency. Rachel turned away from the window and tried to make out the words. Things spoken in the night between her parents were always like this. Just beyond her understanding. Perhaps they spoke another language? Was there some special secret language that only husband and wife could understand? Something that Rachel would learn someday when her own husband took her in his arms? *Someday . . . someday!*

Again she looked up at the wishing star and prayed, "Shine down on my own beloved rabbi so that one day he might teach me too."

The lonely whistle of a train sounded from the Umschlagplatz. Rachel turned her eye in the direction of the sound. Muranow Square was dark and empty. Soft starlight glowed on the wet cobblestones. It was as if Rachel were the only person left in Warsaw. Then, across the square a tiny flame flickered, illuminating a solitary man. One instant of light and then the shadowed figure was lost in the darkness again.

Rachel raised her eyes quickly to the wishing star. Suddenly it seemed cold and remote. An uneasiness stirred within her. A feeling of awful foreboding that she did not understand.

22
Simple Gifts

The request to write for publication was not an unusual one for Samuel Orde. After all, he had published a number of historical monographs during his tour of duty in Palestine.

What was unusual was the subject matter editor John Murphy had outlined for him in the wire from London—the impact of current events upon the members of the Woodhead Committee . . . probable outcome of their inquiry into the demands of the Arab Council . . . any daily events of significance in Palestine.

Orde read the telegram and then reread it a dozen times before he folded it carefully and put it into his pocket. He was certain of one thing: He would have to write under an assumed name if he accepted the assignment from Trump European News Service. His perspective would not be favorable to his own government in matters of their treatment of Jewish immigrants and his own belief that the hopes of a Jewish homeland were becoming more dim each day.

"Winston is behind this," he muttered to himself as Bowen, the duty officer, looked at him curiously.

"Pardon, sir?"

"Nothing. Thinking of an old friend in England." He pretended to be busy at his desk. In truth, he was already composing the lead paragraph to his first story.

It was all very confusing. First Rabbi Shlomo Lebowitz waited in line for three hours at the Office of Immigration in the British Mandate offices.

When he reached the head of the line a very brusque and unpleasant Englishman behind the tall counter told him that he was in the wrong line.

"So this is the line I wait in to find out which line I should be waiting in?" Rabbi Lebowitz thanked him, then moved to the back of yet another line, even longer than the first.

Finally, in a muddled combination of broken English and Yiddish, he explained that his daughter, Etta, had been born in Jerusalem and she needed to come home again with her children from Warsaw. Several minutes of rapid-fire and unintelligible English had followed as a stack of forms had been carefully sorted out and passed across the counter to him.

Such a problem! He did not understand a word of it. Catching the number two bus to Zion Gate, he had shown the forms to two strangers, each of whom had given him different advice. Then a third fellow had joined in the discussion, and an argument had broken out. The old rabbi considered the observations of the sages about his people: Three Jews together mean seven different opinions. True? Of course true!

As the old rabbi walked quickly through narrow Zion Gate, it occurred to him that there were nearly three thousand Jews in his Quarter. This would truly be a confusion. Each one would have at least two different opinions about these papers, and there would be a very big argument about what was the proper way to fill out these things and get Etta and the family from Warsaw to Jerusalem. Such a thought made his head ache.

He tugged his beard and considered the havoc. The shouting. The red faces. He thought about how important it was that he not have to scratch out things on these forms so he would not have to wait in line again.

"So, Lord. I need the wisdom of Solomon, *nu*? Or . . . the wisdom of an Englishman." This made him smile. He looked to the left toward the Armenian Quarter, remembering the nice English Captain Orde who had brought in the hoity-toity Woodhead Commission to visit the school. Captain Orde spoke English. He spoke Yiddish. He spoke Arabic like a native shopkeeper in the souk. Here was a sensible fellow!

This line of reasoning led Rabbi Shlomo Lebowitz to the office of Captain Samuel Orde.

"Pardon me, Cap'n," said the duty officer. "I can't quite make it out, but I think this old Yid has some important documents for you."

Orde did not smile. He glared at his junior officer. "This is Rabbi Shlomo Lebowitz!" he snapped angrily. "A little respect, Bowen, or you'll find you're a private again!"

The tone made the young officer jump to attention. First he saluted

Orde and then he saluted the old rabbi, who merely nodded and bowed slightly. *Yes, Captain Orde is the right man to see—a fellow without confusion on any matter!*

Orde addressed the rabbi with a sweep of his hand. "Sit, please, Rabbi. How can I help you? Is anything wrong?"

"Wrong? *Oy.* No. Everything is *good* in Jerusalem, *nu?*" The rabbi raised his brows and tugged his beard. "The Arabs are *good and mad.* You English are *good and sick* of getting caught in the middle. And then there is me. I am *good and confused!* Things are so *good* in Jerusalem that everywhere I look there is a big *shemozzl!* True?"

Orde laughed in spite of the truth of the remark. "Of course true. And have you come here with a solution for us?"

The rabbi waved his hand as though he were brushing away a gnat. "The only one who can sort this mess out is Messiah!"

"My sentiments exactly."

"And I did not see Him walk in with the Woodhead Committee when they toured the Torah school, *nu?*"

Orde considered the old rabbi with curiosity. Were they speaking of the same Messiah? He agreed with an amused smile. "I was with them all day long in the holy places and I did not see the Messiah among them once."

"Ah." The old man stuck out his lower lip. "Just as I thought. Then they will not find the answer for Zion. That is certain, Captain. So . . . on to another problem. Smaller, maybe, but still I hope the Eternal has some interest."

Within fifteen minutes, the old rabbi had the matter of the immigration forms straight in his mind. This righteous Gentile would be most happy to help him fill out the papers. Indeed! All that would be needed after that was updated passport photos of Etta and Aaron and each of the children, as well as birth certificates. It might also be helpful to have proof that Aaron had lived and studied here in Jerusalem, that the couple had married here. Such papers would not be difficult to furnish and must certainly open the eyes of the English clerks inside the immigration office.

"I will write her a letter," said the rabbi.

Captain Orde considered that suggestion. "Too slow," he concluded, shaking his head. Was that worry in his eyes? Did he know something about this Woodhead Committee? Were they thinking about closing the quotas of immigrants? "Send her a telegram, Rabbi. As a matter of fact, write it out with the address, and I will do it for you. I have also such a telegram to send today."

"*Nu!* Such a generous offer! I can pay, of course, but—"

"No. This one is a gift from a grateful captain to you. Your students were the best behaved in the Old City when I made the rounds with the commission. I had not a moment of worry in the Torah school. That was the only time I breathed all day long."

And so it was settled. *Such a gift!* The rabbi carefully penned his message. Not too many words, lest he cause the English captain unnecessary expense and thus take unfair advantage.

MAZEL *TOV* YACOV STOP SEND PASSPORT PHOTOS, BIRTH CERTIFICATES IMMEDIATELY JERUSALEM STOP GRANDFATHER

Afterward he wondered if he should have added the word *love* before his signature. But he decided they knew he loved them. Otherwise, who would be *meshugge* enough to stand in line all day at the immigrations office?

It was Friday in Jerusalem, the Muslim holy day. The plaintive cry of the muezzin echoed from the tall minaret over the domed roofs and courtyards of Jerusalem.

Within the high, crenelated walls of the Old City, brown eyes turned with reverence toward the Dome of the Rock. Arab merchants shuttered their shops and joined the press of the crowds moving slowly toward the holy mountain.

Here Abraham had offered Isaac to God. Here Solomon had built his Temple, and the glory of the Lord had filled it. Here Jesus had driven out money changers from the courtyards and had proclaimed himself the Living Water that could quench the thirst of Jerusalem and all mankind. Here the battering rams and fires of Roman generals had left the Holy Mount desolate and without one stone upon another until the Muslims claimed it seven hundred years later. A varied history of bloodshed and brutality followed as the site was holy to three faiths.

English soldiers stood as watchmen on the walls now. What did these Englishmen know? They were newcomers. They had arrived to liberate the city from the Turks and the Germans in 1917. It was the opinion of every sector of the Old City that the British were a silly bunch. They would soon be gone. They did not understand the tightrope life here in Palestine. Their military governors were constantly tripping over the boundaries, sending thousands of years of tradition crashing to the stones. City water lines, electric lights, telephones had all come with the British Mandate. But none of it had yet reached through the gates of the Wall into the Old City.

Here, information was carried the old-fashioned way: from mouth to ear to mouth. Who needed telephones? Cooking was done on the little kerosene primus stoves. Lights were lit with matches. Matches were modern enough for the residents of the Old City. Water was stored in cisterns as God sent the rains to the city. It had always been that way, had it not?

Muslims worshipped on Friday. Jews on Saturday. Christians on Sunday. That way everyone got a day of rest of his very own.

On this day, as the Muslims spread their prayer rugs and listened to the resounding voice of their Grand Mufti, the Jewish women of the Old City pondered a modern problem in the local soup kitchen. This problem had been thrust upon them against their will. Crates of small colored boxes filled with powder had arrived in their kitchen from faraway America. The crates did not contain something useful like boullion. No. On the outside of the crates was the word *Jell-O*. This was followed by *Cherry* or *Lime*. The gift had come from a bigwig executive who worked for this company in America. He had visited the Tipat Chalev soup kitchen and gone away with his conscience stirred. *How could children live without Jell-O?* He had sent enough to make certain that each child in the Old City Jewish Quarter would enjoy the benefits of the squiggly stuff and not grow up deprived.

Crates cluttered the dining room. Loose packets overflowed a table, where women kitchen volunteers pondered the generosity of the American.

"*Meshugge!* The man is totally *meshugge!* So why didn't he send shoes to the children?" asked Hannah Cohen as she stacked small packets of cherry gelatin in front of her.

"We can't cook shoes, Hannah." Rabbi Shlomo Lebowitz narrowed his eyes as he scanned the place. "If he worked for a shoe factory he would have sent shoes, *nu?* The man's whole life is Jell-O. True? Of course true! What else would he send?"

"*Oy!* But is this stuff kosher? I ask you," moaned Shoshanna Reingolt. "Can we eat it? I ask you."

Rabbi Lebowitz bit his lip and grimaced as he plunged a finger into an opened box and then into his mouth. "Sour! *Oy!*"

"You taste it without knowing if it's kosher?" exclaimed Hannah.

The rabbi licked his lips. "He seemed like a nice Jewish boy, this Mr. Lipwitz. A nice American-Jewish boy. Why would he send us something that wasn't kosher?" He grimaced again. "Even if it does taste terrible."

Hannah and Shoshanna followed his lead. They dipped their fingers into the package of red powder and tasted. "*Phui! Gevalt! Oy! Oy! Oy!* This nice Jewish boy thinks the children will eat this stuff?"

"He wasn't a boy exactly. Fifty is not a boy. He was old enough to know kosher, so I don't think we need to question the rabbi," said Hannah through gritted teeth.

Rabbi Lebowitz stared hard at the writing on the box. "We need someone who reads English. That is what we need. How are we supposed to figure out how to prepare this if we cannot read English? True? Of course true!"

The rabbi and the women were silent as they considered the problem. Tipat Chalev looked like a warehouse. The stuff might be kosher, but it tasted like poison. They could not read the instructions on the boxes. What had begun as an afternoon of excitement and joy with the twelve-donkey delivery of the crates had turned into sheer frustration.

"Well." The rabbi shook his head. "The modern world has invaded us. *Nu!*" The last syllable was uttered with a sigh of despair.

"Twelve donkeys' worth! *Oy!*" Hannah rested her chin on her hand.

"The children will expect to sample this great gift from the American bigwig." Shoshanna sized up the problem as she gestured toward the windows and two dozen faces gawking in.

"We need an Englishman." Rabbi Lebowitz thumped his hand on the table, sending a tower of Jell-O cartons toppling down. "An Englishman will know how to read the instructions, and I know one who will help."

"Yes. We need an Englishman!" agreed Hannah and Shoshanna in chorus.

Englishmen were as plentiful in Jerusalem these days as this unwanted Jell-O. The trick was to find one who could translate the directions from English to Yiddish. Or at least Arabic, which almost everyone spoke in the Old City. These English fellows seldom bothered to learn more than the rudiments of local dialect. They seemed to believe that English was the first language created by God, and everyone else, therefore, should learn to speak it.

"Such a problem." The old man stood and slipped one packet of lime and one of cherry into his coat pocket.

"Going somewhere?" Hannah asked suspiciously. "Leaving this to me and Shoshanna, are you?"

He squared his shoulders. They ached from the burden of sixty-two years and this long day of work. "I am going to the post office." He produced a letter addressed to his daughter and the new baby in Warsaw. "If I miss the mail it will be Monday before I can get this off to Warsaw." He pursed his lips. "Besides, will we find an Englishman if we just sit here?"

"But what should we do with this stuff?" Shoshanna was not really asking. It was a statement of dismay.

"Send down to the Yeshiva school. Get some young men to move it," he answered as he shuffled toward the heavy wood door. "Tell Eli Sachar we need help moving boxes," he instructed. "He will pick the strongest students and send them to help. And I will bring back instructions for preparing this rat poison."

At that, Hannah put her hand to her throat. Perhaps it *was* rodent poison! Perhaps the nice American Jew had not meant for this powder to be eaten by humans at all. Ah, well. They would know soon enough. Either they would die, or Rabbi Lebowitz would come back with an Englishman!

To any righteous Jew it was a great honor to be chosen *sandek,* or god-father, at the circumcision of an infant. For Aaron and Etta Lubetkin, their choice of sandek for baby Yacov had become a matter of discussion among the community.

Dr. Eduard Letzno, the apostate Jew, the Zionist who no longer believed in the Eternal, took his place in the seat of the sandek as the circumcision ceremony began.

This apikoros wore a prayer shawl. On his head he wore a yarmulke just as any devout Jew must wear, but he had no beard. He fooled no one! His suit was cut like those of the people in Saturday Warsaw. He was no longer one of them. Why then had Rabbi Lubetkin chosen such a man to be godfather for his son?

This was such a question! *Oy!* Frau Rosen led the yentas in the discussion. Would the Eternal bless this occasion? they asked. The kibitzers answered with a thousand clucks of their tongues and wags of their heads. "*Oy! Oy! Oy!* Such *gehokteh tsuris!*"

This phrase had been chosen as appropriate for the occasion of a circumcision; it meant "chopped-up troubles!" The yentas were careful not to let Rabbi Lubetkin and Etta hear their disapproval, however.

Frau Rosen hissed quietly like a steam radiator in the corner. "After all, *nu? Nu!* It is the privilege of the papa and mama to pick the *worst* sort of *trayfnyak* for the sandek if they wish!"

"*Oy!* They have done that!"

The yentas gathered around Frau Rosen as if to warm themselves by a stove.

"God forbid something should happen to Aaron and Etta! *Oy!* To think that the baby should be raised by such a *metsieh!*"

"He is no bargain! *Oy gevalt!*"

"Even if the man *is* as unkosher as ham, what business is it of ours? I ask you."

"Etta's father, the rabbi, would have something to say about this,

I can tell you! You think a rabbi in Jerusalem would stand for such a thing? *Oy!* This Letzno fellow is practically one of the goyim himself!"

"True, true! But I know for a fact that Eduard Letzno comes from a good family. Even if he is a black sheep, he was *also* circumcised! You can't put *that* back!"

Hearts fluttering with the shock of it, tongues wagging with the sensation of it, the yentas of Warsaw lined up to witness the bris milah of tiny Yacov Lubetkin.

A few feet away in the crowded room, Rachel eyed them angrily. She did not approve entirely of Dr. Letzno as choice of godfather for her brother, but the gossip of these women caused her cheeks to glow red with indignation. She, too, wished that he had a beard and dressed like a proper Jew, but Papa said that the heart of Eduard Letzno was sealed in the Covenant even though he lived like a goy! After all, had he not been the first doctor on the scene when the homeless Jews from Germany had been so much in need? His heart was Jewish, Papa said. So maybe he didn't need a beard.

Anyway, Rachel was certain that the baby would not mind who held him during the ceremony. Maybe Dr. Letzno could grow a beard before he saw Yacov next time. Then Yacov would not remember that it was the doctor who held him when Mohel used the circumcision knife! Rachel hated that part of the ceremony. Just the thought of her baby brother feeling pain made her head swim. And she was not the only one!

A chair was provided behind Mama . . . just in case. She had fainted when Samuel had been circumcised. This, too, had given the yentas something to talk about.

At last, all was accomplished for tiny Yacov Lubetkin as it had been for every Jewish male since the time of Abraham and Isaac. The baby slept peacefully in his cradle as the guests filed out with words of *Mazel tov!* In the end it made no difference that Eduard Letzno was sandek. Everyone knew the apostate doctor was leaving for Palestine in three days anyway, so, the Eternal be praised, he would not be around to influence the life of the littlest Lubetkin! *Oy!* Such a relief!

Eduard and Aaron closed the study door and prepared to close a final chapter in their friendship together.

"There are several thousand new refugees in Palestine and a shortage of doctors. But even if I was not needed there, I would not stay in Poland, Aaron. The very fact that your congregation is playing such a part in helping the refugees at—"

"Every Jewish welfare agency in Poland is helping," Aaron protested. "Why would I be singled out?"

"Because you are my friend." Eduard's dark eyes radiated concern.

"Do not flatter yourself, Eduard!" Aaron laughed. "You are not that important, *nu*? The Poles should suspect me because we grew up together and played stickball on the same team?"

Eduard shrugged. He was not laughing. "Men have been arrested for less."

"In Germany, perhaps."

"The voice of Hitler reaches even to Warsaw."

"And to Palestine. One place is as safe as another for us, Eduard. I am no Zionist. My congregation . . . my life . . . is here in Warsaw."

"Where the Catholic anti-Semites despise you."

"And in Palestine the Muslim Mufti makes speeches. Etta and I have decided . . ."

"Etta would like to go home to Jerusalem." Eduard crossed his arms as though this was his final argument.

"Etta is my wife." Aaron lowered his voice. "She will stay here with me and my children in Warsaw." He frowned. "Do not push me too far, Eduard."

The silence between the two men was uncomfortable. Eduard stared up at the leather-bound volumes in Aaron's library—all books of Hebrew literature and law. Aaron Lubetkin was an important scholar in the Jewish community in Warsaw. In Jerusalem, in the shadow of the Western Wall, there was a surplus of rabbinical scholars.

Eduard let his breath out slowly. "Yes. Well, I suppose I can practice medicine anywhere. But I see your point. A rabbi must have a congregation."

Aaron smiled. "My congregation is here in Warsaw. We are three million strong here in Poland. Only half a million in the Mandate. If you find a congregation for me in Jerusalem, then perhaps . . ."

23

Rendezvous

The vaulted stone roof of the Tipat Chalev soup kitchen was an acoustic masterpiece. The clatter of one tin plate on the floor would ring as if an entire shelf of plates had collapsed. The scraping of a spoon against a porridge bowl reverberated like the clanging mess kits of ten thousand half-starved soldiers.

People came to Tipat Chalev to eat, not talk. If they had to talk when the room was packed with hungry diners, they shouted. Or they went outside.

Such acoustics left room for only one speaker at a time to be heard and understood. When the kitchen volunteers were confronted with the sight of people coming through the door, they revved up their speaking volume to full blast.

Perhaps that is why Hannah Cohen now stood before six Yeshiva students and shouted orders at the top of her lungs. "*Oy!* Eli Sachar. Pick up your end of the crate higher! Higher! Now you. Ari. Lower your end. Careful as you back down the stairs! *Oy!* Do not drop this Jell-O stuff. Such a mess. Such a mess."

Her voice ricocheted off the ceiling and slammed around the room, splitting the eardrums of Eli and his fellow students. "EL-I-I-I! Not soooooo high! You'll scrape the doorframe. *Nu!* Josef just painted that doorframe!"

Eli tried to nod his apology around the heavy crate. He backed cautiously down the narrow basement stairs as the densely packed Jell-O crate threatened to break loose from Ari's grip and slam down.

"ELI-I-I! Do not let go! *Oy!* The crate will knock you down the stairs backward if you let go! Careful there! It will knock you over and you will break your neck and then what will I say to your mother, dear Ida, when you are dead from moving rat poison? *Careful*, Ari!"

If Eli had not been in such a tenuous position on the down side of a three-hundred-pound crate, he would have been irritated at Hannah Cohen. She was his landlady. She owned Cohen's Grocery and he could also hear her in the store when she transacted business. Nobody talked as loudly as Hannah Cohen. Mama had said they would get used to her long discussions about bananas and crackers or kosher sausage, but Eli had never quite gotten used to her piercing voice.

To have to listen to her today was almost unbearable! Today was the day when he would meet Victoria in Christ Church! And here he was, when he should have been dressing in his goyim clothes! How could this be? Why him, of all the Yeshiva students?

At the bottom of the stairs they manuevered around sacks of lentils, finally placing the crate according to Hannah Cohen's instructions. Eli mopped his brow. Ari mopped his brow and sighed. Hannah mopped her brow and sighed and thanked the Eternal no one was killed by this cursed stuff.

Panting with exhaustion after watching the dangerous descent, Hannah boomed down to Eli, "I asked for you special, Eli. Such a strong boy! *Oy!* If only I had been blessed with such a strong son to help me at the market, then maybe my back would not ache so bad, *nu?*" She touched her back and grimaced. Just watching the strong young men had made her ache. But it had not managed to lower the volume of her voice.

The knowledge that she had asked for him hit Eli with a hot rush of irritation. But he could not let on. Mama and Mrs. Cohen were friends, after all, and it would not do to have her saying to Mama, *"Something is bothering Eli,* nu? *Tell me, Ida. You can tell me. I love him like a son."*

Eli gulped air and swallowed his first urge to shout back at her. "Always a pleasure to help you, Mrs. Cohen." He regretted saying that. What if she asked him to carry boxes of fruit for her sometime? Ah, well. Better to be polite than shake his fist in her face. "But now I must leave. The others will manage without me. I have a . . . I was studying a passage of the Mishnah and suddenly . . . such a thought! It came to me as I was moving this crate! About the heaviness of a man's burdens. And so I must go write it down."

She clapped her hands once in awe. "Not only strong and handsome, but smart. So proud Ida must be!"

Ari was scowling at Eli as he ascended the steps to take leave of the work crew. Eli bowed slightly to Mrs. Cohen and then gave Ari the sort of look that said, *"Too bad I thought of it first, eh?"*

"Such a rabbi this one will make!" Hannah Cohen finally let her voice grow quiet in awe of the retreating Eli Sachar.

Out on the street and half a block away, Eli could hear her as she resumed her duties as supervisor. "Pick that end up! Lower! Watch out for the doorframe! *Nu!* Watch it! *Oy! Oyyyyyy!*"

The lobby of the King David Hotel seemed nearly deserted compared to the activity during Leah's and Shimon's first day in Jerusalem.

"They've all gone to Galilee to guard the Woodhead Commission," volunteered the desk clerk as he took the receipt of Leah's cello. "They'll be back next week. Probably ready for an encore performance from you. Of course, a good concert will not make as much impression on them as an Arab attack, that is certain."

A portly English businessman overheard his words and volunteered, "That's the difference between the Arabs and the Jews, eh? The Royal Commission will be more impressed by explosions than good music. We'll be seeing the last of European Jews arriving here. I'm sure of that."

Perhaps the man was not aware that he was speaking to recent arrivals. Or perhaps he knew very well whom he was talking to. The thought that Jewish immigration might soon be halted altogether did not seem to be a concern. His expression did not alter when the desk clerk handed the instrument to Shimon.

For a moment Leah considered commenting on the tragedy the closing of Palestine would be to those who remained in Europe with no escape, but the words would be wasted on a man such as this.

At that moment, Victoria Hassan emerged from the administrative wing of the hotel. She glanced toward them. Leah was certain Victoria saw them standing at the counter, but the young woman averted her eyes and hurried on as if they were not there.

Shimon nudged Leah. He had seen her, too. He had noticed the way she hurried from the building. Leah sighed, feeling again that she had somehow insulted Victoria. She would be glad when Tuesday arrived so she could ask her.

Through the glass revolving door, Leah watched her. She was, indeed, beautiful. Sunlight gleamed in her long black hair. She wore a dark blue dress of simple cut adorned only by a silver chain necklace. High heels showed shapely legs. It was no wonder that Eli Sachar was interested in her. She did not seem to fit the Muslim world.

Leah resolved that she would tell Eli they had seen her leaving the hotel this afternoon. Any news of her at all might cheer him up.

Eli hurried toward the restrooms where Moshe had stowed a carefully wrapped set of khaki-colored clothes on top of a high water tank.

He slipped into an empty stall. A feeling of awe filled him. Mama would never suspect that he had gone to visit his Muslim sweetheart in a Christian church! All she would hear was how much he had helped Hannah Cohen. How lucky she was to have such a son! How Hannah Cohen wished she had a crate hauler to call son!

He changed quickly, wrapped his Orthodox garb into the same paper, and slipped it back on the tank. At this moment the first misgivings whispered in his ear. To walk from this place pretending to be anything other than a Jew was most certainly a sin. And to walk into a Christian church! *Oy!* The thought of it made him shudder.

He stared thoughtfully at the green moss on the walls of the lavatory. Outside he could hear merchants and peddlers hawking their wares. Would anyone notice that a Jew had entered the tiny cubicle, but a goy now emerged?

Eli drew a deep breath and winced from the tank odor in the air. Things would be better outside, he decided; he would think more clearly in the street. With that, he squared his shoulders and walked out into the teeming crowds in the souk.

Without the featherlike weight of his yarmulke on his head, Eli felt strangely undressed. In his khaki trousers and shirt, he blended easily with the English civil servants and off-duty soldiers strolling through Armenian Quarter. No one noticed him. No one at all. And yet he felt self-conscious. These English clothes were not for him. They felt sinful against his skin.

He walked quickly down St. James Road toward the Old City wall. Just ahead was the Armenian Patriarchate Street, which ran parallel to the wall. The Byzantine tower of St. James Church was to the left. Christ Church was a short walk to the right, just past the barracks of the British soldiers and the headquarters of the Palestine police. In this ancient stone barracks known as Kishleh, every army since the time of Suleiman had housed its occupation forces. English soldiers with clean-shaven cheeks and short haircuts walked in and out of the building. They looked more at ease than Eli today, even though Jerusalem had always been his home.

He had been a toddler the same year the English General Allenby had stood on a platform in front of Christ Church to accept the official surrender of the Turkish rulers—1917. What a year of hope that had been! Religious tolerance had been proclaimed right in this place as

Eli's father had held him aloft in the cheering crowds. Christian, Jew, and Arab alike had formed committees to clean out the sewage from the moat that surrounded the Old City wall. Eli had grown up believing that one day there would be a Jewish homeland as the British promised. He had grown up with Ibrahim and Victoria and a dozen other Arab children who had mingled freely in their games. No one had been afraid then. Times were better than they had been with the brutal Turkish government. Until Haj Amin became Mufti, there had been peace.

Eli never imagined that one day he would be sneaking out of the Jewish Quarter to meet Victoria in a place like this. In all his years he had never set foot in a Christian church. That thought chafed his conscience just as the strange clothes chafed his skin. He prayed no one would recognize him: *"I saw a goy who looked just like you!"*

He told himself that he was here for Victoria. Here to finish their discussion. To be his wife she *must* convert! And for that one reason he had left his Orthodox clothing wrapped up and stowed on the water tank. On Yom Kippur, Eli would confess this sin to the Eternal and ask forgiveness. Somehow the end would justify his sacrifice of tradition for the sake of love. Would God see it his way? he wondered. Or was the Eternal looking on with disapproval already because Eli was even now breaking laws regarding the proper dress of a Jew? The thought made him shudder. It made no difference that he blended with the crowds. God was still watching. And Eli was about to enter Christ Church and sit quietly pretending to be one of *them* so he could be with *her!*

To his left, British guards stood in stone niches on either side of the iron gate of the citadel. Above them, soldiers patrolled the ramparts of the city wall. Eli halted, pretending to study the young English protectors of Jerusalem. He considered the fact that it was still not too late to turn back. Still not too late to retrieve his clothing from the hiding place and return to Tipat Chalev to move what remained of the crates. He did not have to go through the great iron gate on his right and enter the courtyard of Christ Church.

He had not dared to look at the church. He had averted his eyes from the bell tower during the walk. *I do not have to enter,* he thought now as he pivoted to face the entrance. *Perhaps she will come here from the opposite direction and I will take her by the arm and we will find some other place—any place besides this place!*

Soldiers passed. An Armenian priest passed. Victoria did not come. He stared through the wrought iron into the courtyard of the church, where an enormous oleander bloomed and plum trees dropped their leaves in memory of autumn in faraway England where their mother trees grew. Everything about this place was foreign. The English had built this stone church to lure Jews away from their faith, Eli had heard. He had grown up with the warning ringing in his ears that he must be polite to *them*, but he must not go into their building. Men entered as Jews and left as something else.

Minutes crawled by. Eli was angry at himself that he had thought this was such a good idea. He should have sent Moshe back with an alternate plan! But then, Moshe had also thought the strategy was sound.

A gardener worked beneath a plum tree. He raked and piled purple leaves onto the flagstones. Eli watched him, then turned and looked unhappily up the street toward Omar Square again. If she was coming that way, he would have seen her already. That meant she had either changed her mind, or she was already in *there*.

He drew a breath and stepped forward, laying a hand against the wrought-iron bars of the gate. *Still I have not entered. A silly thing to be this nervous. Moshe would not be nervous. Moshe sees them all the time.*

The wizened old gardener straightened his back for a moment, then leaned heavily on his rake. He was also dressed in rumpled khaki. He was an Englishman. Eli could tell easily by the white straw hat and the bright blue eyes that sparkled out from beneath folds of skin.

"Lovely day, isn't it?" the old man said to Eli.

Eli answered with a nod. He did not wish to give away his origins by speaking.

"Just raking up the last of the plums. The ones the birds got." He stooped and picked out a large half-eaten plum from among the leaves. "What a waste. Paid a boy to shoo them away, but more kept flying in. Finally I gave the tree to the birds. There are no finer plums in Jerusalem. Don't mind sharing with the sparrows if they just wouldn't waste!" The old man stared at the plum, then glanced at Eli. He studied Eli with the same intensity with which he had looked at the plum. "Waiting for someone?"

Eli nodded again. He tried a slight smile for the sake of politeness.

"You won't find her out here." The gardener scratched his head. He tossed away the plum and scowled up at the ungrateful birds.

"Who?" Eli was startled by the old man's seeming knowledge of *her*. . . . He took his hand off the iron gate as if it might burn him.

"Victoria. Are you not here for Victoria? She has been in the chapel." He examined the sky as if it were a clock. "Half an hour. She was early. Come in! I did not notice you there, or I would have told you sooner. Come on. Through the gate and that way." He pointed his rake toward the entrance of the church, then returned to his work as Eli held his breath and plunged that first step into the courtyard of Christ Church.

☜

The letter to Etta was duly deposited into the mail slot at the Mandate post office in Allenby Square. The old rabbi knew that it would take at least eight weeks to arrive in Warsaw. First it would travel by slow boat to England. Once there, it might float aimlessly from this capital to that. *Oy!* The frustration! But at least it was quicker now than it had been when he was a boy. Then it had taken maybe eight months for a letter to go from Jerusalem to Warsaw. And sometimes it did not arrive at all.

Ah, well. Rabbi Lebowitz himself was slowing down these days. The heat of the afternoon seemed to push him backward as he leaned into the incline up toward Jaffa Gate. He raised his eyes to heaven and smiled. The Jell-O in his pockets seemed to call, *"Look up on the wall, old man. There are English soldiers there,* nu?"

"Yes! Enough! I see them already!" The old rabbi passed through the teeming gate and turned right along the road of the Armenian patriarchate. The barracks of the Old City British soldiers were along this road, near Christ Church. Plenty of Englishmen there might be willing to explain the mystery of the lime and the cherry powders.

He yawned wearily and studied the faces of the soldiers in search of *the one* who might meet his eyes and be of service to the cooks of Tipat Chalev.

Soldiers emerged from the stone barracks along the wall. Other soldiers stood in the niches on guard against wild Arab bands and old Jewish rabbis with bombs disguised as Jell-O packets. *Whom to ask?* There was an abundance of Englishmen here, all moving this way or that without stopping.

Rabbi Lebowitz stopped in the center of the cobbled road. He frowned. He squinted. He shaded his eyes against the glare. There, in front of the gate of Christ Church, was a young Englishman dressed all in khaki who looked very much—no, *exactly*—like young Eli Sachar!

But of course it could not *be* Eli Sachar. Eli was back at Tipat Chalev moving crates of this loathsome, troublesome stuff. The old man removed a box from his pocket and held it up to hail the young man at the gate.

Such similarity could not be ignored! God had sent this English look-alike especially to help; the old man was certain. He could say, *"You look just like a young fellow only a few blocks from here! Come see . . . and while you're at it, there is this stuff from America!"*

A crowd of Armenian schoolchildren passed between the old man and the miraculous twin. And at that moment, *Oy!* The young man who looked like Eli Sachar but who could not *be* Eli Sachar stepped through the gate of Christ Church.

This was also proof that the young man could not be Eli. Every old one in the Jewish Quarter remembered the reason all the Sachars avoided passing within the shadow of Christ Church. Some, over the years, had even walked on the opposite side of the street from the building, while the more devout among them took a different route altogether.

But still, might this be some descendant of that early apostate Sachar who had walked into Christ Church a Jew and emerged as something else? Interesting. "Perhaps I should wait," the old man mumbled. "There are reasons why these things happen."

Behind him the horn of a military truck blared loudly. He jumped and whirled as if he were a young man. Then he forgot all about the Sachar relative. He dropped the box of lime Jell-O as he leaped to the side.

The truck pulled up in front of the barracks and the British captain, Samuel Orde, climbed out.

The officer strode directly toward the old rabbi, his hand extended. "So sorry!" he apologized. "The driver was watching the children, and . . . are you all right?"

Rabbi Lebowitz smiled. Everyone in the Old City knew that Captain Samuel Orde was fluent in several languages. No doubt he was familiar with Jell-O.

"Just the fellow!" the rabbi cried happily. "Such meetings are not accidental, you know. You have nearly run me down just at a time when I need your help." He thrust the box of cherry Jell-O into the captain's hand. "A gift from America. Crates and crates for Tipat Chalev. We do not know if we should eat it or clean the sinks with it!" The rabbi paused as Orde grinned broadly.

"It may be difficult without proper refrigeration, Rabbi."

"Proper . . . you *freeze* it?"

Orde laughed. He nudged his cap back on his head. "There might be something down at the quartermaster's warehouse. Perhaps we could make a trade. Tipat Chalev and the British army, eh?"

The old man nodded slowly. These Englishmen were really good fellows. It had been much better in Jerusalem since they had come. First the mail delivery had speeded up, and now this. Who cared so much if they sent their little fact-finding committees—as long as they only talked.

"Powdered milk? Maybe cocoa?" The rabbi grinned slyly.

"Into the truck with you." Captain Orde gave the order. "We'll see what we can do."

The Eternal be praised! All along, the Merciful One had this in mind. Oy! *Still sending manna in strange ways,* nu? *Giving this Englishman an after-*

noon of rest from guiding his silly politicians around Jerusalem. And all so You can bring powdered milk and cocoa to Your children at Tipat Chalev! True? Of course true!

The rasping noise of the rake followed Eli beneath the high stone portals of a building that seemed to have been transported from the English countryside. He knew a little about Christ Church. His great-grandfather had fought against its erection as the first Protestant church inside the walls of Jerusalem. *We fear these English missionaries,* the old man had written in his journal in 1838. *They capture the minds of our youth and pull them from their roots.* The old rabbi's battle against the London Society for Promotion of Christianity Amongst the Jews was still remembered. When the Protestants had opened a medical clinic, so had the Jewish Quarter. Other sects had become worried by the activities of these Protestants. A healthy competition sprang up because of it, and Jerusalem had become a better place. But in the end, a son of the old Rabbi Sachar had converted. He had walked through these portals a Jew and had emerged something else.

Eli looked up at the Gothic arches and wondered what thoughts must have gone through the mind of that young man to make him abandon his faith and his people. Since that day until this, no Sachar had ever set foot on the ground of Christ Church! Not until now! Eli wondered what the old rabbi would have said if he could have seen this moment.

He pushed the doors open and entered the auditorium. Spare and Gothic in construction, the place was one of the few buildings in Jerusalem with a wooden roof. So English! And yet in the center panel of the altar a Star of David and a crown were inlaid in the wood. There was no sign of the fearsome Christian cross in this building. Eli sighed with a release of tension. There were no graven images like the ones sold to pilgrims in the souks. No plaster saints. Only high stone walls and stained-glass windows and wooden chairs on the stone floor, and . . . *Victoria!*

She sat in a shadow at the very back of the church. She did not hear him come in, so he let the heavy door swing shut with a dull boom. She started, turned, and smiled with relief, motioning him to join her.

Every doubt, every feeling of foreboding melted away from him. He forgot about his clothing. He thought no more of his apostate great-uncle and the fury of the old Rabbi Sachar! He rushed down the side aisle. She stood and stretched out her arms to embrace him. And then, even here, Victoria kissed him, and Eli forgot entirely that they were beneath the wooden roof of the much-feared Christ Church! He could think of nothing but Victoria. Why had he ever worried? She loved him! That was all that mattered.

He stroked her soft hair and held her close. Delicate arms squeezed him as if she were afraid to let him go. He whispered her name. It was like a prayer.

"I thought you were not coming," she said at last. "I was so afraid you had changed your mind."

He pulled her deeper into the shadow of a pillar and kissed her again. "I have thought only of you." The words were almost entirely true. The doubts meant nothing now that they were together. It was always like that.

She took his hand and led him to the chairs. "We have to talk, darling. So much to talk about."

He did not want to talk, but he nodded and sat beside her. She leaned against his arm and he held her hand. He was grateful that they were alone in this place. Yes, there was much to talk about, but for a while, he simply wanted to sit here beside her and cherish her nearness.

24

The Barter

It seemed like a long time before Victoria raised her head and spoke. Her words were not about love, however. "Ibrahim is angry with me." Her dark eyes flashed resentment when she spoke the name of her brother. "He says he will not help us any longer."

"But why?" Such news startled Eli. All along he had interpreted lack of communication as a sign that Victoria had decided against his proposal. But it had meant something else.

"Because I would not promise him that I will not go . . . away with you."

"He knows how we feel," Eli protested.

"He hopes that you will join our people. He will not tolerate it if I should be the one to leave." She clutched his hand and stared bleakly up at the red glass of a window. "There is something terrible coming, Eli. My half brothers talk quietly among themselves. They become silent when I enter."

"Do they know? About us?"

Victoria shook her head. "Ibrahim will not tell them. I am certain of that. They would kill you, or have you killed. He does not like it that you have not joined our people, but he would never go so far." She bit her lip. "No. It is something else. Something . . . terrible," she finished lamely, letting her hands fall to her lap.

"Then we must settle this, Victoria." He was resolute. He took both of her hands in his. "I will speak with my parents and with the rabbis. We will settle the matter."

She shook her head. "I . . . I can't. Please, Eli. I just need a little time." She sighed and leaned against his arm again. "I am afraid."

Eli smiled in spite of her fears. He had won. She would be his wife. He would not tell her now that their marriage would mean he could not be a rabbi. He did not seem to hear anything else. "It will be all right now." He touched her cheek. "This is a good place to meet. We will come here every Friday, *nu*? Just like this. Time will pass quickly; you will see."

She nodded. "But still I am afraid when I am not with you." She pressed her face harder against his arm as if she might burrow into him and hide. "I see it in their faces. Little Daud. There is such hate in him now. He was such a good little brother. But now—and Isaak! He hates every Englishman and every Jew. He asks me always to tell him about things the British have me type each day. At night they go to meetings." She paused as if the faces of her brothers were before her. "I am afraid for them." She glanced up at Eli. "They are my brothers, and I am afraid for them! They argue with Father about the Mufti. At the table they shout about the British and Zionists. And my stepmother is one of them. I hear her after my brothers storm from the house."

Somehow Eli could not find it in himself to share her grief about the Hassan brothers. He could think only of the fact that, like Ruth of old, Victoria would leave her people to be with him. His God would be her God. His people, her people. Was there anything else in the world that mattered?

He gazed at the altar of Christ Church as she spoke softly of her brothers. Her voice was a distant sorrow that receded behind his joy. He smiled at the Star of David. Strange to see that symbol in a Christian church. He had not expected it. It seemed as if it had been placed there just for him, a good omen that this was the ideal place for them to meet.

Victoria's voice seemed far away. ". . . and Daud's face was bloody. But not his own blood . . ."

"Don't worry," he cajoled. "We will come here often. Maybe more than just Friday. No one will know. Everything will work out; you'll see."

"They would not tell Father where they had been. And then we heard about the British sergeant killed in Ramle . . ."

"When the time is right we will marry and leave this place . . ."

"It is so hard to think that my own brothers . . . ," she continued.

"Perhaps we will make a life in America."

"They think they are right. They serve Haj Amin, Shetan himself, and yet they think they are right."

Their thoughts poured out like water, but the streams flowed in opposite directions. And so they passed the hour in conversation even though they were not speaking to each other.

"If only there was a way, Victoria." Eli sighed and traced the Hebrew writing on the altar cloth with his eyes: *Incline your ear, and come unto Me:*

hear, and your soul shall live; and I will make an everlasting covenant with you.

She raised her head as though she heard a distant voice. "Perhaps we do not have to wait so long." She squeezed his hand and new hope shined from her eyes as she looked up at the lofty ceiling. "May Allah help us," she breathed.

"I will think what we must do, Victoria. I will send word to you with Leah Feldstein on Tuesday. Maybe by then I will have an answer." He touched her face and gazed into her eyes. "Until then I make a covenant with you. My heart is knit to yours." He gestured toward the altar. "Here, in this place that is neither yours nor mine, there are no rules or laws that would forbid our love. For this moment and forever, I am not a Jew and you are not a Muslim."

"You are not a Jew and I am not a Muslim," Victoria repeated.

Eli smiled wistfully. "I had an uncle who entered this place one time and left it another sort of man. I feel . . . I do not know *what* I feel being here with you on this neutral ground. But I will pray and think."

"I cannot think any longer, Eli." Victoria leaned her head against his shoulder. "You must think for us both, or I will break. I only know I love you, and that I am afraid."

Eli nodded. In his heart he whispered, *I will incline my ear to You, O God!*

Samuel Orde had never seen so much Jell-O—crates and crates of the stuff and anxious, unhappy Jewish faces looking hopefully at him.

"You think he will take it?"

"For milk and cocoa? You think they would exchange such schlock merchandise?"

These words were whispered in Yiddish as Samuel Orde strolled among the boxes labeled *Cherry* and *Lime*. He personally did not care for lime, but soldiers took what they were served and so the Old City troops would eat the stuff and like it. He would arrange the matter with the company cook and quartermaster. Here also was a chance to rid the warehouse of a ton of rock-hard English walnuts that the cooks had been cursing since their arrival a fortnight before!

"The merchandise appears to be in order." Orde peered thoughtfully at a crate in the basement. The whispers at the top of the stairs grew silent with hopeful anticipation.

Can the Englishman be such a fool?

The old rabbi rocked coyly back and forth on his heels in an effort not to appear too eager. "Powdered milk *and* cocoa?"

"Yes, yes."

"And also—" the rabbi held his finger aloft—"sugar? Flour, perhaps?"

Orde considered the request. The cooks would not stand for sugar and flour to be traded. "No." He scratched his chin. "But perhaps we might throw in a few bags of good English walnuts. All the way from England. Very fine nuts they are, too."

Eyes lit up. Women restrained from allowing excited exclamations to escape their mouths. Such a delicacy! Walnuts for the making of baklava and a thousand wondrous things! Could this Englishman mean such a thing?

Rabbi Lebowitz tugged his beard as he pretended to consider. "How many bags of walnuts, Captain Orde?"

Orde mentally calculated. Of course they could have them all. They could use them as weapons against Arabs if nothing else. Perhaps shoot a few pigeons with slingshots. "I believe there are two or three dozen gunnysacks still in the warehouse."

"Not wormy, are they?" The old rabbi scowled cautiously.

"On my word!" Orde declared.

Another moment of hesitation, then Rabbi Lebowitz extended his hand. "A bargain, then! Five hundred pounds of milk. Twenty-five pounds of cocoa. And, God be praised . . . walnuts!"

Eli returned to the Jewish Quarter with his khaki clothes wadded up beneath his arm. He was smiling, relieved that there was no question of Victoria's feeling for him. Time. That was all she needed. Her request did not frighten him.

Two young Torah schoolboys charged past him on the street as if they were being pursued. Soon it would be Shabbat. Everyone in the Quarter seemed to be rushing around to get ready for the holy day of rest!

Eli let his breath out slowly. On this Shabbat he would truly be at rest. He strolled easily through the lanes of his neighborhood. Once again his eyes were able to focus on the faces of the people, on the cluttered shops and the round-bellied merchants who hailed him as he passed. Victoria would marry him. She would convert, and though they might have to leave Jerusalem, his heart would not have to leave his people!

"Eli!" A familiar voice called his name. "Eli! Come quickly!" The rusty voice of Rabbi Lebowitz shouted all the way from the steps of Tipat Chalev. "It will be Shabbat soon and we need to move these bags of walnuts!"

Eli did not mind this interruption. He quickened his pace as the cry of distress demanded, but he felt no resentment as the rabbi waved him up the steps and into the dining room, where heaps of gunny sacks were stacked almost to the vaulted ceiling.

Six other rabbinical students had likewise been hauled into the task of shifting a ton of walnuts to the basement. Eli did not ask where they had come from. Nothing surprised him anymore . . . except the fact that his own black mood had evaporated. He tossed the small bundle of clothes onto the table as Rabbi Lebowitz began shouting instructions.

"Eli! You and Yossi take that stack there, and . . ." For a moment the voice of the rabbi faltered. He looked at the clothes and then at Eli. Confusion crossed his face. He blinked at Eli, swallowed hard, and then began again. "Yes. I was saying . . . that stack there. If we hurry we will beat Queen Shabbat before she arrives, *nu*, Eli?"

If ever Eli had been foolish, this quiet Shabbat evening was the night. The candles were lit. The prayers were recited. The meal was served. All should have been at peace in the Sachar home.

Instead, Ida Sachar sobbed uncontrollably over her plate. "*Oy! Gottenyu!* My own son! The pride of my life, and now he tells us he is in love with a Muslim girl! Hermann! Hermann!"

"Be still, Ida!" Hermann snapped. But she would not be silenced.

Moshe looked at his distraught parents. He shook his head and threw his napkin on the table. "So he loves her! So my brother is in love with a woman who is not born on this side of the Street of the Chain! So what?" he yelled.

Hermann's face was purple with rage. "You be quiet also, Moshe! This does not concern you!"

Moshe defied his father. "Eli is my brother! It concerns me!"

Ida wailed and muttered, "Not one apostate son, but two! *Oy!* Where have I failed? What will the neighbors say?"

"Who cares what they say?" Moshe stood up, knocking his chair over.

"Go to your room!" Hermann pointed toward the stairs. "And if you do not show us respect, leave the house!"

Eli did not look up as Moshe shouted, "I'll do better than that! I will leave Jerusalem! And Palestine! This godforsaken heap of stone! I'm going to England to study as soon as my fellowship comes through, and Eli and his wife may come with me!" He stormed from the table.

"Two sons! *Oy!* Has a mother ever been so cursed?" Ida moaned and blew her nose.

"I love her," Eli said hoarsely. Why had he chosen tonight to tell them? Why had he not presented the marriage as accomplished? Ah, well, it would have been the same now or later.

"But she is not a Jew!" Ida wailed. "There are so many lovely girls in our Quarter! My grandchildren! What will the community say? And I was so proud."

"Maybe too proud, Mama," Eli faltered.

Hermann slammed his fist on the table. "Leave us, Ida!" he bellowed.

"You will take his part!" she cried. "Listen to yourself! You will not be strong in this! That is why it has happened! You let the traditions of the family fall apart! You let Moshe go to Hebrew University instead of Yeshiva! Now look!"

Hermann glared at his weeping wife. "Leave us." His command was quiet, menacing.

"You will be sorry!" she shouted, running from the table and slamming every door in the house as she exited. "This is your fault! *Your* fault!" Her sobs echoed back down the hall from the bedroom.

For a full five minutes, Eli and his grim father sat in silence as they listened to the rise and fall of her grief.

At last Eli spoke. "You would think I died."

Hermann sighed. All the anger had dissipated into weariness. He spoke softly now, Ida's sobs a backdrop of grief to his words. "Do you know what your marriage to her would mean for you? for all of us? All your education, the sacrifice we have made for your schooling. It would not matter, Eli, if she converted. You would not even be fit to lead a congregation of lepers if your wife was an Arab." He paused, then laid down his napkin and rose slowly. "Think about it. You know what it will mean. You do not need the hysteria of your mother or the anger of your father to instruct you. You already know."

Eli nodded with a single jerk. He left his father standing in the dining room and retreated to the room he shared with Moshe.

It was semidark in the room, but Moshe sat in an overstuffed chair and pretended to study. He glanced up to see Eli stretch himself on his bed and turn his face to the wall. Moshe knew Eli wept only by the sound of an occasional sniff.

It seemed as if hours passed before Moshe spoke. "What will you do?"

Eli turned and wiped his eyes with the back of his hand. He sat up and wrapped his arms around his knees as he stared at the khaki shirt draped over the footboard of his bed. "Can I tear out the beard of my father? As long as I am here I must not see her again."

"But why?" Moshe tossed his book on the floor with an angry crash. "Can she not become a Jew?"

"She will never fit in. To marry her means that I turn my back on my faith and my family. You—" he searched Moshe's face—"could no longer call me your brother."

"Medieval nonsense!" scoffed Moshe.

"I would be dead to you. Dead."

"Turn your back on your faith? What are you talking about? So you will not be a rabbi! What has that got to do with anything?"

"You do not understand!" Eli looked away. "There is more to this than you know! More than I can tell you!"

"But you love her!" Moshe laughed in disbelief.

"Yes!" Eli cried. "So much that today I thought—" He did not finish. He did not tell Moshe that he had declared in Christ Church that for her sake he was no longer a Jew. "We shall not speak of it again, Moshe! I have much to think about. What is right? I do not know myself any longer! Too many voices!" Tears came to him again. "The world has gone mad, and we are in the center of its destruction!" He raised a hand to stop any further words from his brother. "No, Moshe! We shall not speak of it again!"

After a time the muffled sobs of Ida Sachar died away. Moshe's breath came in the even rhythm of sleep. The moon rose over Jerusalem, outlining the city in crisp shadow. Only then did Eli get up. He stood at the window for a long time and looked toward the corner where Victoria would walk on her way to work. Then he looked toward the bell tower of Christ Church. He would not speak the deepest secrets of his heart to his family any longer. It would serve no purpose. For the sake of leaving his parents with at least one son in Moshe, Eli would not involve his brother. Moshe must not be implicated in his plan.

There in the moonlight Eli steeled himself for what he must do. He would be alone in his decision. It must be so.

25

Wedding Day

Already the wagons of Warsaw's peddlers rumbled through the streets. The clop of horses' hooves against the cobblestone mingled with the voices of hawking merchants and bargaining housewives.

"Who could sleep with such a racket?" Etta Lubetkin asked as she braided her thick dark hair in the early morning light.

In the mirror she could see Aaron as he quietly recited the morning prayers. He held a finger to his lips, warning her to be silent until he uttered the final Omaine.

She simply redirected her chatter to the air. "Why should I be quiet when every peddler in Warsaw is screaming in the streets?" She studied her own reflection in the mirror. She was thirty-eight. Yes, it was time for those tiny lines around her clear blue eyes. Her skin was still as fair and fresh as it had been when she was a young girl in Jerusalem. Even after giving Aaron four children, her figure still delighted him. No doubt there would be other children if the Eternal, blessed be He, was willing. Aaron was certainly willing enough. He did not seem to notice those tiny lines around her eyes.

She glanced at his reflection in the mirror. He was praying toward Jerusalem, looking very handsome beneath his prayer shawl. He was concentrating very hard. Trying not to look at his wife sitting there in her white cotton shift as she plaited her hair. She was, he often said, his greatest distraction from the things of the Almighty. Still beautiful at thirty-eight. Still as much on his mind as she had been when he had been a Yeshiva student in Jerusalem. He had married her before finishing his studies simply because without her he had been unable to think of anything but her.

And after the wedding? Aaron found that Etta offered him even more distraction and delight. At the advice of her revered father, the Rabbi Lebowitz, Aaron had begun to thank God for Etta every time she popped into his thoughts.

This morning as the sunlight streamed through the beveled-glass window to fall in little rainbows on her skin, Aaron closed his eyes tightly as he finished his prayers. ". . . and thank You, O Eternal, for the blessing of my wife. Omaine!"

At that, he turned and placed his strong hands on her shoulders and stooped to kiss her neck. His beard brushed her soft skin.

She reached up and patted his head affectionately. "You will be late to shul if you do not hurry," she warned as he kissed her again.

"Why are you not like other wives?" He did not move away. "Why are you not fat and shrill and harsh with me so that I can better study the To-rah and discuss the words of the great rabbis without wishing I were here with you making more little Lubetkins?"

Etta laughed. "If you want me fat and shrill, just give me more little Lubetkins too soon, and I will grant your wish. Now really! You will be late to shul. They cannot start without you."

"Let them wait," he whispered. "You have rainbows on your skin."

"And what will you tell them when you are late?"

"That I was looking at rainbows."

"But the sky is clear."

"Then I will weep and say it rains." He kissed her once more as he had not dared to kiss her since the baby was born. "I have missed you," he whispered. "I will not be able to pray any prayer today except the prayer your father taught me: 'Thank You, O Eternal, for my Etta!' I will say it over and over, and everyone will think I am *meshugge*!"

"You must go. You will be late." She said the words but did not push him away.

"Send David to tell them I am sick," he pleaded.

"A lie? You would put a lie on the lips of your son?"

Aaron smiled at his beautiful wife and pulled her toward the un-made bed. "Not a lie. Have you not read Song of Songs? *'I am sick with love. Thou art all fair, my love; there is no spot in thee.'* " A lingering kiss melted her resistance. *"'The roof of thy mouth is like the best wine for my be-loved, that goeth down sweetly, causing the lips of those that are asleep to speak.'"*

Etta drew a deep breath and made one last protest. "The children. Breakfast."

"You have nursed baby Yacov. Frau Rosen will feed Rachel, David, and Samuel." He smiled down into her eyes. "You can tell Frau Rosen that I will allow no one to nurse me but you."

Etta closed her eyes and savored the adoration of her husband. It had been a long time. She felt it too. "I will send David to the shul with the message, and then I expect you to pray twice as hard tomorrow!"

He nodded obediently and released her. She threw on a robe, and fumbling with the sash, she stepped out of the room to call down the hall with the message for young David. She instructed the housekeeper about breakfast and gave strict orders that poor Rabbi Lubetkin must not be disturbed because he was sick and would not be nursed by anyone but his wife!

Frau Rosen, the plump, dour housekeeper, glared up from the foot of the stairs. As Etta finished her directives she thought she caught a hint of a smile on the old woman's face. Had she guessed the nature of Aaron's illness? Would she gossip at the bakery?

Etta raised her chin regally and retreated to the sanctuary of the bedchamber. She hoped that the Eternal would not see His way clear to send along another little Lubetkin today. Everyone in the neighborhood would count backward and remember that they had sent David to the shul with the message that Aaron was ill on that very day!

By dinnertime Aaron had recovered from his brief illness. He took his place at the head of the table and smiled benevolently at the subjects of his small domain.

Rachel, at thirteen, was the budding image of her mother at that age. Her wide blue eyes still carried the innocence and wonder she had as a tiny baby in her pram. Still she talked to the big, rawboned cart horses of the Warsaw peddlers. Stroking the animals on the nose, she carried on conversations as her mother argued about prices of cabbages and chickens with the merchants. Rachel's raven black hair curled gently around her oval face. She was a young beauty. Everyone said so. She was Aaron's firstborn and his pride and joy. Although others might disapprove, he had seen to it that the child was properly educated. She could quote the Torah as well as any boy her own age.

David, who was nine, had also inherited the cobalt blue eyes of his mother. Long lashes accented the clarity of those eyes and made him seem as though he was thinking very adult thoughts. The truth was that this serious boy was usually considering dropping a toad down the back of his sister. Aaron liked the boy. After a particularly diabolical prank and the punishment that must surely follow, Aaron was known to retreat to his own room and howl at the hilarity of David's latest. Of course, he never let David know his true response.

Little Samuel, too, had inherited Etta's eyes, but his features were much more like his father's. For this reason, perhaps, Aaron favored the boy somewhat. He was not pushed quite so hard in his studies as Rachel and David had been at his age. He was not so meticulous about his belongings or his room. Mrs. Rosen still made his bed. The other children resented this fact and called him Prince Samuel.

And little Yacov—at four weeks he was still an unknown commodity. His eyes were also blue, but the women of the neighborhood believed they could still turn brown in time. He was a quiet baby. Stuffed full of his mother's ample supply of milk, he would sleep the whole night through. Aaron described him as well mannered when he spoke of him to the men of the shul.

"What?" came the incredulous reply. "Well mannered at his age! *Oy!* Either you are slipping him a little schnapps at night, or we have the makings of another Baal Shem Tov in our midst, *nu?*"

So. Perhaps this youngest Lubetkin would grow up to be another Master of the Good Name! Baal Shem Lubetkin? The thought pleased Aaron, even though the words were spoken in jest.

Aaron had no doubt that each of his four offspring would somehow grow up to honor God. They were good children. The Eternal, blessed be He, had showered blessings upon Aaron and Etta. The joy they found in each other had been enlarged through these four little lives.

Now, as Aaron prayed over the meal, he remembered to thank God for each of the children as well. He broke the bread and blessed it tonight with such a feeling of contentment that he was certain the Eternal could not be displeased that he had stayed home today.

From the opposite end of the table, Etta, also looking pleasantly relaxed, smiled and winked at him. "Is it not wonderful to see your papa so fit and rested after just one day, children?" A knowing look passed between husband and wife.

"I will still want to go to bed early tonight, I think," he said, feeling genuinely tired.

Young Samuel studied his father with serious eyes. "Today at the bakery I heard Frau Rosen tell Frau Wolff and Frau Heber that what Papa has men *never* get over!"

At this news, Etta choked on her water while Aaron sputtered an incoherent reply and mentally took note that Etta must rebuke their housekeeper for saying such things . . . even if they were true.

"Frau Rosen!" Aaron bellowed loudly toward the kitchen. "Frau *Rosen!*" His voice betrayed his anger, and the housekeeper emerged red-faced from the swinging door. She had heard Samuel's revelation. She looked daggers at the little boy and bowed slightly.

"I . . . would . . . like . . . more . . . chicken," Aaron said through slightly clenched teeth. This was enough to send the woman scurrying back to the kitchen while Etta shook her head and shrugged as if to ask: *So you thought she wouldn't figure it out? A woman like Frau Rosen? Such a yenta!*

"Eh?" Rabbi Lebowitz cupped a hand around his ear as the clatter of spoons against bowls nearly drowned out their voices. "You say Eli Sachar sent you to me?" He considered the young Austrian couple who stood before him amid the clamor of mealtime at Tipat Chalev.

Shimon nodded broadly, as if even a nod might not be understood through such a noise. "We were married in a civil ceremony in Austria."

"Hardly a wedding!" Leah shouted.

The rabbi nodded. What was a wedding without a canopy to stand under? What was memorable about having some magistrate pronounce that the honeymoon was now acceptable in the eyes of the state? "Poor children." He shook his head in sympathy. "So. You should have a proper Jewish ceremony, *nu*? A canopy in Nissan Bek Synagogue! A minyan to witness such a holy moment before man and the Eternal, may His name be blessed!"

Shimon looked pleased. "Then you will do this for us, Rabbi Lebowitz?"

"Such a pleasure for me, children. True? Of course true!"

A small boy squawked and his brother shouted for silence, which drowned out the rest of the rabbi's words. Had he given the time for the ceremony?

"When?" Shimon mouthed as the argument at the table grew louder.

"We will need a little time!" The old rabbi thumped one child on his head, which silenced the entire table. "After the kettles are washed, *nu*? Eight o'clock tonight."

The wonderful wail of the clarinet filled the air of Old City Jerusalem far into the night. There was dancing. There were cakes and cookies. There was even a little wine raised in toast to Mr. and Mrs. Shimon Feldstein in honor of their marriage tonight.

It was true that most of the women in the Old City were more than a bit irritated at Rabbi Lebowitz, however. "How can we provide a proper celebration on such short notice?"

"*Oy!* So you couldn't give the poor girl a little time to prepare for her wedding? It had to be at eight o'clock tonight after the pots are washed?"

"Only a man would do such a thing!"

When all was said and done, however, perhaps it did not make such a difference. The canopy was lifted up. The ring was given. The seven benedictions were recited. The bride was beautiful. The groom was pleased. And everyone in the Quarter came to celebrate the occasion!

"*Mazel tov!*"

"*Oy!* And such a wedding, *nu*? Enough to bring tears from a stone! True?"

"Such a dress she is wearing, Golda!"

"The finest lace from Vienna, I hear. She shipped it to Jerusalem from Austria before the beast marched in! She wanted a proper wedding here in Jerusalem!"

"The girl has a head on her shoulders, I'm telling you."

"And such a heart! Look at the way she looks at him across the room, *nu*?"

"If only I could look at Yosef with such a look!"

"And she saved the real wedding dress until she could stand right here in Jerusalem before a rabbi!"

"She is a real *person*, this Leah Feldstein! I'm telling you! She is a *person*!"

"A credit to our community."

This was the conclusion of every woman among the congregation of Nissan Bek—a unanimous decision in favor of the sweet-faced Austrian refugee who had only a short time before been under suspicion. But even now, eyes narrowed and The Question was whispered behind raised hands: "But do you think she is expecting?"

Still in his wedding coat, Shimon remained two steps below Leah as she unlocked the door to the apartment.

The white lace of her wedding dress showed from beneath her warm coat. *How beautiful she looks tonight*, Shimon thought as he watched her. "Come here and kiss me, Mrs. Feldstein," he said gently, feeling the glow of a dozen toasts mixed with the nearness of Leah.

"Mrs. Feldstein. At last I am a kosher bride." She obeyed, caressing his face with her hands as she pressed her mouth against his.

The warmth of her kiss made him totter on the step. He said her name and pulled her against him.

"How was that?" she asked.

"More. We will discuss it later."

"Perhaps we should finish inside?" She giggled. "But how will you carry me across the threshold with your arm in a cast?"

At that challenge, he simply slung her over his shoulder and carried her laughing into the room. "How is that?"

"Not as romantic as I had imagined. Put me down!"

With a slight heave, he tossed her onto the bed. It was not the narrow cot they had shared but a real bed—walnut headboard, mattress big enough for two, real sheets and quilts and down pillows.

Shimon towered over her as she blinked up at him in amazement.

"How's that?" he asked.

"But how? *Where?*"

"It cost us two place settings from the silver. One wedding present in exchange for another. I thought under the circumstances we were more in need of a decent bed." He lay down beside her. She raised up on one elbow and studied the rugged face of this quiet, gentle man.

"But where did you find such an elegant bed?"

"You do not recognize it? I bought it from the head housekeeper at the King David Hotel." He grinned sheepishly. "He threw in the bedding and the pillows for two serving spoons."

"I will not ask anything else." Leah covered her eyes with her hand and moaned.

Shimon laughed at her reaction to the black-market bed. It was best not to ask too many questions; she was right about that. "Anything for my Leah." He kissed her again and then, with his lips still against hers, he began to unbutton her coat.

"Now I have a surprise for you," she whispered. Her eyes were shining in the lamplight.

"I thought you might. . . ."

"It is not what you think, my darling." Her smile broadened. "You must be the first to know. You are going to be a father, I think. I am practically certain."

He drew back, removing his fingers from her coat. The desire in his eyes softened to something else. Bewilderment? Tenderness? Fear, perhaps? His eyes skimmed over her body to her stomach. He blinked at her in wonder. "A baby?"

She guided his hand to touch her abdomen through the coat and the lace wedding dress. Nothing seemed different, and yet . . . "Part of you. And me. Us, together. Tiny now, just beginning, but I have such hope, Shimon!"

Tears streamed down the big man's cheeks. He embraced her gently, as if he were afraid of breaking something. He saw the face of Klaus Holbein in his mind as the tiny infant Israel had been dedicated on board the sunny decks of the *Darien*. The vision made him fearful. How he longed that their own child could be born in a world of peace.

Leah felt the dampness of his face against her neck. She stroked his hair and held him close to her. "You will be a wonderful papa, you know. I married you because of the way the street urchins gathered around you at the train station in Paris two years ago. That was when I thought, *Such a papa that one would make!*"

They lay together in silence for a long time. He managed to whisper, "How long have you known?"

"I have thought so since last month."

"But you did not tell me?"

"I wanted to be sure you did not feel trapped into marrying me," she teased. Then she kissed his forehead and his cheek and his mouth again. "And so, wake up from dreaming, Shimon. This is our honeymoon."

The joyous music of the wedding had faded. Nissan Bek Synagogue was dark and silent except for the sputtering oil lamps that flickered on either side of the ark.

Eli sat alone on the long wooden bench where he had first read Torah on the day of his bar mitzvah. How the eyes of his parents had shone with pride on that day! And a fire had been kindled in him at that very hour: a desire to serve the Lord here in this place, within the very shadow of the wall where Solomon's Temple had once stood.

Ah, the dreams of a boy. He had imagined the bright Shekinah glory of God as it had filled the holy mountain in answer to the prayer of Solomon. Eli had raised his hands and felt it himself, as if the light had touched him and the words of Solomon had only just echoed from the stones of the holy place to ring in his ears! Eli shouted the words of Solomon:

"*'That Thine eyes may be open toward this house night and day, even toward the place of which Thou hast said, My name shall be there: that Thou mayest harken unto the prayer which Thy servant shall make toward this place.'*"

The shout echoed in the dome of the great auditorium. It seemed to mock him. In this place so near to where Solomon stood, could God not hear him now? Would He not listen to the anguish of Eli's heart?

"Do You hear me, God?"

Silence.

Eli stood slowly and covered himself with the bright silk tallith he had received on the day of his bar mitzvah. He had always imagined that one day it would also be the wedding canopy he stood beneath with his bride. But it would not be so. No rabbi would marry him and Victoria.

Eli stepped forward to face the ark. Shadows and light danced eerily

against the walls. He bowed and placed his lips against the Hebrew letters embroidered on the garment as if it were not night—the darkest
night of his life.

Tears stung his eyes. He quietly tried to recite the Amidah:

> *"'Look . . . upon me . . . in my suffering. Fight . . . my struggles.*
> *Redeem me speedily, for Thy name's sake.'"*

He lowered his head and wept in grief. He had failed. For the love of
a woman he had failed his God and his people. He knew. He would not
serve God in this place. Not here in the shadow of Solomon's wall. He
did not know the One whom he longed to serve. He wanted to know
God, but God was far away tonight. Victoria was real to him. He loved
her.

Forgive my sin against You, I pray, if You can hear me! Forgive me. I can-
not be a rabbi. I cannot serve You in this place.

Eli cried out in physical anguish at this grief. He dropped to his knees
before the flickering lamps, and his sorrow was lost in the shadows of
the cupola.

It is time," Hitler said to Himmler over lunch, "for another demonstration." He toyed with his plate of steamed vegetables as he considered the upcoming anniversary of the Nazi Party's attempted coup of the German government in 1923. That event, celebrated each November, had ended with several of the old-guard Nazis dead and Hitler himself in jail. He had written *Mein Kampf* while in prison, and so counted the time of his isolation as a great advantage for the principles of the Aryan race. This year he decided that the occasion needed an extra touch of violence, something to show the world how far the German people had progressed beneath his guidance. For weeks he had pondered the problem. He had set his Gestapo chief to work on a solution.

"Only a spark will turn a forest into an inferno, mein Führer," Himmler said obligingly.

"And who will strike the match?"

"There is a Jewish boy in Paris. Herschel Grynspan. You remember the name?"

"Ah yes." Hitler chuckled. "The one Hans Schumann used when he killed the French agent. What was the name? Le Morthomme, was it not? The Dead Man. Yes. I recall the incident quite well. The Jew Grynspan was given a gun that he did not know how to fire. He was put on the trail of Thomas von Kleistmann. Hans followed after him with a weapon he then used to shoot the Frenchman."

"Quite efficient. Grynspan himself believed that he had murdered the old man. Hans was able to simply walk away while the boy ran like an assassin and the French agent quietly bled to death." Himmler dabbed the corners of his mouth, then took another bite of cabbage as the Führer chewed on the smoothness of that Gestapo action.

"And where is the Jew now?"

"In hiding. The French officials as well as the British investigated the case. Witnesses reported that the old bookseller seemed to see someone else in the crowd. That there may have been a second shot a fraction after the first was fired. All is speculation, of course, and they are quite unsure who killed Le Morthomme." Himmler folded his napkin and sat back, satisfied. "Hans has remained close to the boy. Hans moves easily among the Jewish population of Paris. He reports now that young Grynspan is more than half mad. Hans has fed him daily on reports of actions against Jews until the mind of Herschel Grynspan is consumed with hatred. His parents were among those deported to Poland."

"Good." The Führer was satisfied. "Then we will arrange a little something to spur him on, Heinrich." Hitler's brow furrowed in thought.

Himmler nodded once. "We should not let this drag on much longer, however. Hans reports that young Grynspan talks of suicide daily now. Hans is afraid he will find him dangling from a rafter before we can find further use for him."

"That would be a pity. To lose such a carefully nurtured assassin at the moment before he can be put to use. Well then, issue the orders."

"Who will be the martyr to our great cause, mein Führer?"

Hitler closed his eyes in deep consideration of who might be the target of the Jewish bullet. "What was Commander Vargen's conclusion about Ernst vom Rath?"

"He is still under suspicion. He was closest to Thomas von Kleistmann among the embassy staff."

Hitler cleared his throat. A decision was imminent. "Vom Rath comes from a good German family?"

"Impeccable."

"His father is of the aristocracy?"

Himmler was always amazed by the details the Führer was able to remember. "Of the purest Aryan bloodlines."

Hitler smiled. "And yet his son may be a traitor." He shrugged. "We should make young vom Rath a national hero before he disgraces his family and betrays his Fatherland, Himmler. I think Ernst vom Rath will serve us better dead than he has served us alive."

Hans had been late in coming with food for Herschel this afternoon. There was a dance tonight, so Hans had left the attic after only a few minutes.

Herschel was alone with the radio. Rain thumped hard on the roof as the roar of cheering Nazis filled the room. Hitler had spoken, and once again the people of the Reich raised their voices in support of all he said. Had any of those among the audience been there when Herschel's family had been driven across the German border into Poland? Had any one of them laid the lash on the back of Herschel's father or pushed his mother into the mud?

Such images first made him angry; then they overwhelmed him with despair. What could he do about any of it? Who was he? *Just another Jew.* In Germany, if he opened his mouth to speak out, the Hitler Youth would throw him to the ground and stuff his mouth with human excrement. Herschel had seen it with his own eyes, watched his friend and neighbor choke and vomit as the strutting members of the Hitler Youth had laughed and beaten him.

One Jew's protest meant nothing, Herschel knew. He could call a newspaper and say, "My family was deported by the Germans! They have nothing left! Everything was taken!" But if Herschel said these things, the newsmen would ask him who he was and where he was and where he was from, and then he, too, would be deported from France.

Martial music blared over the radio. The voice of German Propaganda Minister Goebbels announced that the speech of the German leader would be reprinted in its entirety in tomorrow's paper. Hitler had a voice; the whole world listened and trembled. He commanded persecution of the innocent, and the world fell silent for fear of answering that all-powerful voice!

Herschel stood wearily, bumping his head on the lightbulb that hung from the ceiling. He lifted the mattress of his cot and stared at the rope supports across the frame. He looked from the ropes to the rafters. It would be so easy . . . so easy to end his life tonight. He had no wish to go on living in such a world. If he killed himself, perhaps his voice, his final statement, might be heard as well.

He knelt beside the bed and began to unknot the rope, loosening it from the frame. Threading it through the wood and then through the cross-weave of ropes, he discovered that there was plenty for a hanging. Herschel looked into the shadows of the rafters. He pitied Hans. It would be a terrible thing for Hans to find him strung up beside the lightbulb. Herschel wondered if he should turn out the light before he put his neck through the loop. Or would it be more frightening for Hans to reach for the light and find Herschel instead?

He sat on an upturned wooden box and began to write notes of farewell. One to Hans. One to his uncle. One to his parents. And the last one to the silent world. Yes. At least death would give him one moment to be heard!

He heard the tramp of Hans' feet on the steps below. Quickly he hid the finished letters beneath clean paper. He could not let his friend know his intent. Hans would try to talk him out of it.

"Hey, Herschel!" Hans cried, poking his head through the trapdoor. "I brought you some . . ." His smile faded. He eyed the loose rope lying over the wooden bed frame, then looked at Herschel. "I brought you this," he remarked flatly, holding up a piece of chocolate cake. "And I see you have been busy." He entered the attic and towered over Herschel.

"I . . . the rope support broke. I was just—"

"You were just lying." Hans set the cake down. "Going to leave me, eh? Leave me to find you and then to explain what you were doing here? How I hid you?" Hans was angry.

"What is the use?" Herschel hung his head in his hands. "How else can I make a statement?"

"You are a coward!" Hans spat. "Who do you think will care if you die? There have been hundreds of suicides in Vienna. Thousands of Jews. And who cares, eh? You are going to be just another Jew, buried in a pauper's grave." Hans picked up the blank sheets of paper as if he knew there were notes written beneath them.

Herschel looked away dully as Hans read the first one. "'Thank you for all you have done!' Ha!" Hans scoffed. "You think anyone will care? Why not end your life doing something worthwhile, Herschel? Have you forgotten what you said? To kill a Nazi! Now *there* is a goal! And not just anyone—someone the Nazis care about! Kill one of their own, Herschel, and then they will listen to you! Have you forgotten?"

Hans Schumann's eyes blazed as he spoke, and Herschel hung his head in shame. Perhaps Hans was right. Suicide was stupid, futile, and selfish.

"You took my gun away. You sold it to feed me. Or so you said. How can I kill a Nazi? I have to untie my own bed to get enough rope to hang myself! You think I have not thought of how good revenge would feel?"

"If you kill yourself, Hitler will rejoice that another Jew is out of the way. So make them grieve in Berlin. Steal the laughter from their lips as they steal ours. Steal a Nazi life as they take thousands of Jewish lives. Make them grieve, Herschel, and they will hear you!"

"How?"

"I will help you if you mean it."

Herschel leaned forward, begging for that help. "*Yes!* Tell me *how!*"

Ernst vom Rath could not close his eyes without seeing Thomas' broken body before him. The sound of an automobile backfire outside the Paris Embassy made him jump, spilling coffee at the breakfast table.

Other members of the embassy staff eyed him with curiosity, perhaps suspicion. Obviously, whatever Ernst had witnessed in Berlin had left him shaken and nervous. Had he been involved with the escape of Thomas von Kleistmann, after all? Every glance seemed to ask that question. Was Ernst a part of some anti-Nazi undercurrent, in spite of his denials?

Ernst found himself raising his hand in the Heil Hitler salute with an added gusto these days. At times when his own voice echoed in the vast marble halls, he felt that perhaps he was overdoing his pretended loyalty. But the pretense was inspired by fear, by the vivid and horrible tableau of Thomas pleading for death on the floor of the Gestapo building.

This afternoon a new Abwehr officer was introduced to the staff as the replacement for von Kleistmann. This fellow was of powerful build with stronger Aryan characteristics than his unfortunate predecessor. Fritz Konkel was younger than Thomas had been. Only twenty, he had distinguished himself as a group leader in the early days of the Hitler Youth. He had learned to march and drill with a burnished shovel over his shoulder. Blond, tanned, muscled, young Konkel had once been chosen by the Führer himself from a line of other young recruits. "Here is the ideal of the Aryan race," the Führer had remarked. "It is specimens like this that we should send abroad as representatives of our race!"

Rumor held that Hitler himself had chosen this officer for duty in the Paris Embassy. He had overridden the selection of Abwehr Chief Admiral Canaris with a strong warning: "You chose the traitor Thomas von Kleistmann for the Paris Embassy, did you not? This time I shall trust no one but myself for such an appointment."

As the new man was introduced to each member of the staff, Ernst found himself perspiring. The radiators hissed behind him. As he shook the hand of the Nazi officer, Ernst mopped his brow and blamed the flush of his face on the heating system.

Konkel flashed an arrogant smile. "You do not know heat, Herr Secretary vom Rath, until you have stood in formation for hours in the sun and then looked into the eyes of our Führer."

If Thomas had been alive to hear such a comment, no doubt he and Ernst would have secretly ridiculed the young officer's devotion to sweat and duty and der Führer. But Thomas was not alive. Ernst was alone among the embassy staff in his loathing of such foolishness.

He managed a smile. "No doubt if the Führer were here at the Paris Embassy, we would not need radiators to make us sweat," he mumbled. A foolish thing to say. "His . . . personal warmth . . . would be sufficient, ja, Officer Konkel?" This was a nice recovery. Ernst had managed to put the ball back into Konkel's court.

"That is true," Konkel replied in the only way he could. This handsome Aryan god was strong and devoted, but not clever. His dullness, at least, was a consolation for Ernst.

Konkel proceeded down the line of introductions and then turned as the ambassador clapped him on the back and announced, "Officer Konkel has been personally selected to manage the continuing investigation of the traitor von Kleistmann and his activities here in Paris. I have been instructed by the Führer himself that every staff member is to show Officer Konkel the utmost cooperation in his duties. Some things are known, of course, from the confession given by von Kleistmann before his execution."

Ernst blinked. All other words faded from his hearing. *What confession? Had Thomas made some confession? Whose names were mentioned in some moment of weakness when the torture became unbearable?* Ernst pulled himself back to the droning voice of the ambassador.

"Of course, the unquestioned loyalty of each remaining member of this staff has been checked and rechecked. That is not at issue here. What is requested is even the smallest item of information that might have been overlooked. A name or place Thomas von Kleistmann might have mentioned in passing."

At this, the pretty French maid from the German-speaking province of Alsace raised her hand timidly. Thomas had spent time with this witless woman. He had wooed her, and some whispered that she had unlocked his door on the evening of his escape.

Office Konkel eyed her with the same sort of interest that Thomas had shown. He smiled. Raised an eyebrow. He strolled easily toward her. "What is it, Fräulein?

She blushed, enjoying the gaze of this handsome replacement. "*Bitte*, Officer Konkel . . . Thomas . . . er . . . Officer von Kleistmann once wrote a letter to a woman in London. He burned it. I saw its remains in the ashtray in his room."

Konkel clasped his hands behind his back. He rocked on his toes and eyed the woman with a different sort of interest. "You perform your duties quite thoroughly, Fräulein." He smiled. "I shall remember not to leave correspondence where you might come across it."

A twittering of nervous laughter filtered through the group. Everyone knew she and Thomas had occasionally been lovers. The motivation of her jealous curiosity was evident to everyone but Konkel. "I-I thought you should know," she stammered, flushing with embarrassment. "I thought—"

"Why did you not mention this sooner?"

"I only just thought of it this morning. Preparing your room. It was *his* room and I . . . only just remembered it."

"A woman in London?" Konkel frowned thoughtfully over the top of her maid's cap. "The name was Elisa?"

She nodded excitedly. "Yes. Yes. That was it!"

"Ah." Konkel nodded and grinned. This was not news. This was nothing *they* did not know. "Yes. Thank you, Fräulein. We are aware of this . . . relationship. Quite aware." He swept his hand over the group. "But these details are the sort we are looking for. Things that will help us piece together the puzzle and trace the line to its conclusion. Yes. It is confirmation. And if any of you has such a small incident that you think might assist, the Reich will be grateful, of course."

Ernst's mind went wild with thoughts of all the hints he might have left inadvertently. Would some insignificant word or glance between him and Thomas be remembered and traced? Had Thomas told Elisa about his comrade in the Paris Embassy? If she were captured and tortured, certainly she would not have the strength to remain silent as Thomas had . . . as *they* said he had!

Ernst felt ill. He wondered if anyone noticed the way the blood drained from his face. Was he under suspicion, in spite of assurances by the Berlin Gestapo? In spite of the fact that he had taken the gun from the hand of Vargen and . . .

The ambassador was speaking again, smiling pleasantly, patting the new officer on his back. "We are quite sure that all this unpleasantness will soon be behind us. Forgotten and done with. Then we may all settle in again to our duties for the Fatherland here in France."

Haggard. That was the word Leah would use for Eli Sachar as he took a seat on a packing crate and stared mournfully into his chipped china coffee cup.

"I do not mean to intrude," he said, mindful that arriving at dawn on the doorstep of a just-married couple was an intrusion. "But I have not slept all night."

Shimon sat shirtless across from him and pulled on his socks. "Neither did we," he mumbled in German with a quick look at Leah. She was dressed, but she stood making an irritated face behind Eli's back.

She shrugged. This was not *really* their honeymoon, after all. And the man looked as if he were near death. So she had offered him a cup of coffee on the condition that he would go get the water and give them five minutes to pull on something. Here sat Eli, not wanting to intrude, but . . .

"Your wedding," Eli said through a rusty sounding voice, "was so beautiful. I saw you together last night, and I knew that . . . I cannot . . . that no rabbi will . . . that Victoria and I . . ." He dissolved into tears.

It was embarrassing for Shimon to watch him weep. Leah was instantly ashamed that she had resented his being here when he was in such pain.

Shimon grimaced and glanced nervously at Leah. So? Would she help, already? Say something? Shimon was a touch hung over, and this was too much at 6:15 in the morning. He whacked Eli on his arm. "Pull yourself together, man! Are you drunk? Finish your sentence!" he said gruffly.

Leah started to protest Shimon's roughness, but then she saw that Eli responded instantly with renewed composure.

"Yes. Yes. You are right. I am acting like a . . . you see . . . I told my parents about *us*. Me and Victoria. Of course I will never be a rabbi if I marry her, even if she converts, because it is forbidden for a cohen to marry a proselyte. You see?"

Shimon nodded, a broad *aha* nod. "I had forgotten that one. Yes. Well." Maybe the man had reason to weep. Shimon became more gentle. "So. Have you decided not to marry her, then?"

"What?" Eli sounded irritated. "*No!*" He looked insulted. "It is just that I think . . . we should not wait. There is no rabbi in the entire Old City who would marry us regardless of whether I leave the Yeshiva. And the women were talking . . . there are rumors that you are . . . maybe friends with the English priest at Christ Church? He brought you here, *nu*?"

Leah ran a brush through her hair and walked toward him. "Eli," she said gently, "Reverend Robbins will not perform the ceremony for you and Victoria unless both of you are Christians. At least I think that is the way it works." She bit her lip. "This is very serious business. More than marriage. More than leaving Yeshiva. More than disregarding the wishes of your family." She reached out to touch his hand briefly. "You cannot deny your faith!"

His chin went up defiantly. "But *you* did! I heard what you said about Jesus, the Christ of the goyim, on the night of your concert!" His tone was angry, accusing.

Leah sat down beside Shimon and fixed her clear brown eyes on Eli. "You did not hear me if you think that we have in any way denied our faith as Jews or our heritage."

Shimon interjected, "Hear me now, Eli. Leah and I believe that Jesus is the Messiah of Israel, the Holy One we watch for and pray will come to redeem His people Israel! First He came to redeem us individually, as the prophet Isaiah wrote in the fifty-third chapter. Jesus died for our sins. The Lamb of sacrifice given by God for our sakes. But He will come again as King to redeem the nation Israel. It is written, and we are seeing the beginning of the fulfillment."

Eli frowned, as if a thousand arguments filled his mind. "Christians have slaughtered Jews in the name of Jesus for centuries!" His voice was bitter with the truth of this.

"Those who have done these things have never known *Him*," Shimon answered quietly. "Many who call themselves by Christ's name worship a false Christ created by Evil to serve Evil. The real Jesus said that this would happen."

As Leah prayed for the right words to speak, a thought came to her clearly. "Eli, suppose I say I am a disciple of Eli Sachar, and I take a gun and go into the marketplace and find a baby who is in the arms of its Muslim mother. Then I point the gun at the child and say, 'You are a Muslim. Eli Sachar is a Jew. In the name of Eli Sachar I am going to kill you!' And then I murder that child in your name."

"Never!" cried Eli.

Leah and Shimon exchanged looks. "Well, then? How must the Lord feel when the name of the Holy One of Israel is used so wickedly?"

"But . . . is this a *different* Jesus that you speak of?" Eli blinked at them as if they spoke a foreign language. "Different from the one whose name the goyim invoked as they slaughtered us over the centuries? as they murder us now in Germany?"

"Our Lord Jesus is as different from that false Christ as the bright sun is different from blackest night!"

"Tell me plainly *what* Jesus you mean? How can you say that name beside the word *Messiah*?" Eli looked startled at these words. He ran his hands through his hair, and Leah noticed he was not wearing his yarmulke. She took his cold cup of coffee from the crate and warmed it with a drop from the coffeepot. She gently urged the cup back into his hands and he took a cautious sip.

Shimon began again carefully to explain what he knew as truth. "To cut off the real, historical Jesus from the name *Messiah*, *Holy One of Israel*, *Redeemer*, and *Lord* . . . this is the greatest blasphemy. Many Gentiles who call themselves Christians commit this blasphemy every day. I have felt their hatred." Shimon turned slightly to reveal the scars on his back and shoulder. "I have felt their lash and heard their curses. Seen them destroy others in the name of their false Christ." A strange smile played on Shimon's lips. "They called me Christ-killer even while they were killing innocent children! And inside my heart I heard the voice of the Lord whisper, *It is they who killed Me!*"

He paused and looked deeply into Eli's eyes. "If there is any victory that causes Evil to rejoice, it is to hide our Messiah from us by distortion, brutality, and false doctrine."

Eli's face filled with a hunger to understand. Could it be that Jesus approved of the mercy and truth spoken of in the Torah? Then this was a very different Jesus indeed than the one he imagined!

Shimon reached around to retrieve his Bible. "Through evil men, Satan himself has twisted the Holy Word of God until Jesus is made to appear to be everything we fear. To keep a son of the Covenant from recognizing the Messiah is a great victory against God for Satan, you see. Jesus was a Jew, descended from King David just as our prophets foretold. Put away the Gentile church and Gentile religion and persecution. Empty your mind of their lies and darkness. You must meet Jesus first through the prophets, Eli, and then look at His life! Come to Him as a *Jew*, for the sake of your eternal soul! Face-to-face you must look at the real Jesus, and then you must choose to deny Him or believe Him."

27

Apostasy

His arms piled high with volumes of rabbinical commentary on the book of Isaiah, Eli cautiously climbed the stairs of the Sachar apartment. He kicked the door in an awkward knock. His mother threw open the door. Her face displayed a range of emotion beginning with sullenness, changing rapidly to surprise, and finally relief as she called out, "He is home! Eli is home! God be thanked! And his arms are full of books!"

Eli entered the front room as Hermann peered around the corner from the kitchen. "What's all this?" he asked gruffly, but the relief was also evident in his eyes.

"Books from the Yeshiva library," Eli said as though nothing else needed discussion. True to his vow, he would not mention Victoria's name again to his parents. "I have met an apostate and a liar here in the Quarter, and I will prove his argument false through the words of the ancients."

Ida began to weep and mutter her thankfulness to the heavens. "You see! You see what a rabbi he will be! He is done with this foolishness! *Oy!* It is all over, Hermann. Our son is back home."

"So leave him alone, already!" Hermann Sachar ducked back into the kitchen with a gesture that seemed to say, "*I knew Eli was no fool.*" He was certain the boy would see reason.

Eli did not tell them that this had nothing to do with what he had decided about Victoria. They would know soon enough. Why make things harder? He was angry at what Shimon and Leah had told him. Their gross misinterpretation of the Holy Scripture angered him and challenged his years of education. He had pulled every book and commentary on Isaiah off the shelves of the Yeshiva. In this matter of Jesus, he would not take the word of a Jew from Vienna. A musician from Austria—what could he know?

Throughout the afternoon, Eli studied the sources he spread across the floor of his bedroom. His mother brought him a food tray and left it beside his bed without a word. She did not wish to disturb the study of her son the rabbi. And he did not notice when she entered and when she left as he turned page after page of two dozen volumes.

Moshe finally broke the silence in a tone of derision. "Well, as they say in the world of the goyim, the prodigal has come home, eh?"

Eli looked up at Moshe. He had not understood the jibe. "What? Ah, Moshe. Shalom."

The food tray was untouched. Moshe picked up half a sandwich. "Do you mind?"

"No. I was just studying." Eli wiped his eyes. How different the world looked to him.

"So, you have made your choice." Moshe flopped down on his bed and bit into the sandwich. "Books over true love, *nu*?"

Eli looked down at the yellowed pages of a commentary and then back into the smirking face of his brother. "Sometimes, Moshe, there is more passion and love in the pages of a book." He frowned. "And all the answers are there. Truth."

"Well, forgive me. I am from the real world, you know, where love and truth are very rare these days." He seemed almost angry. "Where Arabs blow up Englishmen, and Englishmen blow apart their promises of a Jewish homeland. And where Jews, even a Jew I thought more sensible than the rest, are afraid to love Arabs for fear of what might be said."

Eli focused on the book. "Be quiet, Moshe," he said wearily. "You do not know."

"I know enough," Moshe said though his sandwich. "I am going to England. You be a rabbi. Victoria will marry some Bedouin camel driver, and the world will be a better place for it!"

"Be quiet," Eli said again more wearily. He had not even thought of all that for hours.

"So where is all the passion and love for you, Eli? My big brother. How will you embrace a book at night and call it by her name? What has made you so happy tonight?" Moshe snatched the reference volume from in front of Eli. He held it up to the light and began to read. "Targum Jonathan on Isaiah fifty-three! Ho! Eli, what love! What truth and light!" He threw the book back on the bed in disgust. "May you be eternally happy with your books, Eli." He reached up and snapped off the light as if to make one final gesture of his contempt.

Eli was too exhausted to argue or explain. Indeed, this reference and several others he had found did change everything for him. He sat in the dark on his cluttered bed for a long time as Moshe kicked off his shoes and lay down to sleep without another word.

Eli did not resent his brother's derision. He expected nothing less. Moshe could not understand. Perhaps Eli would have a chance to explain to him later. Yes. When it was all over Eli would sit him down and explain. Tonight Eli had found truth. And everything was different, even his love for Victoria.

Etta held tightly to baby Yacov as they hurried through the crowded streets of Catholic Warsaw.

"Walk faster, children!" she called over her shoulder to Rachel, David, and Samuel. "We will miss our appointment."

Today's appointment was with a photographer who promised quick passport photos at a reasonable price. It was worth venturing beyond the borders of Jewish Warsaw for such a bargain, Etta reasoned. Besides, this way Aaron would not know she was sending birth certificates and photos to her father in Jerusalem in the hope that her own passport might be renewed in the British Mandate and new British passports acquired for her children.

Aaron would not have consented. So Etta had taken this matter into her own hands . . . just in case.

"How much farther, Mama?" complained Samuel.

"Hush," Rachel demanded in a frightened voice. Two young men leaning against a storefront eyed the little entourage with cruel amusement. They stepped away from the wall and followed after.

"Look! The Christ-killers have come out of their caves today!"

"Ignore them, children," Etta commanded in Yiddish as her back stiffened with fear. She held the baby closer and reached around to pull the other three children in front of her.

"Listen to this, Wochek! The Jewish bitch barks to her litter in Yiddish so we cannot understand!" taunted one of the men.

"She looks very rich, Wolfgang," the second muttered in German. "How do you think she gets her money? You think she sells herself to Poles, eh?"

Etta felt herself color with shame at the man's remark. Her heart began to pound with fear. They could hurt her. Hurt her children and no one would stop them. Such things had been done before. Why had she left the ghetto? *For a few pennies! To keep the passport photos a secret from Aaron! God, forgive me! Help me!*

"Maybe she will give us a free sample, Wochek. You think so?"

"Or maybe she will pay us!" The voice was exultant at the idea.

Other Poles on the sidewalk turned to look and smile with amusement. A few encouraged the young men.

Etta could see that Rachel had grown pale with fear. The faces of the boys displayed a confused sort of anger.

A still-burning cigarette butt was tossed at Etta's face. She ducked and shielded the baby. Rachel turned, her bright blue eyes wide with terror. Walking just behind their two tormenters was the man she had seen in Muranow Square—the watcher! He, too, was smiling. His eyes narrowed with cold hatred.

"Ah, leave them alone!" shouted a thick-framed grandmother walking the other way.

That was all the support they received from the onlookers. Etta walked faster until she was almost running, pushing the children along in front. The long strides of the young men did not seem to be affected by her fearful pace. Still they jeered and mocked Etta. A hand reached out to snag the hem of her dress and pull it up.

Etta cried out and whirled around. The baby began to wail.

"Leave us alone!" Etta demanded.

In response, the men laughed louder and groped for her skirt again.

"Someone help my mother!" Rachel shouted. *"Please!"*

"Just a little taste, eh? I have never had kosher meat!" The amusement turned into a leer. This was no longer a game.

Tears stung Etta's eyes. She tried to speak, but fear choked her as a crowd of men now encircled her on the sidewalk, cutting her off from Rachel and David and Samuel as they screamed for her. Yacov still cried his innocent protest.

The two men walked nearer. Their intent was evident in their eyes. Two other young men stepped between them. "When you are finished with her, I want a turn."

"Don't . . . please!" Etta begged. "Don't hurt my little one!"

The watcher spoke. "Smash the little pig on the sidewalk! The Germans sent us twelve thousand Jews! What do we need with another one?"

The crowd of men grew silent—the silence of anticipation. Who would reach out first? From the outer ring of the growing circle, Etta could hear the weeping voices of her children calling for her. She shielded Yacov, covering his head with her hands. They would not tear him from her; she would die first! Silently she breathed the prayer of the dying. Small bits of the holy words came to her mind as she fought against the panic. *O Israel . . . the Lord . . . our God is . . . where is the Lord?*

The young men reached out as if they possessed one mind. They took her by each arm. She struggled and screamed and fought for her baby.

Two more strong men grasped her ankles and lifted her kicking from the ground. They held her high above their heads like a sacrifice. The crowd cheered her anguish as she shouted to her children, *"Run! Run!"*

She arched her back as she fought against the iron grip of her attackers. In her wild struggle she could see that traffic still moved in the street as people gawked from the opposite sidewalk.

The tiny infant in her arms bleated as she squeezed him too tightly in her fight to hold him. The crowd of Poles roared at the sight of the Jewish woman's struggle. Legs kicking. Pretty head thrown back in a scream. And then the roar began to fade. Still she fought! She shouted out against her attackers as they held her high above their heads. But something changed. First to the right, and then to the left, the circle of men broke and moved back. The laughter died, leaving only those who grasped her. Once again it was their strength against hers. Her voice against theirs. Once again she could make out the sobs of Rachel, David, and Samuel. And then one authoritative male voice cut through the last remnants of her torture.

"Put the woman down! I said . . . on pain of excommunication . . . put the woman down!"

The laughter stilled as she was lowered, weeping, to the sidewalk. A tiny Catholic priest, no more than five feet tall, glared threateningly up at the men who had started it all. At the break in the crowd, the children ran to embrace their unsteady mother. The voice of the baby was hoarse now from his shrieks through the ordeal. Etta could not stop crying. The tears flowed silently down her flushed cheeks.

"We were just having fun with this Jewess, Father," protested the first young man as the onlookers disappeared.

The priest slapped the man hard across the face. He reached up and clutched the collar of the second strong young brute, shaking him as if he were a small child.

"You are animals!" hissed the priest, who seemed very small next to the men. "You call yourselves Catholics!" He raised his voice to include the spectators who remained sheepishly looking on from the fringes. Even those few backed away, stepping on toes, bumping into the crowd gathered behind them. "Call on the mercy of Almighty God, for He is your judge in this!" His eyes burned with rage. He slapped the face of the second man with the back of his hand, then shoved him away. "I know you both," the priest whispered threateningly.

"Oh, Mama!" Rachel cried, holding Etta around her waist. "I want to go home!"

Etta could only nod. They had spent such a long time getting dressed up for the pictures. Now Etta's hair hung down and Rachel's bows were untied. The boys' coats and ties were askew.

The fierceness of the priest changed to calm and gentle concern as he turned his attention to Etta and the children. "Are you all right, daughter?"

Etta shook her head. No, she was not all right. But she was alive. The baby was alive.

"Do I need to take you to a hospital?" the priest asked.

Etta closed her eyes, tying to control the weeping. She could not speak. Rachel replied for her. "Our doctor," Rachel said boldly. She was angry—anger felt better than fear. "Herr Doktor Letzno is our doctor. He lives on Dzika Street. Yes. You may take my mother there."

The priest eyed the young woman with a hint of respect. She had taken charge. This was good. She was a younger version of her mother. Very beautiful, and very lucky that the men had not tried to rape her as well.

"My car is there." He pointed to a small black sedan at the curb. There was never a question that they might refuse to ride in an automobile owned by the Catholic church. Rachel shuddered as she stepped in after Etta. They could not go home like this. Dr. Letzno would be their refuge for a while.

Two plainclothes members of the Warsaw police sat smug and patronizing in the wingback chairs of Eduard Letzno's office. Etta faced them. She looked very alone and small on the wide leather sofa. Eduard sat at his desk. He stared at his hands in anguish. He was sorry now that he had called the police. Was he still so naive as to think that there was a shred of justice remaining in Poland for a Jew, whether a man or woman?

"*You* say," began the thick, red-faced officer as he scanned his notes, "that you were going to a photographer?"

Etta bit her lip and twisted the handkerchief into knots. "Yes. As I told you, we had an appointment." Words came with difficulty.

"And why did you venture out of your own community for a photograph, eh? There are competent Jewish photographers."

Etta glanced at Eduard. Should she tell them that she wanted passport photos? Eduard did not help her in this matter. He simply stared darkly at his clasped hands. "I . . . heard this fellow Wolenski was very good and not expensive."

The officer flipped a page over the back of his clipboard. "Wolenski is

known to us police." He paused. His eyes became hard. "He publishes
. . . certain kinds of photographs. Black market. Obscene photographs."

Etta drew back as if she had been slapped. "But no! Passport photos—he advertises quick work."

The officer smiled. *So the Jewess wanted passport photos.* "We will check
with Wolenski." His words were clipped, officious. "And so, *you* say you
were simply walking along and—"

"But I told you—" Etta's face flushed with shame—"they began to
make . . . remarks. And then . . . advances."

The chin of the officer went up as if to dispute her. "The young men
in question reported the incident to us differently."

Eduard looked up, startled by these words. "They came to you?"

"Immediately," the officer replied. "The . . . incident . . . frightened
them. They say this woman is the one who began it."

"What?" Etta gasped. Again her eyes filled with tears.

"You are surprised?" The narrow grin of the officer was like the leers
she had seen on the faces of the attackers.

"But I . . . w-why would I?" she stammered.

"They were under the impression that you are . . . a prostitute." The
grin remained unchanged.

"But . . ." Etta could not speak. She caught Eduard's eyes.

His dark expression became instantly angry. "Frau Lubetkin is the
wife of a rabbi," he said evenly.

"What has that to do with the charge, Doktor Letzno?" The officer
shrugged.

"It was just as I have told you!" Etta cried.

"We have witnesses who say differently. The two men whom you first
solicited on the street. And then there are many others who will testify . . .

"But the priest! He stopped them! He will tell you!" Etta clenched
her fists in anger and humiliation.

"The priest stopped the little prank. He brought you here. He says he
did not realize that you are a prostitute, or he might have let the men
teach you a lesson." He cocked an eyebrow. "So much for the priest."

"Eduard!" Etta wept openly as she looked to him for some help
against this insanity. How could they say such things? How could they
look at her and think such things?

"Frau Lubetkin is a devoted mother and—" Eduard's voice threatened to lose control.

"Many prostitutes are good mothers," said the officer, smiling. "Soliciting in Warsaw is against the law. We could put you in prison. There
are fifty men who will testify in court as to what you are and what you
were doing."

"But *they* attacked *me*! They threatened the life of my baby!"

"All a part of the sport. Jewish prostitutes should service their own kind. There are hotels near Muranow Square, are there not?"

The doctor rose from behind his desk. He moved to stand between the gendarme and Etta, who now sobbed uncontrollably. The officer smiled up at him. Eduard did not strike the man, although it was an effort to restrain himself.

Eduard's words came in a hoarse croak. "You have made your point," he managed to whisper. "No need to insult Frau Lubetkin or her family further."

"Insult?" The officer glanced innocently at his taciturn partner. Both men were amused with their game of baiting. "I am simply warning this woman that if she ever solicits in the Catholic section of the city again, I shall personally arrest her. We can see to it she is in prison for three years at the least." He leaned around Eduard and fixed his steely gaze on Etta. "Do you understand, madame? Your children will be quite changed when you get out of jail. Much older. The littlest bastard will not remember you."

"Enough!" Eduard shouted. He did not touch the vile man in front of him, lest he also be thrown into prison.

"Remember you are leaving Poland, Doktor Letzno," menaced the second officer. "Unless you violate the law. Or perhaps strike a Warsaw gendarme. You know how difficult it is to leave the country or obtain a passport if you have a police record." At this, the man looked expectantly at Etta. Had she heard his threat? *No passport with a police record. No escape to Palestine, even for the wife of a rabbi.* "You do understand, do you not?"

Eduard stepped back. Yes, he understood. Etta was too broken to comprehend this evil game, but Eduard understood perfectly what they were after.

He cleared his throat and looked over their heads, through the window where a few snowflakes drifted down. These men had not spoken with the attackers. Nor had they contacted the priest. The photographer was a just a photographer. "How much do you want?" Eduard asked.

The officers exchanged glances as if such a thought had never entered their minds. "There are fines, of course. Public disturbances. Soliciting openly . . ."

"There will be no more need of fabricated charges. We all know you can say what you like. You can find witnesses who are not witnesses and they will say what you tell them. I am a realist. Frau Lubetkin is innocent . . . the kind of innocence men like you will not understand. And so, it is time to speak openly. What is your price for leaving her alone?"

28
The Last Waltz

The soft light above the piano shone on Anna's hair. From across the room, Theo closed his eyes to etch this image of her in his mind like a treasured photograph. She played the gentle music of Brahms' Waltz in A flat. She swayed with the music and smiled as though she were dancing. The melody filled the tiny flat with the same elegance and warmth that had once been theirs in Berlin.

Theo knew that the surroundings did not matter. Even playing on a battered old upright piano had not dimmed the brightness of Anna's soul. This melody Theo would take with him; this vision he would cherish.

Outside, a strong wind chilled the city of London, breaking water pipes and sending everyone scrambling for the warmth of a fire. Theo would take his fire with him. Kindled and fueled by moments like these, memories of Anna had kept him warm. When every other image had hardened and died around him, he had stretched out his hands to the face of Anna. Dreams of her had kept him alive. Certainty of her prayers and faithfulness had commanded him to live when it would have been easier to die. And so, once again, he would carry Anna with him in his heart. He would think of her in London, here at the piano, moving to the music of a Brahms waltz.

As if she heard his thoughts, her hands paused in the middle of the melody. Did she feel his eyes loving her? She did not turn around. The wall clock ticked on with the rhythm like a metronome.

"Theo," she asked quietly, "who have they asked to present the plan in Berlin? You did not say."

He did not answer, but continued to gaze at the golden light of her hair.

Her shoulders sagged. "How long will you be gone?" she asked. Her words seemed choked. She would not beg him to stay—would not put her love for him before what she knew *must be*.

He put his strong hands on her shoulders and stooped to kiss her hair. "A short time, they tell me. A few days." His voice sounded light and reassuring in spite of what they both knew. "I will be given a British diplomatic passport. You must not worry."

She nodded and rested her fingers on the ivory keys. What was there to say now? "The Lord will . . . be with you." She began to play again.

Theo sat beside her on the bench. "I have always loved this waltz," he remarked, comforted somehow by her understanding, "loved the way you play it."

She smiled when he looked at her, but tears streaked her face. "We have never danced to it," she managed to whisper.

"Because we hear it only when you play it." He took her hand and stopped the music. Then he lifted her to her feet and pulled her close to him, his cheek against her soft, damp cheek.

She raised her face to his and looked into his eyes—eyes bright with emotion, shining with love forged in the furnace of trials and crafted into an intricate beauty. "Dance with me tonight, Theo," she whispered. "Can you hear it? Can you hear the music? Dance with me, my darling . . ."

Eduard stood framed in the tall window. Beyond him, snowflakes whitewashed Warsaw until it looked clean and beautiful in its baroque splendor. But Eduard and Etta knew what lay beneath that glistening image.

"It is my fault," Eduard said softly. His breath fogged the windowpane. He could not look at Etta. She simply stared at his back in the weary realization of how desperate the situation for Jews in Poland had suddenly become.

"No, Eduard. Silly of me. I wanted only to keep it from Aaron, not let him know about the photos." She brushed her hair from her eyes. "You know how it is in the old neighborhood. Everyone would know . . . passport photos for the rabbi's family. And then the questions."

Eduard gazed at the curtain of snow that seemed to do battle with the black smoke of the chimneys. "I should not have called the police." His voice was filled with self-recrimination. "I had not guessed how corrupt they have become. Three years ago this could not have happened in

Warsaw; before President Pilsudski died, this would not have been toler-
ated!"

He turned to search her face imploringly. "Justice has died in the
hearts of men. You must not stay here, Etta! If such changes have come
to the Poles since the death of one man, what will come to pass in Warsaw in another three years? There is no hand to stop it. With the excep-
tion of one little priest today, the Catholic church would turn its mighty
eyes away from what happened to you."

He shook his head and rubbed a hand over his strained face. "I will
call a photographer to come here immediately to take pictures of you
and the children. We cannot delay in this matter." His eyes scanned the
books of his library as if he was searching for something. "You are right.
The people of your congregation must not know your intent."

Again he fixed his gaze on Etta. "Can you keep all this from Aaron?
He must not know until the passports are an accomplished fact. Then
you will present them to him and tell him what happened to you today."

Etta nodded a difficult assent. "But the children—," she began
doubtfully.

"I will speak to them," Eduard promised grimly. "They will not talk
about this after I explain." He sank down in a wing chair and stretched
his long legs out across the floral carpeting. "Aaron has foolish hope for
the Jews of Poland. And for the Poles." His brow furrowed. "Last week I
stitched up the head of an eight-year-old Jewish child who was beaten
with a metal crucifix because he did not bow his knee to the cross when a
funeral procession passed. Every day there are more incidents. Since the
German deportation, the violence has become more extreme." He did
not add the thought that Etta and the children had been lucky today.
"Now these men have your name. They know you want passports and
exit visas from Poland. They may be back."

Etta visibly paled. "But *why*?"

"More money. Blackmail."

"But you paid them . . . so much, Eduard. And all the money I have
saved is the gold coins I hoped to send to Papa in Jerusalem. In case he
should need them for bribes."

"I will take that to him." He moved to his desk chair and wrote out a
bank draft on his Warsaw account. "I have left this account open so they
will not suspect I am not returning. You must use the money, Etta."

"But Eduard," she protested, "you have paid them so much already.
How can I repay you?"

Eduard seemed not to hear her. He blotted the ink and tore the check
from the book. Then he wrote another and yet another, leaving the dates
blank. The checks lay on his desk. "Do not use them too close together.

Cash them over the next few weeks or months. This will close the account. Hopefully we will have your travel documents in order by then. I will pray that you cash the last check on the day you leave Warsaw forever, Etta—you and the children, and even stubborn Aaron. Perhaps by then he will see that leaving is the only rational course of action."

It was Sunday. Eli walked alone through the crowded streets of the Armenian Quarter toward Christ Church. A stream of Englishmen and their elegant ladies were exiting through the wide iron gates where the Reverend Robbins stood shaking hands, smiling pleasantly in his clerical robes. *He is not the gardener, after all*, thought Eli as he watched the pleasant-faced old man.

But Eli was not disguised today either. He was dressed not in his brother's clothes but in the distinctive garb of the Orthodox.

He wore his black coat, the one he saved for holy days and weddings. The hem of his coat showed the fringes of the garment the Torah commanded the Chosen to wear as a sign of identity. On his head was a black, fur-trimmed shtreimel, no different than a hat one might see on a Jew in Warsaw. In spite of Eli's sandy-colored hair, light brown beard, and pleasant blue eyes, there was no mistaking today that a Jew was walking against the crowd leaving Christ Church, in through the iron gates. He waited beyond the Sunday morning English chatter, until at last, Reverend Robbins raised his head and smiled in kind curiosity in Eli's direction.

Eli stepped forward and extended his hand—a brief and formal handshake. "I have come to discuss an urgent personal matter with you," he said stiffly.

The pastor looked over his shoulder for any stragglers who might overhear such a request. There were none. The congregation had gone to the luncheon buffet at the King David Hotel.

"You are Victoria's . . . friend."

"You have a keen memory."

"She has spoken of you often."

"She has never spoken to me of you," Eli replied, though not unkindly. The news had simply surprised him.

"I knew her mother well before she passed on. A gracious Christian woman. Things might have been very different for Victoria had her mother lived."

Eli was indeed surprised that Reverend Robbins seemed to know so much about Victoria's life. "Yes. Different." There was an awkward pause. What to say?

"Will you join me in my study? Perhaps it would be more suitable for our talk."

Eli followed him through the courtyard to the side of the building. An unmarked wooden door led down a flight of steps to a stone basement beneath the sanctuary. Neither man spoke another word until they were both seated inside a small book-lined room with a high transom window. The pastor clasped his hands on his desk. Eli did not remove his hat in spite of the hatrack by the door. For a moment he faced the pastor without speaking. The old man's eyes seemed to say that he knew already what Eli wanted to say.

"You see," Eli said, "I am a Jew." An obvious statement, but Eli wanted to let this man know that he intended to remain a Jew in spite of what he was about to request.

"And Victoria is Arab. Muslim. A problem for you both."

"You know her well, you say, and I believe you or she would not have wanted to meet me here. She must trust you. And so . . . I trust you."

A nod of thanks. A wave of the finger urging Eli to speak on.

"So, Reverend Robbins." Eli found this more difficult. "I have returned to Christ Church to ask . . . to request your help. You seem to know . . . everything. And so you must know we cannot be married in the Jewish Quarter. Not right now."

"Things are very difficult."

"But we must marry. Things are growing more difficult every day. I am certain that she needs to live beneath my protection."

"And whose protection are you under, Eli?"

"God's protection."

The answer was without hesitation. The firmness of it surprised the old man. "You are not a Christian," he said, as if that was his interpretation of Eli's response.

"And you are not a Jew. But you believe in the Jewish Messiah, as I do. This makes it acceptable to me that you could perform the ceremony for Victoria and me."

The old man's eyebrows arched with astonishment at the reply. "I am not a rabbi—"

"She needs the legal protection of marriage to me. You are authorized to perform the ceremony. Later we will wed in the Old City beneath a canopy after she has taken the appropriate instruction and—"

"She is not a Christian."

"You will tell her about the Messiah. About God's sacrifice of His only Son just as our father Abraham offered Isaac. And she will believe you."

"But . . . how can you know such a thing?"

"Because it is the truth. And Victoria will know that if you explain it correctly. I have searched the ancient references, and it is clear they knew that Isaiah fifty-three spoke of Messiah. Targum Jonathan on Isaiah fifty-three. You know that reference?"

"Why, no . . ."

"Rabbi Jonathan Ben-Uzziel was a disciple of the great Hillel. Surely you know his work?"

"Why, no . . ."

"I will lend you the document, and you will show Victoria and explain to her what it means." Eli felt some irritation at the Protestant clergyman's lack of scholarship in the matter of the Messiah of Israel whom he served.

"Why don't you tell her yourself?"

"I want her to know Him because He is Truth, not because she loves me and I tell her. Women will say and do many things for sake of love. I will teach her other things after we are married."

"You are a confident young man." The pastor leaned forward as if to study Eli in amazement. "And learned."

"Yes," Eli said sadly. "I would have made a good rabbi. But men will give up many things for love, *nu*?"

"Well, I . . . I do not see how I can refuse if Victoria is also . . ."

"Just teach her, and there is no doubt. So. I can offer you some little payment. We cannot delay in our marriage. I request that you keep this matter altogether a secret. Her brothers will kill her if they find out."

"And you as well."

"Maybe even you, Reverend Robbins." A slight smile. "But we are all under God's protection. I will find her a place in the Christian Quarter where she will stay until we find a way to leave Palestine and the Middle East. My brother is going to school in England. Perhaps you will write us a letter of recommendation."

"I would not have thought it," said the pastor dryly.

"What is that?"

"When I first saw you I thought you were a fearful fellow without much . . . what is the word . . . *moxie*."

"Never mind first impressions. I thought you were the gardener."

The last rays of sunlight shone dully on the tarnished green copper dome of L'Opera. On the crown of the cupola, the statue of Apollo played his lyre as he watched the silent intrigues of Paris below.

Horns blaring, taxis rattled past the ornate facade of the building.

"Academie Nationale de Musique," Ernst vom Rath's mother read from the window of their taxi. Her round, pleasant face beamed at the sight of the eight rows of double columns, gilded arches, and colonnades of L'Opera. "The French are *so* . . ." She did not finish her sentence but shifted her attention to her son, who looked away from the building to the rows of restaurants and shops on the other side of the broad avenue. "Ernst—" she patted his hand—"you seem so . . . sullen."

He managed a smile in spite of the resentment he felt at this unannounced visit from his mother and sister. "I wish you had let me know, that is all."

"You sounded so homesick. Lonely." His mother sounded hurt. "We thought you would be glad to see us."

"Glad, yes. But I have no arrangements for you. I . . . I might have gotten tickets for the opera, at least." He did not let them know that to be near this building felt something like standing at the gates of hell itself. It was every reminder of all the things he wanted to forget.

His mother laughed with relief. "Is that all? Well, we have taken care of that already! There will be tickets for the three of us waiting at the hotel concierge's desk. We saw to it in Berlin."

Ernst felt the blood drain from his face. He tried to look pleased. "Ah. Nice. Very . . ."

His mother looked alarmed. She pressed her hand to his forehead. "Ernst. You are not well? Is that it?"

"Tired, Mother. The embassy, you know. So much happening. I am just tired and I have had so much on my mind."

"We have come to help you take your mind off all that. When we saw the postcard, I said to your father, *'He needs a visit to cheer him up, Ernst does!'* And we bought the tickets that same afternoon!" She sighed with contentment. "And we needed a break as well from all the dreary *heiling* of Berlin."

"Mother!" he chided. "You must not—"

"Oh well, not around the embassy, at least, but that is why you are so gloomy. That is why we all are so gloomy. Hermann Göring and his four-year economic plan! Ha! We are ordered to save empty toothpaste tubes for collection. Did you know? They are melting down toothpaste tubes to make their fighter planes! The old elegance of our Germany is gone, I'm afraid, Ernst. But now we are here and we can forget all that for a while, *ja*? No doubt at the opera tonight we will run into all our old friends who had the good sense to leave until *he* is finished with his schemes."

Ernst looked forward at the cabdriver, who just happened at that moment to glance into the rearview mirror. Their eyes caught for an instant, and Ernst was filled with the unreasoning fear that somehow every word his mother had said would get back to Wilhelmstrasse in Berlin. Back to men like Göring and Hitler and . . . Vargen.

Ernst took his mother's gloved hand. She saw the fear in his eyes and immediately felt it too. "Ernst, what is it?" she asked quietly.

He lowered his voice to a whisper. "Not even here. Not even *here* must you say such things, Mother. They are watching . . . everyone."

"I did not mean . . . I would not injure your career or—"

"I am not speaking of my job at the embassy. Mother, you still do not know what they are, what those men are capable of!"

Frau vom Rath studied the face of her son. She brushed back a lock of his hair and then turned toward the opera building as they rounded a corner. Best to talk of light things. Things that did not matter. "Yes. L'Opera. Red silk walls, I remember. We are in the third tier. A box, Ernst. We will be able to see everyone and everyone will see us."

29

No Place to Go

This morning Hans Schumann brought Herschel a stack of outdated copies of the Yiddish daily paper, *Pariser Haint*.

"I thought you would like to read up on all the news," Hans said cheerfully. "These were free, anyway, because they are from last week. The story is so much more complete than just a little word of news on the radio. Of course you want to hear everything about what your family has been through."

At this, Herschel managed a feeble nod. He did not know if he did indeed want the details of his family's torment filled in. He was helpless here in Paris, so impotent against the forces that gripped them. He stared at the stack of newspapers and stood up angrily. "I do not want to read about it."

Hans looked surprised, hurt by the rejection of his helpfulness. "Well, then. As you wish."

"I want to go out," Herschel croaked in a hoarse, desperate voice. "I do not care any longer if they catch me! Let them deport me too!"

"Herschel!" Hans admonished, taking him firmly by the arm. "Have you forgotten? You have things to do! Things to make *them* listen to you! To all of us!"

"I want out!" Herschel tore himself from Schumann's grip, pushed past him, and clattered down the steep stairs to a narrow landing.

Hans called after him. Someone opened a door in the hallway of the rooming house and then closed it again quickly at the sound of Hans shouting down from the attic. "Come back! You have no place to go! Come back here!"

Herschel put his hands over his ears as he charged down two more flight of steps to where the light of day shone through the glass panel of a door.

Herschel had no coat. He slammed the door and ran out into the brisk November wind, but did not feel the cold. He ran along the boulevard, lifting his face to the light. He thought of the streets of German cities. The automobile horns sounded the same. He imagined what he would have done if the Nazis had come for him, if they came for him now in Paris. He would run. They would scream their obscenities at him and shoot their guns, but he would outrun them all and hide. *Yes!* He *must* hide!

He slowed his pace. Hans had not caught up with him. The cold sidewalk was crowded with people who did not see him, did not know why he was running.

He stopped and looked toward the green dome of the great Paris opera house. He remembered music playing in his father's shop and he thought of Elisa Lindheim and her violin. Probably dead, like everyone else in Vienna. Or dying. Or wishing to die.

He turned in the center of the sidewalk like a lost child. Before him was the display window of a gunsmith's shop. Herschel walked forward and leaned his forehead against the glass pane. A display of weapons was laid out on red fabric—large-barrel revolvers and smaller-caliber pistols. Different sizes of bullets down to the short stubby cartridges.

Herschel remembered Thomas von Kleistmann. He thought of the death of the old bookseller. He remembered his own wild firing, and then . . . Herschel frowned. A second gunshot had followed his. Why had he not remembered until now? That other gunshot had crumpled the old man. Then Herschel had run wildly through the bookstalls to escape. He had run and run until he had slammed into Hans and been taken to the attic to hide. And that filthy Nazi von Kleistmann still lived, still strutted in the German Embassy and raised his hand to Heil Hitler and rejoiced at the news of twelve thousand deported to Poland!

Herschel stared at the weapons. He shivered, suddenly aware of the cold. He wanted to go somewhere—maybe to dance with pretty girls at the community center as he had done before. Life had not been so bad. But it was cold now, and he did not have a coat. He walked back along the path to the rooming house where Hans had helped him hide from the immigration people and anyone else who might want to catch him.

Hans was waiting for him in the attic. He was reading the old copies of the newspaper and shaking his head when Herschel returned.

Snow dusted the slate roofs of Warsaw. Wrapped in heavy wool coats and leggings, the Lubetkin family trudged toward the Umschlagplatz, where the great locomotives hissed and shuddered beneath the roofs of the train sheds.

Etta held the baby close against her. The boys' cheeks were red with cold. From behind her muffler, Rachel's breath rose in a steamy vapor as she followed her papa to where Dr. Eduard Letzno waited beside his trunks on the platform.

Aaron raised a mittened hand in greeting. Rachel watched her father's sad eyes as he beheld his friend for possibly the last time.

The two men embraced, clapping each other on the back in a manly, tearless sort of grief.

Good-bye! Was there ever a more difficult word to say? Here in the Warsaw Umschlagplatz, where thousands of good-byes were uttered and millions more were yet to be said, Rachel pitied her father this loss of a true friend. She saw pain in his eyes as Eduard Letzno climbed the steps into his compartment.

"Jerusalem!" Aaron whispered the name like a Shabbat blessing, and Etta thrust a paper-wrapped package into Eduard's hands as the train whistle shrieked and baby Yacov awakened with a startled wail.

"For my father, Eduard!" Etta called through a cupped hand over the din. "Embrace him for us when you see him!"

Eduard held up the package, smiled, and nodded in reply. Yes, he would personally deliver the package to Grandfather. He would embrace the old man for them. *Jerusalem!* he mouthed.

And then as the train chugged and lurched ahead slightly, Eduard Letzno looked over the heads of those who loved him in Warsaw. Those sad, gentle eyes held a moment of recognition, an instant of fear at what he saw.

The train pulled away. He looked at Aaron and then out beyond them. He called something to Aaron, but his words were lost beneath the whistle. He pointed. Aaron looked back, but he saw nothing but masses of people waving and calling out their own sad farewells.

Eduard shouted again! Aaron raised a hand in helplessness. He had not heard. He did not understand.

A minute later the train clacked out of sight, and the crowds of the Umschlagplatz diminished to be replaced by others.

"Two out of three is not so bad," Rabbi Lebowitz said, defending himself against the scowls of the old women in Tipat Chalev soup kitchen.

"What are we to do with them! *Oy gevalt!*" Hannah Cohen pointed an accusing finger to the tables where two dozen Torah schoolboys labored without success over walnuts that were harder than Jerusalem stones!

Hammers raised and crashed down, sending still-intact nuts spinning off dangerously across the room. The wood of tables dented with the blows. When one lucky blow fell hard enough to crack the shell, then the meat of the nut was also smashed into a mere worthless mess.

"Bags of them!" moaned Shoshanna. "Bags and bags and *bags*!"

"Nothing but schlock merchandise!" another woman muttered from inside the kitchen.

"We might have gotten sugar if we had held out," Hannah Cohen said woefully.

This last accusation cut too deeply for the rabbi. As head of the Center for Charitable Distribution of Food, he had done his best. How could he know these English walnuts were of better use as weapons!

A hammer smashed down! A nut squirted out from beneath the steel and hurled toward the disapproving cooks! They squealed and scattered and the nut struck the rabbi on his cheek.

"The final blow," he muttered as the hammer-wielding worker cried out in shame.

"I did not mean to do it, Rabbi Lebowitz! It . . . it was an accident!"

Now all hammers fell silent. Eyes turned in fearful astonishment at the sight of the great Rabbi holding his bruised cheek. The offending walnut ricocheted and tumbled down the basement stairs.

Rabbi Lebowitz opened his mouth. *Calmly. Gently.* These walnuts were fashioned and tempered like steel, but the old rabbi would not curse them. Not out loud, anyway.

"Put away your hammers, my little stonecutters. If the Eternal, blessed be His name forever, wishes for these nuts to nourish us here at Tipat Chalev, then He will have to send us an instrument to crack them for us. True? Of course, true!" Then he turned to Hannah and Shoshanna and said regally, "Still we have milk and cocoa. Two out of three is not such a bad bargain!"

"And this . . . ," Shimon said with a flourish, "will be my finest performance of *The Nutcracker Suite*!"

Before the delighted eyes of a dozen children, Shimon placed a row of walnuts on the wooden table of the mess hall, then raised his cast-encased arm and smashed it down on them.

No one spoke as he smiled slyly and raised his arm to reveal that the nuts had been split perfectly! Shells lay in pieces, while the meat remained intact!

"A-h-h-h-h!" the children proclaimed in chorus. Then, "I told you he could do it!"

"You did not!"

"Yes, I did! Now will you believe me?"

While they argued over his miraculous performance, Shimon handed out the nuts to his audience and emptied his pocket of yet another twelve English walnuts. He lined them up perfectly on the table of Tipat Chalev as the shelled nuts were crammed into watering mouths and eyes turned to watch the plaster cast rise and fall with the precision only a percussionist from Vienna could master.

The crack of nuts brought resounding applause from the Old City children. More o-h-h-hs, and a few oys of amazement echoed from the vaulted ceiling, bringing Leah and the cooks of Tipat Chalev from the kitchen.

"You should see what he can do!" a ten-year-old boy proclaimed to Hannah Cohen.

Proudly Shimon handed out the shelled nuts to the children. He glanced at Leah and winked. Rabbi Lebowitz appeared behind the women and peered over their shoulders as Shimon laid out another row along the crack in the table.

Again the large plaster cast raised up. Two little girls held hands over their ears in anticipation of the loud smash that followed.

Miraculous! Amazing! Cleanly shelled nuts on the table! This giant man from Austria had come to the Old City soup kitchen just in time to relieve the disgrace of the old rabbi's British army walnuts!

The old man raised his eyes to the heavens and thanked the Eternal. He nudged the disapproving Hannah on his right and the scowling Shoshanna on his left.

The two women exchanged astonished glances. "This fellow is better than a hammer!" cried Hannah.

Rabbi Lebowitz stuck out his lower lip in proud victory. "Did I not tell you?" he chided the women. "The Eternal has provided His own device for shelling these stones! Ha!" He raised his gnarled hands up in gratitude.

"More! More! More!" the children begged.

Shimon shrugged apologetically. "All gone, I'm afraid!"

Rabbi Lebowitz pushed his way through the kitchen crew. "Nu! We have plenty more where those come from, Shimon Feldstein! You are sent from God! It is an angel who brought you here!"

At that, the old rabbi rushed forward and took Shimon by the plaster cast. He led the towering giant toward the steps of the basement. Throwing back the wooden door, he snatched up a lantern and stepped onto the narrow landing. Shimon followed, ducking his head beneath the low doorframe.

"There! You see!" crowed the rabbi, gesturing toward dozens of gunnysacks marked *H.M. Walnuts. Jerusalem.* Now the rabbi said very loudly, "These I traded with the British army quartermaster for some boxes of useless American powder called Jell-O." He smiled and patted Shimon's cast. "You may henceforth consider yourself employed, Shimon. From kettledrum to soup kettle, *nu*? Official Tipat Chalev nutcracker."

The rattling furnace inside the offices of the British Mandate had not managed to keep up with the fierceness of the renewed cold today.

Strands of damp mist-covered hair clung to Victoria's neck as she paid her fare and boarded the bus in front of the King David Hotel. Every window of the bus was shut tight, and yet the freezing air of the afternoon seeped into the compartment as the bus lurched forward along King George Avenue toward Jaffa Road.

"Tomorrow will be colder yet," an old woman moaned knowingly. "You would think I would be used to it after seventy-nine years." Her mouth split in a toothless grin as Victoria swung into the empty seat beside her.

"I will never be used to it." Victoria blew steamy breath and brushed drops of mist from her forehead. "And tomorrow the Englishmen insist that all the women in the secretarial pool wear their best English suits . . . short Western skirts!"

The old woman tapped her temple. "They shall kill our women, these English and their short skirts."

"Tomorrow there are important gentlemen coming from London to tour the offices," Victoria offered. "And so we must dress up like proper English secretaries in London. Even though it will be so cold."

Now a young Arab merchant leaned forward. He spoke to the old woman, lest he offend the young woman by speaking directly to her. "Tomorrow will be hot enough. Those Englishmen are in for a big surprise, I hear, and if I were an Arab secretary I might find a reason to stay home tomorrow."

Victoria turned around and frowned at the young man. Such staring was not proper, but she could not help it. Was there to be yet another demonstration? another show of Arab hostility against the English and the Jews?

She glared at him as if it were somehow his doing. He spread his hands in innocence and then looked quickly out the window to where the great citadel and the wall of Jerusalem loomed ahead. He had possibly said too much. And yet did everyone not expect what was to come?

The brakes of the aged bus squealed in protest at Jaffa Gate. It was still several blocks through the Old City to her home. How very different life was here in the Old City than it was where she worked for the British government. In her office it was impolite not to look straight into the eyes of the Englishmen. *How very different!* She sighed and turned her eyes downward in modesty as she walked through the gate and into Omar Square.

To her right she could plainly see the spire of Christ Church, where she would once again meet with Eli. She stopped and let herself imagine him walking up the Armenian Patriarchate Road to meet her. *He will smile. He will touch my face. He will say how desperate the hours have been without me . . . and I will say . . .*

At that moment, her reverie was interrupted by the voice of her youngest brother as he called her name across the square. Her smile faded. Weariness filled her eyes as she spotted not just Ismael but Daud and Isaak with him. These three were half brothers to her and Ibrahim, and the sight of them was never a cause for rejoicing in Victoria.

Short and dark like their mother, they lacked the fine-chiseled features of Ibrahim. Spoiled by their father and mother alike, they did not work in the family rug business but spent their time in the souks and coffeehouses, where they had caught the spirit of rebellion that grew in such places.

"Salaam, Isaak," she said flatly as Isaak took her by the arm.

"You are late," Ismael said. "We came looking for you."

"Worried," agreed Daud, who was the least intelligent and least offensive of the three.

"You need not have worried. The bus is usually late." She shrugged off the hand of Isaak and began walking home as if they had not come for her.

Now began the probing questions. "The English politicians are coming to the King David Hotel again tomorrow." This was a statement of fact.

"What time are they to arrive?"

Victoria laughed. "How should I know who is coming? or when they will arrive?"

"Everyone in Jerusalem knows they are coming back from Galilee tomorrow."

She looked hard at Daud. He was the only one she could intimidate with a look. "Well, *I* do not know of it!" she snapped.

Daud looked confused. Could they have the date wrong? His questioning look was nudged away by Isaak.

"You must sleep all day at your job for the English, Victoria. You never know anything."

She did not reply but pushed her way through the crowds of late shoppers in the souks. *I know enough to have you arrested if you were not the sons of my father,* she thought angrily.

"You can tell us," Daud tried again clumsily. "We are your brothers, after all."

Victoria turned on him. The look on her face made him put up his arms in case she would strike him. "Ibrahim is my brother!" she hissed. "That is all I can be certain of since I see no resemblance to my father in any of you."

Isaak took her roughly by the arm. "You . . . ," he threatened.

She let her voice drop as shoppers in the souk stopped their bargaining to stare at the confrontation. "Take your hand from me . . . unless you wish to deal with my brother."

Grudgingly Isaak released his grip. She glowered at him another moment, then spun around to walk the remaining distance through the vaulted souks to her home, alone.

When she entered the house, Victoria did not answer the shrill voice of her stepmother.

Another cry, "Change your clothes and come fix dinner for your brothers! I have a headache tonight!"

Now Victoria called back over her shoulder, "I have a headache also! They will have to fix their own meal!" At that, she slammed the door of her bedroom and stood panting in the center of the room. She expected her stepmother to pound at the door and then beat her. But the only sound she heard was the ticking of the clock on the night table behind her and the slamming of the front door as the three brothers arrived home.

Theo refused to allow Elisa to accompany him to Heathrow Airport with Anna. "You know how I feel about good-byes," he remarked lightly. "Take care of my grandbaby; now promise me."

Elisa nodded. Her father's eyes were radiant and happier than she had seen in some time. He told her he was going away on business. The nature of the business was not discussed, but Elisa knew her father well enough that his business had something to do with the refugee questions. She did not ask. His unspoken calling gave her peace. Not everyone in the world was silent, after all. While great governments made proclamations and held meetings about the refugees, Elisa knew Theo was *doing something!*

So it was that Theo kissed her good-bye on the sidewalk in front of the Red Lion House. He hugged Charles and Louis and told them that he had left a birthday gift for them with Anna in case he could not get back to London in time. At these quiet words, Elisa thought she saw an instant of pain on her mother's face. Perhaps not.

Anna kissed her and promised to be back in time for a nice lunch at Claridge's Hotel with Sir Thomas Beecham and Frieda Hillman.

"Bring the notes about the next charity concert," Anna reminded her. "We are going to stage it right in the Claridge's ballroom, Theo," she said proudly. "The management is donating the place for the night."

Theo shook his head in amazement. "From Claridge's to a soup kitchen in Prague and a refugee camp in Poland! Only you, Anna!"

The banter seemed almost too superficial. They had talked about this, after all, this morning over breakfast. For a moment Elisa wondered if the record was playing over again to avoid other things being said. *But what things?*

Freddie Frutschy glanced at his watch and then at the threatening sky. "If we don't hurry, sir, you'll not be going anywheres from the looks of the weather." He opened the car door and stepped back as Theo cast one last look at Elisa. Again she thought she saw *something* in his eyes. Sorrow, hope, love seemed thinly veiled beneath light chatter about an already much-discussed event.

Could she ask him in these final moments if there was something more he was not saying? How long would this good-bye be? Suddenly Elisa felt like a small child being left behind on her first day of school. Freddie started the car. Theo raised his hand to her behind the glass of the window.

She stepped forward and put her hand against his through the glass. "I love you, Father!" she called.

He mouthed the words back, *God bless you!* And then Freddie pulled away from the curb.

Ibrahim knocked softly on Victoria's bedroom door. She did not answer, so he knocked again and turned the latch, nudging the door open slightly.

He had expected to find her in the room, but instead she sat on the balcony where the last rays of sunlight had made the western sky a tapestry of bright colors like the fabrics in the souk.

At the sound of the groaning hinges, Victoria turned to look at him. Her dark eyes smoldered with anger. She put her finger to her lips to silence him as she stood, reentered her room, and closed the door to the balcony behind her.

"Have you come to warn me?" she asked coldly.

Ibrahim simply blinked at her in amazement. Indeed, he had come to warn her about the demonstrations tomorrow, but how did she know? "Where did you hear?"

"On the bus."

"The bus!" he exclaimed. That meant that everyone in Jerusalem was aware.

"And—" she gestured back toward the balcony—"our brothers are talking. There. Down in the courtyard where every little bird may carry its voice to the ears of the English."

"The English will know soon enough."

"If they know my brothers are involved, then they will dismiss me from my job at the Mandate administration. They will think I am a spy." Her eyes glistened with tears as she sank onto the bed.

Ibrahim did not move to comfort her. "This is men's business," he said more harshly than he intended. "I came to warn you not to go to work tomorrow; that is all. What difference does it make if you work for *them* or not?"

"It makes a difference to me!" she cried. "That is the only place I am treated like a human being with a mind except for . . ."

"Except for Eli?" Ibrahim finished. She was pouting as women sometimes did. He would not yield to her display of foolishness. "I will not bring him to you until he is *one of us.*"

She tossed her hair in a defiant gesture. "And do you think he will ever be one of us if you and our half brothers are part of . . . whatever is going to happen tomorrow?"

"We wish only for a free Arab State."

"Then go to Jordan! Or Syria! What does it matter? The English are *good* to us! Jews and Arabs! I *work* at the Mandate administration! I *cannot* hear this!" She covered her ears.

Ibrahim did not reply. He waited. She lowered her hands, and then he spoke gently. "There will be no violence."

"So you say each time! Do you think I am blind? or only stupid?"

"Only a demonstration of Muslim displeasure for the English Woodhead Commission. They will see—"

"That we are barbarians."

"Not barbarians! . . . Conquerors! As the prophet has written, as Allah has whispered, '*Jerusalem will belong to the faithful! To those who bow down.*'"

"I have heard the sermons of Haj Amin," she said scornfully. "He promises Paradise for those who die fighting jihad! Holy war!" She moved to the window and looked toward the Dome of the Rock just beyond the housetops of the Old City. "What use is Jerusalem to us if we are dust? Can Allah mean that we are to kill those who have always lived beside us? Can you fight also against Eli because he is a Jew?"

"If Eli is not with us, then I will fight him." There was a coldness in Ibrahim's eyes that made Victoria shudder inside.

"But he is like a brother to you."

"He loves you. That will make him see reason." It was as if Ibrahim was not listening.

"Then you are also one of them," Victoria whispered. "You believe the words Haj Amin speaks to the people."

"He speaks the words of Mohammed. The words of Allah. He will be king over Jerusalem, and those who follow him will be exalted."

"Haj Amin is an assassin!" Victoria drew back. She stared at the hands of her brother. Could those hands do the bidding of a leader like Haj Amin?

"It is the will of Allah—," he began.

"That you murder the innocent tomorrow?"

"There will be no murders tomorrow."

"But you will make certain no more Jews come to Palestine."

Ibrahim shrugged. "A few more tires will be burned in the streets." He attempted to lighten the darkness of her imagination. "A demonstration that will hang in the noses of these Englishmen. Burn their eyes a bit. Black clouds of burning rubber. No violence, Victoria." He took a step nearer. "I came only to warn you that you must not go to work tomorrow."

"Then I will lose my job."

"So be it," he said coolly. "Arab women do not need to work for the English unless they serve their brothers in some way."

Now Victoria turned on him. There was no doubt what he was asking of her. "Get out, Ibrahim! You . . . I thought you were not like our half brothers! I did not think that you . . ." She stammered in her rage against him. "I will leave this house before I consent! Spies are still hanged in Palestine! It makes no difference if they are women! Get out!" She cried too loudly now.

The voice of her stepmother called gruffly up the stairs. "What is wrong with the princess now?"

Ibrahim bowed slightly. "Salaam, Victoria." He backed up a step into the corridor and closed the door, blocking her black look. Then, with a smile, he inserted the key to her room into the lock and turned it as she gave a desperate cry against her imprisonment.

From the tall minaret beside the silver dome of the el-Aqsa Mosque, the cry of the muezzin went out over the dusk of Jerusalem.

Pacing in her small, Spartan bedroom, Victoria did not stop to kneel or bow to pray as her brothers did downstairs. Could she pray to such a god? to Allah? Through his prophet he demanded death and domination over all who did not believe the words, "There is no god but Allah, and Mohammed is his prophet!"

Throughout the city, men with faces bowed low uttered these words. These were the same men who, like the half brothers of Victoria, planned riots and rebellion and plotted for the murders of those who did not follow Haj Amin!

Victoria *would not bow* to this Allah! She raised her chin in defiance as she faced east toward the Dome of the Rock. Fading sunlight shone dully on the tarnished dome as her faith died.

"I will not pray to you," she whispered. "You who have made my life a prison! Never again will I bow to you!"

And so she stood throughout the minutes when all the Muslim faithful touched their foreheads to the ground. All that she had been—everything she had been taught as a child—evaporated like an unheard prayer. Emptiness and anger replaced the words "and Mohammed is his prophet!"

Victoria lay on her bed and watched as the final rays of sunlight faded into the darkness of a moonless night. She wanted to weep but did not allow herself even that small luxury. One sigh, one tear, and her stepbrothers and their mother would gloat and laugh among themselves at the misery of the one they mocked as "the princess."

Hours crept by. The bells of Christ Church tolled ten o'clock; then the key rattled and her door swung back. Daud held a tray of food. Behind him, shadowed in the backlighted corridor, stood his mother.

The woman's bitter voice preceded her into the room. "Is *the princess* sleeping?" Then she commanded, "Set the tray down, Daud, and leave us." She snapped on the light, and Victoria sat up, blinking against the glare.

"I am not hungry." Victoria did not look at the tray of food. She was, indeed, very hungry, but she would not show even that to this woman.

"We did not want you telling your father that we locked you up and did not feed you." The woman narrowed her eyes. There was no hint of kindness. This gesture of food was only to protect herself against the anger of her husband.

"If my father were here—," Victoria began.

"He is not here. And so you answer to me." She held up the key and smiled an unfeeling smile.

"When my father returns—" Victoria spoke carefully. She must not give in to the tears of anger that pushed at her throat. "When he returns from Teheran, then you will answer to him for this."

The smile broadened. "It was your own brother Ibrahim who locked the door and brought me the key, remember? For your own protection, my dear girl."

"You harbor rebellion in my father's house! You encourage your sons and my own brother against the wishes of—"

The woman took a threatening step toward Victoria. "It is you who rebel against my authority!"

"You are not my mother!" Tears brimmed in Victoria's eyes against her will.

This pleased the woman who stood over her. "Your tears do not move me as they do your father. The matter is settled. You will remain here. We will give you no chance to warn these Englishmen you are so fond of."

"*Warn* them?" So this was the reason for her confinement. There was no thought of safety for her, after all. "You think they will not notice when I do not come to work? You think they will not ask me *why* and how I knew? You warn them by keeping me prisoner here."

The reasoning of this penetrated the mind of the woman. She eyed Victoria for a moment longer and then challenged her. "If you tell them of the meeting here today, they will arrest your father."

Victoria did not argue that, even though Amal Hassan hated the politics of his wife and sons. "Just let me go." Victoria was once again in control.

The woman considered the request. "It means a lot to you, this job with the English?"

Victoria chose her words carefully. With this woman, to show too much pleasure for anything meant that the object of her pleasure would be somehow denied her. It had always been so since the day the woman had married Victoria's father. She had possessed a kind of cruel beauty then, but the years had twisted the beauty into ugliness, and the cruelty had only become more harsh.

"My job with the English is just a job. They pay better than anywhere else in Jerusalem; that is all."

The woman understood money. "Greedy little princess. Never enough for you, eh?" Her eyes narrowed as she thought what to do. "You will stay here," she said at last. "I will send word you are ill. And when your father returns, we will speak of finding you a husband. That will quiet your rebellion!"

"*Please—*," Victoria begged.

The begging pleased the woman, as had Victoria's tears. "When your father returns we shall discuss . . . your future." She stepped out before Victoria could reply. The key turned in the lock, and Victoria finally let herself weep.

Jerusalem was still asleep. The sun had not yet risen when the rattle of her doorknob awakened Victoria.

Ibrahim's voice called gently to her. "My sister, are you awake?"

Victoria sat up in drowsy confusion and pulled the blanket around her shoulders. Why had Ibrahim awakened her before dawn?

"Ibrahim?" she questioned, forgetting last night's fears as he unlocked the door. "What . . . ?"

She turned the knob and her brother stood before her, holding a tray with fresh fruit and a small bowl of boiled eggs. He brushed past her and placed the tray on her chest of drawers. He was not smiling.

"We have some bad news," he said quietly.

Victoria felt herself groping for the bed. "Is it Father?" she managed to ask.

Ibrahim smiled slightly. "A messenger came from Hebron last night while you were sleeping. The sister of our mother has died."

She put a hand to her head in relief. "Aunt Antoine?" she managed to ask.

Ibrahim nodded. "We are the only children of this branch of the family. Get dressed. We must mourn for her in Hebron today."

Victoria blinked in understanding. Her relief that it was not her father far outweighed any sorrow she might have had for the loss of her mother's sister.

She examined the breakfast tray and suddenly felt ashamed for her thoughts against Ibrahim last night. Only her dear brother would have thought to bring breakfast to soften the blow of bad news. In the next instant she remembered Leah. *The King David Hotel. Tea at four o'clock.* "My job—," she said, unable to find a way to explain that she had an appointment with a Jewish woman this afternoon.

"I have taken care of all of that." Ibrahim's voice was matter-of-fact. "I sent a messenger to the home of Tasha with word that there is a death in the family."

Well, then, that was taken care of. Victoria could only hope that Leah would think to ask the right department supervisor when Victoria missed their appointment.

A strange light filled Ibrahim's eyes, as if he knew some wonderful joke and yet would not tell her. Yes, there was amusement on his face. "What is it?" she asked. "Why do you smile at such a moment?"

He shrugged. "I suppose I am grateful it is not Father," Ibrahim replied curtly as he left the room, shutting the door behind him.

The morning sun shone through the windshield of Ibrahim's borrowed car as they left Jerusalem. After five minutes passed, Victoria knew that they were not going to Hebron.

"Hebron is south." She shielded her eyes from the bright glare of dawn.

"Yes," Ibrahim replied. "We are taking a different route."

"You are lying, Ibrahim!" Victoria shouted as they topped the rise. The narrow road led east to Jericho and then on down in a twisting rutted track to where Allenby Bridge crossed the Jordan River into the country of Transjordan.

"Yes." Ibrahim smiled again. "I am lying, my sister."

She studied his face, illuminated by the fiery light of the desert sun. "But *why*?" she cried. Her hands trembled. "Why are you taking me away from Jerusalem?"

He pulled down the visor and glanced mockingly at her. "For your own protection, Victoria."

"My protection! From what? From whom? Is it Eli? Ibrahim, are you taking me from Eli?" Tears of frustration came against her will.

Ibrahim glanced at her, a glint of power in his eyes. He was enjoying his sister's tears. She struck his arm with her fist, and he responded with a slap across her mouth. She jerked back against the car door and remained there huddled and sobbing as blood from her lip trickled down the glass windowpane. The mountains of Moab stretched out in desolate monotony before them. An hour passed, and still Victoria wept.

At last Ibrahim answered her. "There are certain . . . *demonstrations* planned for this afternoon. These will occur near the King David Hotel. By tonight it will be done, and we will come home."

"Why?" she wailed miserably. "Oh, Ibrahim. Not *you*! Have you forgotten Eli?"

"If your heart was right, you would turn the heart of Eli like a river into our camp! And you would help us fight the English!"

"I will do neither!" she warned, staying well beyond his reach. "Am I the only child of our father?"

Again Ibrahim raised his hand as if to strike her, but he thought better of it. It would not do to have her return to work tomorrow with a bruised face. It would not be wise to give anyone an opportunity to ask questions of her. Perhaps she would answer their questions; then he and his half brothers would all be hanged at the end of British ropes.

"There are only a handful of us in Palestine," he said. "And yet we send the English foxes running for their dens when the sun goes down! We control the roads. The night is ours. Think what we might do with more men and decent weapons." He was talking for his own pleasure now.

Victoria stared out toward Transjordan where mountains melted into heaps of sand. A thousand questions assaulted her mind. She pictured the faces of her friends and coworkers. If Ibrahim had been frightened enough to carry her away, then what was planned? An assassination? A riot in the commercial district?

"You have done enough already," she muttered.

"We are only beginning, my sister." He licked his lips and squinted through the dust-covered windshield. "Tomorrow you will be grateful that I took you away today. You will thank me that you are alive."

30

Storming the Gates of Hell

Berlin appeared far below as the plane suddenly descended through the gray vapor of clouds. Theo watched out the window with a mix of nostalgia and apprehension. This was a homecoming, to be sure, but not the kind he had dreamed of.

There were no sailboats on the lakes. The Spree River was a colorless line winding through the city. Trees in the parks and woodlands were without leaves. The central city itself seemed torn and ravaged. Heaps of masonry were everywhere mingled with earthmovers and scaffolding that climbed the facades of buildings like barren vines. Tiny automobiles crept like bugs along the roads. The face of Theo's beloved Berlin was being changed, rebuilt to match the monumental ideals of the superrace of Aryans.

Theo smiled as the plane passed over a building that seemed like an old friend. The structure of Lindheim's Department Store remained the same. Now it bore the name *GERMANIA* in bold neon letters across the top floor of the building. Giant swastika flags draped every side from ledge to sidewalk. But still the cornices and arches of the windows were unaltered. The broad doorways that opened to the sidewalks of four different avenues were unchanged. Lindheim's Department Store still roosted firmly on an entire city block of Berlin. What they called it did not matter. Theo still knew the place better than anyone ever could. From the soil beneath the basement to the steel girders and stone facades, Theo had hovered over every aspect of its creation until it had become the finest store in all Germany—one of the finest in all Europe. Today there was no other friendly face below to greet him, only the weathered stones that had once contained Theo's dreams.

He looked beyond, toward Wilhelmstrasse. The house he and Anna had built there was gone. The stones of some new Nazi public ministry were rising up to take its place.

Theo looked back at the old Lindheim store. He would have liked to have one more look around inside, but such a thing would not be possible.

He sighed as the plane dipped lower toward the large square of turf marking Tempelhof Airfield. Not so long ago, he had left that same field with shafts of lightning splitting the air around his tiny biplane. He had almost made it across the border. Almost. The wind had broken a wing strut, and he had managed to land in a cow pasture—in the field of a Bavarian Nazi Party member.

Theo flipped open his passport folder. British diplomatic pass. His face. Citizenship listed as Great Britain. But one thing Göring had insisted on when he demanded that Theo Lindheim return to the soil of the Reich was the change of name—from Theo to Jacob Stern, the name given him when he was interned at Dachau.

Jacob Stern—the sole survivor of the Dachau Herrgottseck! Like the gray stones of Lindheim's Department Store, Theo had been renamed by his Nazi persecutors, but they had never managed to change anything else about him. The stuff that made Theo who he was remained the same.

He wondered if Hermann Göring would see *that* in his face when they met again after so many long and bitter years. He was almost certain that the false name on the British passport would become an excuse for the Nazis to arrest him once again. He prayed that he would at least be given the chance to present the economic plan of the governments he represented. That much alone would make this journey—and what would follow—worth the suffering.

He pressed his lips together as he studied the rooftops of the great German capital. How many thousands of people huddled fearfully beneath those roofs and prayed that someone would help them escape? Theo carried them all inside his heart. He was one of them. He, too, had loved this land that was now determined to destroy him.

Like those who opposed the Führer's evil, the Spirit of the true and loving God had been driven underground. No longer did His love pervade the churches or His beauty fill the woods and rivers of Berlin. The god Wotan lived here now. The Chancellery building on Wilhelmstrasse rose as a new temple to an evil god.

The sound of traffic in Allenby Square echoed inside the large post office. With the clamor of busy Jerusalem in her ears, Leah copied the new post office box number onto the return address of her first letter to Elisa.

As she held the envelope, she imagined her friend holding it in far-away England. Flimsy paper and ink were a tenuous link at best, but Leah found some pleasure in the thought that Elisa's fingers would touch the envelope and cherish the words written inside.

London. A world away. What news would Elisa hear about the Arab demonstrations? She would be concerned until the letter arrived. She would look out on her London street and wait for the mailman just as Leah had seen her do when she had hoped for a letter from Thomas von Kleistmann. How far they had come since those days!

A blue-uniformed mail clerk hurried by. *"Bitte,"* Leah asked, then remembering these were Englishmen, she started again. "Excuse me, please. How long will it take for my letter to reach London?"

The face puckered in thought. The aging civil servant scratched his head. "Several weeks, at least, miss. Depending on what boat it gets on. Military mail goes some faster than the private stuff."

"Ah." A twinge of disappointment rose up in Leah. Several weeks. By then her news would be old and stale. What news would there be between then and now? Would the distinguished gentlemen of the Woodhead Commission have submitted their recommendations by then? Would the matter of Jewish immigration to Palestine have been settled forever by then?

Leah laid her cheek against Elisa's name for a moment. Then, as an Arab man deposited a stack of envelopes into the mail slot, Leah also slipped her hopes and fears down the brass chute.

It would be weeks, or perhaps months, before Elisa's reply came back to Jerusalem. Leah pocketed the shiny new mailbox key. The key would be her link to London, and yet it would be a long time before she could hope to find anything in their box.

There were other matters to tend to before she met Victoria for tea at the King David Hotel. Across from the broad steps of the post office in Allenby Square stood the imposing edifice of Barclay's Bank. Only one hundred and fifty-three dollars remained of the cash Murphy had slipped into Shimon's pocket. It seemed like a small sum to deposit in such a large bank, but the thought of a bank account somehow settled Leah. A post office box. A bank account. They were no longer strangers in Jerusalem, but residents with proof that this place was indeed home! Leah filled out the appropriate forms and passed their American dollars under the iron grid of the teller's window.

At home in Vienna she had known the bank tellers by name. They had known her and smiled in greeting when she walked into the bank on the Ringstrasse. It would be the same here, she decided. *"Guten Tag* . . . hello," she said to the dark-skinned Arab bank teller.

He did not smile or even acknowledge her greeting. "You would like to keep some out?" he asked in a brusque businesslike manner.

This was a small defeat. Perhaps the divisions of the Old City reached into the bank as well, she reasoned. She signed the form and withheld four pounds from the amount. This would buy tea for Victoria and groceries for a few days, perhaps.

The bank was not far from the commercial district of New City Jerusalem and the King David Hotel. An Egged bus sputtered by, but Leah determined she would walk everywhere in Jerusalem. There was no reason to waste money on bus fare when she had two good legs that had carried her over the Alps from Austria!

Walking briskly along the sidewalk, she peered into the shopwindows and mentally made notes about the location of this business or that. In this section of Jerusalem, Leah could almost imagine that she was in Europe again. Window displays showed off the same Paris fashions Leah had seen in the more modest shops in France. A sign in a tailor shop advertised the latest in men's suits, cut after the style of the finest tailors in London and Rome.

Shop signs in English, German, and French gave Leah a sense that she was not so very far from her European roots, after all.

She stopped at the frantic intersection and glanced back toward Jaffa Gate and the Old City walls. Behind those stones it seemed that time had not moved. The passions and conflicts of Mount Zion were ageless and unchanging. She hummed a few notes of the melody from Bloch's *Solomon's Symphony*. Melancholy and poignant, it seemed to fit the timeless tragedy of Jerusalem.

Around her, the horns of automobiles blared. The whistles of traffic policemen directed the discordant symphony. But behind the wall, only the music of Solomon seemed appropriate.

The road sloped away to the weathered headstones of a cemetery. The tower of the YMCA building rose to the south, and Leah could easily make out the fortress-like stones of the King David Hotel across from it. A bus chugged up the slope toward her, then halted at a bus stop, where six people stood.

Leah did not see the two cars until a battered sedan roared around the front of the bus, blocking its way. The bus driver laid on his horn as the doors of the car flew open and two frightened-looking Arab youths leaped out and ran directly toward her before jumping into a second car. A moment later it tore past Leah and sped away.

Instinctively Leah froze as the bus driver crammed his vehicle into reverse and stepped on the gas. The mouths of the waiting passengers opened to scream, and at that moment Leah threw herself to the sidewalk. There was time for nothing else. She did not hear the blast as the white heat passed above her. Suddenly the screams dissolved into silence and bright light. Around her, chunks of debris clattered to earth and she tucked her head even tighter beneath her arms.

The air was filled with the stench of burning rubber and seared flesh. She felt no pain. No fear. A strange, detached calm surrounded her, although she knew that death was everywhere. For an instant she wondered if perhaps she, too, had died, and then she raised her head to the devastation that surrounded her. Where six people had stood, there was a black hole in the sidewalk. Nothing was left of the Arab car. The front of the bus was shattered, the driver vanished. Chunks of metal smoked in the torn asphalt.

Leah tried to cry out, but her own voice was lost in the silence of the destruction. Suddenly people were running everywhere. Two British soldiers spotted Leah where she lay. She raised her hand and called out to them. She could not hear her own voice or their response. Their mouths opened in a soundless shout as they ran to her side.

Only then did the pain scream in her ears, as if the hot metal shards had pierced her head. She wept! She called the name of Shimon! What was wrong with her voice that she made no sound? And then she knew . . . *she could not hear.*

At the sound of the blast, Captain Samuel Orde ran with a hundred others out the entrance of the King David Hotel. A cloud of blue smoke billowed up from what remained of the bombed car. The scent of cordite was heavy in the air. Such a scent meant only one thing to a soldier: Death had come again to Julian's Way.

Stunned, the onlookers gasped and cried out the names of coworkers who had just left the building for the bus. In a matter of seconds, the horror before them sank in, and Orde found himself jogging purposefully across the driveway of the hotel, cutting through blackened hedges and dodging smoking hunks of steel that littered the street and sidewalk like a battlefield.

Cars were already backed up on Julian's Way. Some were disabled by flattened tires and shattered windshields. A green taxi sat sideways in the road. A steering wheel and part of a dashboard lay on the hood. Miraculously, the stunned driver seemed to be moving—and there were other signs of life amid the debris and crumpled bodies.

Orde stepped over the body of a woman. Too late for her. He covered his mouth and nose against the sickening smell that mingled in the smoke. A group of soldiers reached the bus, demolished from the front axle forward. Moans came from inside the wreckage. *Survivors!*

He looked to the right toward another body—a woman on the sidewalk. "Dear merciful God!" he cried, not knowing where to begin. And then the woman moved; she raised her head slightly, then let it fall back against her arm. In that instant Orde recognized her. *The musician! Leah Feldstein!* She was so close to the center of the blast, so near to the black crater! *How had she survived?*

She sat up as Orde ran toward her. Her face was contorted with pain. She covered her ears with her hands as she called out, "Shimon! Help me, Shimon!" And then, "Why? *Oh Jesu! Jesu! Warum?*"

Another officer joined Orde's dash to her. "It is Leah Feldstein!" he exclaimed. As they stepped over the fragments of what had been a living human a few moments before, the officer cursed and shook his fist heavenward as if his curse of the Arabs became a curse against God.

Leah stretched her hand out toward Orde. "*Bitte!*" Her words were all in German. "*Bitte! Hilf mir! Mein Gott!*" Her hands returned to clutch the sides of her head in agony.

"Mrs. Feldstein," Orde said as he knelt beside her and embraced her. "It is over. You are safe." His eyes focused on a victim just beyond her. "By the mercy of God, you are safe."

She sobbed uncontrollably. The wail of sirens pierced the sounds of muffled sobs. The curses. The prayers. The awakening shrieks of agony that came with consciousness.

Leah Feldstein heard none of this. She leaned against Orde's chest and wept quietly until an ambulance came to take her away.

News of the bomb blast on Julian's Way swept through the city within minutes. Shop grates clattered down, and shutters slammed shut before the first ambulances reached the scene. Eyes turned toward the distant echo of sirens and bullhorns. Fear touched Arab, Jew, and Christian alike. From house to house, a census was taken: Who is not here? Who might have been on Julian's Way near the King David Hotel?

In the Jewish Quarter, the name Leah Feldstein was passed from person to person. "She had gone to tea at the King David Hotel, so her husband says. Poor thing. He is sick with fear. Look at him . . ."

Shimon sat beneath the cupola of the Great Hurva Synagogue. His borrowed prayer shawl had slipped off one shoulder and his yarmulke was askew on his head. The men of the congregation sat with him in silent vigil. Eli had forbidden him to leave the Jewish Quarter. Things would be dangerous for a while. Who could say what would happen now?

Shimon turned his eyes upward to the mural of Moses casting down the tablets of stone upon the sinning Hebrews. If it had not been for Moses' prayer to God, all the Hebrews would have perished in that terrible moment of wrath. Shimon ran a hand over his eyes. *Remember Your Covenant, O Lord,* he prayed silently. *And remember Leah for my sake.*

Hours passed. As others drifted off for dinner, Shimon and Eli sat in silent vigil. Eli's agony was as intense as Shimon's. He could think of nothing but Victoria. And how could he know if she was safe or dead?

Near dusk, urgent whispers sounded behind them in the foyer. English voices!

"Shimon Feldstein . . . told he was here . . ."

Cold fear swept throughout Shimon's body. His breath came too quickly as he stood and tried to reply. "I . . . am . . . Shimon . . ."

The face of an English officer turned toward him. The eyes were kind and weary and full of sadness. "Mr. Feldstein," the officer began, "I am Samuel Orde, captain of the Highland Light Infantry here in the Old City. I—"

"Is she dead?" Shimon blurted out. He did not care who this fellow was. He wanted to know. That was all.

"No. She is . . . she sustained only slight injury. She is . . ."

Shimon's shoulders sagged with relief and he slumped back down onto the seat. "Thank You, eternal and merciful—" He jerked his head up. "Where is she?"

"Hadassah Hospital. She is asking for you. I have a car—"

Shimon was at the side of Captain Orde before the officer finished the offer of a ride. He took a step and then turned back toward Eli.

The young man had not moved. His shoulders were still hunched forward in grief and worry. *Victoria!* Eli could not even say her name out loud.

Theo had not forgotten the sense of heaviness that clung to the city of Berlin, but he had not felt it until he stepped once again onto the soil of Tempelhof Airfield.

The night he had attempted escape from this place, even the storm had not seemed as dark as the evil presence he had fled from. Still the Darkness remained—almost a tangible, physical oppression that caused Theo to falter in his steps and pray silently that the Spirit of the living God would surround him. He looked up at the flat gray skies above the city with the feeling that even now an ancient and unseen war was taking place. The battlefields were the hearts of all who remained in this desolate land.

Long ago Hitler had struck at the Christian pastors. Most of the shepherds of Germany were dead or imprisoned, and so the flock was scattered, devoured by fear and beaten by the staff that was crowned with the crooked Nazi cross.

Strangely, Theo felt no bitterness as he made his way toward the doors where Gestapo agents stood in trench coats to scrutinize each passenger. Perhaps these creatures of darkness had once been men, but they were men no longer. Like Faust, they had sold their souls for a price. Now they walked the thin wire of brutality and hatred above the hell that waited eagerly for their fall.

The end would come for them. Theo had seen that truth during his days of suffering in Dachau. But the end was not yet. The battle for these tortured souls had been won by Nazi darkness, and now hell yawned open and cried out to be fed with innocent sacrifices.

For this reason, Theo had returned to Berlin. Agreeing to this mission represented his individual attempt to storm the gates of hell. If even one innocent life could be saved by this journey, then heaven would rejoice. The Darkness would flee before the light of even one remaining candle of the Covenant!

The mist clung to Theo's face like tears—the tears of a holy and loving God for those in Germany who had sold themselves to an ancient idolatry. Hitler was right in what he claimed. The ancient Nordic gods lived on. They demanded Aryan worship. They craved human sacrifice.

Theo looked toward the edge of the airfield. Rows of bright new bombers and fighter planes were on display there. Like hounds of sport in a kennel, they waited for the command to kill. Theo knew the command would come. There would be no peace. The German god of creation was also the god of destruction. What Hitler could not have he would destroy.

Theo whispered the name of Jesus, loving Savior and Messiah. The true Jesus bore no resemblance to the brutal masters who had driven the Spirit of God from the German churches. "I believe in the Lord, the true God of Israel," Theo said softly, as if the words protected him from the heaviness around him. "And I know the end of the Book! The Lord will reign in Jerusalem and every knee shall bow. It is written!" His words were not audible to any of those around him, and yet Theo felt that the words of his heart were heard. The candle was small, but the light was alive! The Darkness fled back from him.

He presented the British diplomatic passport to the tall, thin Gestapo agent at the gate. The officer scanned the document and then peered down at his list. "Yes. Herr Stern." He raised an eyebrow and appraised Theo coldly. "We heard you were coming to Berlin. British Ambassador

Henderson is waiting for you in the next room. You may pass through inspection. Your luggage will be sent separately to the British Embassy."

"*Danke.*" Theo tipped his hat. His leg ached from the weather, and he limped more slowly than usual toward the door.

Behind him he heard the Gestapo agent remark loudly to a clerk sitting to his left, "You know which Jews are kikes? Every Jew, once he has left the room." The joke was punctuated with a roar of laughter that followed Theo out of the customs area to where Neville Henderson waited impatiently for him.

31

Even in Sorrow, We Will Believe

Etta did not see them come. Aaron had gone to the shul and she was upstairs bathing Yacov when she heard them knocking on the door. Moments later Frau Rosen appeared in the doorway, out of breath, eyes wide.

"It is two men from the Warsaw police, Rebbitsin Lubetkin! They say they must see you. Not Rebbe Lubetkin, but *you*! A personal matter, they say!"

Etta felt ill, but she managed a feeble smile all the same. "Probably nothing. I mislaid my handbag the other day and reported it."

A bad lie. Frau Rosen's eyes narrowed. No one had asked her about a handbag. Why had she not heard of it if this happened? "I let them into the study," she said. Caution had replaced alarm. Curiosity pulled her mind toward a thousand different possibilities, and she knew a missing handbag was not one of them.

Etta maintained her composure. "Thank you. Finish washing the baby and dress him. I will be back in a moment." She turned the little one over to the housekeeper and swept past her as if this were nothing unusual at all.

Now that Eduard was gone from Warsaw, Etta was alone in her conspiracy to keep Aaron from hearing about her ordeal. She would not tell him until the Mandate passports arrived from Palestine. But what if these men wanted something more from her than Eduard had given them?

Her heart pounded hard as she slid back the doors to the study. The two men were pretending to look at the books on the shelves. They could not have understood any of what they saw. The thick, red-faced officer was flipping through a book of Hebrew poetry from back to front as if it were written in Polish.

Etta eyed them for a moment. Fools and buffoons. Brutal and unscrupulous. And now they held something of their own making over her head. Fear left her suddenly at the sight of such ignorant lumps thumbing through books they did not understand. Indignation took the place of fear. It gave her courage to confront them.

"What do you want?" she asked with surprising harshness.

They turned and coolly appraised her. "So," said the red-faced man in a thick peasant speech, "Herr Doktor Letzno has gone off to Palestine."

"Yes. You seem to know everything. And what you do not know you make up. In this instance, you are correct. He is gone. What has that to do with me? Why are you interrupting my work?" This tone was startling. The blue eyes of Etta Lubetkin flashed her outrage.

"Well, my pretty Frau Lubetkin." The red-face man smiled. His teeth were decayed, his face lumpy, and his nose discolored from too much cheap brandy.

Etta smelled the brandy on his breath. "How dare you address me in such a manner?" she snapped.

"Why don't you have us arrested?" laughed the man.

His partner sneered and nodded at the jest.

"You are in my home. If you have something to say, say it and leave." Etta crossed her arms defiantly.

"Well then, to the point, Ivan." The red-faced man deferred to his partner, who stepped forward.

"Frau Lubetkin," the second man said patronizingly, "we were talking about the matter of fines just now. We let you off too easily, you see. Such an error could cost us our positions."

"Yes, blackmail could get you fired!" Etta retorted. She felt strong in her defiance of them. She had recovered from her ordeal now. She could handle them. "Shall I call your captain and report what you have done?"

The red-faced man chuckled and rubbed his bulbous nose. "It was the captain who informed us of the error. Not enough money, you see. Not enough to keep you out of jail for prostitution. You did not pay a big enough fine, Frau Lubetkin. And so we are here to arrest you."

Etta's self-composure faltered only an instant. She swallowed hard and raised her head in such an aristocratic gesture that the grins of these bullies faltered a bit. "You are swine," she said in Yiddish.

They exchanged looks. Angry. Instantly threatening. "We know what you said, you Jewish whore, and now you will pay us or we will take you to jail. There is a cell for women like you. The men of the police force visit it often."

Etta could not find her voice at this threat. For a full minute she stood in the center of Aaron's study. She glared at them, and they seemed frozen by her look. She thought through all of it. All the implications of what they said. Probably they could do what they wanted with her. Put her in a place like that. Keep the key in their own pockets, and . . .

The thought sickened her. She must tell Aaron. There was no other way. But until she could tell him she must pay them.

Eduard's checks! She looked through the door to where her handbag sat on the sideboard beside the silver tea service.

"A nice place you have here," said the red-faced policeman. "You Jews are wealthy people. You live better than honest, hardworking Poles, don't you?"

Without a word she turned her back and went to her handbag. She pulled out the first of Eduard's checks and held it in her hands. The movement of a rustling petticoat sounded on the stair above her. Frau Rosen glared down at her—questioning, angry, revolted by whatever was happening with the mistress of the house.

"Frau Rosen!" snapped Etta. "You will see to baby Yacov now, please."

Frau Rosen nodded reluctantly and turned from her eavesdropping.

Etta did not go back into the study. She waited in the foyer and held the check for the blackmailers to see. When they came out, she preceded them to the front door. Opening it to a cold blast of air, she stepped out and they followed. Then she stepped back in and handed them the check. "There will be no more," she warned.

They looked at the amount on the check and seemed pleased.

She glared at them for an instant. "You may drink that up as well, but there will be no more for you. Do not come back into my neighborhood or on my street or to my home. There will be nothing more for you here."

With that, she closed the door, shutting them out. She slid the bolt and peeked out around the lace curtain of the foyer window and watched as they clapped each other on the back and tramped through the snow across the square.

The bomb blast had killed indiscriminately. Four Arabs were dead. Five Jews. The numbers of wounded were equally divided as the ambulances screamed up Mount Scopus to Hadassah Hospital. Twelve seriously wounded. Eight of those critical. Thirty-two came into the wards listed as stable. Leah Feldstein, with ruptured eardrums and a miscarriage in process, was one of those in the last group.

Eduard Letzno had not anticipated this horror as he had toured Hadassah Hospital on his first day in Jerusalem. When word came of what had happened and the ambulances had begun to arrive, the resident physicians had looked upon Eduard's presence there as providential.

While teams had worked together on the critical patients, Eduard and three medical students had labored to assist those with superficial wounds—cleaning, stitching, and bandaging those who were in no real danger.

In the case of Leah Feldstein, there had been little to do. She had told Eduard she thought she was pregnant. Her bleeding was certainly not heavy enough to threaten her life, but miscarriage was inevitable. An IV was administered. She was put to bed. Eduard was more concerned with the possibility of loss of hearing in her right ear, which was damaged more severely than her left.

He explained all this to her grieved husband as they stood together outside the crowded ward.

"She is . . . she has lost the baby?" asked Shimon.

"She is lucky that she sustained no other injuries—or worse." Eduard tried to comfort Shimon with the realization that she might have been in the morgue right now instead of in the hospital ward. This thought only struck the big man with a more terrible kind of grief—what might have been, what almost was!

"But she is *all right*?" He clutched Eduard's arm in a viselike grip.

"I see no reason why she will not have other children. The pregnancy was in the very early stages. She tells me she had not even consulted a doctor yet. We will keep her here for observation, of course." Eduard could not escape the intense and searching gaze of Shimon.

"But her hearing . . ." Shimon rubbed his eyes. "She is a concert musician, you see. A cellist." His voice broke. "Herr Doktor! This is all my Leah knows to do. Music is her life, you see, and—"

This news alarmed Eduard more than the young woman's spontaneous abortion. She would probably conceive again, but he could not be optimistic that there would not be at least some damage to her hearing. And there was nothing at all that could be done if that was the case. "We will monitor her progress, of course," he replied almost curtly. It was a habit he had formed to shield himself from the emotions of his patients. "In the meantime, Herr Feldstein, there are many dead and seriously wounded here today. Count yourself and your wife lucky in this case that she is alive."

Mercifully, a nurse called Eduard's name, and he was spared further discussion. "You may see her." He managed a near smile as he brushed past the big man to confer with the mother of a young man who had lost his right arm in the blast.

Shimon was shaking as he entered the large ward of twenty beds. Some were surrounded by white curtains. The air smelled of antiseptic and floor wax. The soft murmur of voices filled his ears. He stood unmoving as he scanned the rows for Leah. He wished he did not feel so weak, so frightened and sick. She was the one who was hurt, not he. Why did his knees feel as though they would buckle if he took even one step?

A nurse emerged from behind a curtain. "You are looking for someone?"

"Leah Feldstein."

"On the end. By the window." The face was kind and sympathetic.

Shimon heard a baby cry. Only then did he realize he was in an obstetrics ward. He put a hand to his head. The sound made him feel faint. It seemed too cruel to put her here where she would hear the babies.

He walked unsteadily to the end of the ward and peeked cautiously in through the slit curtain. *Yes. Leah.* She looked . . . awful. Glass bottle. Needle in her arm. Pale and tiny. Her head bandaged. Ears covered with gauze. She will not hear the babies after all. The realization made tears come to his eyes. His throat burned with the agony of emotion he felt he must master.

White iron rails guarded her bed, as if she were a small child and might fall out. He stepped into the cubicle. The curtain clung to him as he sidled up toward the head of the bed. He did not want to wake her. *Why did we not stay in England? or America? Lord, did You bring us here for this?*

He stood beside her for a quarter of an hour and mourned. For their lost life in Vienna. For their lost child. For lost innocence. Once he had believed that the world was mostly good—people mostly good-hearted, nations just, governments trying their best. But standing by Leah, he remembered again the child Ada-Marie. The faces on the *Darien.* Evil was somehow personal and real. It had chosen to destroy the People of the Book because to do so would be to make the Covenant of that book a lie and God a liar!

Shimon clenched his fist and raised it slightly in anger at this personal Evil that had killed their child and the children of the *Darien* and now nearly Leah. "No matter what you do," he whispered hoarsely, "we will not curse God! Give up! You cannot defeat Him! Kill us and we will be with Him! Drive us into the sea and He is there! You will not have your way with Shimon and Leah Feldstein or our children! Even in sorrow we will believe in the promise of our Holy Messiah!"

Such words were nothing Shimon had learned in synagogue as a boy. They were not a prayer, certainly, but instantly a heaviness lifted from him. He took a deep breath, as if he had just run and won a terrible race against his own despair. Only now did he feel that somehow he would have the strength to encourage and comfort Leah. He squared his shoulders and prayed for help. He touched her arm and her brown eyes opened in confusion. First relief, then sorrow shadowed her face at the sight of Shimon.

It was her turn to cry. Silent tears dripped from the corners of her eyes. "I am so sorry," she whispered, reaching up to him. "No baby, my darling . . . so sorry . . ."

He knelt beside the bed and touched her face, careful of the bandages. "We will have others, the doctor says."

"I cannot hear you," she replied, fumbling beneath the blanket to pull out a clipboard with paper and a pencil attached to a string. "I cannot hear anything." She closed her eyes with a sob and covered her mouth. Then she looked at him. "I am so sorry," she choked.

He was shaking his head, speaking words she could not hear. "I love you. Everything will be fine. Do not be afraid. We will have a family. You will hear your own music again. You are alive, my dearest, and nothing else seems important right now."

"I cannot hear you, Shimon." She managed a pitiful smile through the tears. "You have to write it down." And as he nodded and began to write, she talked and told him what happened. "So fast . . . so fast . . . I saw them. Arabs. They left the car and trapped the bus, and then I fell down. Maybe someone pushed me down. A light flashed; I couldn't hear but there were people hurt everywhere. The English soldier came and shielded my eyes. I did not get to Victoria. Eli's note is still in my pocket. I . . . started bleeding in the ambulance and I knew . . . the baby was . . . going away . . . I'm sorry."

Shimon finished his scrawled note. He had written down all the things he had said to her and then added:

> This is the eighth blessing of the Amidah—the Shemoneh Esrei. I prayed every week in synagogue and never believed it before now. But now I am praying this for you, Leah.

He finished the note in Hebrew:

> Heal us, O Lord and we shall be healed,
> Save us and we shall be saved
> For You are our glory.
> Send complete healing for our every illness.

And then he wrote in German:

> *For Leah's ears, for her womb, and for her heart, we ask healing and we will give You thanks.*

Then again in Hebrew:

> *For You, divine King, are the faithful, merciful Physician. Blessed are You, Lord, who heals the sick of His people Israel!*

In German he wrote:

> *I do not know any other prayers for such a moment, but now I pray it in my heart and not just on my lips. The Lord will hear and answer. Be comforted, my love!*

Leah read the prayer out loud and in those ancient words of the *Shemoneh Esrei*, she found the comfort her heart longed for. "I will keep it here beside me in bed. Will you bring my Bible?"

Shimon nodded in reply.

"And will you also bring me good stationery? Elisa will hear about this in the newspapers. I must write and tell her."

He nodded again, then gave her a warm, relieved embrace. He pressed her strong, calloused fingertips to his lips. Leah's soul was music. He heard it even now in the antiseptic clatter of Hadassah Hospital, amid the sweet cries of babies that were not their own.

Samuel Orde had returned to the hospital with Shimon Feldstein. His purpose for doing so was more than an act of mercy, however.

He waited in a small anteroom set aside for medical consultation. It was urgent that he speak with Dr. Letzno about the woman's condition. There were a number of questions she could possibly answer. The sooner Orde was able to speak with her the better.

Impatient and haggard-looking, Dr. Letzno pulled open the door and confronted the British captain. "There are injured people here, Captain Orde," he said sharply. "Make this quick."

"Leah Feldstein . . ."

"What about her?"

"She was closest to the blast. She is the one survivor who was close enough to see the terrorists."

"A fact I am certain she would like to forget."

"I need to speak with her about it. If she can identify the men—"

"The woman has undergone a miscarriage, an emotional loss as well as physical. Tonight she is not a witness but my patient, Captain Orde."

"I do not mean to appear calloused," Orde began.

"Then save your questions at least until tomorrow!" Dr. Letzno snapped.

"If I do that, the perpetrators may get away."

"It seems that they have already done so."

"We have roadblocks on every road leaving Jerusalem. But roadblocks will do us no good if we do not have a physical description of the terrorists who have done this." Orde was firm. "If we catch them, perhaps it will prevent others from being hurt in the future."

The doctor seemed to hear him. He sighed and mopped his brow. There was so much grief here today. So many hurt. They must stop such a thing from happening again, catch the animals who had done this thing! He nodded. "She is sedated. I cannot guarantee anything. Come on, then." He opened the door and expected Orde to follow him to the ward.

The halls were quieter now. Some still sat on the long benches at the end of the corridor, waiting for word, but most of the relatives had gone home. Orde had not realized that it was nearly midnight until he glanced at the clock above the nurses' station.

The doctor walked quickly toward the ward where Leah rested. The long room was dark except for the dim lights on the call buttons beside each bed.

The countenance of the doctor changed as he stood silently over the sleeping form of Leah. His face became tender and in the shadowy light, Orde saw a transformation from brusque impatience to compassion. The doctor did not shake her to awaken her but simply took her hand in his and waited for two minutes before he rubbed it gently.

Leah inhaled and turned her head toward him. She opened her eyes to blink up in bewilderment at Dr. Letzno. Only then did he turn on the light above her bed. He wrote out the purpose of Captain Orde's visit.

"Yes," Leah said sleepily. "I saw them. Am I the only one who saw them?"

Orde nodded and took the notepad. Could she describe what she saw? the faces of the men?

"It all happened so fast." She closed her eyes.

The doctor continued to hold her hand. "She may be too exhausted," he said to the captain. "I cannot allow you to push her."

Leah opened her eyes again. They were clearer. More aware. And they were filled with the memory of what she had seen. "I saw them both quite clearly," she said in a strong and certain voice. "Both of them. Young Arab men. And a third man who drove the getaway car."

Orde smiled with relief. Would she know them if she saw them again? He scrawled the words in large block letters.

"I could never forget their faces," she replied. "You must catch them. Such men . . . anyone who would do such a thing." She paused as if to regain composure, and then as Orde took down every word, she described the details of what she had seen. Everything was clear before her. "They were hardly men. Very young. Not twenty years old. The driver of the second car was older. He wore a red fez hat, and when he shouted, I saw he had a gold tooth in front."

An hour later Orde hurried to the telephone to contact the officers on duty at headquarters. Leah Feldstein's mind had taken a perfect photograph of Evil. Faces were etched indelibly into her mind.

He read the descriptions to be transmitted to the soldiers manning the roadblocks. Fifty-one Arabs had been detained for questioning. A strict curfew was in force. And now there was a witness who even remembered the color of the cuffed trousers of both younger terrorists.

This news turned the dismal gloom of military headquarters to hope. *The cellist Leah Feldstein saw everything! We'll catch the blighters, then, won't we?*

32

Dark Counsels

The sounds of light surrounded the Dead Sea where Ibrahim had parked the car to wait. A warm breeze swept across the waters from Transjordan, and in Victoria's dream she heard the shouts of millions on that wind: *"There is no god but Allah, and Mohammed is his prophet! Drive them into the sea! Jews to the sea! Eli! Eli, be one of us . . . one of . . ."*

The million raging voices blended into Victoria's voice, and she thought she called the name of Eli out loud as she slept. A sudden fear took hold of her. She must not speak his name. Not in her sleep.

"Victoria."

She heard Eli's voice.

"Victoria! Wake up. Victoria!" It was not Eli but Ibrahim who called her. "Get out of the backseat. *He* is coming!"

Victoria opened her eyes and fought to remember where she was. *The Dead Sea. With Ibrahim. Waiting for someone.*

In the distance she could hear the soft sputtering of a motorboat engine on the water. Ibrahim flicked the headlights once. Twice. A third time. The steady thrumming of the engine replied in a slight change of course, and now it cut an unswerving path toward the automobile.

Victoria sat up quietly and brushed her hair back as she studied the intense profile of her brother. Even in the darkness his eyes glowed with a strange light. Excitement, as if he were watching two mongrel dogs fighting to the death in the street while the men shouted wagers around him. Victoria had seen that look before on the face of Ibrahim. It had frightened her then, and it frightened her now.

The motor thumped louder, and again Ibrahim flicked the lights.

A fraction of a second was enough to illuminate a small, dilapidated boat carrying three men with faces turned toward the shoreline of Palestine. Two were Arabs, dressed as the Bedouins who camped around Amman. The third man was of fairer skin. His bald head had no covering. Victoria knew by this that the man was European. His mouth was a cruel, hard line, lips pressed together in disgust.

The bald man's face seemed to burn into Victoria's mind. That second of light filled her with foreboding. "Praise be to Allah," Ibrahim whispered. "He has come at last!"

So the man with the cruel mouth was the one they had been waiting for. Victoria shuddered as the motor of the boat coughed and died. There were words murmured at the shoreline. The guttural accent of German was plainly distinguishable. She stared forward, trying to find some movement in the darkness outside the car.

Footsteps approached. The man was invisible in the blackness. And then hands touched the half-open glass of the window. Victoria drew back from the thick pale fingers that almost touched her face. And then the voice spoke. "I am Commander Vargen, here at the command of the Führer of the Third Reich. Heil Hitler!" Without further speech the door opened, and the man with the cruel mouth slid in beside Ibrahim.

Freddie lifted Charles and Louis up on his shoulders as they waited in the wings of the theatre for Elisa. Her box was stuffed with mimeographed sheets containing notes on the score and changes of rehearsal schedules. She tugged on the stack of papers, then groaned as they tumbled out onto the floor. Frieda Hillman looked on, amused.

Freddie placed his young charges down on the stage and stooped to help her retrieve her papers.

"Well, missus . . . ," he said, holding up an envelope and squinting as if to look through the paper, "what's this now?" Frieda leaned over for a glance, then returned to adding still more papers to the other boxes.

Elisa took it from him, frowning as she recognized the neat German script of the handwriting, then the postmark. Paris. Her hands began to tremble as she passed it back to Freddie. "You open it," she said hoarsely.

He nodded and stood slowly to his full towering height as he slit open the envelope with a penknife. His face was a scowl of disapproval as he silently scanned the letter. He shook his head and then shook it again as if he could not comprehend the meaning of the message.

"What is it, Freddie?" Elisa managed to ask.

He did not answer for a long time. He opened his mouth, then closed it again as he considered what to say. "Do you know anyone

named von Kleistmann, missus?" He put a big paw beneath her arm and
guided her to a bench as the boys played on a backstage platform.

"Thomas," she replied dully.

"That's the same. Now sit down, missus. Sit before you read; will you
now?"

Rachel did not mean to listen. The door of her parents' room was slightly
ajar. Mama sat on the yellow coverlet while Papa paced at the foot of the
bed. Papa's eyes were full of pain and worry as Mama pleaded with him
in a voice so desperate that Rachel scarcely recognized it.

"I sent the documents to Father in Jerusalem. Eduard will make certain he receives them."

"But Etta! *Why?*"

"I am a daughter of Jerusalem! My birth certificate, my old passport
can be renewed. For the sake of the children, Aaron! We *must* be prepared!"

"You are a citizen of Poland now, Etta! We will have to take our place
at the end of the quota line like everyone else!"

"Father will do what he can for us in Jerusalem! He is a rabbi! They
will listen to him! At least we can send the children—"

"You have been listening too much to Eduard!" Papa took off his
coat and threw it onto the bed.

"You said they were following Eduard. But *look!*" Mama jumped to
her feet. She went to the window but did not pull back the curtain. Fear
crossed her face. "You know we are also being watched, Aaron. Ever
since you came back from the refugee camp, you have been followed! I
cannot go to market without some horrible man trailing along behind! I
am a woman, but still I have eyes to see what is happening! You bury
your head in the sand, Aaron, and you may well bury us, too!"

Rachel had never heard them argue. The sound of it, the sight of their
faces, made her stomach churn.

Papa's face was red. "Read the newspapers, Etta! Do you think we
will be safer in Palestine than we are here? In Warsaw there are no riots!
We have not had a pogrom in months! Jerusalem has violence every
day! I cannot leave the congregation! I *will* not! The police may follow
us all day long, but there will never be a crime for which they can arrest
us! I am a rabbi! A humanitarian, not a politician." His own words made
him falter. He fell silent suddenly and rubbed a hand across his face as
Mama glared at him unhappily.

And then Papa looked toward the door. He saw Rachel. He saw by
her wide, terrified eyes that she had heard everything. His anger ex-

ploded. "What are you doing there?" He stalked to the door. "Why are you sneaking around the halls!"

"Oh, Papa!" Rachel cried as if his anger was a physical blow. "I did not mean to—"

"Go to your room!" He slammed the door in her face, and she ran weeping up the narrow stairs to her bedroom.

The volume of the argument dropped low. It hissed up through the floor like escaping steam. It did not stop for hours until, at last, Rachel fell into an exhausted and restless sleep.

Three other wire services already placed the name of Leah Feldstein at the top of the list of wounded in the Jerusalem bombing. Murphy read Samuel Orde's dispatch aloud as it clacked the full story over the TNS office wire.

> "RENOWNED CELLIST LEAH FELDSTEIN SUFFERED MINOR INJURIES STOP THE INVOLVEMENT OF FOREIGN INSTIGATORS SUSPECTED BY BRITISH OFFICIALS STOP"

This was an element no other reports had even mentioned. Murphy inwardly cheered Orde's thoroughness as the story added a dozen minor details that transformed a flat tale of violence into a three-dimensional portrait.

> "COMMENTS OF THE ROYAL COMMISSION OF INQUIRY HEADED BY SIR JOHN WOODHEAD IN JERUSALEM HAVE EXPRESSED CONCERN FOR SAFETY OF ALL RESIDENTS OF PALESTINE MANDATE STOP SUCH EVENTS HAVE GIVEN RISE TO QUESTION OF HOW AN INDEPENDENT JEWISH STATE WOULD SURVIVE SUCH ONSLAUGHTS ON ITS OWN WITHOUT PROTECTION OF BRITISH MILITARY FORCES STOP"

Murphy frowned at this paragraph. "In other words," he said dryly, "Ol' Woodhead thinks maybe a Jewish homeland is not such a grand idea after all—eh, Orde?"

The dispatch continued:

> "BRITISH MILITARY SOURCES IN JERUSALEM HAVE DRAWN PARALLELS BETWEEN ACTIVITY OF FOREIGN MERCENARIES IN SPANISH CIVIL WAR AND RECENT EVENTS IN PALESTINE STOP NEARLY 20,000 BRITISH TROOPS NOW OCCUPY MANDATE TERRITORY IN ATTEMPT TO KEEP PEACE STOP"

Murphy had been in Spain. He had seen the planes of the German Luftwaffe over Madrid and Barcelona. He had watched the weak Fascist armies of Franco become strong and brutal with Nazi men and equipment. The same thing was happening in Palestine. This time it was twenty thousand British soldiers who would be tied up away from whatever might happen in Europe. And Murphy was certain that Hitler's "last territorial demands in Europe" were really not the last. How convenient to intimidate England into remaining tied up in Palestine while at the same time closing off further hope of a Jewish homeland!

"Hitler really is a genius," Murphy remarked to Harvey Terrill. "Diabolical. Evil. And brilliant."

"You want to edit Orde's piece, or shall I?" Harvey scanned the page.

Murphy shook his head. "Print it word for word the way he wrote it. We can hope there will be a few out there who can read between the lines, Harvey." Murphy pocketed a copy of the story. "Anyway, I'm going home. Leah Feldstein is okay. That is the only news my wife will care about. I need to tell her before somebody else calls her with only half a story and word that Leah was hurt."

Harvey saluted. He knew Murphy had been working for fourteen hours straight today. "You want me to call if there's anything else, Boss?"

Murphy nodded wearily. He needed a shave and a shower and a good night's sleep, but there was enough implied in Samuel Orde's story to keep him wide-awake. The gates of hell were slowly swinging open in Palestine. Churchill had called the Mandate Hitler's second front against British foreign policy. After today, Murphy believed that Palestine might well be the first front against England and certainly against the Jewish people.

"I'm going to sleep light tonight, Harvey. Keep me posted on this one." He frowned and stared out the dark window, where the bright headlights of a bus swept over Fleet Street like searchlights. "Something's coming," he muttered.

All the lights of the Red Lion House were blazing when Murphy arrived home. Freddie Frutschy greeted him at the top of the stairs. The big man's expression was an unhappy scowl as he wrapped his enormous hand around Murphy's.

"She's heard the news, huh?" Murphy asked quietly.

For a moment Freddie looked perplexed. "Yes, sir. And an unhappy way to hear such a thing, too. I stayed right here with her an' the boys 'til you come home."

She was not in the front room. Murphy stepped past Freddie. The radio in his study played Benny Goodman live from the Algonquin Hotel in New York. Murphy remembered how much Leah liked Benny Goodman.

Elisa appeared in the doorway. Murphy could tell she had been crying. "Oh, Murphy!" she said softly.

Murphy put his arms around Elisa, and she began to weep softly. "Don't worry," he said. "She's okay. I got the story from Jerusalem, and she's . . ."

Elisa stiffened. "Jerusalem? What—"

"Leah," he answered. "You heard about the bombing. But Leah is—"

"Leah? Bombing?" A look of such anguish swept across her face that Murphy knew she had not heard.

"You *don't* know!" He turned to look at Freddie, who stood at the door wringing his cap. "What's happened?"

"A letter for the missus. From Paris again." Freddie frowned. "Some bad news. I thought it best I stay close until you arrived."

Elisa was still digesting the fact that Murphy had mentioned Leah's name in connection with a bombing. It was almost too much. She sat down and tugged the rumpled letter from her pocket. "Leah," she whispered.

"She's all right, I tell you!" Murphy sat down beside her. He raised a hand in farewell to Freddie. "Thanks, pal." A nod of acknowledgment and the big man left them alone.

"Was she hurt, Murphy? Was Leah—" Elisa asked.

"Only minor injuries." Murphy opened the letter. He scanned the words. Each phrase was like a shock of cold water.

> *Thomas von Kleistmann died the silent death of a hero. Gestapo in Paris mentioned the name of Elisa Murphy in connection with the activities of von Kleistmann opposing the Nazis. Take every precaution for your safety and for the sake of those who remain in Germany whose names you know. Their lives depend on silence. Please destroy this communication. God bless you. God restore our nation. Heil Deutschland!*

Murphy lowered the letter and took Elisa's hand. "I'm so sorry, Elisa."

Elisa could not speak. Tears brimmed in her eyes, and she pressed her lips together and shook her head as if to resist any more crying tonight. She leaned against Murphy, letting him cradle her in his arms. She was glad she had not heard the news about Leah in Jerusalem from anyone but him. She could trust him that her friend was all right. Somehow that also comforted her in the grief she felt for Thomas tonight. It had drawn her away from the knowledge that he was dead. *Leah is alive!*

Murphy did not speak for a long time; he simply held her. "The postmark is Paris?" he finally asked.

Elisa nodded, then sat up to search her pockets for the envelope. "I . . . must have thrown it away. Or . . . I don't know. But it was Paris."

Murphy moved to open his rolltop desk to retrieve the first postcard of warning that he had received. He had tucked it beneath the edge of his desk blotter. It was not there. "Did you see a postcard here?" he asked in a puzzled voice.

She joined him to search for the postcard. "No. I never . . . what is it about?"

Murphy looked at her thoughtfully, then explained. Sir Thomas Beecham, conductor of the orchestra for which Elisa played, had received the postcard from Paris. He had become alarmed when he read its terse message and had phoned Murphy at his office. The message had simply said, GEFAHR. Danger. Murphy had never told Elisa about it, but he had hired Freddie immediately as a bodyguard.

Elisa and Murphy looked in every drawer and cubbyhole in the massive desk. The postcard was not there.

Murphy tried to think. He might have gathered it up accidentally with something else. Taken it to the office. Maybe it did not matter. He took the letter from his pocket and knelt before the glazing hearth. He touched a corner of the paper to the flame and held it there until it flared up, then yellowed and blackened. *The silent death of a hero.*

Carved out from the labyrinth of stone corridors and secret tunnels that honeycombed the mount beneath the Dome of the Rock, a small square room lay hidden deep below the surface. In the room, a square table, bathed by a single shaft of light, held a black leather letter case.

Three sets of hands ringed the fringe of light around the table, the faces shrouded in shadow. It seemed as if the light had come into the room only for the sake of the letter case—as if this leather folder were on display, and the men had come to worship it.

"Open it," instructed the voice of Dr. Hockman to Haj Amin. "You will find it as I promised."

Delicate hands and embroidered tapestry sleeves reached for the letter case, hesitated, and then opened it. "I was expecting . . . hoping for Officer Georg Wand. He trained my men." Haj Amin Husseini was not pleased by the arrival of Commander Vargen.

Vargen spoke up, not to defend himself, but to explain. "Wand is dead. In service to the Fatherland. But you may read for yourself my rank and experience."

The swastika and the eagle were emblazoned on the letterhead of the paper. The greeting was a personal one from Adolf Hitler to the Mufti. In the shadow, a hint of a smile tugged at Haj Amin's narrow lips. "Ah," he said at last. "You fought with the Turks against the English in the war."

"He aided in the disposal of the Armenians at that time, Your Excellency," Dr. Hockman spoke up quickly. "He did not fight against the Arab armies."

"It would not matter if he had," said Haj Amin lightly. "I fought with the British against the Germans and the Turks, but you see now how time has changed all that. The English are our enemies, and you are now here in Palestine—perhaps hoping to claim the territory once again for Germany?"

"Our goal is the same as your own," Vargen said coolly. He would not be baited. "We wish to see the end of British power here and the end of the Jewish problem. For that reason the Führer sent me as his personal representative."

"And what do you think of our efforts? We have claimed the roads and fields for our own after dark. The streets of Jerusalem are under my control. One word, and—" Haj Amin was pleased with himself.

"A good beginning. Small and unprofessional, but a beginning nonetheless."

Haj Amin ignored the jibe and scanned the papers without emotion. Lists of the names—Jews—Englishmen—Christian Arabs . . . targeted for assassination. Riots planned for Safed. Haifa. Jaffa. Galilee. And Jerusalem, of course. Routes for the rioting mobs to follow. Shops to be destroyed. Everything was clearly laid out with German precision.

Haj Amin read and read again. He laid the sheaf of papers back in the light. "All this planned for the same day, the same hour. It is not possible."

Hockman cleared his throat as if the word *impossible* was blasphemous. "Commands are not given that are impossible to follow."

"I do not have men enough or army enough for such widespread actions," Haj Amin protested.

Vargen smiled. This little Muslim knew much but he had much to learn. "Your *people* will be your army! Call on them! In every city and town they will come."

Haj Amin shook his head slowly. "Not even the voice of the prophet could arouse them to *this* in one moment! They will not be moved . . . not this *far*!"

"You must provide the reason." Vargen's voice was patronizing.

"I have called for a holy war. Some fight for the sake of Allah because I demand it, but most—"

Vargen leaned forward until the light illuminated his face. He was the teacher, Haj Amin the pupil. "Not alone for the sake of a *god*! Only fools will fight and die for the sake of a god alone. In the Reich—" he paused for effect—"our Führer has learned that the love of a god and love of a country will not turn the hearts of men to his will." He crossed his arms and sat back again. "Ah, but when the enemy defiles a woman! Perhaps not even a woman of your house, not wife or mother, but a woman of your own race—you see? In days of old a virgin was presented as a sacrifice to the gods. There are lessons in legend, Haj Amin. Find me a woman to sacrifice to the gods, and the people will be yours!"

Haj Amin sat back in confusion. "But . . . we worship Allah. The law forbids such—"

"You worship your own ambition," Vargen hissed, "the god of yourself! The god of the adoration of your Muslim followers!"

"I will not be insulted by this . . . madman!" Haj Amin stood.

Hockman raised a hand to calm him. "Please, Your Excellency. Herr Vargen speaks . . . in a figurative sense! He is a poet who teaches you the way to achieve your goals!"

Haj Amin did not sit. "Speak on then, poet," he warned. "But remember I have only to raise my hand and *you* are the sacrifice!"

Vargen laughed. He was unafraid of the threat. "Find me a woman, Haj Amin, and I will find a Jew who will violate her. This small act will give you an army that will roar over the English and the Jews of Palestine with a storm of revenge!"

There was a long silence in the square stone room. Haj Amin sat down slowly in his chair. His hands flitted into the light and picked up the papers. "A simple matter of rape?" There was amusement in his voice.

"The rape of a Muslim woman *by a Jew*." Vargen grinned. "Even a prostitute will suffice. It is the subject matter that will create the explosion—a proven method in the Reich."

Haj Amin rarely laughed. Outside the dark corridor, his bodyguards exchanged wondering glances when the laughter of their leader reached their ears.

"There is time to consider the characters in our play." Haj Amin wiped away tears of mirth. "Hitler is right! Was there ever a match struck that could cause a greater fire? *A rape!* Indeed, this poet understands men's passions!"

There were other matters of business to discuss, but Haj Amin was still chuckling to himself as he made his way through the passageways to his private residence just beyond the courtyard of the Dome of the Rock.

33

A Chink in the Wall

A thick fog blanketed Berlin. The British Embassy was dank and musty-smelling as the moisture permeated the walls.

Ambassador Henderson sat at the breakfast table in a heavy wool tweed jacket. He cracked his soft-boiled egg with a nervous tapping of his spoon as he discussed the bombing in Jerusalem with Theo.

"My dear Mr. Stern . . . Mr. Lindheim," he said in an amazed tone, "you cannot expect the British government to turn over any portion of Palestine to the Jews after something like this! Good heavens! Why would a Jew wish to live there? They cannot protect themselves, certainly."

"Where else are the refugees supposed to go?"

"Go? I ask you why that matter has fallen squarely on the shoulders of Great Britain? Why are we supposed to decide such a thing?"

"Because Great Britain occupies Palestine. And the various commissions have whittled down the land area that was promised as a Jewish national home. Acre by acre, the area for Jewish settlement and purchase of land grows smaller."

The spoon smashed irritably down on the eggshell. "But *why*, in heaven's name, do the Jews wish to settle there?"

"Chaim Weizmann has said that there are two places in the world for the Jewish people: the countries where they are not wanted, and the countries where they cannot enter. Where are they to go then?"

"Well, if I were a Jew, I would not choose Palestine!"

A sad smile. "I would not choose Palestine either if there were anyplace else to go."

"Ah, well." Henderson smiled patronizingly as he lifted the dripping spoon to his lips. "Maybe your little talk with Hermann Göring will change all that, eh? This little trade arrangement should open the doors to a few more places. The United States? Certainly with all their self-righteous prattle about our management of Palestine, they will open their own doors for immigrants if your plan is successful, eh? That is why you have come." He raised his coffee cup as if to toast Theo's mission. "And so, here is to your success, Mr. Lindheim. May you get the monkey of immigration off the back of Great Britain." He slurped as he drank.

Theo found it a waste of time and energy to argue with a man as shortsighted as Henderson. Instead he ate his breakfast and listened politely as Henderson gabbed on about what a nice fellow Hermann Göring really was, what a splendid sportsman and hunter, what a droll and witty fellow, always ready with a joke.

Theo did not respond with the information that he knew Göring well. He knew enough to be certain that Göring's idea of what embodied a good hunt would no doubt be found in their meeting at Karinhall.

For two hours after breakfast, the staff artist of the Palestine British military intelligence sat beside Leah's bed and sketched portraits according to her direction. Orde looked on silently over Harry Smith's shoulder as eyes were widened and eyebrows altered to meet in a solid line. Lips too full were erased and made thinner.

"Yes. Yes. That is more like it," Leah whispered in amazement as the picture in her mind became a tangible reflection of the men she had seen on Julian's Way. The images were not exact likenesses, but they were close, she said. And the face of the burly, unshaven driver with his gold tooth was very close indeed.

When she was satisfied with Smith's efforts, she looked eagerly at Orde. "Find these fellows in Jerusalem, and you will have the murderers."

Orde thanked her with a nod, and suddenly her strength left her. She lay back wearily on her pillow and closed her eyes. She had been working very hard, and she was tired. She did not say good-bye.

The two soldiers left her sleeping as they hurried off to headquarters to reproduce the faces Leah had given them. They would appear on a thousand posters to be posted throughout the city.

Lucky, Tasha and Mr. Parks had called Victoria when she returned to work in the transportation department. She was lucky she had not been there. It was terrible. The explosion was horrible. And that nice cellist who had played so beautifully and liked Victoria enough to give her tickets to the Woodhead concert was also among the injured. She was in Hadassah Hospital, they said. And Victoria was very lucky she had not been there!

There was nothing else talked about all day. Hardly any work was done. Victoria tried not to listen, tried to forget that her own brother had known enough about what happened that he had not let her come to work!

By the time the Mandate offices had closed, Victoria was ill from all she had heard and all she knew but did not say. The guilt of her brothers had somehow blackened her own heart. Because of her, Leah Feldstein was in a hospital! Because Victoria did not run to the Palestine police with the word that *something* was planned, people had died.

At least that is the way it felt. *Was there anything I could have done?* she asked herself a thousand times. The answer came in the memory of a locked door. A lie with which Ibrahim had carried her away from Jerusalem. No. There had been no chance. But what about now? Should she go to someone? tell them that Ibrahim had been worried about her because he knew about the terrible *something* that had happened?

She scanned the lobby, crowded now with uniformed British soldiers. Every bag and parcel was searched as residents entered the hotel through the revolving doors. Should she tell someone now? tell them that Ibrahim *knew*? But others had known something was coming. The man on the bus had been talking about it. A demonstration, everyone had thought. What could Victoria say to these English soldiers? *Arrest my brothers. Imprison them. Maybe they know who bombed the bus on Julian's Way!*

Victoria did not know what to say. Ibrahim had denied that he knew any details. He swore to her that he had heard the rumors and was frightened for her well-being. But what of the man they had picked up on the shores of the Dead Sea? Victoria was certain that Ibrahim was not innocent, but she did not dare accuse him since she could not be sure of the scope of his involvement and guilt.

Such thoughts made her exhausted, yet she must do one thing before she went home to bed. She caught the bus to Hadassah Hospital. Leah Feldstein was injured, and Victoria knew she would not sleep unless she saw her. After all, Leah had been coming to meet her, coming for tea at the hotel! Victoria felt responsible for Leah's condition, too, and so she hurried through the glass doors of Hadassah and asked for Leah's ward number. The Jewish staff looked at her oddly, but Victoria didn't care. She had to see Leah—no matter what.

It was almost noon. Dr. Eduard Letzno had not slept in thirty-one hours. Sunlight had not touched him since he had entered Hadassah twenty-six hours before. It seemed much longer ago than yesterday since he had come here. He had seen lifetimes end. He had heard the stories of the wounded, watched the tears of families fall, given hope, and taken hope away. Before he had even had a chance to see the stones of Jerusalem, he had become as much a part of the city's history of grief and travail as the stones themselves.

His smock flecked with blood of Jerusalem's wounded, Eduard caught a glimpse of his own reflection in a window. Beyond this ghost-like apparition of his face was the Dome of the Rock. The city wall encircled the holy mountain, embracing houses and shrines together. Christian. Muslim. Jew. All gathered into one unyielding ring of stone. Ironically, Eduard saw the great sight for the first time with his own face superimposed upon it. He had helped to save an Arab boy while he had been helpless to do anything for a Christian child the same age. A Jewish merchant had died in his arms. Yes. Eduard was part of the stones and flesh of Jerusalem, a fragment of living history after one day in Palestine. *I was there. I tended the wounded and dying.*

He ran a hand over the sandpaper skin of his unshaven cheek. In the reflection of the window he did not look like a physician, but a butcher.

A strong hand clapped him on the back as he stared at the glass and beyond at his new city. "Go on, man! Go get some rest," said the guttural voice of Dr. Johann Kleinmann. Dr. Kleinmann had once been the head of a great German hospital. Once . . . a long time ago. Much longer ago than the lifetime that was Eduard's yesterday.

"So, Herr Doktor—" Eduard managed a smile—"I am finished then?"

"It was good you were here. Good for us. Maybe not so good for you on your first day here, eh?"

Eduard did not share what he was thinking, did not tell the doctor that since yesterday Eduard considered himself a native of the city. "I made one more round. There are several among the wounded who can go home. I have taken the liberty of signing their papers for discharge. They will need follow-up care, of course."

"Fine. Yes. So now you go home, too. Sleep. Eat something. I will tell Nurse Cominski to make the outpatient appointments beginning tomorrow at eight o'clock for you." Another thump on the back. "I would hate to lose you to exhaustion before you have even started officially."

"Yes. I need to unpack." Eduard looked again toward the Old City. "There is an old man I must see. Father of a friend in Warsaw."

"Fine. Fine. But pay your calls after you sleep a few hours or you will be of no use to us here in Hadassah Hospital—unless you plan to donate your body to science. I had a few hours' sleep last night, and now so must you. An order from the chief of staff, eh?" A finger tapped against Eduard's chest to make the point, and then Dr. Kleinmann hurried down the corridor as his name was called over the PA system.

Eduard's dull fingers fumbled with the ties of his smock as he made his way down the steps to the physician's locker room. He showered at the hospital and put on his same clothes. He smelled mildly of his own sweat tinged with antiseptic as he made his way outside to the bus stop. He carried Etta's precious package beneath his arm. He had intended to visit her father in the Old City immediately following the orientation tour of Hadassah. His orientation had simply taken a bit longer than he expected. He would sleep later.

The fresh air smelled good. He filled his lungs with it as the bus rattled toward Jaffa Gate. The slanting rays of the sun trapped light and shadow on the wrinkled complexion of the wall and suddenly it did indeed seem ancient. On the ramparts, British soldiers patrolled, while pigeons waddled along the crevices without concern for whose stones these really were.

The printed words on the yellow notepaper were comforting to Leah, better than a wish for speedy recovery or the heaping basket of fruit on the bed beside her:

> *Do not worry for anything. We are feeding that husband of yours at Tipat Chalev, along with the other children, so rest and be well.*

This was written in the firm hand of Hannah Cohen as she and Shoshanna Reingolt and Ida Sachar gathered around Leah's bed. The fruit was presented with strict instructions that Leah must eat so many of this and so much of that each day lest her bowels become sluggish while she was in the hospital. After all, sluggish bowels had killed many more Jews that Arab bombs could ever kill, *nu*?

Leah happily informed them that she had been released by Dr. Letzno to return home to her own bed tomorrow. This information resulted in a long discussion among the ladies about who would prepare and bring the meals in what shift. Leah could make out something about menus and what sort of herbal teas were best in cases of miscarriage. Suddenly the animated conversation came to a halt.

The eyes of Ida Sachar narrowed as she watched Victoria enter the ward. Leah observed the interaction of characters like someone watching the drama of a silent movie. Victoria seemed quite nervous as she walked toward them. At the sight of Eli's glaring mother, she paled visibly and paused, as if considering which way she might escape.

Perhaps Leah should have let her go, but she called out Victoria's name impulsively. The three visitors frowned at Victoria, then at Leah, as if she were a traitor.

"Victoria is my interpreter," Leah said cheerfully. "And my first friend in Jerusalem." She motioned for Victoria to come forward. The ladies seemed stunned. It was obvious that they knew this was *the girl* who had nearly lured Eli from the fold. They did not approve. Not at all. Indeed, the Hassan family was well respected in the Old City, but the unwritten law had been violated, and Victoria had crossed the boundary. It had to be *her* fault. Everyone knew what a good boy Eli was, *nu*?

Leah put out her hand to Victoria. She welcomed her warmly as a blizzard of cold disapproval blew across the little space.

"Well then," said Hannah crisply, "she does not need *us* here."

Smiling through tight lips, the three women made their farewells to Leah. They nodded acknowledgment to Victoria and then walked stiffly from the ward.

Victoria looked ill, as if she might need to lie down. Leah patted the bed. "Sit, before you fall."

Victoria nodded and obeyed. *Eli's mother.* Her lips formed the words. Leah did not need to hear in order to understand. *She hates me.*

Leah gazed at the beautiful young woman in sympathy. Then she took a note from under her pillow. "I was praying that you would come, Victoria." Leah handed her Eli's note. "I was bringing this to you at the hotel when *this* . . . happened."

Victoria began to weep silently. She held the note with trembling hands and shook her head from side to side. "I am so sorry," she said again and again. "There was nothing I could do."

Leah could not hear her, but she patted Victoria's arm and tried to comfort her. Leah could not know that Victoria wept not because Eli's mother was so hostile, but because Leah was hurt and somehow Victoria felt responsible.

"Rebbe Lebowitz?" The red-bearded Yeshiva student eyed the rumpled European suit of Eduard Letzno. "What do you want to know?"

Eduard held up the brown paper package as if it was proof. It, too, was rumpled from its long journey in train compartments and ships and finally an airplane. "I have brought a gift for him from his daughter, Etta, in Warsaw," Eduard explained.

At the mention of Etta the young man's face brightened. He grinned broadly, showing widely spaced teeth like missing keys of a piano. "*Nu!* Why did you not say so? The Rebbe Lebowitz has gone to the Western Wall to pray! This is his custom each day at this time," he said, as though he was letting Eduard in on a family secret. "And he prays for his daughter and son-in-law and the grandchildren there."

Eduard's head pounded with exhaustion and dizziness. He felt as if he had drunk a gallon of wine. He swayed slightly. "The wall? You mean the Wailing Wall?"

"The very same." The pale blue eyes wandered up to Eduard's hatless head. Surely Eduard was no Jew. "Would you like to wait for him?"

Eduard shook his head in a firm no. To sit would mean not getting up until he slept. "Which way?" he asked, looking up at the weathered stone blocks and cracking plaster of Nissan Bek Synagogue. There were no English soldiers, even though the Dome of the Rock was plainly visible just beyond the thick fortress walls of the synagogue.

Only pigeons strutted above the arched windows. The cold winter sky was a clean blue contrast to the dusty earth and the jumble of buildings of Jerusalem. Today there was no black smoke. No burning tires or explosions; as yet, the streets and alleyways of the Old City were almost deserted.

The memory of yesterday was still a fresh wound. There were funerals to be held outside the walls of the city. Jerusalem again mourned her dead.

Eduard focused on the clean patchwork of the sky as he trudged up the slope of a narrow street. Framed by the grimy facades of the houses and shops, the sky seemed like a clear river to Eduard's weary mind. In spite of what he had witnessed yesterday, he had no doubts that Etta and Aaron must come home to Jerusalem.

Dr. Letzno's conviction brought tears to the eyes of Rabbi Shlomo Lebowitz when Eduard stood at his side along the deserted stones of the Western Wall. The gnarled hands of the old man reached out to take the package from Eduard. His frail arms embraced it as if it were a child. He thanked Eduard and then turned back to face the stones, which seemed almost the same color and complexion as he was. In a singsong voice he began to pray, holding up the package before the hovering angels and the Shekinah glory that seeped down through the crevices of God's throne room. A slight wind stirred. The fringes of the old man's shawl twirled and the fabric tugged against him. Ah, the wings of the angels fluttered. The photographs and birth certificates had finally arrived! Was this not some chink in the wall of British bureaucracy? And from this

chink, might a door be carved for Etta and Aaron and the little ones to
enter?

To this end Rabbi Lebowitz prayed as Eduard looked on patiently.
Eduard knew the prayers, but he did not say them. He shut them from
his mind as the superstition of an old man. It was this sort of superstition, he believed, that would be the death warrant of the Jews of Poland.
Eduard did not believe any longer that there was a God who heard their
prayers. Not even here at the chink in heaven's floor. He had no hope in
miracles or prayers any longer. Without any emotion, he watched the
old man sway and hum his requests.

At last the rabbi turned and embraced Eduard with a kiss on his
cheek. "I have been praying you would come with an answer just today. I
have been asking the Almighty if perhaps I should leave them alone in
Warsaw, already. If they are not maybe better off there after such things
happen right here in Jerusalem, *nu*?" The old man sighed and took
Eduard's arm as if they were old friends. "But now at the hour of my
darkest doubts and fears God has sent you to me, Doktor Eduard Letzno.
And so, you must come home with me. Share a meal. You have come a
long way to answer the prayer of an old man. And now I will not rest until Etta and my dear ones are here in Jerusalem with me."

34

Twilight of the Gods

Eli had arranged it all: a wedding at Christ Church! A furnished room in the Mahaneh Yehuda district of the New City where she could hide until Eli managed to find a job in Tel Aviv. And money enough for her to buy a pretty dress to be married in!

The note was like a reprieve from the doubt that had imprisoned her these last awful weeks. Now the plots of her brothers would mean nothing to her! She and Eli could move far away from Jerusalem!

Her hands trembled with joy as she wrote her thanks to Leah and the request that Leah and Shimon might come to a very small wedding at Christ Church next week. A happy nod, a quick kiss, and Victoria hurried out to catch the bus home.

Suddenly the whole world looked different. Sunlight pierced through the circle of clouds, illuminating the Old City in light as Victoria's bus moved down the slope of Mount Scopus and then on to Damascus Gate.

Sheep bleated in their pens outside the gate. Heavily laden donkeys moved among the press of shoppers. Women with baskets on their heads and thin veils covering their faces walked with effortless grace in spite of their burdens. Crates of fruits and vegetables were stacked beside open sacks of lentils and coarsely ground flour. Victoria saw it all today as if she were seeing it for the first time. And yet she knew this would be among the last times she walked these crowded, cobbled lanes. She felt no remorse or regret, but amazement that at last she was leaving. Eli was taking her away, and there was no one in the entire Old City whom she could tell about it!

The tall minarets pointed skyward like lances among the shops and houses. The voices of the muezzins silenced all conversation in the marketplace except for the braying of the animals. Rugs were placed on the hard ground and the faithful all knelt and bowed. Here and there English soldiers and a few brave or foolish tourists in the Arab Quarter watched as the population sank to its knees. Victoria hesitated. Not to bow would make her more foolish than the tourists who had come here in their ignorance of danger. Victoria was well aware of the eyes that watched every corner of the Arab Quarter from the Damascus Gate. She also bowed and knelt toward Mecca as she hid her intentions from those who might question the look of happiness on her face.

She called on the name of Eli as if he were her god now. When she finished and raised herself once again, she looked up into the face of Ram Kadar. His black robes and keffiyeh seemed especially black today. There was no speck of dust on him. Except for his thick mustache, he was clean-shaven and scented as if he had anointed himself for an occasion. His white, perfect teeth smiled at her. She averted her eyes from his tanned face.

"Salaam, Victoria." He bowed graciously. "Have you heard the news? Your face has such joy. I have been watching. I followed you from Damascus Gate." So many words from Ram Kadar seemed strange.

"Salaam," she answered, still not looking directly at his face or daring to smile. "I am just home from work, and . . . what news?"

"Your father is home! I have spoken to him already." He lowered his voice slightly. The clamor of the Quarter resumed around them.

"My father?"

"Home from Iran. And he will have a surprise for you!" Kadar seemed giddy. His nearness made her own joy dissipate. The note from Eli felt warm and dangerous in her pocket.

"Then I must go," she said, turning away from him.

"I will walk with you." It was not a question or request. He stepped a pace ahead of her as if to clear her path. His head was high and proud. His eyes swept the stalls within the twilight of the covered bazaars as if he, too, were seeing them for the first time.

He knew the way to the Hassan home. Through the streets of the tinsmiths. Past the shoemaker's shops. Along the street where prayer rugs were heaped up on display. The finest rugs were sold by Victoria's father.

Ahead of them she could see that the new Persian carpets were stacked just inside the shop. Yes, her father was home. That knowledge brought her no pleasure. The presence of Ram Kadar and his self-assurance as he walked with her gave her a sense of foreboding.

Within the shop, Victoria's father stood talking to Ibrahim. He still

wore his business suit, English-made pin-striped, and on his head he
wore a red fez. He was clean-shaven and unrumpled in spite of his journey, but when he looked up to see his daughter in the doorway, he
seemed weary and sad.

Victoria pushed past Kadar. "Father!" She ran to him and embraced
him. She clung to him longer than she might have if Kadar had not been
there.

"Victoria, my daughter. You have missed me, eh? Allah be praised, I
have come home to find you all in health in spite of the many reports
about Palestine."

"She was praying just inside the gate when I saw her," Kadar said. "I
wanted to walk with her here. An unveiled woman alone in the Quarter?
Well, soon we will remedy that Western rebellion."

Victoria turned to face Kadar. What did he have to say about her lack
of a veil? And why had he been so presumptuous as to walk with her to
her own home? "I thank you, Kadar. And now I wish to spend time with
my father."

"Victoria!" Her father sounded shocked. "You forget your manners!
Fix us tea."

Victoria blinked up at her father in surprise. She looked at Ibrahim,
who had not said anything at all to her. He would not look at her. His
hands brushed over a deep red carpet, and he pretended to study the
threads and pattern of it.

"But, Father," she began.

He smiled at her strangely. "Do you not know, Daughter?"

"Know what, Father?"

He laughed nervously. His glance flitted from Ibrahim to Kadar, then
back to Victoria. "Allah has willed that you are to be married."

Her breath came hard. *Could they know about Eli?* "What . . ."

"You have not spoken of this with Ibrahim? Just an hour ago we settled the contract. You and Ram Kadar are to be wed."

Her eyes widened. She felt the blood drain from her face. What could
she say? To be ungrateful or rude would result in a beating, a locked
room. And yet tears of outrage came to her eyes in spite of her battle for
self-control. "My father . . . ," she began.

"Ram Kadar is a man of substance. He will treat you well." Her father
looked aloof, beyond discussion. Ibrahim glanced at her with an uneasy
guilt. Could her brother see on her face the accusation of betrayal?

Victoria wanted to shout her refusal. She wanted to beat her fists
against her father and brother, to run from the arrogant self-assurance of
Ram Kadar. Somehow she managed to master herself. To do otherwise
would have been foolish.

"I had not imagined such . . . an honor, my father. Forgive me if I seem . . . ungrateful." She dared to meet the steady gaze of Ram Kadar. "I simply had not expected Allah to answer my petition in such a way."

Her answer pleased Kadar. It also pleased her father, who sighed with relief. Only Ibrahim dared to look at his sister with open suspicion. Only he knew better.

Her father clapped his hands together happily. "Then we shall set the date."

"As soon as possible," Kadar replied with a gracious bow. "Soon there will be pressing business that I will be required to attend to."

"Please—" Victoria calmed the sense of panic that threatened to break through her voice. "A woman needs time for such important arrangements as this. I must prepare myself."

Ibrahim's eyes seemed openly hostile. He shook his head. He knew she would not consent or submit willingly, and yet Victoria was smiling pleasantly. Her hands trembled. Her eyes were pained behind the soft words and nod of compliance.

"Ram Kadar is an important man," Ibrahim blurted out. "He is a member of the council, and Victoria must fit his schedule, not expect him to fit into matters that are so trivial. The wedding should be soon. This week."

"No!" Victoria turned on him with a fierceness that startled her father and Kadar. "It is none of his business, Father. Tell Ibrahim it is none of his affair! I need time, I tell you! I must not be rushed!"

"Well . . . " Amal Hassan straightened his fez and shrugged in apology for his daughter's outburst. "In this matter it is the bridegroom who suffers as the days pass on, and so—"

Kadar seemed amused. He liked her spirit. He would tame it soon enough, as a man tames a headstrong horse. "I have waited this long. I can wait two weeks more for her."

Victoria swallowed hard. She felt her cheeks flush with the thoughts of her deception. In two weeks she would be the wife of Eli Sachar, and all this would mean nothing. A bad dream to be forgotten.

"You are gracious," she said softly, letting her eyes linger on the face of Kadar.

He took her hand and bowed to kiss it. "My darling," he replied. "*Habibi* . . ."

It was difficult to keep her composure. Difficult not to jerk her hand away. Somehow she managed to maintain her smile.

"And now, my father—" she bowed—"it has been a long day. A difficult day at the offices. There were many innocent injured and so the workload is greater for those of us lucky ones." She let the venom she felt toward Ibrahim pierce him with a hard look.

Ibrahim smiled. Yes. This was better. More what he expected from Victoria. A look of hatred and rage. Much better than this simpering acceptance of a marriage she certainly did not want. He touched his hand to his forehead in a nearly imperceptible salute. Enemy to enemy. Betrayer to the betrayed. Ibrahim preferred this to Victoria's charade.

"Perhaps Ibrahim will prepare your tea, Father. I am unwell from the difficulty of the day." She smiled up at Kadar. "Forgive me."

Kadar offered a deep bow. She stiffly embraced her father before she walked silently back to the stairs that led into the house. She passed her stepmother in the hallway.

"Well, if it isn't our princess! Soon to be a wife! Soon to be gone from this house. Allah be praised."

Victoria did not reply. She went straight to her room and lay down on her bed while the bitterness of her anger washed over her. She stared up at the ceiling and considered Ibrahim's betrayal of her and Eli. If she had a gun, she would kill him. Or a knife . . .

But Victoria had no weapon tonight except her ability to pretend that a marriage to Ram Kadar was just what she wanted. She would play the game. She would disguise the truth that the thought of such a marriage revolted her. And she would think what she must do.

After dinner Ibrahim entered the room of his sister. He did not turn on the light.

"What do you want?" she asked angrily.

"I want to let you know that I am no fool."

"It will take more than words to prove that to me now, Ibrahim," she hissed.

"What I have done is for your own good."

"And for the good of the Arab rebellion, I suppose."

"You will come around."

"You *are* a fool."

"I am watching you. Know that. Every move, I am watching."

"Then watch me tomorrow, my dear brother. Watch me buy a pistol and load it and shoot you."

"Then you will hang."

"Not if I say you tried to molest me."

"You would not do such a—"

"If ever you come to my room again, I will inform Ram Kadar, and then I will not have to kill you myself."

Ibrahim was silent. Ram Kadar was a loaded gun, and Victoria could

indeed point that weapon at Ibrahim's head. He bowed in salaam and
backed from the room. He would not bother her here again.

The moment Etta had been dreading arrived. The strain showed on her
face as she watched Aaron lead the two Polish policemen into his study.
He slid the door shut, letting his eyes look up quickly to where she stood
trembling on the landing. He frowned, nodded to her in a gesture of reassurance. But she was not reassured. Aaron did not know why they had
come. She had never told him what had happened. What would he say
when those men laid out their wicked slander before him?

In a few minutes, she knew.

From behind the door, Aaron's voice roared against their impudence
and crookedness. "Get out!" he shouted. "Leave my home and do not
bother to come back! I shall report your blackmail to the proper authorities and then we shall see how long you carry a badge in Warsaw!"

Another voice shouted back. "You will be sorry. We have the justice
of Poland on our side. She has a police record, you know! And so will
you if you are not careful!"

The second thug joined in. "You know what your chances will be to
emigrate if you have a police record!"

The door crashed back with a startling noise. Aaron's face was tight
and flushed with fury. He stepped out of the study. "Get out!" he said
again. "I am a citizen of Poland, as free as any man. I will not leave my
country, nor will I live beneath the threat of stray dogs like you!" He
clenched and unclenched his fists. The men wanted him to strike out,
but he did not.

"Filthy Jew," muttered the red-faced man.

"I would stay off the streets if I were you," said the second.

Aaron flung open the front door. Snow flurries blew in as the policemen stepped out. The house seemed very cold. Aaron looked up at Etta
as he slammed the door shut. He said nothing as he stalked back to his
study and closed the door behind him.

The postcard from Paris, addressed to Elisa Murphy in London, lay on
the desk of the Gestapo Chief Heinrich Himmler. Beside that was an envelope with the same address—the same distinct handwriting, the same
postmark from a Paris post office not far from L'Opera.

Himmler flipped open the thick file of correspondence from the German Embassy in Paris. There were handwritten requests for additional
stationery, rubber stamps, and office supplies. The Gestapo chief sorted

out the nondescript memos according to handwriting. Those written by
Ernst vom Rath were placed neatly beside the Paris postcard and the
plain white envelope addressed to Elisa Murphy. Himmler replaced the
rest of the material and deposited the file in the refile basket.

Himmler did not need a handwriting expert to see that the script on
the embassy memos matched the writing on the letters to Elisa Murphy
exactly. For Himmler, this was a relief. Of course, Ernst vom Rath had
been suspected of disloyalty to the Nazi Party. These communications to
Elisa Murphy were simple proof of the man's guilt. Himmler only
wished he had been able to acquire a copy of the letter that vom Rath
had sent to the woman. Its contents might have shed some light on the
extent of vom Rath's disloyalty.

He dialed the Führer's private line as he tapped his pen beside the
name of Elisa Murphy. A male voice answered. Himmler stated his
name, and after a moment the voice of Adolf Hitler came on the line.

"Good news, mein Führer," Himmler said cheerfully. "We have
made a definite connection between vom Rath and the traitor Thomas
von Kleistmann! Yes. Now it is certain that our sacrifice for the celebration of the November Putsch is not innocent. We are simply executing a
traitor against the Reich."

Hitler seemed pleased by this information. He liked things well
planned out. Even now he was discussing the routes and targets of the
rioters for the demonstration against the Jews. Trucks would be on hand
to transport the demonstrators out of their own neighborhoods and cities so there would be no personal feelings involved when they attacked
various Jewish homes and establishments. Of course, all this must seem
very natural and spontaneous, the response of German outrage against a
Jew murdering a member of the German Embassy. It was good to know
clearly that vom Rath would die a martyr for their own cause. He was a
minor actor in the play against Hitler, anyway. As for Elisa Murphy, she
was more useful alive now than dead.

Himmler was amused by the enthusiasm in his leader's voice. Hitler
was directing the entire November celebration as if it were a Wagnerian
opera. He had already made notes on Ernst vom Rath's funeral service.
All this would fall on the anniversary of the Beer Hall Putsch, Hitler's attempted coup in November of 1923. Germany needed martyrs.

Himmler wrote a few notes on the back of Ernst vom Rath's envelope; then he gathered it all up and placed it in a new file that he labeled
Götterdämmerung—"twilight of the gods"!

35

Best-Laid Plans

A single thought obsessed Herschel Grynspan now: to take vengeance on the Nazis for the persecution of his family.

He pored over the accounts of the situation in Poland until the lines published in the *Parisian Daily* were memorized like the script of a play in which he must act.

> *Critical situation of Polish Jews deported from Germany. Overnight, more than twelve 12,000 persons have been rendered stateless. Rounded up and deported to Zbonsyn, the no-man's-land between Germany and Poland, their living conditions remain inhuman and depressing. Twelve hundred of them have fallen ill and several hundred are still without shelter. As there is a risk of epidemic, Red Cross doctors, with the help of private doctors, have distributed typhus vaccinations and 10,000 aspirin tablets. A number of instances of insanity and suicide have been recorded.*

These vivid images were reenacted in his mind with the face of his mother and father and sister placed alongside words like *epidemic, typhus, aspirin, insanity . . . suicide.*

He was fed and sheltered, yet even here thoughts of his own suicide plagued him. Would not death be easier than living like a hunted animal? Had it not been for the urges of Hans to give his life a purpose in revenge against the Germans, Herschel would have used the rope from his bed to end the torment.

The obsession of his hatred kept him alive through these days and nights. Tonight, Hans gave him a date to look forward to. A day when his desire for vengeance would be accomplished.

Hans passed him a cigarette; his eyes seemed animated as he explained his plans. "These filthy Nazis." Hans swaggered as he paced in the tiny cubicle. "They have their big celebration coming up. The one where they celebrate the failed coup in the Munich beer hall. You remember?"

Herschel did indeed remember. Every year in mid-November the strutting Brownshirts and their SS companions roamed drunkenly through the streets of every German city looking for Jews to bash. Herschel nodded. The thought of it made him angry with new intensity. "Yes. It is the same each year."

Hans lifted his head like a hunter sniffing the wind. "They celebrate the deaths of their comrades. They glorify the fact that Adolf Hitler was tossed into prison. They make speeches and spew their venom. And they will surely find more Jews to beat up this year, too."

"If I could." Herschel's eyes smoldered with hatred as he conjured up the images. "If only . . . I would shoot them all down! Every one of them! A machine gun in their stinking beer hall, and they would be sorry! All of them!"

"Ah, but you are in Paris," Hans said. "They are back in Germany. We must think what you can do here to disrupt their little celebration, eh?" He patted Herschel on the back. "We must give them a new martyr. And where will you find him in Paris, eh?"

Herschel's eyes glazed as he thought of it. He had made deliveries to the embassy before. It was a simple matter. "The German Embassy!" he whispered, as if the idea was his own, as if the idea had not come straight from the dark minds of those he most wanted to hurt. Suddenly the idea spawned in Darkness became Herschel's own plan. "I know of someone in the embassy in Paris. If I could find him—"

Hans frowned and shook his head. "It does not matter who dies as long as it is a German, eh, Herschel? Providence will direct you to the one you are to teach a lesson! We Jews are not dogs—we are humans! They will hear that in their Nazi meetings. Let their speeches be tainted with sadness as they lose one of their own kind! Have we not lost hundreds?" Hans picked up the newspaper to make his point. "And now, how many more are dead? Even today? Maybe your own family, Herschel. Who can say?"

Herschel clutched his sleeve. "You must help me!" His voice was shrill with desperation. "It is the only thing to do—the only thing I *can* do. There is no other way!"

Hans sighed with relief. No more needed to be said. The frail young

Jew had finally reached an end. Herschel Grynspan would follow every instruction, say every word that was put into his mouth. On November 7, he would walk into the German Embassy of Paris with one goal in mind.

Victoria's eyes flashed a warning to Ibrahim as she left the house for work. *"Do not follow me or bother me,"* the look seemed to say. He simply stared at her in sullen reply.

It was cold this morning. Water had frozen on the stones of the streets, making them slick. Fires burned in smudge pots throughout the Old City, and Arab merchants stretched out their hands to the warmth as they spoke about the curfew and discussed the faces on the posters that had appeared magically on the walls of houses and shops last night. These English were offering a large reward for the capture of the terrorists. A thousand pounds for each of the men who had bombed the bus on Julian's Way. Such a reward made every man search the face of his neighbor to see if perhaps a murderer was lurking there.

Victoria passed through the pedestrian entrance to Jaffa Gate before she noticed the faces on the posters. She looked away and then looked again harder. She frowned and stepped back, trying to deny the similarity to Daud and Isaak she saw in the sketches. The chin of this one was too round, the lips of the other too thin, the cheekbones not defined enough. And yet, there was enough to make her breath come faster with apprehension.

She boarded the bus and paid her fare mechanically. *It could not be, and yet . . .* The posters were also taped up inside the bus. Passengers squinted into the penciled eyes of the sketches. Did everyone see someone they knew in those faces?

Victoria forced her eyes away from the posters. She focused on the busy intersection of Allenby Square—the post office and Barclay's Bank, taxis and civil servants hurrying because of the chill that swept over the city.

The bus turned onto Julian's Way. A section of the road was under repair. Scorch marks were evident on the cracked sidewalk near the bus stop. The broken-off trunk of a sapling was being trimmed back. On the pocked wall of a building, the wind blew a poster up and then back down, showing glimpses of the faces. Chin. Eyes. Mouth. Nose.

Victoria stepped from the bus and stood transfixed before the flapping paper. *Isaak's nose and mouth. The eyes of Daud!* She felt sick. She wished she could sit down someplace.

She put a hand to her forehead, aware that her half brothers stared back at her, daring her to speak—accusing her of betrayal just as she now accused them of murder.

She turned back toward the bus and impulsively raised her hand to stop the driver from closing the doors. She hurried back on and paid her return fare. She did not need to look at the posters again; she was certain now.

Staring at her hands, she tried to think where she should go, whom she should talk to. At Jaffa Gate she inclined her head toward the ramparts of the citadel of David, where British soldiers stood bundled up against the icy wind. Their eyes scanned the buses. Of course they would look at every bus today. It could happen again, couldn't it?

Victoria tucked her scarf tightly around her neck as she walked quickly back through the gate and into Omar Square. She glanced over her right shoulder toward the bell tower of Christ Church. In that moment she knew what she must do.

The voice of Reverend Robbins was gentle and reassuring as he introduced Victoria to the British captain. "You have done the right thing in coming here, Victoria," he said. "And now if you will tell Captain Orde everything, just as you told it to me."

Holding a cup of tea in her hands for warmth, Victoria found that she still trembled as she repeated the story of the midnight trip to the Dead Sea, the German man who had ridden back to Jerusalem with her and Ibrahim . . . and then the posters. Victoria could not bring herself to say that she was certain. Somehow the fact that Isaak and Daud were the sons of her father made it impossible for her to accuse them openly.

"I am afraid they have gotten themselves into something," she said haltingly. "I do not know what it is. But . . . I am afraid for them. Things are so uncertain these days, and young men are so full of passions. I . . . cannot tell you more than this."

Samuel Orde sat on the edge of the pastor's desk as he considered the words of the young woman across from him. She was brave to say anything at all. It would be difficult enough to speak up if one suspected a stranger in the street. But to have to talk about her own family! The strain showed on her face, and Orde pitied her.

"Miss Hassan, I would like you to return to your home." His words were also gentle.

She looked up sharply. "I am leaving there soon."

Reverend Robbins nodded. This was the only mention of the upcoming marriage.

"If possible, I would like to ask that you return to the house just for a while. Keep your ears and eyes open for us," Orde said.

She bit her lip and searched the face of Reverend Robbins for some hint as to what she should do. He answered for her. "Victoria is to be married here on Friday."

Orde rubbed a hand over his cheek and frowned. "Would you be willing to help us until then?"

"I did not intend to become a spy in the house of my father." She paused, then added, "And you must understand, my father is not part of this. He is a good man. He would not . . ." Her voice faltered. She realized that there were many questions in the eyes of Captain Orde. Had he somehow seen that there was more that Victoria was not willing to say?

"No need to report anything to us but something unusual, Miss Hassan—for instance, if that German fellow should come around again. You understand? If there is some involvement on the part of your brothers with the perpetrators of the rebellion, the best thing for everyone in Palestine is to put the rebels where they belong." He smiled reassuringly.

Victoria was not reassured. Her head moved in acknowledgment. "I have a job at the Mandate offices. I am missing work even now."

"I can square it with the office. I will tell them you have a special assignment with me. You will still have your job when you return."

"All right then." She looked fearfully at the captain. "I do not want my brothers harmed because of . . . because I have come here. Please?"

Reverend Robbins cleared his throat at the sight of tears in her eyes. "The captain is a fair man, Victoria. You have done—are doing—the only thing you could do." With that, he stood and saw the captain out. When he returned, Victoria sat staring thoughtfully at his desk.

"I had hoped that this would be the week of my freedom," she said. "That I could leave the Dome of the Rock and have no shadow or guilt follow me away."

Reverend Robbins placed a hand on her shoulder before he sat down again. "I think your hope has been realized, Victoria," he said, opening his Bible. "God is clearly showing you the Darkness you leave behind." He patted the open book. "I have seen the hunger in your eyes for the Light. The same Light your mother knew; God rest her soul. I should have told you sooner," he murmured, as if talking to himself. "But I was afraid for you. I saw no way for you to escape as long as you lived in that house. But it is time now. Time for us to speak honestly, dear girl. This is the week of your freedom. Yes. I am certain of that!"

A handful of posters had been torn from the walls in the souks. They lay faceup on the table between Leo Vargen, Hockman, Ram Kadar, and the

Hassan brothers. In a corner of the room to the right of Vargen, Ibrahim's father sat with his head bowed. He wept silently as his wife stood over him.

Vargen's voice was cold and unfeeling as he directed his question to Ibrahim. "Where did your sister go after she left Christ Church?"

"She is coming home. I left her in the souks. She was walking slowly. Shopping. Looking at things as if she were a tourist." He shrugged. "I do not know."

"You think she has recognized the faces of her brothers?" Hockman first eyed the poster and then the hunched figures of Isaak and Daud.

"My sons," Amal Hassan said quietly. "*Why?* Why *my* sons?"

Vargen ignored the man. Such sentimental nonsense did not address the issue of Victoria Hassan. Why had she gone to the King David and then returned immediately to the Old City? And why had she gone to Christ Church?

"You assumed she would be of service to us, Ibrahim." Vargen raised an accusing eyebrow. "Now you believe she could be our undoing?"

"All I know is that she was behaving strangely this morning. I followed her, as I have told you. She was behaving strangely."

Vargen stuck out his lower lip and sat back, crossing his arms in thought. He turned to Hassan's wife. "Go upstairs and take her clothing." He snapped his fingers and the woman hurried away, leaving her broken husband to shake his head in grief and amazement at what had come upon his house.

Vargen directed his attention to Ibrahim. "When she comes home, see to it she is locked in her room."

Kadar straightened. "I do not believe ill of her." He scowled at Ibrahim. "No harm must come to her. There is an explanation to this."

"Until we have the explanation," Vargen said quietly, "your beloved will have to remain under our watchful eye. Anything less would be foolish." He raised his head angrily, "Just as you have all been foolish and careless in your handling of the situation here in Jerusalem." His eyes narrowed. "Before we have even started, the British could stop us. All it would take is one word from a silly young woman, and all our plans could come crashing down." He pointed toward the weeping father. "And what about him?"

All three brothers leaned forward fearfully. "He will not say anything!" declared Daud.

"Is that true, Mr. Hassan?" Vargen asked with amusement in his tone. "Your sons will hang, you know, if word of this gets out. You understand?"

The elder Hassan nodded silently. He understood only too well.

Victoria hoped that at this odd hour of her midmorning return, no one would be home. She had not taken two steps into the foyer before she realized what a mistake she had made to return here at all.

Ibrahim, Isaak, and Daud stared openly at her. Her stricken father did not look up. The German and another man were smiling curiously at her as if they knew something about her that she did not know yet. Ram Kadar stood. His face looked pained.

"Salaam," she managed to stutter.

There was no reply. Ibrahim answered after a long silence. "Salaam, my sister. Why are you at home at such an hour?"

"I did not feel well," she answered. "I came home for a few minutes only. To take some aspirin. I am gong back to work." She pretended not to notice the face of her father.

The German smiled more openly now. "You are a clever girl," he said in a low, menacing voice, "but you will not be returning to your job at the Mandate office this morning."

She tried to act indignant. "Who are you to say?"

"You will escort her up to her room, Ibrahim," Vargen instructed. "Go along, Kadar. Teach your bride-to-be obedience."

"Father!" Victoria cried as Ibrahim took her by one arm and Kadar by the other. "Father!" But her father did not lift his eyes to her.

She did not fight them, realizing that they would hurt her and she would still be locked in her room. They did not speak to her. Passing her stepmother in the hallway, Victoria caught a glimpse of her dresses and clothes for work on the floor of Ibrahim's bedroom. "What are you doing with my clothes?" she protested.

Kadar grasped her arm more tightly, a signal for her to be silent. "You will wear the traditional clothes of a Muslim now," he said. "There is no reason to wait."

They let go of her arms in front of her bedroom. Ibrahim turned the latch and stepped aside for her to enter. The closet door was open, the rack empty. Drawers were empty and lay piled on the floor. On the bed was a stack of folded robes and veils.

Ibrahim gave her a slight push forward as he stepped out and closed the door, locking it behind her.

It was barely light in the tiny apartment of Leah and Shimon. Leah rolled over and wrinkled her nose. Something smelled strong and unpleasant. She resisted opening her eyes.

Leah heard music far away, as if in a dream. She sensed the light of morning filtering through her eyelids. Was she dreaming? Opening her eyes, she peered around their tiny apartment. Shimon was cleaning the dingy glass of the windows. The pungent smell of ammonia filled the room and made her eyes water, awakening her against her will.

Still the music played. Beethoven. "Sonata for Piano and Violin." *A dream?*

The lid of the phonograph was propped open. Leah could see the tone-arm bobbing across the record. It was a recording she had packed with special care. The violinist was Elisa on a recording made years ago in Salzburg.

Leah sat up. She put her hand to her head. One of the bandages had come undone during the night. "Shimon?" She laughed.

He turned and bit his lip as he searched for the notepad and pen they had used to communicate for the last few days. He held up a finger for her to be patient. There it was, beside the phonograph. He held it up. A message was already written: *Would you like coffee or tea?*

"Tea this morning, please. And after Elisa is finished playing, I would like to hear a little Benny Goodman, if you don't mind."

Victoria was dressed in the traditional robes of her Muslim sisters. A veil covered her face. She studied her reflection in the half-light of morning. She looked the part of a Muslim woman, but she knew her heart had forsaken that life and begun a new one. She was a prisoner, and yet this morning she finally felt free.

It was a twenty-foot drop from the rail of Victoria's balcony to the flagstones of the garden below.

Sheets and blankets were knotted together, then tied to the railing and threaded down to the ground. She stuffed a pillowcase with clothing and tossed it onto the stones where it landed with a dull thud.

For a moment Victoria peered over the edge of her prison. A cold wave of fear gripped her. The rope passed just outside the window of the room where Daud and Isaak slept. Had they heard her? Were they waiting below to catch and beat her? She prayed for help.

Somewhere in the city a rooster crowed. Soon the merchants and peddlers would awaken. Jerusalem was stirring. If she intended to escape this house, it must be now!

She held her breath and swung herself over the railing. For an instant she clung tightly to the makeshift rope, unable to move.

The bells of Christ Church chimed six as the sun began to push up over the horizon.

"Help me, please," Victoria whispered. She did not address her prayer to anyone in particular. Allah, the god of her fathers, she now hated. Eli's God she did not know. Once more she looked over the railing. Once more she heard the chiming of the bells from Christ Church. "*Go,*" they seemed to urge. "*Go now!*" Taking a deep breath, she slipped down and down, finally collapsing onto the stones at the bottom.

A light flicked on behind the curtains of her brothers' room. Stifling the urge to cry out, she gathered up the pillowcase and fled toward the high wooden gate of the courtyard.

They will hear you! Her heart thumped a desperate warning. She forced her trembling hands to pull back the bolt carefully and quietly. The hinges groaned as she slipped through the narrow opening and eased the gate back in place.

First Victoria scanned up the street and then down. She couldn't decide which way she should run now that she was free. She had not really believed she would get this far.

She could not go to work today. Perhaps her brothers would look for her at the King David Hotel. Perhaps they would come into the offices and pull her out from behind her desk while the shocked Englishmen looked on.

Eli! Did she dare run to his home for shelter and safety? It could not be! The fury of Haj Amin and her brothers would turn there, and the day would become a day of massacre in the Old City.

She raised her eyes to the crowded skyline of the Old City. The purple sky lightened, and a beam of light crashed against the bell tower of Christ Church. "*Come!*" the bells seemed to say. "*Come in.*"

That was it! She could hide in the garden of Christ Church. She could crouch behind the shrubs in the courtyard until Eli came for her! And then . . . ?

Victoria could not think that far ahead. Over the wall she heard the voice of Daud shout the alarm: "Victoria is gone!"

She began to run wildly through the deserted streets. Her robes clung to her legs, holding her back as if she fled in a nightmare.

Her breath pushed and pulled against the veil that hid her face. Just ahead she could see the crowded souk where farmers stacked their produce for a day of selling. There were no Muslim merchants in the souk today. The stalls were ominously empty. There were no Muslim women shopping early beneath the vaulted roofs. Only Christians. Armenians. Jews.

Victoria was frightened. She did not stop to listen to whispered words of warning that passed from one merchant to another.

"Something happening today . . ."

"I will not stay open long this morning!"

Victoria emerged on the other side of the souk into the Christian Quarter. She glanced back over her shoulder to see if she had been followed. *They will come! They will come looking for me! Any minute they will be here!*

She began to run again, bursting through a group of startled Copt priests, past the entrance to the Church of the Holy Sepulchre, and finally into Omar Square, where Christian Arabs already thronged on their way in and out of Jaffa Gate.

She dashed across the square, bumping into two British soldiers.

They shouted something to her, then laughed. She did not hear their words. And then, when she was certain she could run no longer, *Christ Church*!

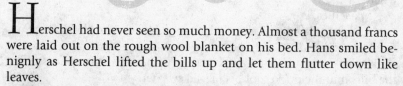

Herschel had never seen so much money. Almost a thousand francs were laid out on the rough wool blanket on his bed. Hans smiled benignly as Herschel lifted the bills up and let them flutter down like leaves.

"But how?" Herschel asked in amazement.

Hans shrugged evasively. "Let us say a collection. From friends."

Herschel ran his hands over the money. He could scarcely believe it. This was much more than he expected or needed. "All of this . . . so much!"

"You will need a new suit of clothes. You cannot check into the hotel in the rags you are wearing. You will need a large trench coat, something with deep pockets for the gun. And the gun. Of course, you will need to buy a suitable weapon. The rest is for your escape."

Herschel managed a smile. "Escape." He repeated the impossible word. Then he frowned. "I have decided that I must see my uncle and aunt again. And my friend Nathan, before—"

Suddenly Hans looked angry. "You will jeopardize everything if you go back there! I forbid it!"

Herschel blinked stupidly at him. "Forbid? But I . . . I want to see my family at least before—"

Hans raised his eyebrow and studied Herschel. "Who found you this room, eh? Who has been your friend? You are worried to show your face, and who takes care of you? I do!"

"I wish only to know if they have any word about my parents."

"Why? So you can back out now? After I have brought you all this?

Made it possible for you to be a hero and avenge your family and your people?"

Herschel was silent.

It began to rain again. It had not stopped raining for two weeks. He looked at the money and thought about the new coat he would buy. The business suit. The gun. "You have been my friend," he said with a note of shame at his obstinacy. "I will not fail in this." Thus he dropped the issue of visiting his uncle and his friend Nathan. But he had made up his mind. There was a good chance he would not see them again. A very good chance that he would not walk out of the German Embassy alive. There were things he wanted to say. He would go to them after Hans left Paris for good tomorrow.

"I am grateful you see reason." Hans appeared relieved, although Herschel had not told him his intentions. "I am leaving tomorrow. I will read the papers and wait for word. When you escape, you will know where I will be."

"Marseilles."

"And then Portugal. Lisbon." He tapped his forehead. "You memorized the address?"

Herschel nodded again and began to gather up his fortune, stuffing the bills into the pockets of his ragged sweater.

No footprints marred the virgin white snow of Muranow Square this morning. Beautiful and glistening, the pristine blanket looked soft enough to sleep on.

Beyond the borders of the Warsaw ghetto, the goyim children would be building snowmen and pitching snowballs at one another.

But today was a special day in Muranow Square. Parents helped little boys and girls dress in the clothes they had laid out yesterday for the bar mitzvah service at the synagogue. Here in Muranow Square there would be no snowball fights, no noisy shouts or soggy mittens.

Rachel did not envy the raucous freedom of Catholic Warsaw. She loved the peace of their way of life.

Papa, looking more worn than peaceful, descended the stairs.

"Baby Yacov has a sniffle, children," he said avoiding Rachel's eyes. "Your mother will not be going to services this morning. Rachel, the boys will stand in the upper gallery with you, *nu*?"

Rachel felt ashamed. She could not forget the anger of her father's voice toward her. She had not meant to listen in. She was wrong to have done so. She must ask God to forgive her this morning. She must pray that Papa would also forgive her.

He opened the door to a blast of wind; then, as the boys walked ahead, Papa touched Rachel on the arm and lifted her chin until his warm brown eyes held her sorrowing gaze.

"Forgive me for shouting, little one," he said gently. "To speak harshly is more a sin than drawing blood. This morning I asked God to forgive me, and now I ask you."

"Oh, Papa!" she cried, wrapping her arms around him. "Oh, Papa! I am so very sorry!"

He laughed, and everything was all right again. Mama called that they should go out or stay in, but at least shut the door! The voice sounded bossy and confident. Mama was all right again. Rachel followed Papa quickly out the door.

From every house, black-coated figures emerged. Cheeks were bright with cold. Little trails of footprints crisscrossed Muranow Square. All feet pointed toward the steps of the great domed synagogue at the end of Przebieg Street. Mamas and papas. Old men and women hobbling on canes. Strapping young men in proud new beards and broad fur-trimmed hats.

Papa's face was peaceful as Rachel looked up at him. *Black hat and coat. Black beard and dark eyes. Breath a vapor that kept time with each crunching step. All this framed by the white backdrop of the snow.*

Yes. Everything felt normal again. Rachel would not worry. Perhaps everything Papa had said was right. After all, she did not see any sign of the watcher this morning in Muranow. Had he given up? Decided that the Jewish rabbi was not worth watching, after all?

And then, as the peace seemed to descend over them, something in her father's face changed. There were murmurs now instead of greetings. Children focused sharply on their parents' faces as big hands clamped tensely around little fingers. The rhythm of her father's breath quickened, and his eyes flicked nervously toward the end of Pokorna Street. Then he swung around to look over his shoulder at the far end of Muranowska Street.

Instinctively Rachel followed his gaze. Samuel and David also mimicked the searching glances of their father and the other adults walking toward the synagogue.

"What do we do?" shouted a short, round man. "Rebbe Lubetkin?" he called to Papa.

"Ignore them." Papa's voice was calm, almost patronizing.

In that same instant, Rachel saw them at the ends of the streets. There was a wall of them: Poles, Saturday people. They glared down toward Muranow Square. They did not speak among themselves. There were some men on horseback. Policemen?

"Papa!" David cried in alarm.

"Ignore them," Papa said in that same too-calm voice. "Keep walking, children. Into the synagogue. Do not look back. Do not act as though you are frightened."

Rachel was frightened. She had heard of pogroms. Such demonstrations were common in the outlying provinces—Jews attacked and beaten by the Saturday people.

Rachel felt her heart beat faster as they neared the steps of the synagogue. The great carved doors loomed up like a fortress. They swung open, and families hurried up the steps.

"Slowly," Papa warned again. "We do not see them."

Rachel wanted to run. The silence of the Saturday people was ominous. There were hundreds of them. Why did they stay just beyond the ghetto border? Were they content to send their hatred through the morning air on looks alone? Would they attack?

One step at a time, Papa nudged the children ahead of him. The color was gone from his face. There were others walking behind them. The doors of the synagogue would not be closed and bolted until every Jew on the street was safely in.

"Women and children upstairs to the gallery," Papa instructed. Still rational, he helped the more frightened of his congregation to remain calm.

"Oh, Rebbe! Is it a pogrom? Are they coming? Are the goyim coming here too?"

Papa raised his hands to quiet the murmur that bordered on panic. "We will have our Shabbat service. Morris? Is everyone in?" A long last look out at the square. A nod. "Then close the doors. Slide the bolt. Lock up tight."

Eli stood with his cheek against the stones of the Western Wall as the sun rose. Lists of the dead and wounded had been posted. The name of Victoria had not been among them. For this, Eli gave thanks.

The faces of the young Arab men on the posters above the lists troubled him. He could not be certain, but two of the terrorists bore a marked resemblance to the two youngest brothers of Victoria and Ibrahim. *Her brothers?* What, then, was Eli to do if this was so? Surely someone else in the Old City would identify them! Someone would report this to the British authorities, and they would be arrested if the sketches on the posters *were* Isaak and Daud! Such a thing was not Eli's responsibility, after all. There would be many in the Arab Quarter who would recognize the likenesses.

Almost as soon as that hope entered his mind, another thought chased it out. What Muslim would dare to report that the faces on the posters seemed like those of the Hassan brothers? Even for money, it would take a brave man to speak up.

How could Eli report them and still look Victoria in the eye? They were her brothers, after all! And yet, if they did this thing, many innocent people had died at their hands. The unborn child of Leah and Shimon was among the lost.

This morning Eli had watched from a distance as Shimon helped Leah up the steps of their flat. The women of the Quarter had whispered among themselves: "She was expecting, poor thing." Eli had not gone to visit. How could he face the couple with the images on the posters burning in his mind? *"Shalom, I hope you recover. Oh, by the way, I think I know who bombed Julian's Way, but I am not talking."*

Was it enough for Eli to pray that someone else in the Old City would recognize them and be courageous enough to speak up?

Eli stood before the wall and prayed that very thing. But when he had finished, he realized that a prayer for justice was not enough. If other men went to the authorities, Eli would be one more confirmation of their report. If no one else went, then Eli alone would do what he knew was right. He would pray now that Victoria would understand and not hate him for it.

Victoria was gone. She had vanished into the crooked streets of the Old City like a vapor. Ibrahim released the knot of her makeshift rope and let it fall to the cobblestones of the courtyard below. His brothers stood behind him, angry. They spoke of finding her, of taking her far away so that she could not betray them. But where to find her?

It was time, Ibrahim reasoned, to tell them.

"She will be with the Jew, Eli Sachar," he said in a low, menacing voice.

Silence fell over the three brothers as they considered Ibrahim's words and wondered how he could know such a thing.

"Eli? The Jew friend whom you have put above your own brothers?" asked Isaak.

"How do you know such a thing?" Ismael demanded, putting a rough hand on Ibrahim's shoulder and spinning him around.

"Eli?" Daud asked stupidly, "Eli Sachar? The Jew?" He could not understand.

Ibrahim licked his lips. His mouth felt dry, and he tasted the iron taste of fear. "Victoria loves him."

"But he is a Jew!" Daud declared.

Ismael shoved Daud. "Shut up!" he hissed. Then he stepped close to Ibrahim. "She loves this Jew, Eli Sachar? Tell us how you know this."

"I have known for a long time. I did not discourage it, thinking he would join us."

Ismael's face contorted with rage. He spit into Ibrahim's face. "You are the flesh of swine. You have given our sister to a Jew?"

Ibrahim wiped the spittle from his cheek. He clenched his fists and considered using the dagger beneath his shirt, but he restrained himself. "If we find Eli Sachar we will find Victoria. That we must do first. For the sake of Daud and Isaak, we must find her and bring her back." He glared into the smoldering eyes of Ismael. "Later, I will settle with you. When we have her back, then I will fight you."

Ismael nodded brusquely. He turned to Isaak and Daud. "You two go to the caverns beneath the Dome of the Rock. You must hide there in case she has already betrayed you. Ibrahim and I will find her and bring her back. No word of this must be told to Ram Kadar or Vargen. Do you understand? We will need this marriage as an alliance." He grabbed Daud's shirt. "Before Allah and the prophet, you must swear that you will say nothing to them! Swear it!"

Trembling, Daud raised his hand. Then Ismael repeated the demand to Isaak, who also agreed.

"Get out of here then," Ismael demanded. "Ibrahim and I will find the Jew and Victoria."

The frost of winter mingled with the breath of worshippers to fog the windowpanes of the Warsaw synagogue. Rachel watched through the lattice of the women's gallery as the men of the congregation, heads covered by the wool of prayer shawls, faced toward Jerusalem. The words inscribed above the ark proclaimed an awesome warning: *KNOW BEFORE WHOM YOU STAND.*

Although women were not required to pray the *Shemoneh Esrei,* Rachel let her lips move silently with the lips of her father as he recited the eighteen blessings. She had done so all her young life until the prayer was carved in her heart as clearly as in the heart of any man.

> *"Blessed are Thou, Lord our God and God of our fathers,*
> *God of Abraham, God of Isaac, and God of Jacob. . . ."*

Like a flock of birds across the sky, other names filled the silent prayer of Rachel. *God of my grandfather who worships you in Jerusalem, God of my own father, Aaron Lubetkin* . . . She changed the words each time and so never tired of finding new ways of tracing her family lineage to the God of her fathers. She did not trust her own heart to reach out to this great and awesome God, but she had family connections, after all. So maybe God would listen—even though she was just a woman and perhaps not even that yet. Perhaps the great, mighty, and awesome God would turn His attention for an instant to the women's gallery and hear this woman-child as she whispered her blessings and requests:

> "Master of all,
> Who remembers the gracious deeds of our forefathers,
> And who will bring a Redeemer with love to their children for His
>   name's sake.
> King, Helper, Savior, and Protector."

With this last word, *Protector*, Rachel shut her eyes and grasped the lattice tightly as she prayed. *Protect us please. My papa . . . I heard him and Mama talking. I am afraid. I am afraid for all of us. I am just a girl and You are the awesome God, but I am here praying like the men. I hope You do not mind. Papa says Doktor Letzno has been followed, and now for a week I have seen a man outside in the street watching our house, too.*

Rachel opened her eyes with a start. She had fallen far behind on the recitation of the blessings. Papa had already repeated the sixth blessing of forgiveness:

> "Forgive us, our Father, for we have sinned. . . ."

She tried to bring her lips back in time with the voice of Papa:

> "Blessed art Thou, Lord, Gracious One who forgives abundantly."

She stared hard at the smoke rising from the silver lamps that hung above the heads of the men in the auditorium. Did God hear their prayers or were these words just like the faint traces of smoke? There was no room to doubt. *No room!* The look on Papa's face told her that a terrible Evil stood even now at the gates of the Warsaw ghetto! Darkness had cast its long shadow over the house on Muranow Square. It touched the rabbi who prayed with his people in the voice Rachel loved like no other.

"OPEN UP, CHRIST-KILLERS!"

> "Sound the great shofar to proclaim our freedom! . . ."

Voices and shouts rose up outside the synagogue, the pounding of fists against the doors resounded in the hall. But Rabbi Lubetkin did not raise his voice to compete with the sound.

> *"Lift up a banner for the ingathering of our exiles. . . ."*

The booming sounded more urgently on the doors. The heads of worshippers jerked slightly upward. Eyes widened with fear. *They have come! The Poles have come to the ghetto! The Saturday people have come! They are here! Pogrom! Pogrom!*

"Open up Jews, in the name of the Polish jurisdiction of Warsaw!"

"We demand that you open the doors!"

"Jews! . . . Jewish Bolshevik swine!"

Cries rang out in the women's gallery. Mothers pulled their children close as the locked doors strained against the force of a bench used as a battering ram.

Rachel clung to the lattice. Her brothers, mute with fear, hung on to her arms in desperation. She did not look at the straining doors; she could not focus her eyes on the confusion of the men below as they turned to one another and shouted words no one could understand. She looked only at Papa. He stood with his feet together. Still he faced Jerusalem. Still his lips moved unfailingly in the *Shemoneh Esrei*:

> *"Rule over us, Thou alone, O Lord*
> *With kindness and mercy,*
> *And vindicate . . ."*

No one else was praying. No one except Rachel and Papa. Her own voice was drowned out by the shrieks of terror within the synagogue, but she prayed aloud—she prayed with Papa!

> *"And let all wickedness instantly perish.*
> *May all Thy enemies be quickly cut off. . . ."*

Boom! The hinges of the doors splintered! *Boom!* The frame crashed crazily inward. The voices of hatred swept in on the winter wind. Talliths were blown off and heads bowed against the force of this cold breath.

Others surged around Papa as he stood unmoving in the presence of the King. Children wailed as the roar of the Poles crashed over the congregation like a breaking wave.

"Poland for Polish! Jewish scum get out! Back to Russia, filthy Communist swine!"

Rachel cried out as clubs fell on the heads of the men. Talliths became red with blood. She shouted as two Poles spotted her father and charged toward him, their clubs raised high.

> *"Establish peace, well-being, blessing, grace, loving kindness, and mercy upon us and upon all Israel, Thy people!"*

"Get the Christ-killing pig! Kill him! Kill him!"

Rachel tried to scream, but the scream caught in her throat as the men raced over the wounded Jews toward Papa. Her breath came in short jerks. "Papa . . . Papa . . . ," she managed to whisper. Then, "God. God . . . oh . . . oh, *God!*"

But God did not seem to be listening that day in the synagogue of Muranow. Blackjacks landed on the rabbi's shoulders and back. Red blood soaked through the white of his tallith even before he crumpled to the floor.

Rachel clung to her terrified brothers, their faces buried in her skirts. They did not see their father fall. From this high view, perhaps Rachel was the only one who saw as the rabbi was dragged out the side door into the bloodstained snow of Muranow Square.

As she watched, the prayer on her lips became a scream that went on and on far into the night.

It would not be said by future historians, Herschel reasoned, that the avenger of the deported Jews of Poland had died in rags. After all, Herschel's father had been one of the finest tailors in Germany. Should his son now put him to shame?

Herschel chose a fine dark blue wool suit from the rack, a coordinating necktie, shirt, new socks, and shiny black shoes. He tried on a dozen overcoats, finally deciding on a camel-colored trench coat of the cut worn by the American actors in the detective movies he had seen in Paris. He paid cash and tossed his tattered old clothing into a trash can in the alley behind the shop as he left through the back door.

The winter air of Paris felt good on his face. He felt renewed, alive again, like a man with an important mission to fulfill. In his seventeen years he had never had such a sense of control and power as he felt right now, walking through the St. Martin district of Paris toward the home of his uncle. He carried a secret with him! Hans was long gone, and now the plan, the idea, the courage were all his own. No one else would take

credit when it was accomplished! He would go down in the history of
his people as a man like David, facing the Nazi Goliath—or perhaps Bar
Kokhba, fighting against the tyrants of Rome. He might fall, as Bar
Kokhba had, but at least he would not be forgotten as those nameless
thousands who now languished in the deportation camps.

Herschel stopped for a haircut and a shave, although he scarcely had
a beard. He tipped the barber, who stared at his young customer with the
curiosity of the old toward a young man of means.

The money in Herschel's pocket gave him a sense of freedom and
power. The immigration authorities of Paris would not think to chase
down a fellow dressed this well and carrying so much cash. Herschel
stopped at a haberdashery and bought a fedora, which he pulled down
slightly over one eye. His reflection in the mirror pleased him.

Only one item remained for him to purchase: the gun. Once again he
found himself looking over the weapons in the window of the gunsmith's shop. He could afford to pick carefully. He could purchase the
best. But he would buy the weapon later, after he visited his uncle one
last time.

Eli buttoned his overcoat around him as he hurried down the Street of the Chain toward the citadel at Jaffa Gate. Every few yards the posters glared accusingly at him. The shoppers had returned to the marketplace. They haggled over prices as if nothing had happened. Did anyone but Eli notice the eyes that stared out beneath the bold letters: *WANTED IN CONNECTION WITH THE JULIAN'S WAY BOMBING!*

Heaps of baskets against a wall half concealed the faces on the posters. The eyes of young Daud looked out at Eli. *Victoria's brother!*

Eli's heart beat faster as he stepped around a group of four Arab men who stood in the center of the street as they glanced furtively at the sketches and then spoke among themselves in low, urgent tones. They knew—maybe everyone in the Arab Quarter knew. But they would not speak up.

Eli focused straight ahead, for fear his eyes lingering on the sketches would betray that he also knew. Past heaps of citrus fruit, sacks of beans and lentils, he hurried. From the corners of his eyes he saw the white posters—like opaque windows from which those familiar, threatening faces stared. He turned to glance back as conversations behind him fell silent and the scuffling of feet clattered over the cobblestones.

A dozen Muslim boys were jogging through the bazaar, tearing away the posters. No one tried to stop them. No one dared protest. The faces of the guilty were crumpled up, tossed into the air by one boy and batted playfully by the next and then the next until the paper ball fell into a puddle.

Eli stepped aside as they shoved past him and nearly knocked a

Greek Orthodox priest to the ground. They made it seem like a rough game, the sport of adolescents jostling through the streets. But everyone knew. Everyone understood that the game was a warning concealed beneath the raucous laughter of defiant youth.

Eli wiped his brow as the boys continued up the steps, leaving a trail of crumpled paper behind them. He was grateful that he would not have to look at the glaring white faces of Daud and Isaak any longer.

He emerged into Omar Square. Even beneath the watchful eyes of British sentries on the wall, the posters had been torn away. Only those on the wall itself remained.

In spite of the cold, Eli was sweating. He looked up at the soldiers on the ramparts. Their presence did not reassure him. He ducked his head slightly and cut across the square to the entrance of the citadel, where two sentries stood in niches on either side of an arched doorway.

"I-I wish to see—," he stammered, then began again—"Captain Orde, please."

Eyes narrowed with suspicion. "Your business?"

There were hundreds of pedestrians in the street. Eli could not speak his purpose. "I am from the Jewish soup kitchen, Tipat Chalev. You know it?"

"Yes."

"Good. Well, we are having some trouble, you see, with the English walnuts we were traded. I will need a word with Captain Orde since we feel we have been cheated."

Indignation was a certain way to get in to speak to the British officer in charge. This worked well. The eyes of the soldier widened. The Jews of the Old City feel they have been cheated by the British government in an issue of food?

Within minutes Eli stood before Captain Samuel Orde.

Shimon heated water on the primus stove and helped Leah bathe in a tin washtub as the music of Benny Goodman played on the hand-crank phonograph. In her head Leah could hear an irritating ringing over everything. "Like a trumpet hitting high A," she explained to Shimon. "But I can hear you beneath it. You don't need to shout, my darling."

Shimon felt like shouting for the joy of having Leah home. She was thin and shaky, but she insisted on dressing this morning and sat curled up on the bed as she drank her tea while Shimon finished the windows.

He waved broadly at two British soldiers whom Captain Orde had stationed as sentries on the roof across the street. Their constant gazes in this direction had made him get up before dawn to clean the windows and take them a pot of steaming coffee. He had not meant to awaken Leah with ammonia, even though she accused him of waving the bottle beneath her nose like smelling salts. Later, she insisted, he would have to go into the New City to telegraph Elisa in London that Leah was at home and well. She must not worry.

He was just finishing the last panes of the front windows when he caught sight of Reverend Robbins walking quickly up the street. The minister also spotted the soldiers on the rooftop. He looked from their perch toward the apartment, and his expression displayed a grim approval at their presence.

"The Reverend from Christ Church is coming to pay a call," Shimon said over his shoulder.

"You think he will come inside this time?" Leah asked, remembering his hesitance to enter the apartment the first day.

Shimon shrugged. Reverend Robbins was climbing their stairs and seemed quite anxious to reach the top. Shimon gathered up Leah's nightgown and shoved it under a pillow as the minister banged urgently on the door. "This is the way Christians knock when they visit someone they think is deaf?" Shimon asked wryly, amused but surprised by the demand of the gentle pastor's fist on the door.

"Coming!" Leah replied. She got up and opened it herself as Shimon stood smiling proudly behind her.

Reverend Robbins did not smile back. He seemed not to notice at all that it was Leah who had answered—Leah who addressed him, Leah without the bandages on her head.

"Shalom," he said, having somehow forgotten entirely that she had been injured in any way. "May I come in?" He glanced nervously over his shoulder, then slipped in before they could reply. "I am glad to see you have sentries here." Then, "Oh. You are up?"

Leah nodded, baffled by his agitation. "Is something wrong?"

"Please sit," Shimon offered. "We have coffee. You would like coffee?" The lightheartedness of the moment before had vanished with the anxiety the minister brought into the room with him.

"Something has happened," he began without introduction. "Victoria came to me this morning at Christ Church. We need your help."

"And so, you see," the pastor finished, "her brothers took all her clothes. Every modern dress that she owns. They locked her in her room without explanation."

"I will pack some of my things for her," Leah said in quiet consternation.

"She would like to see you, if you are able," the minister said to Leah.

"And—" he eyed Shimon—"I need your help locating Eli. I cannot go ask for him without arousing curiosity in the Quarter—probably even hostility. There is no time to wait in this situation. If Victoria is married to Eli, her family will have no legal recourse in the matter of forcing her to marry anyone according to Muslim law. I am prepared to perform the ceremony immediately."

Shimon nodded. It must be accomplished for her safety. At least then Eli would have the legal right to ask protection from the British for his wife. Except for the signatures, Reverend Robbins had already completed the legal forms. It was a simple matter of finding Eli and bringing him to Christ Church today.

Eli left the citadel as Captain Orde called the British military headquarters with the news that a possible identification had been made of the two primary terrorists in the bombing. The apprehension of the Hassan brothers would have to be carried out in an orderly fashion during what looked like a routine patrol.

Orde believed that the brothers were still at their Old City residence. He requested that additional troops be sent to the citadel in case there was a violent response to their arrest by the Muslim population. To Eli's satisfaction, Orde mentioned that several members of the household were innocent, and special care must be taken that they were not hurt in the operation. Orde did not tell Eli that Victoria had come to see him. The less the young man knew, the safer the two of them would be.

For a moment, as Eli emerged from the citadel, he was tempted to walk back along the Old City wall to Christ Church. He stood in the crowded street of the Armenian Quarter and gazed solemnly up at the bell tower. Then he looked to his left toward Jaffa Gate. Victoria would be getting off the bus there, he reasoned. He would intercept her at the pedestrian entrance and guide her quickly back to Christ Church, away from whatever horrible things were happening within the Arab Quarter and her own home.

He began to walk slowly toward Jaffa Gate and Omar Square, trying to think how he could explain to her that she must not go home, that her two youngest brothers were about to be arrested for the bombings. He could only pray that she would forgive him, that she would not blame him. Perhaps in time she would thank him.

Rabbi Lebowitz's kitten perched on his shoulder and leaned against his head as he stood in the doorway of Tipat Chalev to answer Shimon, who towered above him.

"Eli Sachar? I have not seen him all morning. He was not in class. Is he ill, perhaps? Did you try his house?"

"His mother says he left before dawn this morning. She thought he was on his way to morning prayers." The usually pleasant face of the big man was lined with concern, even urgency.

The rabbi scratched the kitten beneath her chin as he considered where Shimon might look. "Perhaps he has gone to the Western Wall. I am just going there myself to pray. We can walk together, *nu*?"

A light of impatience flashed across Shimon's face as he considered the request. "I will run ahead and look in the souks for him. If you see him later at the Wailing Wall, please tell him that it is most urgent that I see him. I will meet him at my apartment. Will you tell him that if you see him?"

The rabbi's face clouded. He nodded and put the cat on the floor. "Some time ago I saw him enter Christ Church. His mother says he has become involved with a girl from the Muslim Quarter. Is that what this matter is about?" There was no unkindness in his voice, only concern.

Shimon took his hand. "I cannot say. Truly, I cannot."

Rabbi Lebowitz nodded in understanding. "If you see Eli before I do, tell him I pray for him today at the Western Wall. Tell him no matter what happens, my door is open to him. So. I hope you find him, whatever this is about."

Muslim houses faced the Wailing Wall, so it was not unusual that Ibrahim and Ismael strolled along the street where old and young Jews gathered in the cold to pray.

Ibrahim scanned the black coats and hats. He paused to examine the swaying forms beneath their silk or woolen prayer shawls. He watched. He waited until a slight movement displayed beard, hair color, or profile which was not that of Eli.

The Wailing Wall stretched on. Ismael was impatient and angry. The hilt of his dagger was hidden beneath his jacket, but he kept his hand on it as he walked. "He is not here," Ismael said gruffly. "I say we go into their Quarter and demand she be returned."

"Shut up," Ibrahim commanded. "That is not the way we will get her back. You think Eli will hand her over and let us leave the Jewish Quarter as if nothing is unusual?"

The singsong chants of a hundred Jewish prayers rose up. Eli's voice was not among them.

Ibrahim turned to walk back the other way. He stopped a young Jewish boy and asked about Eli Sachar. "We are trying to deliver an important package to him," Ibrahim said. It did not matter that the lie made no sense. The boy believed it.

"I think he went that way." The boy pointed toward the street that led to the souks.

Ibrahim thanked him and then very calmly and deliberately left by the same way.

Shimon ran ahead of the old rabbi to scan the worshippers along the Western Wall. He asked a young Orthodox man if he had seen Eli Sachar.

"Very early," said the fellow. "He was just leaving when I arrived."

"Did he say where he was going?"

"He did not say. But he left in that direction. Toward the souks. Not unusual. Maybe to go to market for his mother." He tugged his earlobe in thought. "He seemed preoccupied; I will say that." Then he smiled. "Like you!"

Shimon did not comment. He thanked him as he left, feeling foolish. Certainly the Protestant pastor of Christ Church could not have aroused any more curiosity than Shimon was managing to do right now.

Shimon walked quickly along the street of the Western Wall to where a narrow alleyway climbed up toward the Street of the Chain and the bazaars of the Old City.

Victoria's eyes were shining happily into the mirror of the choir-robing room at Christ Church. Leah's beautiful burgundy dress and matching pumps fit Victoria perfectly. The rich color made her smooth olive skin glow with the excitement she felt.

She turned and embraced Leah, who seemed pale and wan compared to Victoria. "Oh, Leah!" she cried. "It is perfect! And today is perfect!"

Leah stepped back to appraise her with a pleasantly critical eye. She tugged at the collar making it straight. And then with a broad smile she agreed with Victoria. "Perfect. Now all we need is the groom and the best man, yes?"

Victoria nodded nervously as she glanced at the clock. It seemed that they had been waiting hours. Surely her brothers would have turned the city upside down looking for her. Would they think to come here as well? Would they take her away before Shimon came with Eli? The strain of these fears showed on her face.

"I have no regrets," she whispered, as if to herself, "except that we did not do this sooner." Then she gazed into Leah's eyes. "I have always loved him. Since we were children, you see. He was always so big and strong, yet gentle. Not like the other boys. And yet I did not think it could ever be."

She sighed and looked toward the ceiling. "But now our hearts meet here in truth before the one true God. And suddenly the things that kept us apart and fearful for so long do not matter anymore."

Victoria closed her eyes as if to drink in the truth of what she had just said. "I am not afraid, Leah. God is not a terrible God of vengeance and hatred to me anymore. I have found His nature in Jesus." She turned to rummage in her pillowcase and pulled out a small Bible bound in mother-of-pearl. She held it gently in her hands for a moment and then held it out for Leah to see. "You see? The prettiest one!"

Leah frowned in thought. It was identical to the Bible she had given to the little beggar in the souk on their first day in Old City Jerusalem. "Yes. It is . . . did you . . . ?" She hesitated to ask.

Victoria nodded happily. "I went back to find him after I left you. I paid him twice what you paid for it." She held it to her heart. "And it is the greatest bargain, the greatest treasure of my life. I was ready, you see, before anyone told me! I was ready to meet the living Jesus! It was so easy for me to believe, Leah," Victoria said. "I am going to find that little boy after all this is over, and I am going to return this to him and teach him to read."

Radiant. That was the word for Victoria today. Leah was certain that Eli would be pleased with the beauty of his bride.

Etta watched it all from the upstairs window. The shouts and obscenities echoed throughout the square like a howling, evil wind. She saw the upraised fists, watched the heavy brass crucifix high atop a staff as it waved over the mob, encouraging them forward to the steps of the synagogue.

The shouts of "Christ-killers!" became a chant that fell in rhythm with the crashing of an upraised bench against the doors of the synagogue.

She dashed down the stairs to pile chairs in front of the door. But the mob never came to her house. They vandalized the great Warsaw synagogue, but when they finished, they drifted off, laughing into the snow-covered side streets.

Silence overtook the square. Snow began to fall again as men and women staggered out to help the injured in the street. The cold nearness of death stood beside her. She did not weep as she watched; it was all too much like a nightmare, unreal in its madness. Her children. Her husband. What had become of them? Fear for their safety drove everything else from her mind.

Baby Yacov slept peacefully in his cradle throughout the pogrom. She did not pick him up for fear even a small cry from his innocent lips would call the Darkness here to devour him.

A group of women and children emerged from the synagogue. They were surrounded by men with bloody faces, who formed a circle of protection for them as they moved down the steps and across the square. They were coming here; somehow Etta knew even before they had directed their staggering legs toward the house. She put on her coat and hat and pulled mittens over her trembling hands as she ran down the hallway to pull away the heap of chairs from the door.

In her mind she replayed the faces and forms of the desperate human circle moving toward the house. Her children. Frau Rosen among the women. But Aaron was not among them. She had not seen the face of Aaron in the dark ring that glided soundlessly across the stark white snow.

Chairs were scattered everywhere in the foyer. She pulled back the bolts and threw open the door; then she heard their weeping—not just the voices of women and children, but the men as well! Their sobs ascended on the vapor of their breath. They were not individuals now, but one single unit of moving anguish—black coats torn, bright red blood clinging to beards and soaking white collars. The scarves on the heads of the women were untied. Buttons dangled; shoelaces trailed in the snow. Hands grasped fabric and flesh around them. No one let go, and the expression on every face was the same. The horror in each pair of eyes was identical. No one was untouched. No one separate in their grief.

Etta spread her arms as she stood on the top step. As she cried out to them and urged them to hurry, she seemed to embrace them, to join the circle of anguish.

Rachel clung to her little brothers. "Mama!" she sobbed, and the boys joined her cry. "They took Papa! They took him away! Oh, *why*, Mama? They have taken Papa!"

Etta wiped her tears. Her legs would not carry her forward to them. They had to come to her. "My children! Rachel! Oh, my Rachel!"

Rachel broke off from the slowly circling group. Her arms out, fingers wide, she ran to Etta and embraced her. The boys followed, and a smaller circle was formed in the snow of Muranow Square.

"Where have they taken him?" Etta wept as she called to the men. "Where did they take Aaron?"

"To the prison on Ginsea Street!" someone replied. "They called him a Communist! They beat him! They took him from the pulpit as he prayed. His blood marks the way!"

Across the square, Etta could see other small circles moving in their own orbits toward other houses and side streets. No one was alone. Not one. .

"Who else? Who else did they arrest?"

"Only the rabbi! Only Rebbe Lubetkin!"

Etta shook the housekeeper by her shoulders as she sobbed uncontrollably in the parlor. "Listen!" Etta demanded. "Enough of this!" A slap across Frau Rosen's cheek quieted her at last. "Listen to me! You must stay here. Lock the doors when I leave and do not open them until I return!"

"Yes . . . yes, Rebbitsin," the woman sniffed. "It was so terrible!"

Etta would hear no more. "Stop it! Think of the children! Feed them now. Take care of the baby. I will be back."

"But where are you going? Rebbitsin? You cannot go there!"

Etta's look was stern. She picked up her handbag and demanded that Frau Rosen obey her. There was some sanity in obedience, at least.

Without a backward glance, Etta left the warmth and safety of the house and trudged off alone across the empty square. The snow crunched beneath her boots while fine flakes swirled about her head, stinging her cheeks and clinging to her eyelashes.

She had no more tears to shed. She would find Aaron. She had learned the game of the Warsaw police. She knew well why Aaron had been arrested. *No immigration papers if one has a police record. No country will admit a criminal . . . not a prostitute or a Communist!*

Inside her handbag, Etta carried Eduard's bank checks. If they were lucky today, she would speak to the right officer, someone corrupt and filled with greed. And then perhaps Aaron could come home again.

The shops on both sides of the street were closed. An artificial twilight hung over the Jewish district of Warsaw today. There was no sign of human life here except for Etta, bent against the snow and wind.

Two blocks farther, she reached Ginsea Street, where the great stone facade of the prison loomed over every other building. This was in Catholic Warsaw, and Etta could clearly see automobiles and red streetcars ahead in the busy intersection. She had worn her camel-colored coat today, the one with the red fox collar. The Poles would not know she was Jewish by these clothes. She would be safe today. Until she opened her mouth in the police station, she would be safe!

Let them bring a crucifix before her—she would kneel and kiss it for the sake of Aaron. She would do what they asked. She would pay them. She would beg them!

She reached the corner of the street to Catholic Warsaw. They had flowed down this very street this morning—a vile flood of hatred. They had chanted the name of their Christ as they battered the doors of the synagogue. How Etta hated them! How she hated them all as they passed her now!

She looked up at the web of electric wires that crisscrossed above the street. Snow fell onto those wires and balanced there above the crushing chaos of the traffic below. Neat perfect lines of snowflakes clung to the wires while other flakes were trampled and soiled by the feet and tires of the Catholic Warsaw on this Sabbath day.

We are those snowflakes on the wire, Etta thought. *How narrow is our world, how precarious our balance!* And then she closed her eyes in a wordless prayer for help from the God who fashioned each snowflake. *Let not my feet slip from Your way! Not even for the sake of Aaron. Let me kneel only to You, my living Lord!*

To the left was the prison where Aaron had been taken. To the right was the spire of a magnificent cathedral—the very one whose priest had come to her aid in the street when the Poles had taken her. That priest— also a very fine snowflake perched on the wire. Had he not risked his own safety to help Etta that day? And the Darkness had parted for him. At the sound of his voice the men had put her down and backed away.

Etta turned to the right. She walked through the thickening snow flurries toward the Catholic church. She smiled, confident that there was more inside that building than the cold metal image of a dead god. Inside the cathedral was a living man who somehow must have understood the compassion of the Eternal One and taken the Law into his heart! One righteous Gentile in all of Warsaw! Yes, Etta would ask for his help. Such a brave man would not refuse her.

She thanked the Eternal as she quickened her step, praying that the priest would be there. She didn't even know his name, only that of his church. Somehow she knew that was enough.

38

Faith in the Shadow of Death

The number two bus from Mount Scopus and Hebrew University emptied its passengers outside the city walls near the pedestrian entrance of Jaffa Gate.

Eli was so busy looking for Victoria among the women passengers that he did not notice the glum face of his brother Moshe as he approached.

"Well, Eli," Moshe said, his voice still bitter, "you have come to wait for me?" He slung a bag of books over his shoulder and stopped before the niche where Eli waited.

"I was just—" Eli could not offer him an explanation. He did not want Moshe to know his plans until everything was settled. Over with. "I will walk with you a ways. You are going home?" He fell in stride with Moshe, entering Omar Square to continue along the Street of the Chain.

"Home. Yes." Moshe sounded regretful, almost apologetic. "For a few days, anyway." He did not look at Eli.

"What are you saying?"

"My fellowship has come through. I am going to England. Oxford. I begin this coming semester."

"I envy you," Eli said as they pressed on through the narrowing street into the clamor of the marketplace.

"You? Envy? You have all this. What more do you want? So certain of your life, Eli. Serve your God in the Old City of Jerusalem. Carry on. I do not know what I believe anymore." His words were not accusing, but still there was an unmistakable edge of bitterness.

"Mama will miss you," Eli said.

"She will have her son, the rabbi." Bitter amusement. Almost mocking.

Eli did not reply to that. He longed to tell Moshe the truth, but his brother would know soon enough. "We will all miss you, Moshe."

The clanging of hammer against metal in an iron foundry drowned out Moshe's response. Eli raised his head to look through the human current moving up the street ahead of them. He stopped, grasping Moshe's arm.

"What?" Moshe looked up to follow Eli's gaze. He frowned at the sight of Ibrahim Hassan and his brother Ismael pushing their way purposefully toward Eli. There was no mistaking that they wanted to speak with him. Their faces seemed hard and set with anger.

"Come on," Moshe said. "We'll go back."

The clank of the hammer beat out a rhythm above the murmur of the crowds. Eli shook his head. "I have to speak with him sometime," he replied, sensing there was no escape.

Angrily Ibrahim shouted out Eli's name. His face was menacing. A few seconds and the two Arabs stood scowling before Eli and Moshe.

"Where is she?" shouted Ismael. He reached out to grasp Eli, but Ibrahim shoved his brother back.

"I will handle this!" Ibrahim roared, and the heads of strangers turned to look.

"Where is who?" Eli replied sharply.

"Victoria! What have you done with her?" panted Ismael, clenching and unclenching his fists.

"I do not know what you are talking about!" Eli shouted back over the roar of the foundry fire. The pounding of hammers behind them fell silent as the Arab ironmonger raised his head to see the confrontation between the Jews and his own countrymen.

"You son of a Jewish pig!" Ismael screamed. "Where is my sister, Victoria?"

Again Ibrahim shoved Ismael away. "I said I will—"

Eli responded in equal anger. "I do not know where she is!" He feigned unconcern. "And why should I? I am a Jew! I will remain a Jew! She is Muslim! I have no interest in—"

"You lie!" Ismael slammed forward against Ibrahim, who held him back.

The crowd of onlookers grew. Arab faces glared with sullen hostility at Moshe and Eli. Dark eyes considered them from beneath checkered keffiyehs. Hands drifted to the hilts of hidden daggers. And the murmur of conversations and haggling began to grow silent.

"I am going for help," Moshe whispered hoarsely from behind Eli. Then he backed up one step and another, passing through the smoldering crowd until he emerged through the fringes to run wildly back to-ward the citadel to the British soldiers.

Eli felt the knot of fear in his stomach. A circle of Muslim faces ringed him as Christians and Jews alike scurried away from what looked like certain murder.

Long coats were pulled back at the waist and the hilts of daggers were in plain sight. Brown hands grasped the daggers, ready to unsheath the weapons at the right moment. Behind him, Eli felt the heat of the iron foundry. The fires hissed and made a dull roaring sound.

Eli spread his empty hands. "I have not seen her for a long time, Ibrahim, *my friend*! Not since I was with you. You remember?"

The blame shifted to Ibrahim. Ismael spat on the ground. "I have heard of the foolishness of Ibrahim. But now I will settle with you, Jew."

Eli managed a weak smile. There were beads of perspiration on his brow. "Tell him there is nothing to settle, Ibrahim!" He gave a short, nervous laugh. "I have not seen her since we were all together. I have no interest."

Ibrahim's face tightened with indignation. "No interest! You are a swine, indeed. To trifle so with us. To pretend."

"Ibrahim!" Eli put a hand on his arm. "*Brother!* We are beyond these things, you and I!"

Ibrahim now spat and tore Eli's hand away. His eyes were full of hate. He stepped forward. The ring of rough Arab men tightened. It was settled. There would be a killing today. Blood was hot. Hearts raced with the smell of imminent death.

Eli moved into the shadows of the foundry. The smell of molten metal filled his nostrils. The blacksmith stepped aside as Ibrahim and Ismael unsheathed their knives.

"Where is she?" Ismael's voice was low. "What have you done with her, Jew?"

"N-nothing," Eli stammered. "I . . . swear. I do not know where she is!" He looked to Ibrahim for help, for some sign of the friendship that once had seemed so strong.

A cold smile was frozen on Ibrahim's face. "He is mine," Ibrahim growled. The steel blade of his dagger glinted with the orange reflection of the fire.

"Ibrahim!" Eli shouted, backing up until he tripped over a large piece of metal and fell to the ground.

Instantly a resounding roar erupted from the spectators as Ibrahim leaped forward, falling upon Eli. With a cry, Eli grasped the wrist of Ibrahim, pushing against the downward thrust of the knife that hung inches above his neck.

The shouts of encouragement for a quick death of the Jew merged into a roar, hovering over the struggle taking place on the floor of the foundry.

Eli's face was contorted with the effort. Ibrahim's sweat dripped onto his cheeks. Ibrahim smiled above him, confident of his strength.

Eli jerked his knee hard into Ibrahim's groin, sending him sprawling back in startled pain. The roar grew louder. This was not a simple slaughter; the Jew could fight, after all! It was more sport for the spectators, even though the end would be the same for the Jew!

Eli lunged toward Ibrahim, knocking the raised dagger from his hand. He slammed his fist against Ibrahim's throat, and the Arab's face filled with pain. He struck at Eli, a hard blow of his forearm across the bridge of Eli's nose. Blood spurted out, spraying Ibrahim's clothes with red.

The cheers rose—the first blood was Jewish blood!

Eli grasped Ibrahim's shirt and slammed him onto the stone floor. Blood. There was blood everywhere. Ibrahim broke Eli's grip as the fabric of his shirt tore apart, and both men rolled away from each other for a fraction of an instant. Eli clambered to his feet and lunged for Ibrahim, who had only managed to climb to one knee. They fell to the stones again, rolling over and over as they struck equal blows.

Ibrahim reached for the dagger that lay just beyond his grasp. Eli cried out as he slammed his fist against Ibrahim's jaw. Ibrahim looked up to where hot pokers of iron protruded from the fire. He reached up, grasping a poker.

In that same instant Eli screamed and threw himself at Ibrahim, clutching him by the hair and slamming the Arab's head hard against the firepit. Ibrahim's face convulsed in agony. His mouth opened to cry out. Once again Eli lifted his head and crashed it down on the stones. Ibrahim's eyes rolled back. He went limp, his chest rising and falling in convulsive breaths.

The cheering died. The rush of the fire was the only sound. Eli released Ibrahim and turned slowly. He was heaving with exertion. Only a few seconds elapsed before he managed to focus on the grim hostile faces that glared at him from the semicircle just beyond the foundry entrance.

Ismael stepped forward. He kicked at the foot of his unconscious brother. He held up his own dagger. His mouth curved in a smile of contempt as he considered the exhausted Jew on the floor before him.

"Now it is *my* turn," he said. A new cheer erupted as he crouched to spring with his knife upraised.

Instinctively Eli reached up to the rough stones to pull himself upright. Instead, he grasped the end of a poker, pulling its glowing tip from the white-hot coals. It turned a fiery arc in his grasp, ending slightly up-turned. The gleaming orange tip was driven into Ismael's belly as the Arab lunged forward to kill Eli. Ismael's scream drowned out the tumult of the cheering Arabs as the metal spike pierced him through. His eyes widened in anguished surprise; his fingers spread, dropping the dagger. Working open and shut, his mouth formed soundless screams.

As if caught in time, Ismael hung there, impaled above Eli, who looked on with horror at what he had done.

"*No!*" Eli shouted. "No! *Victoria! Victoria!*"

In one final convulsion, Ismael grasped the steel of the poker and fell backward to the floor.

Eli scrambled to his feet. There was total silence now as the Muslim crowd considered the quivering body at their feet. "Allah!" The whisper rippled through the crowd. And then a cry of new rage swelled up against the murdering Jew who trembled before them. "*Allah Akhbar!* Kill the Jew! Kill him!"

"I did not mean to!" Eli cried. "Oh, God! *God!*" He knelt beside the body of Victoria's brother and wept, not caring anymore that he was soon to die.

The toes of scuffed shoes moved slowly forward. There was no hurry. Who would strike the first blow? Knives were drawn. They would make this Jew pay for what he had done!

Suddenly, from the pack, another cry went up.

"ELI!" the bellowing voice of Shimon Feldstein cried as he smashed through the mob, using his cast as both shield and weapon. Men were flung to the right and left with startled cries of indignation. Others scrambled back from the formidable giant with the plaster arm.

Then the shrill whistle of a British soldier was heard. The crackle of gunfire passed over the heads of the mob. "In the name of His Majesty, you are ordered to disperse!"

The order came late. Already the mob was running back through the labyrinth of the souk. Thirty Arabs scrambled over toppled baskets and upturned wares to dissolve into the shadows of the marketplace.

Shimon, his jaw set, blood dripping from his cast, stood towering in front of Eli, who still wept and cried out the name of Victoria.

Captain Samuel Orde rushed into the foundry. Moshe was at his side. The soldiers did not pursue the fleeing spectators. Two dozen soldiers stood ready before the door, their weapons loaded, their eyes scanning the rooftops.

Shimon stepped past the unconscious form of Ibrahim and the dead body of Ismael. He clutched Eli by his bloody shirt front, wrapping his thick arm around him in an embrace. "Come," he said, looking down at the dead man. "We must hurry."

Etta Lubetkin's eyes took in every fearsome detail of the great Gothic cathedral that towered over the street. A white vapor of snow concealed the uppermost sections of the spire, but the faces of demons and gargoyles leered down at her from pillars and buttresses.

Standing in the niches of the facade, stone images peered down at her with unfeeling eyes. Were those stone hands raised in blessing or curse? Did they direct the myriad of hideous demons carved into the vast structure of the church?

For a moment she considered abandoning her quest for the one righteous Gentile in Warsaw. How could a man so kind and brave serve within the walls of a place so adorned with idolatry?

She prayed again before she put her foot on the bottom step of the steep stairs, then looked up at the figure of the Gentile Christ on the cross. That symbol had led the mob that battered down the doors of the synagogue. She feared and loathed that symbol. And yet, beyond these fearsome portals was a man who had called on the name of God in his compassion for her.

She raised her hands to push through the massive bronze doors. Inside, the cathedral was almost as cold as outside. Great arches reared up to join at a peak in the vault three stories above the ground. Rows of wooden folding chairs filled a vast auditorium of stone and beautiful stained-glass windows. The carved image of Mary, a crown on her head, sat above the altar. Rows and rows of red votive candles decorated the steps beneath that image. To either side of the main auditorium were small niches where saints gazed over their own candles.

Etta shuddered at the sight. She scanned the vast, echoing interior of the cathedral in search of the priest. Here and there men and women knelt in their own private petition to some saint or another. Etta did not see the priest among them. Had she made a mistake to come here? Surely to enter such a place was a violation of Torah.

She would walk no farther forward into the gaze of these stone images. Etta was certain now that she had made a mistake by coming here. She turned to go, lowering her eyes from the baleful glare of a being who scowled at her from a cluster of carved leaves. She looked only at the floor as she silently repeated the Shema: *Hear, O Israel, the Lord our God, the Lord is one!*

Then she heard her name. "Frau Lubetkin?" The voice of the priest sounded startled, yet he seemed pleased to see her.

She gasped as she looked up to see him emerge from the shadows of an arched alcove just off the foyer. "I . . . I do not know what to call you," she said awkwardly.

He smiled gently. "I did not properly introduce myself that day. Father Kopecky. But . . . why are you *here*, dear lady?"

"Please . . . I should not have come. Forgive . . ." She turned to go.

"Frau Lubetkin!" The kindness in his tone stopped her, just as he had stopped the evil men by his voice. "Please wait. Is there some way I may help you?"

She stood with her back to him. She could not move. Not a step. And then she began to weep. She turned to face him, and in spite of the leering, laughing stone faces above her, she told him everything.

Inside the thick walls of the citadel, Orde led young Moshe Sachar to one side as the medic examined Eli in the infirmary.

"Go home now. Tell your family what has happened—that your brother is unhurt, but that for a while he will have to stay in hiding."

"He had no choice. He did not start it." Moshe felt compelled to defend his brother, although no defense was necessary. It was obvious what had happened.

"We understand that. But—" Orde paused and gestured toward the door and the city that lay behind—"you know as well as I what may be made of this. It is best if we place him in protective custody for now."

Moshe nodded, still defensive. "They wanted to know where their sister was. But my brother, you see, is going to be a rabbi, and so he has decided he cannot marry her, and so he has not seen her. We were just walking along, you see, and they came up, and then . . ."

Orde nodded and guided the distraught young man to the door. "It's all right. We know. Tell your parents we understand self-defense around here."

Moshe looked pained as he left. It was such a nightmare. He left the citadel and ran through the Armenian Quarter toward home.

Shimon looked on from the doorway. His clothes were splattered with blood, but he was uninjured. He'd listened to the quiet reassurance of Samuel Orde to Eli's brother, and he waited until the young man hurried away before he entered Orde's office.

Orde exhaled loudly as he faced Shimon. "So you know where the girl is?" he asked wearily.

Shimon nodded. "I was looking for Eli when I came upon the fight. She ran away to take refuge in Christ Church this morning."

Orde nodded curtly. "I thought as much. Her half brothers are suspects in the Julian's Way bombing. They have vanished. The stepmother said the two other brothers had gone to find their sister who had run away." He spread his hands. "Does Eli know any of it?"

With a shake of his head Shimon replied, "They are to be married. She is waiting there now for me to bring him to her."

Orde pressed his lips together in thought. "Get him cleaned up," he said quietly. "There are clothes in my locker; we are about the same size." He frowned. "I'll just jog over to Christ Church and have a word with her. Explain what happened. Maybe it will be easier coming from me."

Dressed in the uniform of a British captain, Eli entered the office of Reverend Robbins, where Victoria waited for him. The captain had already told her about the attack on Eli at the foundry. The death of Ismael was clearly self-defense. Yes. Victoria understood all that. Yes. Eli must be told that she loved him. That she still wished to marry him.

Orde, Shimon, Leah, and Reverend Robbins waited outside in the hallway. Muffled sounds of grief penetrated the door. Eli wept. Victoria comforted him. Half an hour later the two emerged from the room hand in hand. Their eyes were red from the tears they had shed together, but radiant peace shone from their faces.

"We wish to be married," Victoria said with her head held high. "Please. We do not wish to delay any longer."

The minister looked questioningly at Orde, who nodded. At this point the marriage seemed more important for keeping the peace in the Old City. If Victoria was Eli's wife, who could then say that the Hassan brothers had been defending her honor?

Reverend Robbins led the couple to the small chapel enclosed by stained-glass windows. Shimon and Samuel Orde held Eli's prayer shawl aloft as the wedding canopy. There, beneath the covering of God, Victoria and Eli became husband and wife.

There was a tinge of grief to this moment of fulfillment. For all knew that beyond the walls of Christ Church the first howls of sorrow and rage were rising above the Muslim Quarter of the Old City as the body of Ismael Hassan was carried home.

Bitter, silent, hungry for revenge, Ibrahim Hassan followed after.

39

Peace within the Walls

It had been absurd, of course, to think that Haj Amin and Ram Kadar would not hear of Victoria's connection to the Jew, Eli Sachar.

Beneath the Dome of the Rock, Ibrahim sat with his two remaining brothers. Commander Vargen, Hockman, and the Mufti looked on as Ram Kadar stalked angrily from the meeting. He had been deceived by the Hassan brothers. He had been made to think that Victoria was unsullied and pure, fitting to be a wife. All along Ibrahim had known otherwise. Ram Kadar left the room rather than satisfy his impulse to kill the man.

Vargen eyed the grieving brothers with a mixture of disdain and amusement. "And you still believe she is with this Jew?"

Ibrahim nodded. "We have checked everywhere. I do not see how it could be otherwise."

Hockman sighed thoughtfully. "But the Jew is under the protection of the English. In hiding."

Haj Amin spoke up. Until this moment he had listened without comment. "Yes. The English have him. The Arab Higher Committee has already demanded justice for the murder of Ismael Hassan. The British refuse to divulge the Jew's location. They claim the incident was a matter of self-defense." The Mufti let his eyes linger on Ibrahim's bruised face. "Of course, this issue of self-defense makes no difference to the propaganda we are making of the incident to the Woodhead Committee. I plan to declare Ismael a hero and a martyr before the assembly." He nodded toward Ibrahim. "You may find some comfort that your fool of a brother will not have died in vain."

Vargen smiled broadly. "*Excellent!* And as for the girl, we may wish to whisper that she is believed to have been kidnapped and murdered by this Jewish swine, Sachar." He clapped his hands together with pleasure. "It is all working much better than we planned, Haj Amin." He indicated a stack of lists and plans for the upcoming actions throughout Palestine. "You should inform the Arab Higher Committee of our conviction that the girl has come to harm. They may make the public announcement. It should also be relayed to Radio Cairo as well as to our leaders in Damascus and Amman."

Ibrahim stared at him in amazement. "If she is with Eli, it is of her own choice!"

Hockman shrugged. "Does that matter? It serves the cause just as well either way. Remember, Sachar killed your brother and now perhaps he laughs at you as he lies in bed with your sister. No doubt she laughs as well."

These words caused Ibrahim to cry out in fury. He held his head in his hands. *I have been betrayed! Betrayed by a man I once called friend! Betrayed by my own sister! They will pay for their betrayal!*

Haj Amin looked upon Ibrahim's anguish with some pity. He addressed the two younger brothers. "You are being taken north to Haifa to fight against the British there. As long as your sister is alive and in the hands of the English and the Jews, you are not safe in Jerusalem. And then there is the matter of the posters . . ."

"*Insh' Allah,*" muttered Daud and Isaak with one voice. "If it is his will." They gazed reproachfully at Ibrahim. He had brought this upon them. Death and disgrace. It was his fault for trusting the Jew. Now they would all pay for the folly of Ibrahim Hassan.

Haj Amin clapped his hands, summoning a bodyguard to the door. "You must call Ram Kadar back into our presence," he instructed. "He must be made to play the role of the anxious, grieving bridegroom left without his bride." Haj Amin inclined his head toward Vargen. "I am certain Kadar would kill the woman himself if he had a chance, but this will be better for the sake of appearances."

"You have learned much from the Führer," Vargen said. "Of such small incidents, whole governments and nations topple, and new kingdoms arise."

Haj Amin raised his hand languidly as he looked toward the heavens. "*Insh' Allah,* Commander. May it be his will."

Herschel wished that he had listened to Hans and never returned to the home of his uncle. The meeting had not been the sentimental farewell of one man to another as Herschel had envisioned. It had ended in an awful argument. Without any apparent regard for the fate of Herschel's parents, his uncle had stormed and raged and called him ungrateful. Herschel had run from the house, slamming the door behind him, closing that chapter of his life with irrevocable finality.

For a moment his old depression returned. He was alone. Utterly alone. Perhaps, he thought, he should return immediately to the shop of the gunsmith, buy a gun, and turn it on himself! Then no matter what happened, he would never again feel pain or fear or loneliness.

"Wait! Herschel! Stop, will you?"

Herschel stopped on the sidewalk but did not turn around. He looked down as the slap of his old friend's shoes sounded behind him. Nathan Kaufman, breathless and flushed, nudged him hard on the shoulder. He stood panting before Herschel, admiring the new clothes and the new Herschel.

"I will be late," Herschel told him brusquely.

Nathan appeared very young compared to Herschel. "Late? Late for what? You stay away all this time, and the first thing you tell me is that you will be late! What is all this?" He tugged on the overcoat and grinned at the gleaming shoes. "You look like a rich man."

"I have a job. I cannot be late." Herschel began to walk and Nathan walked beside him.

"There is a dance tonight at the Aurora Sports Club. You want to come? Remember the carefree days, Herschel?"

"They have never been carefree days for me. At least your papers are in order. Mine have never been." He raised his head, resisting any memory of happiness. "No. I have business. I cannot meet you."

"You look different," Nathan said, and the tone of respect in his young voice once again instilled a sense of mission in Herschel.

"We all have to grow up." Herschel sighed and looked away, a dramatic and mysterious gesture that made Nathan frown and nod as if he understood.

"Well, yes. But at least come to the dance, will you?"

Herschel's feeling of importance was evident in his voice. "I have things to do."

Nathan did not argue further. "Then will you meet me later? At the restaurant Tout Va Bien? You know it. On boulevard de Strasbourg."

"Yes," Herschel agreed, although he knew he would not go there. It would save any further questions from Nathan, who seemed very much a child now.

"Good! Nine o'clock. All right?"

Herschel shook Nathan's hand in farewell and boarded the Metro, getting off at Strasbourg–St. Denis as Hans had instructed him. He ran up the steep steps. On his right was the Scala Cinema, where he and Nathan had watched dozens of subtitled movies in the carefree days. The sight of the marquee made him shake his head in wonder. Could such entertainment still go on when the world was such a terrible place?

To the left was the sign for the Hotel de Suez. Strange that Hans had recommended that he stay in a hotel patronized by Arabs from the French colonies of North Africa. This had always been a place Herschel and his friends avoided. They had often stepped from the Scala Cinema and seen men in strange red fez hats enter the lobby of that mysterious place. Ah, well. It was close to the Metro station.

He shoved his hands into his pockets and walked resolutely toward the hotel. The gold lettering on the door was flaking, the tiles of the foyer marked with muddy footprints. A handful of guests sat reading their papers written in the flowing Arabic script. The ancient clerk behind the counter did indeed wear a red fez, although no one else did. The hooked nose of the proprietor almost bent over his upper lip when he smiled at Herschel.

"How may I help you, monsieur?"

"A room." Herschel's voice quavered and he began again, consciously trying to strengthen and deepen his voice. "A room, please."

"You are not French?" asked the old man, turning the register for Herschel to sign.

"No. German." Herschel remembered Hans' instructions. When the green registration card for foreigners was presented for Herschel to sign, he was to explain that he was a salesman from Hamburg and his luggage was still at the station. "I will complete the formalities when I collect my luggage."

The old man bowed slightly in acceptance as Herschel counted out payment for the room in advance. Three francs. The old Arab, still smiling, placed the key in his hand and directed him toward the wrought-iron cage that served as the elevator.

"A pleasant stay . . ." He looked at the signature on the register and repeated the name Herschel had given. "Herr Heinrich Halter."

Herschel smiled, trying to shrug off the feeling that the old man somehow doubted that he was a salesman from Hamburg. It did not seem to matter much anyway. It had been easy. Hans had told him there would be no problem.

The message from the proprietor of Hotel de Suez was short and to the point. At the Berlin headquarters, Gestapo Chief Himmler sighed with relief as he read it. With a cheerful nod he picked up the telephone and dialed the private quarters of the Führer in the Chancellery.

"We have just received an update from Paris. Yes. The guest has arrived at Hotel de Suez on time. He has said and done everything exactly as he was instructed. Like a trained dog, this little Jew. He mimics every word, just as he was told."

This information and the anticipation of the drama to be played out in Paris and in Germany strengthened the outline of the Führer's speech for the coming celebration. It was now very clear that a hand stronger than that of a mere mortal was guiding this war against the Jews. An earlier dispatch from Vargen in Jerusalem indicated that events were happening all on their own, quite without a need for premeditation. The English Woodhead Committee trembled in their hotel rooms at the sound of a balloon bursting. Small incidents were gathering into an avalanche that would soon sweep the enemy from the face of the earth. "First in Jerusalem," Hitler said, "and then to the ends of the earth."

A murmuring darkness slid over the walled enclave of Jerusalem. Samuel Orde had been waiting for the darkness before he dared to move the newly married fugitives.

With his beard shaved, and dressed in the uniform of a British officer, Eli was not recognizable. Victoria was also dressed in the uniform of a British soldier. Her long black hair was tucked up under a pith helmet, and she carried a rifle slung over her shoulder as she climbed into one of the armored cars in front of the Old City barracks.

They all felt the eyes of the Mufti's watchers following the progress of the vehicles. There were six armored cars in the line of a convoy. Outside Jaffa Gate, they split off two by two, each pair taking different routes to various destinations in the New City.

Eli held Victoria's hand as their armored car swept through the residential district of Rehavia, past the Montefiore windmill, then around the city walls toward the Mount of Olives and the Garden of Gethsemane. Eli had explained that he had rented a small room for him and Victoria, but Orde protested. There was no place in all of Palestine safe enough—except one place that Orde knew.

Through the slit windows in the vehicle, Eli could see that place nestled on the slope of Olivet at the edge of Gethsemane. The seven golden onion-shaped turrets of the Church of St. Mary Magdalene glowed in the moonlight like a gingerbread castle in some Russian fairy tale. Each dome was topped by the cross of the Russian Orthodox church. Surrounded by aged pines, the compound was populated by Russian nuns and a handful of followers of the Russian czar who had managed to escape the massacres of the Bolshevik Revolution.

Here, on the hallowed slopes of Olivet, this small core of Russian faithful had found refuge and a sanctuary while men like Joseph Stalin murdered their Christian counterparts by the millions. Still living within the green iron gates of the compound was a general who had led the Imperial Cossack Guard of Czar Nicholas into exile after the royal family had been murdered.

Samuel Orde explained these things to the couple as he drove. He knew these people, knew the Mother Superior well. They were people who understood as well as any sect in Jerusalem what it meant to be hunted. Eli and Victoria certainly qualified for such a classification. The old nuns would take them in, give them a place to sleep and provide them with the privacy they needed. More important that that, there was no possibility that the men of Haj Amin would think of searching for them beneath those seven golden domes. Never would they imagine that Eli Sachar, the Jewish rabbinical student, would take his Muslim bride to a Russian convent!

Orde was quite pleased with himself for the idea. Besides, there was no more beautiful place in all of Jerusalem. Tonight they would close their eyes and smell the scent of the pine trees. Perhaps somehow, near the place where Jesus prayed, Eli and Victoria would find one night of peace within the safety of these walls.

The British armored car followed the stair-stepped stone fence that surrounded the Russian convent. A lane crept up the slope of Olivet at the back of the compound. Lights were still shining warmly in the windows of the residence buildings. The nuns were waiting for the arrival of their guests, Orde explained. Mother Superior had been notified early that afternoon and had prepared a place for Eli and Victoria that same hour.

Gravel crunched beneath the tires of the vehicle. The lane was so narrow that there were only inches on either side of the steel plate.

Orde stopped in front of a green wrought-iron gate. He turned off the lights and let the engine idle. Moments passed before the gate swung inward. Only then could he drive forward so the doors of the armored car could be opened.

"Here she is," Orde said as he peered out the slit at a tiny figure dressed completely in white from head to foot. "Mother Superior." A lined, pleasantly smiling face welcomed them as they stepped from the protection of Great Britain directly onto the soil of the Russian convent.

The old woman touched Victoria on the arm. "Welcome," she said in a voice much younger than the lined face. In the lantern light, the slightly hooded eyes of the old nun twinkled kindly. "Welcome. Welcome, Captain Orde."

No one spoke as she locked the gate and led them along a well-worn path. The two-story buildings of the compound nestled in the lower corner of the property, surrounded by pines and Cyprus trees that whispered and swayed above their heads. She did not seem to need the lantern for herself. Her feet knew the path well. She held it out for the others who stumbled along the shadowed ruts and bumps of the uneven path.

She did not stop at the main building, but continued down a short flight of steps to a flagged courtyard, then across to a small structure that she called the guesthouse. Beneath its simple archway she recited the names of the Russian aristocracy who had stayed here at one time or another during their long exile. "Not a palace," she said with a warm look meant for Victoria, "but comfortable."

And so it was. She opened the door to a sitting room illuminated by soft candlelight. A Victorian settee was placed in front of a fireplace where broken boughs and hissing pinecones burned, infusing the room with warmth and fragrance. Photographs of emperors and patriarchs and Russian aristocrats occupied the spaces on one entire wall. The names of these fell from her lips like the names of old friends. Looking down from among them was a large photograph of the Grand Duchess Elizabeth Feodrovna, who had carried out the plans for the building of the church before she was killed by the Bolsheviks. She was buried in a chapel on the grounds, explained the old nun.

When she had made the introductions, she looked at Victoria's clothing with pity. Men's trousers and shirt. Heavy coat and boots. Not the sort of wardrobe for a woman's wedding night. "There are nightclothes on the bed for you, dear," she whispered conspiratorially. "And some for your husband as well."

"We could not bring their belongings out of the Old City," Orde explained. "I will bring the things Leah packed for you when I come back tomorrow to pick up Eli."

Victoria gripped Eli's hand. "Pick him up? But why?"

"Statements. Depositions about the struggle. Your brothers. There are still questions that must be answered for the official record. We can't take the risk of bringing officers and equipment out here during the daylight hours. It will be simpler—and safer—for Eli to come into the city."

Eli squeezed her hand. "It will be all right. A formality only, and I will be back here."

The Mother Superior raised a crooked hand. "Tonight is not a night to think of business, children." She opened the enameled green door that led to the bedroom. Thick down quilts were turned back. A bowl of fruit and cheese and a small bottle of wine, along with a plate of bread, sat on a sideboard lit with candles. Victoria looked at the plain white-washed walls, thankful that there were no photographs gazing mournfully down at her. Above the bed hung a Russian Orthodox cross that seemed to glow in the flickering candlelight. "And so, children, the good captain and I bid you good night. God's blessing."

Orde smiled self-consciously as he shook Eli's hand and muttered, "Good luck, *Mazel tov*, and *shalom*." He tipped his hat to Victoria and then followed the frail old nun out of the house, closing the door behind him.

Eli stood with his hand resting on the footboard of the intricately carved olivewood bed. Still in the pith helmet, Victoria lingered at the side of the bed.

The crackle of the fire in the sitting room was the only sound inside the house. Outside, pine branches tapped against the roof and high windowpanes. Candlelight made shadows dance on the clean stone walls of the bedroom.

Victoria bit her lip and looked away self-consciously toward the open door of the sitting room. It seemed hard to believe that at last they were alone.

She lowered her eyes, feeling suddenly shy at the warmth of Eli's gaze upon her. She reached out and felt the fabric of the long white cotton nightgown the old nun had laid out for her on the coverlet. It was beautiful—trimmed in soft eyelet lace, with tiny buttons all the way down the front, and full, loose sleeves.

She touched the buttons of the borrowed khakis she wore and looked up at Eli, who smiled at her. She laughed and pulled off the pith helmet, letting her long black tresses tumble over her shoulders.

She smiled as his eyes filled with emotion—bright, loving. All the months of longing, and now they were here.

"Funny," Eli said in a hoarse whisper. "Every night I fell asleep dreaming of you. Of this moment. Now I am afraid to reach out. Afraid to hold you. Afraid this is only a dream." He did not move toward her, so she walked slowly around the bed to where he stood. She took his hands in hers and lifted them to her lips in a kiss.

"I am not a dream, Eli. But if I were, I would wish that you would never awaken." She held his hand to her heart and raised her face to his as he bent to kiss her. "No dream, my love," she whispered. "Touch me . . . touch me."

40

Hell Has Nothing Better Left to Do

Field Marshal Hermann Göring sent his private car to fetch Theo from the British Embassy. Long, sleek, and glistening black, even the raindrops stood at attention on the highly waxed finish. Two stiff swastika flags flanked the front bumpers. The chauffeur wore the black uniform of the SS. He saluted with a "Heil Hitler" as he held the door open for Theo.

For a moment, Theo hesitated before the curving driveway of the British Embassy. He turned to look at the softly glowing lights of the old mansion. It was not too late to turn around. Not too late to go back inside and send word he could not meet with Göring. Perhaps he could even catch the morning plane back to London. To Anna. Elisa. His children and grandchildren yet to be. Everything within him yearned to live only for those who were his own family. But what of other families? How many prayed tonight within this very city? How many prayed for help? for a way out? for a voice that might speak for them since their own voices had been so ruthlessly silenced?

Theo tossed a quick salute at the British Union Jack that hung limp in the evening mist. He eyed the plush red-velvet interior of Göring's car and then took one last deep breath of air before he plunged in. As he exhaled, he whispered a secret farewell. *Jacob Stern.* There must be a reason Göring has insisted his passport be issued in the name of the Dachau prisoner. Was Theo to become that prisoner again? Or worse?

He caught himself, restraining his mind from thinking about the possibilities as the limousine slowly drove past the floodlighted Reich Chancellery building on Wilhelmstrasse. He found his eyes looking toward a balcony that opened off the Führer's private quarters. The balcony was a new addition—designed so the Nazi god could review his marching troops and adoring masses.

Theo shuddered. The heaviness of Hitler's living nearness was oppressive. The Evil on this street was a thick black curtain that made Theo long for one more clean, untainted breath of air. He whispered a prayer against the Darkness, but here, where the backlighted windows gleamed as if illuminated by a lampless power, Theo's prayers were whispered with difficulty. A great weight pressed against his chest. He could not take his eyes from the dwelling place of the one who had made life more terrifying than death for so many. *What words are being whispered behind those curtains? What plans are being made? What demons hiss their commands against the People of the Book? against true Christians who protest? This is not the evil of a mere man,* Theo reasoned. He tore his eyes away from the crooked cross of the swastika flag that hung everywhere. *The broken cross. Symbol of ancient evil. Everywhere!*

The car continued down Wilhelmstrasse and turned at Leipziger Strasse, where the building that had been Lindheim's loomed up. Had the route been chosen on purpose? Had Göring laughed and instructed the SS driver to take Theo past the grand old building for one last look?

The windows held displays that were only half as full as they had been in the old days. Theo could see that the German economy and Göring's four-year economic plan were in trouble.

Theo was glad they had driven this way. Seeing the barrenness in the windows of Lindheim's Department Store gave him courage and a sense of hope. Perhaps Göring might be serious about a trade agreement. Foreign money for Jewish lives.

He caught the glance of the driver in the rearview mirror. Was the man in the SS uniform studying Theo so that he could report reactions later?

"The displays at this store are quite bare," Theo said, hoping that his words would indeed be repeated to Göring. "I am surprised to see such a grand old place stripped down. It must be difficult for the German women after so many years of good shopping here."

The eyes in the rearview mirror hardened. The amusement and curiosity sharpened to resentment, as if to say, *"How dare anyone criticize— even if it is true!"*

Eventually the cluster of city lights dwindled to a sprinkling of lamps scattered across the farmland beyond Berlin. Theo had been told that he was to be in Göring's home, that it had been his wish and he intended to discuss the ransom of human life over a quiet dinner at Karinhall. Theo had not questioned the reason for that request until the broad gates of the estate were swung open. As the car rolled up the drive, Theo could see that the front of the house was illuminated not by electricity, but by an enormous bonfire on the lawn.

A ring of SS and Brownshirts stood solemnly around the leaping flames. Their colorless faces turned to watch as the limousine pulled to a stop in front of the large house that Göring had named after his late wife. Lights glowed in every room. On the upper story, a shadow moved in front of a tall arched window. The shadow looked out as if to measure the effect on Theo as he emerged into the night air. Then the shadow moved away.

Theo looked toward the members of Hitler's private legion. They still watched him with lifeless eyes. Theo did not move from beside the automobile. He watched until the front doors of Karinhall opened, bathing the porch in light.

"Herr Stern?" asked a deep and resonant voice. "Herr Jacob Stern?"

"Just admiring the beauty of the bonfire."

Theo glanced over his shoulder at a tall SS officer who wore the insignia of a colonel. The man was unsmiling. "The field marshal is keeping a vigil in memory of the slain who died in the November Putsch."

Theo nodded. He remembered all that. He turned away from the flames, from this mystical appeal to the spirits of the dead Nazis.

The heat of the flames clung to his back even as he walked into the mansion. The light of the fire still burned as an afterimage in his vision when the hulk of Field Marshal Hermann Göring appeared in the foyer to welcome him.

From his passport folder Herschel pulled a black-and-white snapshot of himself. He held it up to the dim light of the lamp on the bed table.

Herschel. Smiling and happy as he stands beside the banks of the Seine River in Paris, he mused. *The river is still there. Unchanged. But where has that boy gone? Was I ever there at all? I cannot remember what it was like to smile.*

Nathan had taken the picture—so long ago, it seemed. Herschel studied the features of his image and wondered if that was really himself. Perhaps that hour of happiness was just a dream.

But he had awakened. He looked at his watch. Nathan would be waiting for him at the restaurant. Waiting for the Herschel who no longer existed except in this photograph.

Herschel turned the photograph over and then neatly wrote his farewell on the back:

My dear parents,

I could not do otherwise. May God forgive me. My heart bleeds at the news of 12,000 Jews suffering. I must protest in such a way that the world will hear me. I must do it. Forgive me.

Herschel

He propped up the photo, face out, smiling at him from the bed table. This picture of happier days was all he had left—a sort of miniature memorial of what life might have been for him, for thousands of others who never dreamed it would all come to this.

Herschel fell asleep with the light still burning. He slept with the fitful howling of twelve thousand desperate voices ringing in his mind. The faces of his mother, father, and sister rose up in tortured images, interposed with smiling black-and-white photographs of the better days. The stark contrast of what had been somehow made what was now seem all the more evil.

The world will hear me. I must do it. Forgive me. Herschel.

The majority of the staff members had left Paris to attend the coming celebrations of the November Putsch. Ernst vom Rath was left as the senior staff member in charge of the German Embassy in Paris.

The days had been long and uneventful. Tonight when the gates closed and the Nazi flag was lowered, Ernst changed into his dark brown suit and traveled on the Metro to the Strasbourg–St. Denis station. There was an American musical film playing at the Scala Cinema. The marquee was emblazoned with the title:

MARIE ANTOINETTE

Starring

Tyrone Power – Norma Shearer

The film was the talk of Paris because of its atrocious portrayal of the life of the French queen who had been beheaded just a few miles from the theatre where the film now played. In France, the film had become a poorly dubbed comedy, and the audiences had left the packed theatre every night with their sides aching from the American interpretation of the mindless queen.

Ernst needed a laugh. His life in Paris had taken on the same depressing monotone quality it had in Berlin. Of course, in Paris he was not required to strut and heil and applaud the Nazi superstition as long as he was not in the embassy.

A fine mist cooled his face as he walked to the end of the line that snaked down the sidewalk and ended just at the door of Hotel de Suez.

Ernst was sorry that he had come alone. Of course, lately he had gone most places alone. Tonight in the midst of the Paris theatre-goers, however, his loneliness seemed a heavy burden.

Couples were everywhere. Pretty girls held tightly to their escorts. They kissed beneath a forest of umbrellas and laughed about things they had been told about the movie.

"Ah, yes! And in the news film there is a section showing Charles Lindbergh as he accepts the Nazi service cross from Hitler. Imagine! Who would think he would do such a thing? Remember how we cheered him when he landed? It is a betrayal—a betrayal of France!"

So even here in the line of a movie theatre, Ernst could not escape the rotten propaganda of his nation's Führer. A young woman stared at him from beneath her umbrella. Could she see that he was German? Perhaps the cut of his clothes, his unsmiling face. . . . She whispered to her companion in a barely audible voice, "Be quiet. He is one of them. A filthy *bosche*! Do not speak about the Germans."

Ernst looked away as if he had not heard. For several couples in front of him there was silence along the line. He glanced up at the marquee and down at his shoes as if he were considering something. Without a word, he left the queue and walked quickly back to the Metro station to take the next train back to the embassy.

Once again Etta rode in the black automobile of the Warsaw priest, Father Kopecky. She stared out the window at the brutal streets of the city and yet she felt safe within this tiny ark.

Father Kopecky was indeed a man of great authority. His indignation had rattled the iron cages of the Warsaw jailers, causing them to turn around and point fingers of accusation at everyone besides themselves.

"I will send the car to fetch you at your home at nine o'clock tomorrow morning," said the priest. "Then the director of the police will be back in Warsaw. He is not a parishioner of mine, but his mother is faithful. The fellow will listen to me." He smiled slightly. "Or I will have a word with his mother. A formidable woman."

Etta managed a smile at his words. She was tired. So weary. Had there ever been such a day of fear and trial? She prayed that Aaron was unhurt. She prayed that a deep and peaceful sleep might come upon him so he would not know he was in a jail cell. As for herself, to think of sleep, in spite of her exhaustion, made her feel guilty. How could she sleep with Aaron in prison?

As if he heard her thoughts, Father Kopecky said, "You must let your heart have peace now, Sister Lubetkin. The prophets of old suffered much more than this, and yet the Lord was with them."

She nodded and averted her eyes from the cross he wore around his neck. It surprised her that he spoke of suffering prophets. Those could not be the same as the prophets of Jewish Warsaw.

"Besides," he continued, "I am your witness; am I not? I only wish you would have come to me sooner and we might have ended this blackmail business before it got started." He considered her silence and then began again more cheerfully. "Ah, well, it will be finished tomorrow. This is Warsaw, not Berlin. You will see. In Poland we have our fanatics, but the law is still the law. Go home now to your children and rest. Tomorrow night your husband will be at your side. I promise."

For the thousandth time, Ernst considered vanishing from his Paris post. If he left, he decided, he would do it with more success than Thomas von Kleistmann had done. He would have a plan. Passports made up under several different names. A destination far away from the probing eyes of Gestapo agents and SS goons like Officer Konkel.

Only one thing stopped him from leaving, from vanishing into the woodwork: his family. Still in Berlin, they might fall under the punishment of Hitler's law that if any one member of a family transgresses, all are held accountable. His aging father was already known for his disapproval of the Nazi Party and the crushing of the Reichstag parliament. His father had warned him during Ernst's last visit to Berlin that he must tell no one about the death of Thomas, that he must not speak out again or he might find himself also crucified in some dark Gestapo torture cell.

Tonight, the face of Ernst's father swam before him as he lay down on his bed. The old Prussian aristocrat would be hunted down and arrested in place of Ernst. If the Gestapo could not catch Ernst, they would take his father and mother hostage, and . . .

What was the use? Ernst was trapped. He turned over and stared at the wall. He should be grateful, he reasoned, that he was serving in Paris instead of Berlin. The only thing that could be better is if he could go to America. *If only I could somehow go to America and take my family there!*

He fell asleep with that prayer on his lips, and dreamed sweet dreams of freedom.

Over an elegant supper of veal and asparagus, Hermann Göring chatted with Theo as if they had never met before, as if the name Jacob Stern was really Theo's name. Surrounded by half a dozen ministers from within the Nazi Economic Ministry, polite conversation drifted toward the possibility of expanded trade for Germany and the lifting of the international Jewish boycott against German goods.

In all of this, no mention was made of the exchange of Jewish assets for increased trade. Nothing seemed to connect the two intertwined subjects. It was as if Göring was saving the real purpose of this meeting for after dinner, after his flunkies and assistants were sent their way and Goring and Theo were alone.

The large grandfather clock in the study struck ten o'clock. Theo half smiled. He recognized the chimes of that old clock, just as he had recognized paintings taken from the walls of his own house.

At last only Theo remained. He was a captive. He had come in Göring's car and so must leave the same way, if he were to leave at all.

That thought crossed his mind as he followed Göring into an enormous library. One entire wall contained the collection of rare books that had once been Theo's prize possession. How insignificant such possessions seemed to him now!

Göring turned to face him. Smiling, he addressed Theo by his real name for the first time. "A brandy, Theo?" he asked, pouring two snifters with amber liquid before Theo answered. "You always did appreciate fine things." He extended the glass to Theo, who took it with a nod and then looked at the wall of books.

"Yes. In some things our tastes are the same, I see."

Göring swirled his brandy, then sipped it. "In aircraft. In books." He smiled again, without any pretense or sign of embarrassment. "In paintings. And . . . in women."

Theo met his gaze. There was bitter amusement in Göring's eyes. Old friend turned enemy. "You have done well, Hermann," Theo replied, feeling pity for the man he had once known.

"And how is Anna?"

"Better than you would imagine, I am sure."

"Did she know you would be meeting with me?"

"She knew I would have discussions with Field Marshal Hermann Göring. Second in command only to the Führer himself."

Hermann lowered his bulk onto the sofa as he spread a hand for Theo to sit opposite him.

Theo continued to stand. He turned to look out the window to where the bonfire blazed with renewed vigor and the sentinels of the morbid vigil began to sing the "Horst Wessel."

Göring broke the silence in the room as the distant voices served as backdrop. "You never were a very good Jew, Theo," Göring said. "When first I heard you were one of them, I defended you. Said it couldn't be that such a patriot of the Fatherland was one of them."

Theo tore his gaze from the flames as he turned to face Göring. "Strange. I was also surprised when I heard you were a part of this . . ." He lifted his hand toward the bonfire. "You have come a long way with your Führer. A long way from yourself."

Göring laughed. "You just did not know me, Theo. I was always this."

"No, Hermann. Brash and foolish perhaps. The perfect candidate for a hero in Germany. But you were not *this*. To be what you are now takes years of slow hardening of the heart."

Resentment twitched on Göring's face. "Sometimes one must be hard for the sake of one's race and nation. For the cause of victory, Theo, we Aryans make ourselves hard. We must root out and destroy, you see—kill even the roots of those who do not belong among us." His eyes narrowed. His face hardened beneath his jowls. "You were never one of us."

"I am grateful for that, since I have learned from you what such belonging means."

"We are the power of Germany now, and you see what we accomplish," Göring countered.

"The death of freedom."

"Freedom is not dead in the Reich."

"Only those who desire freedom."

"Freedom is redefined by the standards of race and purity of blood. If we do not rule over you, then surely you will rule over us."

"You have forgotten that God rules over all."

"Which God? The Jewish God? The Christian God?"

"They are one and the same."

"We have chosen another god who will rule over millions across the world. Those who follow your weak and worthless God of love will die, Theo, because they have no strength to fight."

Theo did not answer him. He looked first at the fire outside on the lawn, then at the shelves of gleaming leather-bound books on the wall just behind them. Göring had taken them from Theo's shelves and replaced them in exactly the same order. He ran his finger along a row of books until he gently touched the small blue and gold volumes containing the complete works of the poet Lord Bryon. There were seventeen volumes in the set.

"You are familiar with these books?" Theo asked.

Göring nodded, pleased at his own memory. "The definitive edition. Published in 1833, I believe. Quite valuable."

"But have you read them?" Theo chose one book, took it down, and opened it.

"No. But I am familiar enough with the value of such editions that I did not allow them to be burned."

"The value is not in the binding, Hermann, but in the words within."

"A fundamental difference between you and me. We see value in different ways."

Theo thumbed through the pages. "Yes. And that tragic reality separates us."

"Tragic to whom?" Göring scoffed. "Not tragic to the Aryan race. Only tragic for those over whom we rule and those over whom we will rule around the world very soon."

"And after your rule ends? What then, Hermann?"

"The Third Reich will reign for one thousand years."

"So I heard. But you will not. And so, what then?"

Göring flushed at the mention of his own end. "Others of our race—they will remember what we have done here."

"Yes. I do not doubt. I pray they will remember." Theo lowered his gaze to the pages of the book. "It is a pity you have not read—"

"To what purpose?"

"A vision of judgment. It is written here. The words of a man long dead still speak in these pages." Theo's gaze silenced Göring. "Here Lucifer had much to say to God about the souls of kings who stand in judgment." He began to read:

"'On the throne
He reigned o'er millions to serve me alone. . . .
They are grown so bad
That hell has nothing better left to do
Than leave them to themselves: so much more mad
And evil by their own internal curse,
Heaven cannot make them better, nor I worse.'"

Theo raised his eyes.

Göring's face was set with defiance. "What has *that* to do with me?" he demanded.

"Surely you must listen, Hermann, before it is too late for you!" Theo sat down across from him. "You say the whole world must serve you, bow to you, slave for the sake of your Aryan god and ideals."

"Yes! That is how it will be!"

"You reign over millions."

"Yes!"

"But you serve only the Prince of Darkness and Death!"

Göring paled. Had he heard the whisper of some warning in his own soul? He did not answer. Thoughts—and even a shadow of fear—crossed his face. And then . . . the hardness descended like a curtain of steel. He snatched the book from Theo's hand and stared at its pages, then stood and stalked to the window, throwing it open to the chill of the night.

He shouted to the men who ringed the fire. "Come in!" he called. Then he shut the window and turned, smiling, to Theo. "I have brought you here to kill you," he said in a cheerful voice. "And I find that you have strengthened me. Deepened my convictions as to certain *values*." He strode to the fireplace and, in a gesture of contempt, tore the pages from the book and tossed both book and pages into the flames. The fire roared hungrily, devouring the pages and the book cover as Theo watched.

A dozen SS troops crowded into the room. They looked at Theo with the same hunger as flames for fragile paper.

"Tonight we are going to offer a sacrifice to our gods." Göring swept a hand over the wall of books. "You are right, Theo. Our ideas of value differ. I should be more careful what I consider worthwhile." He turned his gaze on the eager young Titans. "Burn these books. All of them. Not one page of this filth shall remain in the Reich."

Theo stood. He stepped back and watched grimly as the men shouted and threw the precious volumes down in irreverent heaps on the floor and then carried them out by the armload to the funeral pyre.

Göring clasped Theo by the arm and led him to the window to watch as sparks of truth rose up to appease the god of Nazi ignorance.

"That is you burning out there, Theo Lindheim. All your thoughts. Everything you are. See how the flames of our fury consume you. And you are dying there. Page by page, word by word, letter by letter, you blacken and shrivel and perish! I don't have to kill your miserable Jew body—I have a much better plan! You can take word of your death back to England. Tell them that you have witnessed the death of your God and yourself tonight."

"Someday you will stand before Him in judgment, and then you will know that every word you tried to destroy and every innocent life you took is eternal," Theo replied. "You are the one who burns out there—your last chance to cling to Truth."

Göring's face registered disdain. "What is truth? Truth is what we make it to be." He smiled cruelly. "Tomorrow you will see the truth of our Reich, and you will believe in the power."

41

Plotting the Course of Destiny

The embers of a thousand books sparked in the night air, reflecting on the shining finish of the black Nazi limousine as it pulled slowly from the driveway. From the window of the automobile, Theo could see Hermann Göring presiding over the conflagration of books. He gloated in his window. Somehow he still believed that by destroying the pages, he had destroyed the Truth that accused him and would, one day, condemn him.

Göring had never seriously intended to consider the exchange of lives for trade agreements. Theo had been brought here for a far more sinister purpose. He would be Göring's personal mouthpiece to carry back to Britain the message of death.

Theo looked out the back window. It was a miracle that the automobile was indeed speeding back to the British Embassy with him alive inside it. He could still see the orange glow from distant Karinhall. Foreboding filled him as he wondered what answer had been planned for the world and the Jews of Germany tomorrow. God was still alive, but Reason was indeed dead. Hitler, Göring, and the rest ruled over millions, but they ruled to serve only the Prince of Darkness.

Victoria awoke in the half-light of predawn. Eli was already dressed. She watched him from the bed as he stoked the fire with a fresh supply of pine boughs.

"Eli?" she called sleepily to him.

He replaced the poker and stood slowly. His face was shadowed with the regret that he had to leave her on this, their first morning together. He returned to the bedroom and stroked her hair as he sat on the edge of the bed.

"Why are you up?" she asked, taking his hand and laying it against her cheek. "Come back to bed."

"I can't. It is almost light."

"It's the middle of the night. Come back to bed." She smiled dreamily and pulled him down against her on the bed. She wound her silky arms around his neck and kissed him until he kissed her back with an unresisting hunger.

"It is almost light," he mumbled.

"It is just the moonlight. Come back." She fumbled with the buttons of his shirt.

"Captain Orde said . . . he said . . . I should meet him at the gate before the sun comes up."

She kissed him harder. "It is the moonlight, Eli."

It was hopeless. At her urging, he was helpless to leave her. "All right. I'll stay. Even if they see me leave. Even if the Mufti himself should spot me from the city wall. If you say it isn't dawn but the moonlight, I will stay with you. What is anything compared to this?"

Suddenly she released him. She sat up, leaving him panting, his shirt half buttoned. "No!" she exclaimed, wide-awake. "You cannot leave the convent in the daylight! The whole area will be filled with Arabs by morning! You must go now, Eli!"

He protested. He kissed her neck and resisted leaving. "It is the moonlight."

"It is the dawn! Almost morning! You must go now by the cover of dark!"

"But, Victoria," he whispered, in pain.

She leaped out of the bed and quickly buttoned her gown as she searched for his jacket. "You must hurry." She held it for him to put on. "If the Arabs see you, they will know where we are. We will have to find some other place, and—oh, hurry, Eli, before the sun comes up!"

"I will be back tonight." He sighed with resignation. Gathering her close against him, he muttered, "May we have an eternity of nights and morning and days together."

"I will be waiting here for you."

"Dressed like this, I hope." He stroked her cheek and smiled down into her eyes.

"Waiting for you."

Still out of breath, the Arab messenger was shown directly into the bed-chamber of Haj Amin Husseini. He wiped sweat and mist from his brow as he bowed low before the Mufti.

"What word?"

"As you predicted," the messenger said. "I watched the British captain bring Eli Sachar into the British headquarters. Sachar wears an English uniform. He has shaved."

"And the woman?"

"I did not see her. She was not with them, but I followed Captain Orde. He picked up Eli Sachar from the grounds of the Russian convent."

"You are certain of this?" The Mufti's eyes were animated in thought.

"No. I mean, I did not see Sachar at the convent, but the armored car pulled up to the gate in the back. It stopped a moment. The gate swung back and then the armored car drove away. It did not stop again until it reached British headquarters, and then Sachar got out."

This news pleased the Mufti. "She is there, then," he said under his breath. "At the Russian convent in Gethsemane." He was smiling, a rare smile. This all seemed so easy. "We shall have to think of a way to draw her out." He tugged his earlobe.

"The walls are ten feet high. She will not come out from their safety," protested the messenger.

"We will send her news." The Mufti clapped his hands, summoning the muscular bodyguard into his room. "Go wake Commander Vargen," he ordered. "We must discuss the nature of our announcement about the trial of Eli Sachar."

The messenger frowned. Trial? The Jew was obviously under British protection. "A trial?" muttered the man.

"People will believe anything they hear on the wireless; will they not? The wording must be perfect. She will come. You will see. Victoria Hassan will come to this very door and plead for the life of Eli Sachar."

"But that would be suicide."

"A small matter when love is involved."

As if anticipating a coming conflagration, citizens of the Old City Jewish Quarter had begun building barricades across every street into their Quarter.

Eduard Letzno had volunteered to set up an infirmary in the Jewish Old City; he arrived just after dawn with a carload of medical supplies.

Rabbi Lebowitz helped him set up in a back room at the Great Hurva

Synagogue; then both the young doctor and the old rabbi had joined the crews who filled sandbags and also canisters with water.

There would be a Muslim funeral in the Old City today, and the rage would no doubt flood the narrow banks to sweep away any within its path.

On this day, Rabbi Lebowitz would not travel to the Western Wall to pray. He would not mail his letter to Etta and Aaron in Warsaw. He would not pass beyond the boundaries of the Quarter. There was no question of that.

Within the great synagogue, he led prayers for Eli Sachar. Everyone knew the truth of what had transpired in the foundry. But truth had little meaning when weighed against blind fury and a rampaging mob.

There was no radio here to spread the word of Muslim outrage. No radio was needed. Not one shop opened. The bells of the Christian Quarter tolled the hours over empty streets. The British soldiers were doubled in force along the wall. Everyone knew what was coming. It was only a matter of when the violence would erupt.

For a moment Herschel could not remember the name he had signed on the hotel register.

"Monsieur?" asked the man on the other end of the telephone line.

"Ah. Yes. This is . . . Heinrich Halter. Room 22. Please send up strong coffee and croissants."

As he took the room-service tray and paid the porter for breakfast, it seemed strange to Herschel that he felt so calm this morning. And hungry as well.

If he had any remaining doubts, they had dissipated last night. Herschel had not eaten anything since noon yesterday; he devoured his breakfast hungrily. His depression was gone. A resolute excitement replaced it. Today was the day! The Nazi monster Adolf Hitler would hear Herschel's message. He would raise his head and know that at least one Jew was not a lamb to be led quietly to the slaughter!

Dressed in his new suit, Herschel took one last triumphant look at himself in the mirror. His one regret was that Hitler himself was too far away to be his target. His one fear was that he would not be allowed into the German Embassy, and that all of this would come to nothing.

He placed his fedora on his head and pulled the brim low. Then, carefully filling the pockets of his overcoat with his identification in case he was shot dead, Herschel left the Hotel de Suez and walked briskly toward The Sharp Blade, the gunsmith's shop.

He lingered outside for a few moments, trying to decide which weapon in the display window would be best for his purposes.

Then the smiling face of the proprietor appeared at the other side of the window, welcoming the young customer into the shop.

So many guns. Herschel had not imagined that there could be so many weapons to choose from.

The owner of The Sharp Blade, a man named Carp, showed him nearly every revolver available in the store. Herschel's head was spinning. He did not know what would best kill a man. Should he choose an automatic or a small-caliber pistol?

He picked up one and then another, measuring the weight of each weapon in his hand. He could not decide. An hour passed and still Carp labored over his one lone customer.

At last the diminuitive, balding shopkeeper asked in exasperation, "You are so young. Why do you need a gun?"

How could Herschel explain? The reply Hans had given him to such a question entered his mind. "I am a foreigner. I have to carry large amounts of money for my father."

Carp nodded with relief. He would help the boy decide. "Something to frighten away thieves, eh, young man?"

"If they should attack I would wish to do more than frighten them."

"Ah, well, any one of these will wound and kill. You need something easy to handle."

"Yes."

"Easily concealed and quick and simple to use!"

"Exactly," Herschel nodded seriously as he imagined attempting to conceal one of the larger weapons in his pocket. They were so heavy, certainly someone at the German Embassy would spot the bulge.

Carp held up his trigger finger in pleasure. "Then I have just the thing for you. A small-barrel, 6.35-caliber pistol." He held up the gun. It looked like a toy compared to many of the others.

"But will it do the job?"

Carp laughed at the question. "Would you not run if someone pointed this at you and began to pull the trigger?"

Herschel smiled also. He nodded. Yes. This would be perfect.

The pistol had cost Herschel two hundred and forty-five francs, including ammunition. He had plenty to pay for it. He inwardly thanked Hans for providing the money that made all this possible.

He smiled as he left the shop. Monsieur Carp had showed him how to load the weapon and how to fire it. Herschel strode quickly to the Tout Va Bien restaurant and went directly into the restroom. With steady hands, he loaded his gun with five bullets and then held it. Soon these bullets would enter the body of a Nazi. Herschel nodded. *Yes!* All his own pain would be transferred to the enemy through these five tiny bits of lead!

He slipped the weapon into the left inside pocket of his coat before he left the restaurant and descended into the Metro. At Strasbourg–St. Denis station, he caught the subway train for the Germany Embassy.

Ambassador Neville Henderson was visibly agitated when he returned from an early morning telephone call. He sat across the breakfast table from Theo Lindheim on the morning after Theo's trip to Karinhall.

"What did you say to Field Marshal Göring? He's normally such a jolly fellow. I've never heard him so distraught before."

Theo did not reply. Instead, he stared out the window of the ambassador's residence into a murky gray Berlin morning. *How appropriate*, he thought. *The world is dividing itself between light and dark, and only the British are still attempting to see shades of gray.*

"How could you antagonize the Nazis so?" Henderson continued.

Without answering the question Theo replied, "Exactly how did Göring express his displeasure?"

"He's ordered—no, *demanded*—that you be expelled from Germany at once. Twenty-four hours, he said. If you're not off Reich soil in twenty-four hours, he's going to have you arrested!"

Ernst looked up from where he sat at his desk in the embassy to find an immaculately uniformed Konkel staring at him from the doorway. The Abwehr officer had an odd smile on his face. *Definitely an unpleasant smile*, Ernst thought.

Ernst decided that a touch of bravado was required to overcome the quaver he felt in the pit of his stomach. "Getting a late start for the celebration, aren't you? The ambassador and the others have left without you."

"I have been detained briefly by important business for the Reich," replied the officer haughtily. "But now I find that all matters are in order and proceeding as they should, so I am free to leave. I shall certainly arrive in time for the solemn remembrance ceremony."

"Well, then," Ernst said, with as much nonchalance as he could manage, "Heil Hitler! Naturally, I will be here giving my full attention to the words of the Führer's speech as it is broadcast to the world."

That same curious, mirthless smile evoked a small shudder in Ernst's frame, despite every effort he could manage to repress it.

"Before I can depart," added Konkel, "I must give you instructions about a matter of importance to Reich security."

"Certainly, Officer Konkel."

"We have had reports to the effect that there is a violent uprising being planned by gangsters of international Jews. We even have reason to believe that such violence may be directed against Reich property here in France. I have certain contacts who have pledged to bring me advance word of any such activity, and I do not intend to miss receiving the information because of my absence."

He fixed a piercing stare on Ernst. "Naturally, it falls on your shoulders, vom Rath, to accept such an important message. You must not, under any circumstances, be absent from your post. Is this obligation completely clear?"

"Quite understood. I'll do my utmost to aid military intelligence in this delicate and important matter. How will I know this individual when he arrives?"

"I have instructed both the housekeeper and the porter to be expecting someone who will indicate that he has an important message to deliver to the person in charge, whereupon the fellow will be shown immediately to you."

Ernst was puzzled by the apparent change in Konkel's high regard of him. *Perhaps it's a trap to see what I'll do,* he thought. "And what do I do with the message when I receive it?"

"Have no fear," said the Abwehr officer bluntly, "you'll receive explicit instructions that will leave no doubt about what to do." He gave a Nazi salute of textbook precision and spun on his heel to leave.

Ernst called after him, "Be thinking of me working away here all alone."

Through the same strange smile Konkel agreed, "I can promise you we will all be thinking of you." Then he was gone.

Beyond the walls of the Russian convent, all Jerusalem simmered. Emotions, like white-hot coals, waited for even a light breeze to whip them into a frenzy.

Proclamations were made from the Dome of the Rock, and Ismael Hassan became a holy martyr to the cause of the jihad against the Jews. From Damascus and Amman and Cairo, radio broadcasts declared that the murderer Eli Sachar must be turned over to the Arab Council for justice! The return of the kidnapped Muslim bride of Ram Kadar was demanded. Speculation was made as to whether Victoria still lived or if the murderer had killed her as well after he had violated her.

In reply, the BBC of Palestine announced that Eli Sachar was in custody and being detained for questioning. So a war of accusation and defense was being made over the airwaves of the Middle East. Vengeance was demanded with a new fervor. The dreaded winds of rumor and lies began to whip against the coals of hatred.

Behind the walls of the convent, Victoria heard none of this. Dressed in the borrowed habit of a novice nun, she walked freely about the compound. She felt no apprehension; there had been no reason for fear. After all, Eli had been taken to the British military headquarters for routine questioning. A deposition. A simple statement of fact about the attack. He would be back as soon as the sun went down again. Victoria longed for that time.

She sat down on the low stone wall surrounding the flagstone courtyard. The sun had broken through the heavy piles of clouds in the east over the mountains of Moab. Shafts of light beamed down on the bulbed domes of the Russian church, as if that place alone was in heaven's spotlight.

Victoria watched the shifting light and shadow for a few moments, then opened her precious mother-of-pearl Bible. The wind rustled over the onionskin pages until they flipped open to the story of Christ's agony in Gethsemane. She began to read:

> *My soul is exceeding sorrowful unto death: tarry ye here, and watch.*

She raised her eyes to ponder the ancient olive trees whose roots, it was said, dated back to before this prayer was uttered.

> *Abba, Father, all things are possible unto Thee; take away this cup from Me; nevertheless not what I will, but what Thou wilt.*

Within the peaceful enclave of this convent, the suffering of Christ in the garden seemed tangible and immediate. Somehow she felt that if she climbed the tiny footpath up the slope tonight, she would find Him there. Perhaps tonight, when Eli came back, they would steal away together to Gethsemane and talk to Jesus about suffering.

She turned her face toward the gentle slope of Olivet as it rose behind the church. In these whispered memories of Christ's suffering, Victoria found a measure of peace.

Herschel had changed trains at the Paris Metro station rue Madeleine, and arrived at the Solferino station near the German Embassy a few minutes past ten o'clock.

He stood across the street from the embassy, staring up at its grim walls and the bloodred flag waving lazily from the flagpole above the entryway in the middle of the block.

Herschel nervously fingered the pistol in his coat pocket and thought about the five little messages it contained. He raised his right foot, preparing to step down from the curb and cross the street, when an oncoming truck made him draw back. It passed without stopping, but Herschel did not immediately move again.

What am I standing here for? he pondered. *Why don't I just go in and get it over with? This all seems too easy; it can't possibly be this simple to kill someone. Maybe I should go around the block to see where the guards are located.* Then a horrible thought struck him. *What if this isn't the right entrance and I can't get in?*

At that moment a voice behind him startled Herschel. "Pardon, monsieur, may I be of assistance?" It was a short, trim man in the dark blue uniform of a Paris gendarme.

"Yes. I mean no—that is, no. I'm all right, thank you," blundered Herschel. He kept himself from running away only with the greatest difficulty, reminding himself that he was dressed as a prosperous businessman.

The policeman was apparently taken in by the disguise, for he continued in a helpful tone, "Ah, you are German, are you not?" He followed Herschel's nervous gaze across the street to the embassy. "Can I be of some help?"

Herschel grasped at the first reply that came to mind. "Is this the main entrance to the embassy? I didn't realize that it was so large and I am supposed to meet someone . . . to . . . to discuss business. I am a businessman from Hamburg, you see," he concluded lamely.

"But of course," the gendarme replied. "You have arrived correctly at the main entrance, just there beneath the flag."

Herschel still hesitated, still held back from crossing the street.

"Was there something else, monsieur?"

I've got to go in now, thought Herschel. *He's expecting me to cross the boulevard and enter the building. I've got to go in now.* "No, nothing, thank you, Officer. I was just admiring the building and the way the flag moves in the breeze."

With that, Herschel finally stepped off the curb and crossed the street to ascend the steps into the German Embassy.

These Germans! thought the policeman fiercely. *What ugliness they must have in their souls!* He continued on down the block, swinging his nightstick jauntily as he went.

The horrifying news about Eli blared over the radio of the Russian convent and sent the Mother Superior out searching for Victoria. How would she tell her? How could the old woman break such news to one so young and hopeful as Victoria? The Mother Superior found her sitting quietly in the courtyard.

Victoria walked beside the frail old Mother Superior across the grounds. Here, on the fringes of the garden where Jesus had suffered and prayed alone in agony, Victoria felt a peace she had never known. The old nun pointed toward the gnarled trunks of the ancient olive trees where He had prayed and then been betrayed.

"They say the Romans cut down the trees when they destroyed Jerusalem. Ah, but the roots of olive trees live on, you see. Buried in the soil, hidden, they live on and then send forth shoots and live again. Yes.

Those are the very trees. Their roots go deep into the centuries when He was here."

She looked up at the onion domes of the Russian church. "The trees are a better reminder of His agony than all these buildings." She paused and toyed with a small silver cross that hung around her neck. "I knew the Grand Duchess who built this church. She was killed with the rest of the Czar's family when the Bolsheviks took over. Her body came to rest here, as she wished." The old woman held up the silver cross. "This was hers. It is passed on from each of our Mothers Superior to the next." She smiled at the memory. "Now I wear it."

"Such sorrow you speak of," Victoria said. "And yet I feel such peace here, as if even now the Lord prays there in the garden."

The old woman turned her eyes upon the young woman. "Then you have found the secret of Jerusalem. City of sorrow. City of hope. We are not bound by time in this place." She lifted her head as the wind brushed over them. "Time, after all, is not a thing you can touch. This moment as we speak—where is it?" She spread her hands as though letting a bird fly free. "It is gone. And so, we can look forward to eternity from here. We can see what Jerusalem will be, what is promised and sure. We can choose not to think about the dark side of faith, but know that Christ has called us to be friends. And the Russian word for friend is *drougoi*."

"*Drougoi*," Victoria repeated.

"The word gives a sense of being reflected in somebody, like a mirror. A friend, you see, is in a way *another of yourself*. Of all creatures on earth, we are made in God's image and are given His freedom."

"It seems no one is free in Jerusalem," Victoria said quietly.

"Men are even given the freedom to hate instead of love. To destroy instead of create." She frowned and looked deeply into Victoria's eyes. "And for those who love, freedom can mean suffering. As Jesus suffered there." She raised a hand, as gnarled as the olive branches, to point to Gethsemane. "It was because He loved us that He suffered. Suffered for our wrong choices and the freedom we abuse. And if you suffer, my child, you will learn! You will reflect Him even more. *Drougoi*. That is how the great saints and martyrs came to be like Him."

"I am a coward," Victoria said softly. "I do not want to suffer. I want only to stay in a place like this. Very close to heaven. And I want to love my husband and live in happiness."

The old woman patted her hand. She sat in silence and gazed at the ancient trees where Christ prayed. She needed help to say what she needed to say! How could she tell Victoria the news that blared over the radio every half hour?

"Sometimes the best dreams vanish," the old woman offered gently.

"I remember when I was sixteen, living in Moscow. The Bolsheviks murdered the husband of the Grand Duchess."

"The woman buried here?"

"Yes. He was the Czar's uncle, and they murdered him to make a
point. No other reason than that. I remember kneeling beside her. Beautiful woman. All in black. And their sons . . ." In a gesture of despair, she
raised her hands. "They suffered. All of them. But . . . you must remember, even suffering is not permanent. Time will pass and so will the moment of your greatest agony . . . my dear . . ." She faltered.

"What is it?" Victoria drew back, suddenly aware that all this had not
been idle talk. Mother Superior had been trying to tell her something.
"Tell me. *What?* Is it Eli?"

The old woman nodded. "I heard it on the radio. I did not wish you
to hear it alone."

"Please?" Victoria begged. Tears filled her eyes.

"They say, on the Radio Cairo, he has been handed over to the Arab
Council for trial. They accuse him not only of the murder of your
brother but also the rape and possible murder of a woman they claim is
the wife of a Muslim named Ram Kadar. Could they mean you?"

And so it was said. Peace vanished, cut down to the roots like the olive trees. Victoria's dreams and hopes were tossed as kindling onto the
fire of the Mufti's ambitions. She turned her eyes from Gethsemane toward Jerusalem, where Jesus had been tried, condemned, and crucified
even in innocence. So, it was to be done again in Jerusalem. Once again
an innocent man was to stand in the house of the Mufti on the spot
where the Sanhedrin had judged Jesus. The hour of agony had come.

Herschel stepped through the heavy doors to the lobby of the German
Embassy. He found himself facing a reception desk topped with a telephone and an ornate fountain pen in a marble holder. A tiny replica of
the Nazi flag waving outside stood on one corner of the desk, while the
wall behind it was occupied with an enormous and fierce-looking
bronze eagle clutching a swastika. The room was completely empty of
people, however.

Now what do I do? thought Herschel. "Hello?" he called hesitantly in
French, and then somewhat louder in German. "Hello. Is anyone here?"

Down the corridor to his right, a door opened and an elderly man
shuffled into view. Herschel grasped the butt of the pistol in his pocket,
then relaxed as he noted the man's age.

The man moved with his head looking down at the floor. He was
buttoning the fly of his trousers as he scuffed toward the lobby. When he

finally caught sight of Herschel, he straightened his back as best he could and attempted to look dignified. "Your pardon, monsieur. I did not hear you come in. May I help you?"

"Is there no one here except you?" inquired Herschel in an anguish of frustration.

"No one, monsieur. They've all gone to some sort of celebration or something."

Herschel could no longer keep the desperation from his voice. "But I must see someone in charge!"

This phrase seemed to penetrate the old porter's brain. "Someone in charge . . . of course, of course, how stupid of me! Third Secretary vom Rath is here. He is in charge."

Herschel actually breathed a sigh of relief, until he realized what the presence of "someone in charge" meant. "Can you take me to him? I have an important message to give directly to the person in charge."

"Certainly, I'll show you right in," offered the porter, turning to shuffle toward the stairs at the left of the lobby.

No! Herschel's mind screamed. *He can't go with me!*

"That's quite all right," said Herschel, attempting to sound calm. "If you'll just point me in the right direction, I'm sure I can save you the bother."

"How very kind of you," agreed the old man. "Secretary vom Rath's office is just up the stairs at the top. You can't miss it; all the other offices will be closed."

Herschel thanked the man, who turned away without further comment and seated himself at the reception desk.

Herschel took the stair steps two at a time. Inside his coat pocket he kept his hand pressed tightly on the pistol to keep it from bouncing against his leg. He wished he had a hand that he could keep pressed against his pounding heart as well.

All at once he arrived at the head of the stairs and an open doorway. Herschel marveled that his body seemed to be moving so rapidly when his mind seemed to be dragging along so slowly. Abruptly he found himself facing another desk, this one with a thin, aristocratic-looking man seated at it, reading a newspaper and smoking a cigarette.

"Yes, can I help you?" asked Ernst vom Rath.

Herschel made no reply. His body, which a moment earlier had been all in rushing motion, seemed rooted to the floor. His tongue stuck to the roof of his mouth. He could not even will himself to speak, much less draw the gun from his pocket.

"Did you have a message to deliver?" prompted Ernst. "Something to do with Jews?"

As if Ernst were reading the script for his own destruction, the words *message* and *Jews* exploded in Herschel's brain, freeing his mouth to work, his body to move. *My father,* he thought wildly, *at last I can strike a blow for you . . . for you!*

Drawing the pistol from the pocket of his overcoat, he pointed it at vom Rath even as the secretary was rising from his chair to gesture to his visitor to seat himself.

"You filthy Nazi!" shouted Herschel, pulling the trigger. "Here, in the name of twelve thousand persecuted Jews, is your message! *Here . . . is . . . your . . . message!*" he repeated, punctuating each word he screamed with another shot from the gun.

Vom Rath collapsed backward into his desk chair as if suddenly overcome with extreme weariness. His mouth opened and shut but succeeded in producing only one syllable over and over. "Why? Why? Why?"

The old porter reached the top of the stairs and stood panting for breath. He had come up as fast as he was able after the shots were fired, but he had heard no other sounds since. He peered cautiously around the doorframe into Ernst's office. Herschel Grynspan still stood in the middle of the room, the empty gun hanging from his hand as if it were a useless appendage.

Herschel made no movement except to sway slightly. He seemed to be looking at vom Rath, who was now slumped to the floor, his white shirt a soggy mass of crimson. The porter turned and stumbled down the stairs as he ran to telephone the police.

The old nun embraced Victoria as she left her at the door of the guesthouse. Victoria entered the sitting room alone. More alone than she had ever been.

She closed the door behind her and stood in the center of the room. The fire had died out. The charred end of a pine bough lay on the cold hearth. Victoria thought of Eli as he had stoked the fire just this morning. Where had that moment gone? It had vanished even as they lived it. All that was left now was the eternity Mother Superior had spoken of. Victoria must cling to that faith, that whisper of truth, or she would go mad.

Eli had been betrayed, handed over to the Mufti and the Arab Council for judgment. The cup of sorrow had not passed; she must drink it, here in Gethsemane.

Victoria's eyes lingered on the white nightgown lying on the neatly made bed. "Eli," she whispered, wishing she could call their moment back.

She opened the top drawer of a writing desk to find clean white paper and a pen. Carefully she wrote her farewell and thanks to Mother Superior. She did not want to tell the old woman what she had in mind. She folded the sheet and slipped it into an envelope, which she propped on the mantel. Beside that she left her Bible and a second note: *For Leah Feldstein.*

She looked out the window. A gentle fog was drifting over the Mount of Olives and Gethsemane as if to shield the world from the sorrow that was there.

The courtyard was deserted. Victoria looked back one more time at the little house where she had known one night of happiness. Then she slipped out the door and made her way through the clinging mist toward the gate at the rear of the compound that led upward to Gethsemane.

Still in the habit of a novice, she might have been just another member of the small Russian community going to pray. Ghostlike, she glided out of the safety of the convent grounds and disappeared among the gnarled trees of Olivet.

Adolf Hitler was holding court in the formal reception room of the Rathaus building in Munich. He was wearing a simple brown uniform with a single lapel ribbon and swastika armband to show his solidarity with the crowd of eager national socialists. He was greeting delegations from all corners of the Reich as each German state sent representatives to the memorial service of the Beer Hall Putsch.

The bespectacled head of the Gestapo, Heinrich Himmler, stood unobtrusively in a corner of the room watching the proceedings. An aide in the uniform of the SS entered the hall and scanned the crowd briefly before locating Himmler. The aide strode quickly to Himmler's side and bent to whisper in his ear. Himmler nodded twice, grimaced once, and dismissed the aide with a jerk of his head that was as close to anger as the calculating chief of Internal Security ever betrayed.

Catching Hitler's eye, Himmler received a look that indicated the Führer had also seen the aide's arrival. A moment later, the two withdrew to a private office.

"Well," demanded Hitler at once. "The sacrifice—has it taken place as planned?"

"Yes, mein Führer," Himmler began. "Only—"

"Only what?" growled Hitler ominously, his petulant anger bubbling just beneath the surface.

"Vom Rath is not dead. The Jew Grynspan shot him—excuse me,

mein Führer, shot *at* him—five times, but only two bullets struck him. One of the wounds is only minor, having lodged in his shoulder."

"And the other?"

"Much more serious. The last bullet penetrated both stomach and spleen, as well as grazing a lung. It is considered very unlikely that he will survive the combination of injuries."

Hitler lapsed into thought, gazing off into a silent contemplation that Himmler did not even dream of interrupting.

A few moments passed; then Hitler spoke. "Certainly he will not survive beyond two days. I sense this. I have a vision of him lying in his coffin surrounded by wreaths of flowers and grieving comrades-in-arms." The Führer paused to favor Himmler with his most direct and intense gaze. "However, it would be inconvenient if our martyr of the Fatherland lived. We will dispatch my personal physician to attend to him immediately. Is my intention clear?"

"Completely, mein Führer." Giving a precise salute, Himmler exited to see that Hitler's directive was put into immediate execution.

43

Last Chances

Etta kissed each of the children good-bye and left them with the reassurance that Papa would be home today. The good priest, Father Kopecky, had promised as much, and they must pray and believe.

The expression on Frau Rosen's face was doubtful, almost accusing. After all, had it not been some folly of Etta's that had brought this disaster down on the household and the community? There was much that needed explanation.

Father Kopecky did not get out to knock on the door. He simply waited as the engine idled and exhaust fumes rose through the snowflakes.

Etta, feeling lighthearted and confident in the veracity and respect her witness commanded, felt better than she had since the incident in Catholic Warsaw had happened. The priest was correct: She and Eduard should have called on him when the threat of blackmail was first made!

She threw open the door and climbed into the car. She greeted him with a cheerful smile, but this morning the priest seemed subdued. The radio was on. News from Paris. The priest was shaking his head in distress as he turned up the volume to drown out her optimism.

The director of police eyed Etta with some doubt. How could he not believe her story with Father Kopecky sitting here to back her up?

He turned his gaze on the priest as if Etta were not there. "You have heard the news from Paris?" the director asked, rubbing a hand across his paunch as if he had indigestion.

"Yes." The priest nodded, not certain what that had to do with two corrupt policemen and the arrest of a rabbi in Warsaw.

"This is all tied up with those Jewish deportations, you know," explained the director.

Etta jumped in. "My husband headed a relief committee for the Jewish deportees."

The director eyed her coolly. "The arrest of your husband has nothing to do with the unfortunate incident you had in the street. I can promise you, if you had come to this office when you were first approached by the corrupt officers, I would have personally dealt with them." He seemed to say this for the benefit of the priest. "And they will be dealt with now." A quick frown of sincerity.

Father Kopecky nodded as if he knew it all along. "Your mother is such a pious woman. I knew her son would also be fair. The Rabbi Lubetkin will be released then?"

"I have nothing to say about that," said the director. Yet another finger was being pointed. "You will have to speak with the head of Internal Affairs. That matter is in the government's jurisdiction, I'm afraid."

"What?" The priest leaned forward.

"As I told you, Father, this has to do with the deportees. There are other leaders of the Polish Jews who are being detained for questioning."

Etta was stunned. "But why? What have they to do with government affairs?"

The director sighed wearily. He did not know everything, but he offered them the explanation he had gotten. "Apparently the Jews have begun their conspiracy of assassination. We were warned . . . the government was warned by the intelligence service of another country that the next few days might be days of violence of the Jews against other races." He nodded at the bewilderment in Etta's eyes. "Your husband has been known to have strong connections with a leader of a Zionist group here in Warsaw. You have connections yourself."

"Doktor Letzno?"

"Yes. That is his name. He is suspected to have contacts with the Communists in Russia. Of course, the Communists would like to take over Prague. The Jews will help them."

"Propaganda from Hitler!" Etta proclaimed. "Nonsense!"

"All the same, you see what happened in Paris this morning. And in Palestine. The Jews have begun to assassinate public officials." The director was adamant in his belief that the shooting of Ernst vom Rath was somehow connected to events in Poland.

"My husband is a humanitarian, not a politician. He certainly has nothing to do with any violence against public officials."

"He has had some contact with the parents of the young killer. Grynspan. Herschel Grynspan is the boy's name."

Father Kopecky leaned forward. "But the shooting only happened this morning! If Rabbi Lubetkin was somehow related to such a thing, why was he detained yesterday? *Before* the shooting?"

The director shrugged. "Not my department. How do I know how they know these things? We have just been advised to keep an eye on the leaders of the Warsaw Jewish community because there is a widespread Jewish plot under way." He shrugged. "Your husband has been implicated."

"Aaron would never harm anyone," Etta protested. "You cannot hold him."

"I do not hold him!" exclaimed the director. "You are talking to the wrong fellow!"

The junior officer at the British headquarters brought in yet another communication from the Arab Higher Committee and the Arab Council.

Orde and Eli sat with the secretary taking his dictation. They sipped steaming cups of coffee as the story of the fight in the souk unfolded.

"I was trying to pull myself up when he lunged," Eli said wearily, as if reliving the moment was too much for him. "The poker was above me. I grabbed it and it whipped forward. He fell on it. It was an accident."

Orde leafed through the stack of typed Arab demands. "They have a different story, and—" Orde frowned and pulled out a contract, written in Arabic and signed by Victoria's father and Ram Kadar, with Ibrahim as a witness. "Marriage contract," Orde said. "Reads more like a business transaction for cattle."

Orde passed it to Eli, who read it and shook his head. "Well, at least I've got her free of all that."

Orde was still frowning. He scratched his cheek in thought as he pulled out a second document sealed with the official seal of the Arab Higher Committee. "A marriage certificate," Orde said. "They are claiming that her marriage to this fellow already took place."

Eli did not need to wonder why the document had been forged. It was part of the propaganda that was only beginning. Already he had heard the claims that he had kidnapped the sister of Ismael Hassan and that the kidnapping had then led to murder. "If such tricks were not so deadly, they would be laughable."

Orde sighed and sipped his coffee. "Deadly. Yes. I'm afraid we will have to move you out of Palestine as soon as possible. I spoke with the high commissioner. No one in the government is fooled by this."

Once again the junior officer poked his head into the room. He had an astonished look on his face. "Captain Orde! Wait until you hear this one!" He motioned for Orde and Eli to follow to the radio room.

The frantic voice of Radio Cairo crackled over the airwaves:

> *"The body of Victoria Hassan has been found in an alley in the Old City. The murderer Jew, Eli Sachar, is being handed over to the Arab Higher Committee for trial. Ram Kadar, husband of the murdered woman, vows that he will personally take revenge for the killing and rape of his wife."*

Orde looked first at the junior officer and then at the radio operator. "Propaganda."

"That's not all." The radioman turned up the volume.

> *"In Paris this morning, a young Polish Jew has shot a high-ranking member of the staff of the German Embassy. Hitler has proclaimed that the incidents in Palestine and now in Paris are part of a world-wide conspiracy of the Jewish Bolsheviks, and that responsible government must unite to stop such . . ."*

At this point the reception whined and howled, obscuring the words that followed.

Victoria made her way through the stones of the cemetery on the slope of the Mount of Olives. On the crest of the hill she looked back toward the masses of people who already crowded into the Old City through St. Stephen's Gate. There were fewer mourners moving through the south entrance of the Dung Gate. There, the sheep destined for slaughter milled in the stock pens. A few donkeys were corralled as their masters were searched by English soldiers before they passed into the Old City on their way to the funeral.

Englishmen would not dare to search a woman in a nun's habit, she reasoned. She set off cross-country toward the Dung Gate on the south side of the Dome of the Rock.

It was an hour before she reached the entrance to the Old City. The questioning stares of the young soldiers greeted her.

"Today is not a good day to enter the Old City, Sister," one said, tipping his cap in respect.

"I have need to go to the Church of the Holy Sepulchre today," she said piously. "I have a vow to fulfill."

The soldiers exchanged worried glances. A few more Bedouin shepherds fell in line behind her, waiting to be searched. "No one is being searched at St. Stephen's Gate," an old Bedouin whispered behind Victoria. "There are too many people there. Too many. But they have nothing to hide from the English, anyway. It is a small inconvenience."

"Sister, today is not a good day to enter the city. There is a funeral for a Muslim brother and sister today. Didn't you see the crowds? From all over Palestine. The Mufti has made a regular event out of it."

"It surely will not be started before I can walk to the Church of the Holy Sepulchre. That is, unless you detain me here longer."

One of the soldiers rubbed his cheek. He would warn her one last time. "Well, you ought to stay there until this thing blows over. Maybe all night, if you have to."

"If there is trouble I will not leave."

He waved her through. "There will be trouble all right! Be careful, Sister."

Victoria inclined her head slowly and crossed herself as she had seen the sisters do. She hurried past the shuttered butcher shops and picked her way around the animal droppings for which the Dung Gate was named. Except for mourners heading toward the entrance to the Haram and the Dome of the Rock, the streets were empty. There was no sign of Christian or Jew here today.

She stepped into a public restroom and removed the wimple from her head. Then she loosened the scarf that tied back her hair and draped it loosely over her head like a veil. She could only hope that the Muslim crowds would not notice that the clothes she wore were those of a Russian convent novice.

Victoria stepped outside into a crowd of mourners who spoke angrily among themselves about the words of the Koran in regard to vengeance in such a case. "This Jew should die a slow death. He should be made to suffer as the families of those he murdered will suffer!"

Victoria walked with her eyes downcast until they passed through the Armenian Quarter to the Wailing Wall. There was not one Jewish rabbi there today.

"They are afraid," said one old man in a fez. "And rightly so! We will cause them to suffer as well. The Koran demands it. A tooth for a tooth!" Victoria noticed he had no teeth, but he pulled out a dagger from his belt all the same. "How can this Sachar fellow pay all the penalty himself? No matter how he suffers, it will never be enough. I say all the Jews should suffer!"

"Brother and sister both killed by the same hand! She was raped and beaten, they say! We will make certain the Jew violates no one else."

For a moment, Victoria considered revealing herself to them, but then she thought better of it. When the crowds fell silent to listen to the Mufti, then she would speak. She would pull off the scarf and run to her father. She would reveal to all of them the truth that Eli had not done what he was accused of.

"They will bring in the coffins side by side," a tattooed old woman whispered to Victoria.

"Brother and sister," added another old woman. "Jerusalem has never seen such a thing as this!"

Victoria looked away. She could not answer. Would even her revelation stop what was to come? These people had no concern for her brother Ismael. They did not know the family or Victoria. She walked among the people who had come to mourn and bury her, and they did not know who she was!

It was unsettling. The side street into the Street of the Chain was packed. The crowd from her street backed up as entry to the Haram slowed to a crawl.

Victoria looked up at the spikes of the minarets. The Mufti's men stood there, rifles slung over their shoulders, looking down on the crowds. Their gazes seemed without emotion, like a cat eyeing a wounded bird and waiting. . . .

"But she is gone, I tell you!" The voice of Mother Superior shouted to Eli over the telephone, causing the other nuns in the office to stare at her. Had they ever seen Mother Superior so upset?

The hands of the old woman trembled as she held the note Victoria had written.

> *Thank you for your kindness. I will remember. . . . Must return to my home and family to prove I am well . . . for the sake of my husband.*

She read the words to Eli, who had also heard the Arab broadcast and telephoned so that Victoria would not worry. But the call had come too late.

"I do not know when. I stopped back by the guest cottage only a few minutes ago and found this note of farewell and a Bible left beside it for her friend Leah. But she was gone, and no one at all saw her leave."

From the upper-story windows of the Tankiziyya, the Mufti could look straight down on the crowds who moved along the Wailing Wall as they jostled toward the entrance to the Haram. The Haram itself, courtyard of the Dome of the Rock, was filling up fast. Estimates were made of twenty thousand and then thirty and now forty thousand, with thousands more clogging the roads on their way to the shrine.

All this, and it was still two hours before the appointed time of the funeral. It was more than he had hoped. Allah had given bountifully to the ranks of the army of the jihad! Today the name of Allah would be *He Who Destroys!* In every city and village in Palestine the muhqtars were ready to release their wrath at the same moment the spring uncoiled here in Jerusalem!

Haj Amin turned to Vargen and Hockman in his pleasure. "It will take only a word," he said. "They have come here for this! This show of death is what they have been waiting for to enliven their spirits! Today will be a day they speak of for generations to come."

"The second coffin adds a little something, I think," Hockman said as he looked out a side window into the courtyard where the two coffins lay side by side. "The rape and murder of a woman. It is the stuff great explosions are made of. You have done well."

"She was a prostitute," Haj Amin explained. "My men disfigured her face enough so that even those who know Victoria Hassan would not be sure who it was."

"The crowds do not care, anyway. They have come for a show. A dead woman is good enough, lying at the side of the brother who tried to save her. Now, that is splendid!"

Word had already come of the bungled attempt on the life of a German official in Paris by a young Jew. The timing was impeccable, even if the Jew's aim had not been. Vargen had no doubt that the Führer would make good use of the incident regardless. The planned violence in the Reich would erupt at the same time as the demonstrations here in Palestine. Such events would leave the world—especially Great Britain—reeling.

"Tomorrow the Woodhead Committee makes their announcement about the immigration question," Haj Amin muttered with pleasure. "We will make certain they are aided in their decision."

Etta stood trembling in the anteroom of the office of the minister of Internal Affairs. Beside her stood the little priest, Father Kopecky. "Courage, my child, courage," he whispered.

The door into the minister's private office opened and the secretary emerged. "You may go in now, Father." The tall, thin-faced woman, with her hair pulled back severely from her face, addressed herself to the priest as if Etta were not even present.

They walked into the office together and stood before the desk of Poland's minister of Internal Affairs. The man gave them no word of acknowledgment, nor any offer for them to be seated. He continued to scan the contents of a file folder that lay spread out in front of him.

At last Father Kopecky broke the silence by asking, "In the light of the evidence you undoubtedly have read, Minister, surely it's clear that Mrs. Lubetkin's husband should be freed."

The minister finally looked up from the papers to scrutinize Etta and Father Kopecky from under heavy eyelids and bushy eyebrows. "I'm surprised at you, Father, getting yourself mixed up in such an affair. Do your superiors know of your involvement?" Before Father Kopecky could reply, the minister continued, "Aren't you aware of what is happening in Germany? At this moment, the Germans are taking steps to eliminate the problem of the Jewish Bolshevik conspirators in their midst. We here in Poland will do even better than that. We will not let the problem grow to the size that it has in Germany. We will take steps right now to ensure that we do not have any difficulty controlling our Jews."

Father Kopecky was almost speechless with disbelief, and into the silence that followed the minister's remarks, Etta blurted out, "But I can pay—I can pay for my husband's release!"

Father Kopecky looked at her with horror, and Etta stopped abruptly, but the minister only shook his head slowly and gave a single snort of disgust. "You Jews!" he said. "You think your money will save you—well, no longer. We are rounding up all Bolshevik agitators, and we'll round up many more before we're through. You'd do well to keep that in mind, Father."

"Is that all?" gasped Etta. "Is there no appeal?"

"In due time, your husband's case will be considered," concluded the minister. "And now, I have more important business." With a negligent wave of his hand he indicated that they should leave.

44

At the Hour of Our Death

The Bible on the mantel convinced Eli of Victoria's real reason for leaving. She was going to the Muslim Quarter, yes, but she was not going home. As he replaced the receiver, he stared out the window to the panorama of Jerusalem beyond. The Muslim crowds, they said, were beginning to gather in the courtyard of the Dome of the Rock for the funeral of Ismael Hassan. That was where Victoria was going. She would show herself there to convince the people of the lies of Haj Amin Husseini.

In such a place, at such a time, there would be no one to help her. Even the British soldiers along the wall took their posts behind the stones and peered out at the multitudes with a sensible fear.

It was easy for Eli to walk past the sentries of British military headquarters and out of the building. Dressed in the uniform of Captain Orde, the men saluted as he passed on his way to the motor pool.

"Captain Orde asked me to bring the car around," he explained nonchalantly to the same sergeant who had parked the vehicle for them this morning. A salute and an obedient nod were followed by a set of keys being placed in the palm of Eli's hand.

Within two minutes from the time he left the building, he was driving alone toward the Old City walls. From the Hill of Evil Counsel, Eli could plainly see the onion domes of the Russian church and the Dome of the Rock across the steep Valley of Kidron.

Fog moved like currents of water around the low spots on the road ahead. It snagged on headstones protruding from the hillside beneath the Muslim holy place.

From every side road, Eli could see shadowy forms of the Muslims who were coming to mourn and to express their outrage today. They poured onto the main road in front of the car. Keffiyeh-swathed heads turned to stare with resentment at the British armored car that forced them to move to one side as it crept past. He drove by the convent and cast one searching gaze over the pine-studded grounds. *She was gone! Gone!*

Eli found himself searching every woman's face. He slowed the speed of the vehicle until it moved no faster than a walk as he looked for Victoria among the crowds. When he was certain she was not among one group, he sped ahead to the next. It occurred to him he did not even know what she was wearing. He had left her this morning in the white cotton shift. Would she have put on the uniform of a British soldier again? He scanned the mob for a helmet, but then realized that no sane Englishman would dare to come among this group.

Thousands jostled before St. Stephen's Gate. Like grains of sand through a funnel, they poured into the Old City and onto the Via Dolorosa as they inched toward the Dome of the Rock.

Still a hundred yards from the Old City gate, the crowd no longer moved to one side for the armored car. Like the fog, they surged around him, bringing him to a dead stop. He inched forward, reluctant to park and climb out to make his way on foot.

"Victoria," he muttered as he tried to search the sea of intense faces that swept by. "I am here, Victoria. Come on. Please! Please, pass by me!"

But she did not pass. He waited and watched for ten minutes as the mourners walked around him and then closed off the road. *Would she be wearing a veil?* He narrowed his search to a study of eyes. She was not there. She could have walked from the convent to the gate in half the time that had passed since he left the British headquarters.

He blasted the horn. Faces turned angrily to stare at the steel-plated vehicle. He inched ahead and blasted the horn again until the growing resentment on Arab faces caused him to simply pull to the side of the road and wait for a few more precious minutes.

Eli whispered the words of the Shema as he switched off the motor and set the brake. Pocketing the keys, he opened the door and stepped out into the human current. He looked back at the hundreds of faces moving toward him up the slope. He could not see them all, but he knew she had already entered the Old City. She was inside the gate of St. Stephen. Perhaps even in the courtyard of the Dome of the Rock.

His mouth was dry with fear. He stepped into the mass of surly Arabs who surrounded him with hostile glares and unspoken curses. He tried to push ahead, tried to break through the slow deliberate pace. The ring of resentment tightened around him, holding him back.

Moving with tiny, shuffling steps, he reached the high arched portal of St. Stephen's Gate, where the closeness shoved him against those he walked with. The Arab stares became more obvious. The questions were asked among themselves:

"What does this son of an English pig have to do with us?"

"Must they come here to threaten us even as we weep?"

"What is he doing?"

"Why is he here?"

"A spy!"

"Then a poor spy. Why is he dressed like that?"

Eli pretended not to understand them. He lowered his head and pulled the brim of his cap down over his eyes. Only at this moment did he realize that he was now among the mourners of the man he had killed. He had concentrated so intensely on finding Victoria that only at this instant did he remember why the thousands packed the narrow entrance.

Just as many thousands surged forward from the opposite direction of Via Dolorosa. Eli tried to think where Victoria would go. To her home? Had she meant that? Was she returning to her home?

That could not be. She was an outcast. Ibrahim would not kill her, but the others would not hesitate. The thought made him shudder. A sense of hopelessness descended on him. *To find her in this. To hope to take her safely away!* But what other hope was there for them? Better to die here searching for her than to live with the knowledge that she had simply vanished into the maw of the schemes of Haj Amin Husseini.

He turned to enter the Haram with the rest. A gruff Arab voice challenged him. "Hey, English! What do you think you are doing?"

"I have come—to pay respects."

"No son of the prophet needs your respect. You intrude! You are not welcome here!" growled another emotion-laden voice.

Eli replied carefully. "I knew him well. Did you know him?"

"No," he answered. "But the family is known."

Eli's voice now cracked with emotion. He did not stop or look as if he might turn back. "I knew him well. Like a brother. I have more right to weep than any."

Yet another voice demanded, "And did you know the sister also? Victoria? The wife of Ram Kadar?"

Eli frowned. Fear stirred in the pit of his belly. "Not so well."

"They are bringing her coffin now," the voice called back from the portals of the Dome of the Rock. "I can see it. *Ya Allah!* There they bring two coffins into the gates!"

Eli gasped for air at those words, even though he knew it could not be. She had left the convent only two hours ago. She could not be dead. Another trick! It was another trick!

All around him wails rose up—cries to Allah, cries for mercy, cries for vengeance! Through the gates, Eli caught a glimpse of two coffins bobbing over a sea of heads already packed into the courtyard. The screams increased in volume as the wooden coffins glided inward toward the sanctuary. "Brother and sister! Brother and sister!" cried a toothless old man who clutched Eli's sleeve and sobbed hysterically. "*Ya Allah!* Two of them murdered! Two in the same family!"

Eli felt sick. Waves of nausea swept over him. He tore himself free of the old man's grip and leaned against the stones of the portals. *It could not be! She left the convent only two hours ago! Oh, God! Could it be? Could it?*

The caskets were closed. It was another deception, an added fuel to the fire of passion. Two from the same family, they said, and yet the second casket could not contain Victoria! Or could it?

Eli raised his eyes. Three rough-looking Arabs strode confidently along the ramparts of the wall that encompassed the courtyard. They openly carried their rifles. There could not be a Muslim burial without the firing of rifles. Eli looked across the vast field of shrieking mourners. There were men with rifles at every station along the stone enclosure. These men displayed no emotion in the midst of the hysteria. They had not come to watch the mourners. They had come for other reasons—for what was to follow the funeral.

"Two coffins!" shrieked a woman. "*Ya Allah!* Oh, God!"

Eli pulled himself straight. He began to move forward with the rest. Victoria was not dead! His heart gave him courage. He would get close enough to see. Somehow. She was alive! Somewhere in this mob of teeming thousands, she too was making her way forward to declare the deception, to stop what was to come upon Jerusalem! How many would die today? How many would fall if it happened as the Mufti planned it?

Eli had never before set foot on the grounds where Solomon's Temple once stood. Where Jesus preached and prayed. Where the Romans had made the glory of the Holy of Holies desolate.

It was still a place of desolation. Darkness had come to hover where the Shekinah glory had descended. Death was near in the chanting hysteria of the waiting masses who crammed together until moving became almost impossible and breathing itself, difficult.

"Allah! *YA ALLAH!*" shrieked a hysterical woman who tore her clothes and beat her face at the sight of the coffins.

Madness!

Eli pushed forward as yet another woman convulsed and frothed at the mouth as she stood wedged upright among the others.

The entire courtyard was a powder keg, and Eli was a lighted match slipping cautiously by. The wind of insanity was already rising into a confused roar.

He tried not to think of his own death. If Victoria was here, if she was alive, he must find her and take her to safety. And if she was indeed within the plain wooden coffin that sailed above him like a ship, then he would die with her! He would die gladly and count his own death among the millions of Jews who were slain upon these same stones.

He shouted against the gale, yet no one heard his voice. No one but God. Eli wept as well, sensing not only the tragedy of what was happening to him and Victoria, but a greater, heart-rending tragedy that had begun with the corruption of this once-holy place.

He felt desperately alone. Mourning for Victoria. Mourning for Jerusalem. Mourning for his people who longed for the Return. Mourning for the Messiah who had wept for what He knew would come upon the Holy City.

"For the Temple that lies desolate," he cried, "we sit in solitude and mourn!"

He wedged his body between two men and inched forward toward the platforms where the coffins were being lowered.

Eli shouted at the top of his lungs this ancient lament for the fallen Temple:

> "For the walls that are overthrown,
> I walk in solitude and mourn!
> For our glory that is departed,
> For our wise men who have perished!
> For the priests who have stumbled!
> For our kings who have despised Him,
> We sit in solitude and mourn!"

Yet no one could comprehend what he said. They seemed not to notice his uniform. Certainly, no one guessed that a Jew walked among them. Or that it was the very Jew accused and already judged by the Arab Council. "Look down on me, O Lord!" Eli cried. "May I see her face before I see Your face! O Lord, save her! Help me find her!"

As Eli slowly pushed forward from the north toward the coffins and the raised platform, Victoria moved with difficulty toward the same goal from the south. It did not matter, she realized, what she was wearing. Each individual within the shrieking and wailing crowd had some private vision of death that preoccupied them. Men and women seemed to see only the coffins—and only themselves. They scratched their own faces with fingernails or bits of stone until frenzied eyes peered out from bloody cheeks.

Victoria did not mourn, not even for her brother who she knew lay in one of the wooden boxes. Her only thoughts were of Eli—of stopping the madness around her.

She found strength in this. Her father would surely sit on the dais beside the coffins. Did he know she still lived? Victoria wondered. Or did he believe the lie?

He would know soon enough. He would stand beside her and proclaim an end to this deception!

This thought, *this goal*, strengthened her to push forward. Foot by foot she gained ground. She turned sideways to squeeze between bodies. She stopped and stood on tiptoe to peer over the bobbing heads to where four men removed the lids of the caskets and propped them up for all to see the dead bodies within.

A new howl arose, loud enough to be heard throughout the British Mandate. Victoria paused in her struggle to look at the ashen-faced body of her half brother. Only now did the reality of his death settle on her. The finality of his end. Such a wasted, evil life. There was no more hope for him and that indeed caused her to grieve.

The face of the dead woman beside him was covered by a thin veil—thin enough so that those around the platform could see the mutilated features. Victoria cried out at the sight. This was meant to be her! The body was the same size and build. But even her dear father would not know by the face that it was not Victoria. *Poor woman! Who was she? What animals they are to do this to her!*

Some among the masses fainted, only to be held upright by the sheer press of those surrounding them. The howling was deafening, the hellish misery of those who were dead inside even while they still breathed.

Victoria pressed on with renewed determination as she looked up to see her father emerge from the doors of the Dome of the Rock and slowly climb the steps of the platform to take his place behind what he thought were two of his children. Such grief on his face! Had there ever been such sadness in the eyes of any man?

Ibrahim followed. Their stepmother came after that, veiled in mourning robes. She leaned heavily against a woman who walked beside her.

Impossible as it seemed, the noise of the tumult increased in volume. Death had given the Muslims of Palestine one voice. Surrounded by his bodyguards, that voice emerged in the form of the Grand Mufti, Haj Amin Husseini.

Victoria pushed harder to move forward.

The Mufti did not try to discourage the madness raging before him. His blue eyes measured the success of weeks of planning. If every man of Britain's twenty thousand troops in Palestine were to come against this crowd, the British would fall. A hundred thousand packed the courtyard of the Haram. Thousands more pressed upon the gates to be let in. Soon, the voice of Haj Amin would release them.

The woman! Eli had to see! Had to get closer! Someone flailed out wildly and struck him in the face as he groaned and pressed closer to the platform.

Haj Amin stood still and silent above his faithful followers and those who had been suddenly recruited into his fold by the call of death.

None of that mattered to Eli any longer. If they had sacrificed his beloved to their strange and terrible god, then Eli wished to die as well.

It took all his strength to crowd forward. A few inches at a time, he gained his way to a mere twenty yards from the platform where Ibrahim sat between his parents. Eli had not stopped looking for Victoria—a living Victoria among the multitude.

He stared at the figure of the dead woman. There was little that was visible, except for her hands. They were not the hands of Victoria! No. The sacrifice was not her!

He turned around once again, hoping to glimpse her face. *She is here;* he knew it now! *But where!*

He turned toward the platform again to stare at the face of Ibrahim. *Once friend.* Had he allowed this terrible deception, knowing that Eli would come, that Victoria would also fall into the trap?

Haj Amin raised his hands, and a massive shudder convulsed the crowd.

Ibrahim stood. He stooped and plucked a flower from a basket and walked forward to place it in the hands of the dead woman. Then he turned as the ripples of howling began to subside in anticipation of the Mufti's words.

In that instant, Ibrahim's eyes caught Eli's. He looked away and then back again. His eyes locked with Eli's, and he *knew!*

With a shout of recognition he pointed and shouted Eli's name. He ran to a row of bodyguards, who all sparked to life. Eli managed to turn.

He tried to work his way back. *Back where?* Without knowing it, the crowd of people around him pressed tighter, pinning him where he stood.

More urgent words to the Mufti, who then stepped forward to the microphone. The silence was not complete yet. He could wait. The rabbit was caught in the snare. Kicking and struggling to get loose, it was, nonetheless, trapped.

Eli cried out. His voice carried, and faces turned to stare at him. Men looked up at the gesturing Ibrahim and then down at the man in the English uniform who struggled and shouted as he attempted to get away.

"Allah is good to us, my children," intoned the Mufti. "*Allah Ahkbar!* God is great, and here is proof for us today! Allah the Avenger has sent to us the murderer of these two faithful . . ."

From her position to the right of the platform, Victoria's eyes followed the Mufti's gesture.

Eli! Arms pinned. Hat off. Hair falling over his pale forehead as he struggled.

"No!" she shouted at the top of her voice. "I am Victoria Hassan! I am not dead! It is a mistake! That is not Victoria Hassan in the coffin!"

Some turned to stare at her. Was she insane? Ah, well, there were many here today who were insane.

"You have come to mock us!" the Mufti roared. "Allah is just! Eli Sachar, you are delivered into our hands for justice as the prophet commands!"

Victoria continued to shout and push against those around her. "Eli!" she screamed in horror.

He heard her voice. Called out her name. "Victoria! Victoria!" His eyes searched wildly for her. Hands reached out for him. *Yes! This is the one the Mufti is addressing! This is he! The one in the English uniform!*

"Eli!" she screamed. The loudspeaker of Haj Amin drowned her out. Ibrahim saw her. His eyes darted nervously. He rose again and whispered to the Mufti. There was no time for the cat to play with the wounded bird. They must strike now or perhaps be discovered in their deception.

"There is the man who killed them!" Ibrahim screamed and pointed to Eli. His face was contorted by hatred, as if he believed the lie.

The crowd went wild! Those surrounding Eli tore at him from every side! They lifted him high above their heads, as they had the coffins, for all to see. "*Allah Akhbar!*"

"Victoria!" Eli cried as he saw her only yards away. His fingers spread wide as he reached for her. She strained to touch him. The gulf was too great. His eyes embraced her one last time.

"No!" She pounded on those between them as she struggled to reach him. "You cannot do this! Cannot! He is innocent! Innocent! I am Victoria Hassan! He has murdered no one!"

Those around her did not notice the fury of her fists. They did not hear her above the tumult. Even if they did hear, they did not care.

Daggers were unsheathed by the thousand and raised skyward to receive the Jew as he was passed above them. Leaving a wake of blood, Eli was swept away from her over the heads of the mob, carried on a current of rage.

45

What Is a Lifetime?

Murphy stepped off the red London omnibus at three minutes after six in the morning. The Fleet Street office of TENS had been running wide open since yesterday when the news of the Paris assassination attempt and word of the Palestine riots had both clacked over the wires within minutes of each other. Murphy had gone home for three hours of restless sleep while Anna and Elisa had sat up and listened to the news on the BBC.

Elisa still did not know that her father was in Berlin, but mention of Herschel Grynspan as the would-be assassin was enough to keep her wide-awake. Murphy had left her with the promise that he would call the moment he heard anything new.

He had not counted on the fact that every few minutes word of fresh violence would be clacking over the wires into Trump European News Service.

Twenty of the best American journalists in Europe sat at their desks, with their eyes riveted to typewriters. Murphy took a deep breath before he pushed through the swinging door and into the thick of it.

No one seemed to notice that the boss had arrived. The unrelenting tap of fingers on keys and the blue haze of tobacco smoke filled the newsroom, reminding Murphy that this office was a reflection of the battles taking place right now in Palestine and in the hospital room of Ernst vom Rath in Paris. Both events, though seemingly distant and unrelated to each other, could affect the fate of millions of Jews trapped within the Nazi regime. Murphy knew that well enough. The truth of it made him shudder and pray that Ernst vom Rath was still hanging on to life.

Harvey Terrill, night desk editor, had never left the office. The weary, frantic little man raised his bald head and scowled in Murphy's direction. Three cold cups of coffee stood amid the devastation of his desk.

"Hi-ya, Boss," he said glumly.

"Bad night, huh?" Murphy swung past him and motioned with his briefcase for Harvey to follow into the glass-enclosed office.

Harvey gathered up a stack of transmissions and hurried after Murphy. He kicked the door shut and sat down, looking like a man suffering from shell shock. Then he laid the sheaf of transmissions on Murphy's desk.

"The German diplomat has been promoted by Hitler."

"Vom Rath?"

"Right. Now he's the head of the German Embassy in Paris. Nice job if the guy lives."

"And?"

"He might make it. Hitler has sent his personal doctor to take care of him. We can hope."

"And Palestine?"

"Twenty new incidents since last night." Harvey rubbed his bald head forlornly. "Mostly in and around Jerusalem for the worst of them. One major attack in northern Palestine near Mount Carmel. Twenty-four hundred troops of the Royal Scots Grays Horse Regiment arrived in Haifa yesterday from India and spent their first night in the Holy Land fighting Muslims."

Harvey passed the next few minutes ticking off the incidents one by one, counting on his fingers twice through.

"Any word from Captain Orde?" Murphy asked quietly, with a sense of foreboding.

Harvey passed the short dispatch across the desk to Murphy. "Just this."

Murphy scanned the page:

ARAB REBELLION BELIEVED BY BRITISH INTELLIGENCE SOURCES
TO BE FINANCED AND LED BY FOREIGN AGENTS STOP MANY
INNOCENT KILLED ON ALL SIDES STOP NO PEACE IN OUR TIME
IN PALESTINE STOP

Murphy pondered the brief message, putting it all together. "Foreign agents. No peace in our time." He shook his head and looked up at Harvey. "We don't have to think very hard to figure out who the foreign agents are, do we?"

"We can't print it, Boss, until we have proof. They gotta catch a Nazi in Jerusalem before we print it. Otherwise they'll say we're just a bunch of paranoid journalists."

"Like Churchill?"

"Exactly."

Murphy scowled at the message. He read it again, then picked up a wire describing the struggle of Ernst vom Rath to live. Another told of the anguish of the Jewish adolescent who pulled the trigger. Still another related violence against Jews in Poland. Beyond the glass window of his office, the machine-gun rattle of the typewriters waged a war of words. "Seems as if only the innocent get hurt, doesn't it, Harvey?" He narrowed his eyes and looked out on the rain-slick London streets as he remembered German bombers over Madrid. "We're not paranoid. England is already at war with the German Reich in Palestine, but Chamberlain is too dumb to know it." He handed Orde's dispatch back to Harvey.

"What do I do with it?"

"Give it a banner headline, Harvey. 'NAZI AGENTS INSTIGATE RIOTS IN PALESTINE.' Got it?"

"But, Boss—"

"And get me a line through to the British colonial secretary. I want a box right below that with a story about the Woodhead Commission's decision on Jewish immigration."

"But they haven't decided yet."

"They decided before they ever set foot in Palestine!" Murphy snapped. "Now *do* it."

Hitler was conferring with Dr. Joseph Goebbels, Reichsminister of Propaganda, just before his limousine was scheduled to take him to address the horde of Brownshirts gathered to hear his memorial address.

Heinrich Himmler, unmistakable satisfaction beaming from his round face, entered the room. "Mein Führer, I have the latest dispatches, which I thought you should hear before attending the ceremony."

"I have been expecting you," remarked Hitler. "Stay, Goebbels. You should hear this also."

"The BBC has just announced the findings of the Woodhead Commission's review of British plans for a Jewish state in Palestine."

"And?" encouraged Hitler.

"They have concluded that to go forward with such a plan would unnecessarily antagonize the Arab population. It is the commission's strong recommendation that the partition plan be scrapped."

The Führer's eyes began to glow with anticipation.

"Furthermore, reports have arrived of new violent outbreaks in Palestine that are taking place even as we speak. It seems there is a massive Arab uprising in response to some Jewish atrocity."

The light in Hitler's eyes intensified.

"Finally, it is my painful duty to inform you that Secretary vom Rath has tragically succumbed to the wounds inflicted by the Jew assassin Grynspan."

Hitler could not repress the urge to give a little jig-step of delight. He beamed at the two men with him in the room.

Rumors of vom Rath's death were already circulating in the packed hall. A growing rumble was heard as Brownshirts exclaimed in louder and louder tones: "What are we waiting for? The Jew dogs must be taught a lesson they'll never forget!"

The official announcement that vom Rath had, in fact, died came just before the Führer strode onto the platform to speak. A tense silence fell over the crowd in anticipation of the Führer's words.

Hitler approached the microphone. The Brownshirts leaned forward almost as one in anticipation. They waited, but still Hitler did not speak.

Some in the crowd could not stand the tension any longer and began to murmur again: "Kill the Jews . . . break their heads . . . all Jews are guilty . . . kill the Jews."

The Führer, obviously in the grip of the strongest emotion at the death of the fine young Aryan, vom Rath, indicated with a shake of his head that his grief was too powerful; he could not speak.

The Brownshirts could no longer restrain themselves. They surged from their places and out into the streets of Munich, shouting, "Smash the Jews! For one dead German ten thousand Jews should die . . . no, a hundred thousand . . . no, millions . . . smash them all!"

The Führer stood on the platform, his head bowed in silent, personal suffering. In a soft aside, spoken just for the ears of Reichsminister Goebbels, Hitler remarked, "The Storm Troopers must have their fling."

A sharp and urgent rapping on Theo's door pulled him from sleep.

"Mr. Lindheim!" It was the voice of Ambassador Henderson. "Wake up, my good man! For heaven's sake!"

As Theo moved to open the door, he could hear the rumble of a fleet of trucks outside the embassy gates. *Could it be,* Theo wondered, *that Göring has gone back on his promise to allow me twenty-four hours to leave Berlin?*

The face of Henderson was gaunt and pale in the corridor. He pushed past Theo, closing the door behind him as he took Theo's arm and guided him to the window overlooking Wilhelmstrasse.

"What is it?" Theo asked, startled by Henderson's intensity.

Henderson pulled back the curtain and gestured for Theo to look.

Most of the windows at the Adlon Hotel across the street were dark. The street itself was deserted except for a line of trucks that passed in slow procession around the corner from the Interior Ministry to Wilhelmstrasse.

"That German chap has died in Paris," Henderson explained, his voice hoarse from agitation. "Those trucks are coming from Gestapo headquarters."

Theo could see the open-backed trucks were loaded with men. He quietly finished Henderson's thought. "Then there will be reprisals, demonstrations." He frowned. Would one of those trucks stop outside the British Embassy? Had Göring arranged for his arrest tonight?

"Quite." Henderson nodded curtly. "It has already begun in Munich. There is not much time, I'm afraid. Please gather your things as quickly as you can. I have arranged for you to leave early. There is a British transport plane fueled and ready at Templehof. The car is waiting for you in the drive."

"Five minutes," Theo agreed and Henderson left him. Then, as if to signal that even five minutes might be too long, an eerie orange glow lit up the night sky somewhere beyond the Adlon Hotel.

Theo buttoned his shirt as he took one last look out the window. *Berlin was burning!* Herman Göring's bonfire of books had been only a small demonstration of the conflagration that the Nazis planned for the Jews of Germany. *Kristal Nacht,* the "Night of Broken Glass," had begun. Perhaps this night, too, was meant to be just a taste of what Hitler planned for the People of the Covenant.

Theo would carry the warning back to England. He could only hope that someone would listen, that something might be done before it was too late.

A fine mist drifted over the Mount of Olives. Two white-robed figures walked slowly among the ancient trees of Gethsemane. One, an old woman, clung to a small silver cross that hung around her neck. The other, young and beautiful, carried the sorrow of the ages in her eyes as she studied the Jewish cemetery below.

The old woman reached up and plucked a gray green leaf from the branch of a gnarled tree. She held it out to the young woman and pointed to a single raindrop on the leaf.

"*Drougoi,*" said the old woman. "The Lord is also weeping for you today."

The young woman held the captured teardrop gently in her hands as she watched the body of Eli Sachar being lowered into a grave surrounded by a cluster of black umbrellas. A ring of British soldiers led by Captain Orde stood guard around the perimeter of the mourners, lest an Arab sniper fire on them as they grieved. Leah and Shimon stood to one side.

"The captain has spread the story that you took your own life rather than endure a forced marriage. For your safety it is best that no one knows the truth. Not Eli's loved ones. Even your own." The old woman looked back toward the mourners.

"I have no loved ones," Victoria said quietly. "Captain Orde is right about Eli's family. Let them believe what they need to believe. They must not carry the burden that he loved me. That he would not have been a rabbi after all . . ." Her voice faltered. "They must have their own illusions. It makes no difference."

"What will you do now?" asked the old woman. The distant sounds of sobbing drifted up to them. Ida Sachar called the name of her son again and again. Eli's brother, Moshe, stood apart, unshielded by an umbrella. His hair dripped water onto his grim, hard face. No one looked up toward the two women on the knoll of the hill.

The young woman did not answer for a long time. She looked again at the teardrop on the olive leaf, proof that the Lord suffered with her. "Yes, in the Old City they say that I am dead," whispered the young woman. "And so I am, in a way." She smiled sadly toward the grave. "It is just as well."

The old rabbi intoned a prayer in Hebrew and then tossed a handful of dirt into the grave. The sobbing grew louder. Moshe's face broke with emotion. Angrily he brushed away his tears.

The young woman did not weep as she watched. "They suffer," she said, "but they do not know that time is nothing, do they, Mother?"

The old woman shook her head in pity for the mourners. "It is a blink of an eye since Jesus wept here. It will be that long until He returns to this very place, Victoria."

"Yes. I believe that. And so . . . I would like to wait here for that moment. To be near Eli while I wait. To grow more in the likeness of my Friend."

The old woman touched the silver cross. "You may be waiting a lifetime."

"What is that?" Victoria raised her hands as if releasing a bird. "It will be gone. Is that not the secret of Jerusalem? All the lifetimes. All the grief. It will end, and I will stand before my Lord with Eli again at my side. Please, do not send me away. I want to serve here until then."

The old woman nodded her assent. "His will be done," she said softly.

And the two women walked back home along the path where Jesus walked.

Digging Deeper into *Jerusalem Interlude*

In August 1938 Hitler's forces sweep across the borders of the Sudetenland, ultimately swallowing the entire land of Czechoslovakia. His goose-stepping soldiers seem humanly unstoppable. Other nations who had promised to protect Czechoslovakia back down, fearing for their own safety, thus making it easy for Hitler to carry out his evil agenda.

More Jews are forced to flee their homelands. Some are forcibly removed in cattle cars, such as Lazer, Rifka, and Berta Grynspan. And all for the unforgivable sin of being born with Jewish blood! Other Jews flee to Palestine, the Promised Land of their dreams . . . only to be imprisoned in barbed wire as they disembark from rusting ships. Shimon and Leah Feldstein are two of the "lucky ones" who are approved to live in Jerusalem.

However, even in the Holy City, Hitler's darkness lurks. Two unlikely bedfellows, the Muslim Grand Mufti of Jerusalem and Adolf Hitler, secretly join in a common goal: to eradicate the Jews from the earth.

It's no surprise the Jews would wonder, *Is there no place on earth that's safe for us?* For people like Leah and Shimon Feldstein? for Rabbi Lebowitz in Jerusalem and his beloved family in Warsaw? for young people in love, like Eli Sachar and Victoria Hassan, who are separated by the highest walls of religion and tradition?

Yet in the midst of such broken dreams, violence, and death, God's miracles—both large and small—still reign. Baby Yacov is born, and the Grynspans survive—both events a testament to God's covenant with the people of Israel. In a time of evil, kindness comes from surprising sources. Before she dies, Shimon's great-aunt leaves him four months free rent on her flat, allowing the homeless Shimon and Leah to have a place of their own. A compassionate priest picks up a dead child in his arms and gathers the grieving refugee family to take them back to his parish. God allows the tough yet compassionate British captain Samuel Orde to be in the exact position to help the Jews of Jerusalem. The diminuitive but feisty Father Kopecky prevails over the Nazis who are determined to rape Etta Lubetkin.

And then, to show His caring about even the smallest of details, God sends Shimon and his cast-encased arm to answer Rabbi Lebowitz's request for an instrument to crack the hard English walnuts! How right Rabbi Lebowitz is when he writes, in all capital letters, *GOD IS AN OPTIMIST* and posts the message on the walls of Tipat Chalev!

And that takes us to you, dear reader. You may be in a situation right now, or have faced a situation in the past, where you wonder whether there is a God at all, whether He cares, or whether He's simply unable to help. Our heart goes out to you. We prayed for you as we wrote this book and continue to pray as we receive your letters and hear your soul cries. No doubt you have myriad life questions of your own.

Following are some questions designed as a starting place, to take you deeper into the answers to your questions. You may wish to delve into them on your own or share them with a friend or a discussion group.

We hope *Jerusalem Interlude* will encourage you in your search for answers to your daily dilemmas and life situations. But most of all, we pray that you will "discover the Truth through fiction." For we are convinced that if you seek diligently, you will find the One who holds all the answers to the universe (1 Chronicles 28:9).

Bodie & Brock Thoene

SEEK . . .

Prologue

1. Have you loved—and lost—someone (as Charles lost Edith—p. xii)? If so, how has that experience affected your ability to love again?

_____

_____

2. All her life Tikvah has longed for some word from the mother she never had a chance to know (see p. xiii). What do you long for? (Rabbi Lebowitz prays that his family will be able to join him in Jerusalem—see p. 99.) Why?

_____

_____

Chapters 1–2

3. After being such close friends—like sisters—Elisa and Leah find it very difficult to say good-bye (see p. 1). Aaron Lubetkin also feels the loss of his good friend, Dr. Eduard Letzno (see p. 265) as the doctor boards the train for Palestine. Have you found it hard to say good-bye to a particular person? Who? When?

_____

_____

4. *"Men will do for religion what they would not do for mere economics! Clothe one's purpose in the robes of a religious cause, and they will gladly die for you"* (p. 5). Do you agree? Why or why not? What evidence do you see in today's world to support your conclusion?

_____

_____

5. "That which was most forbidden had now become that which Eli desired more than anything else in his life" (p. 10). Have you ever struggled with wanting something that was forbidden? What was the result?

_____

_____

Chapters 3–4

6. All of us long for soul rest, as Elisa did (see p. 27). A place where we can "cocoon" for a while, away from pressure and trouble. When you long for such a place, where do you go? How is that need for rest met?

_____

_____

7. Shimon Feldstein was the only one who survived the SS _Darien_ (see p. 30). Theo Lindheim was the sole survivor of his block in Dachau. In such situations, do you believe "there must be some reason" (p. 34) for their survival? Or is it simply the luck of the draw? Explain.

_____

_____

8. Have you ever been "overwhelmed by the vastness of the problem" (see p. 34)? In what situation? Looking back now, in what ways would you respond differently today to "make a difference even to one," if given the opportunity?

   Some encouragement from Anna Lindheim:

   > _"Those people, the numbers you speak of, they are each precious in the sight of God. The very hairs of our heads are numbered—so it is written. We must only be willing to dedicate our hands to the service of God's love. Then He will assign our tasks to us. We must not be overwhelmed by the vastness of the problem."_

   _____

   _____

Chapters 5–7

9. Leah feels ashamed for complaining about their arrival in Palestine when she realizes so many Jews were not given the freedom to enter the Promised Land (see pp. 44–45). It's easy—and quite human—to feel sorry for yourself until you meet someone who is in a worse situation. When has someone else's situation put your own sorrows and worries in perspective?

_____

_____

10. Have you ever, like Rabbi Lebowitz, felt "lucky to be alive" (p. 49)? If so, when?

_____

_____

11. "The best interest of nations is not the best interest of individual human life," says Winston Churchill (p. 63). Would you agree? Why or why not? Use an example or two from today's headlines.

_____

_____

12. How would you answer these two questions if someone asked you?

    *What value have we put on honor these days?

_____

_____

    *What value have we put on human life? (p. 64)

_____

_____

Chapters 8–9

13. Why do you think so many forces have tried to possess the city of Jerusalem over the years (see pp. 19–21, 70, 155)?

_____

_____

14. Have you lived through a time when "no place feels like home," as Leah did (p. 75)? Describe the situation.

_____

_____

15. You have always lived in one house. Then one night soldiers come to your door and say, "You had nothing with you when you came here, and you will take nothing out!" (see pp. 82–84). They force you to leave immediately and send you to a land where you know you will be persecuted. What thoughts would run through your mind on such a night?

Chapters 10–11

16. Have you experienced a rift in a relationship due to differences in spiritual beliefs (see p. 91)? How have you handled those differences? What has worked? not worked? (Longtime friends Eli and Ibrahim come to blows over their differences. It ends with Ibrahim being beaten unconscious, his brother Ismael's death, and ultimately Eli's death, since he was a Jew who killed an Arab. See pp. 357–360 for a reminder.)

17. Berta Grynspan was only fifteen years old when she stood with her parents at the German border station of Neu Bentschen. And yet, in this darkest moment in her young life, she was able to find a bit of good. "It is good that we have rain," she says (p. 96). What glimmer of good has come from a dark moment in your life?

18. If you, like Eduard Letzno, were faced with a group of refugees, what would you do? What small kindness could you extend to a needy person in your area today?

Chapters 12–15

19. Do you believe that there are "great cosmic forces behind" (p. 109) what happens in the world? And that men (such as Adolf Hitler) and women are the tools of spiritual forces? Why or why not? (See page 372 for an explanation of what the swastika symbol really means.)

_____

_____

20. All of us face times of discouragement, when we wonder if anything we do is for any good purpose. Even the great Christian leader, Theo Lindheim, did. "My hands are tied," he says (p. 111). When have you felt that way?

_____

_____

    Anna, his wife, encourages him by saying, "Your heart is willing . . . and so God has some other task for your hands."
    The Mother Superior at the Russian convent echoes this, saying to Samuel Orde, "Perhaps you do not yet see how you may help. . . . It is not always clear until the Lord puts it right in front of you" (p. 119). Are there any answers right in front of you that you're not yet seeing?

_____

_____

21. "We mortals have a small and troubled view of time. If the wicked could have one glimpse of their eternal future, perhaps they would repent. . . . And if the righteous could have one glimpse of their eternity with God, they would no longer fear what evil men might do to them in this life. No. I think we might pity the wicked man for the price he will pay for his sin" (p. 120). Do you agree with this statement? Why or why not?

_____

_____

Chapters 16–18

22. Have you ever helped someone "further a romance" as Moshe helped his brother, Eli (he carried messages to and from Victoria Hassan—see pp. 140, 144)? What happened to the relationship? Would you do the same thing again?

_____

_____

23. Do you believe Leah's statement to be true: "It is a miracle, you see, that even one of us [Jews] has survived to come home. It is proof that God exists and that He does not lie! He has not forgotten His Covenant with Israel" (p. 156)? Why or why not?

_____

_____

24. If a friend pleaded with you to kill him (as the battered Thomas von Kleistmann pleaded with his friend Ernst vom Rath—see pp. 159–160), would you? Could you? Explain.

_____

_____

Chapters 19–21

25. Eli is faced with a difficult choice. If he marries Victoria, the Arab woman he loves, he will lose his life's dream—to become a rabbi (see p. 177). If you had to choose between a person you love and your career, what would you choose? Why?

_____

_____

26. Have you ever been in a position, like Eli, to envy the love other couples have (see pp. 182–183)? Explain. Perhaps you're single, and you long to be married. Or perhaps you're married, and you wish you had married someone else, that you weren't married at all, or that you shared a deeper, more understanding love with your spouse. . . .

_____

_____

27. Theo Lindheim comes up with a plan—"a trade agreement with Germany that would allow refugees to depart with a portion of their assets" (p. 191)—to help the thousands of Jews who must leave their homeland. But in order for the Germans to even consider the plan, Theo must return to Germany and present it himself. If you were Theo, would you go—risk your life to save thousands who share a common heritage with you? Why or why not?

_____

_____

28. Imagine you are Victoria Hassan. You discover that your family has been involved in a sinister plot, leading to many deaths (see p. 193). What would you do? Would you warn the English of a potential demonstration (see p. 275)? Would you inform them that your own brothers were involved somehow in a bombing (see pp. 327–328)? Why or why not?

_____

_____

Chapters 22–23

29. The kind Eduard Letzno was misjudged by the Jews of Warsaw since he lived like a goy. Yet the rabbi, Aaron Lubetkin, sees Letzno's true heart. He was the "first doctor on the scene when the homeless Jews from Germany had been so much in need. His heart was Jewish" (p. 206). Have you or your motives ever been misjudged? How did you respond? Have _you_ ever misjudged someone else? What was the outcome?

_____

_____

30. When the Americans sent Jell-O as a gift to Tipat Chalev (unusable in the unrefrigerated conditions of Jerusalem), the kind Samuel Orde traded with Rabbi Lebowitz for something more useful— milk, cocoa, and walnuts. The rabbi thinks, _The Eternal be praised! All along the Merciful One had this in mind. Oy! Still sending manna in strange ways, nu?_ (p. 216). When have you received something you didn't expect in a strange way?

_____

_____

Chapters 24–25

31. Have you ever made a decision that made those you love angry? a decision that they couldn't understand (as Eli Sachar did in choosing to love an Arab girl—see pp. 223–224)? What happened in the short-term? the long-term?

_____

_____

32. "I have too much to think about. What is right? I do not know myself any longer! Too many voices!" (p. 225). Have you ever had this same heart cry as Eli? When? What did you do as a result?

_____

_____

33. "Do You hear me, God?" Eli asks, but receives only silence. "He wanted to know God, but God was far away tonight" (pp. 234–235). Has God felt far away to you? When?

_____

_____

Chapters 26–28

34. At one point, Eli Sachar claims that believing in Jesus would deny his heritage as a Jew, and he accuses Shimon and Leah of doing just that. Here is Shimon's response:

> "Leah and I believe that Jesus is the Messiah of Israel, the Holy One we watch for and pray will come to redeem His people Israel! First He came to redeem us individually, as the prophet Isaiah wrote in the fifty-third chapter. Jesus died for our sins. The Lamb of sacrifice given by God for our sakes. But He will come again as King to redeem the nation Israel. It is written, and we are seeing the beginning of the fulfillment" (p. 244).

If you are of Jewish heritage, do you believe that acknowledging Jesus Christ as the one and only Son of God would deny your heritage as a Jew? Why or why not?

_____

_____

35. Eli says, "Christians have slaughtered Jews in the name of Jesus for centuries!"

"Those who have done these things have never known *Him*," Shimon answered quietly. "Many who call themselves by Christ's name worship a false Christ created by Evil to serve Evil. The real Jesus said that this would happen" (p. 245).

If this is true, how can you identify the *real* Christians from those who just claim to be Christians? (See also Matthew 7:20; John 3:19-21.) Contrast the actions of people like Theo, Anna, Elisa, Murphy, and Samuel Orde with Victoria Hassan's half brothers and Haj Amin, who "promises Paradise for those who die fighting jihad! Holy war!" (p. 273). What do their actions say about what they believe in? (See also 2 John 1:6-11)

Remember Shimon's statement: "If there is any victory that causes Evil to rejoice, it is to hide our Messiah from us by distortion, brutality, and false doctrine" (p. 245).

---

36. Shimon challenges Eli (p. 246):

> *"Jesus was a Jew, descended from King David just as our prophets foretold . . . .Empty your mind of . . . lies and darkness. You must meet Jesus first through the prophets . . . and then look at His life! . . . Face-to-face you must look at the real Jesus, and then you must choose to deny Him or believe Him."*

Have you chosen to investigate for yourself who Jesus is? Why or why not? What encourages you? hinders you?

If you wish to investigate more about Jesus, the following Scriptures will help you begin your search:

*Isaiah 53

(Written over seven hundred years before the Messiah walked the earth, this book of the Bible records the characteristics and actions of the real Messiah)

*Matthew 1:1-16

(The genealogy of Jesus that goes back many generations to Abraham)

*Matthew 1:18–2:23; Luke chapters 1–2

(Jesus' conception and birth, the Magi's search for the king of the Jews, Jesus' and His family's flight to Egypt, and Jesus' growing-up years)

*Matthew 3:13-17

(Jesus' baptism, when God the Father claims Jesus as His Son)

*Luke 4–9

(Some of Jesus' miracles and teachings; note especially 4:38-41 and Peter's confession in 9:18-20)

*Luke 13

(Especially Jesus' sorrow for Jerusalem in verses 34-35)

*Luke 21

(The signs of the end of the world, when the kingdom of God is near)

*Luke 22–23

(The betrayal, arrest, trial, and crucifixion of Jesus, His death and burial)

*Luke 24

(The resurrection of Jesus, His appearance on the road to Emmaus, and His ascension to heaven)

*1 John 5:1-21

(Who really believes in God and follows Him? The answer here is clear.)

Chapters 29–30

37. Little did Shimon, the kettledrum musician, know that he would be called upon to become Tipav Chalev's nutcracker (see pp. 266–268). Anna Lindheim had no idea that she would be involved in a soup kitchen in Prague or helping refugees (see p. 271). When have you carried out a role that surprised you? Has it fit into the larger picture of your life in any way?

_____

_____

38. "Theo had been renamed by his Nazi persecutors, but they had never managed to change anything else about him. The stuff that made Theo who he was remained the same" (p. 280).

    Theo Lindheim's name was changed to Jacob Stern when he was interned at Dachau. How would you feel if someone in authority suddenly changed your name? Why is a name so important?

_____

_____

39. Because of a terrorist bomb, Leah, a musician, can no longer hear music (see p. 283). And she also is losing the baby she is carrying (p. 292). Yet her response is simply, "Why? *Oh Jesu! Jesu! Warum?*" (p. 284). If this happened to you, how would you respond (anger, self-pity, fear . . . something else)? Why?

_____

_____

40. Do you believe that it's worth saving even one innocent life? That one person holding the light of God's truth can make Darkness flee (see p. 286)? Why or why not?

_____

_____

Chapters 31–34

41. "Once he had believed that the world was mostly good—people mostly good-hearted; nations just; governments trying their best" (Shimon, p. 293).

    At what point in your life did you begin to understand that not everyone or everything in the world is good? How has that realization affected you?

    _____

    _____

42. Jews have been persecuted by numerous forces (including the Egyptians, the Romans, the Nazis, the Arabs) over thousands of years. Shimon finally realizes:

    "Evil was somehow personal and real. It had chosen to destroy the People of the Book because to do so would be to make the Covenant of that book a lie and God a liar!"

    Simon pinpoints Evil for what it is, and shakes his fist at it:

    "No matter what you do . . . we will not curse God! Give up! You cannot defeat Him! Kill us and we will be with Him! Drive us into the sea and He is there! You will not have your way with Shimon and Leah Feldstein or our children! Even in sorrow we will believe in the promise of our Holy Messiah!" (p. 293)

    Do you think Shimon is right, or is he simply believing blindly, so he won't be disillusioned by life? Explain your answer.

    _____

    _____

43. "Chaim Weizmann has said that there are two places in the world for the Jewish people: the countries where they are not wanted, and the countries where they cannot enter. Where are they to go, then?" (Theo, p. 33).

    Step back into 1938. If you were in charge of finding homes or a homeland for the Jews, what would you do? Where would you decide they would go? What about the people currently in that land?

    _____

    _____

Chapters 35–39

44. Have you ever wondered, like Herschel Grynspan did, if dying would be easier than living (see p. 325)? What, if anything, has changed since you had those thoughts? What motivation has kept you alive?

---

45. Do you hunger, as Victoria Hassan does when she talks to Reverend Robbins (see p. 329), for the Light? Do you long to leave Darkness behind? If so, why not start today?

> *"For God so loved the world that He gave His one and only Son, that whoever believes in Him shall not perish but have eternal life. For God did not send His Son into the world to condemn the world, but to save the world through Him." (John 3:16-17)*

Can you say with Victoria, "I am not afraid. God is not a terrible God of vengeance and hatred to me anymore. I have found His nature in Jesus" (p. 351; see also 1 John 4:11-18)? Why or why not?

---

46. When Etta Lubetkin, a Jew, walks into a Catholic cathedral, she is going against everything she has been raised to believe. Yet she is compelled to go to the "one righteous Gentile in Warsaw" (p. 360). Do you, like Etta, fear those who believe something different than you do—even if you both believe in God? What is one way you can go out of your way to reach out to and understand someone, of a differing faith? to think beyond the borders of your own "faith world"?

---

47. "You have forgotten that God rules over all." (Theo)

"Which God? The Jewish God? The Christian God?" (Göring)
"They are one and the same." (Theo, p. 378)
Do you believe there is only one true God who is over the world? Why or why not?

---

48. Göring suggests that "those who follow your weak and worthless
    God of love will die . . . because they have no strength to fight"
    (p. 378).

_____

_____

The prophet Isaiah says:

> Do you not know?
> Have you not heard?
> The Lord is the everlasting God,
> the Creator of the ends of the earth.
> He will not grow tired or weary,
> and his understanding no one can fathom.
> He gives strength to the weary
> and increases the power of the weak.
> Even youths grow tired and weary,
> and young men stumble and fall;
> but those who hope in the Lord
> will renew their strength.
> They will soar on wings like eagles;
> they will run and not grow weary,
> they will walk and not be faint.
> (Isaiah 40:28-31)

Whom do you agree with—Göring or Isaiah? Explain your answer, using an example from your own life or from someone you
know.

_____

_____

49. "Someday you will stand before Him in judgment, and then you will know" (Theo, p. 380). The Bible is clear: Every person will stand before God someday in judgment. Every word of ours will be known; every deed will be revealed:

> For we will all stand before God's judgment seat. It is written:
> "As surely as I live," says the Lord,
> "every knee will bow before me;
> every tongue will confess to God."
> So then, each of us will give an account of himself to God
> (Romans 14:10-12, quoting Isaiah 45:23)

When you stand before God, what will you say about yourself and the way you have lived?

> It is by the name of Jesus Christ of Nazareth, who you crucified but whom God raised from the dead. . . . He is "the stone you builders rejected, which has become the capstone." Salvation is found in no one else, for there is no other name under heaven given to men by which we must be saved. (Acts 4:10-12)

_____

_____

50. "Men are . . . given the freedom to hate, instead of love. . . . It was because He loved us that He suffered. Suffered for our wrong choices and the freedom we abuse. And if you suffer, . . . you will learn! You will reflect Him even more" (Mother Superior of the Russian convent in Jerusalem, p. 392).

How will you choose to live your life—right here, right now?

_____

_____

About the Authors

Bodie and Brock Thoene (pronounced *Tay-nee*) have written over 45 works of historical fiction. That these best sellers have sold more than 10 million copies and won eight ECPA Gold Medallion Awards affirms what millions of readers have already discovered—the Thoenes are not only master stylists but experts at capturing readers' minds and hearts.

In their timeless classic series about Israel (The Zion Chronicles, The Zion Covenant, and The Zion Legacy), the Thoenes' love for both story and research shines.

With The Shiloh Legacy series and *Shiloh Autumn*—poignant portrayals of the American depression—and The Galway Chronicles, which dramatically tell of the 1840s famine in Ireland, as well as the twelve Legends of the West, the Thoenes have made their mark in modern history.

In the A.D. Chronicles, their most recent series, they step seamlessly into the world of Yerushalyim and Rome, in the days when Yeshua walked the earth and transformed lives with His touch.

Bodie began her writing career as a teen journalist for her local newspaper. Eventually her byline appeared in prestigious periodicals such as *U.S. News and World Report*, *The American West*, and *The Saturday Evening Post*. She also worked for John Wayne's Batjac Productions (she's best known as author of *The Fall Guy*) and ABC Circle Films as a writer and researcher. John Wayne described her as "a writer with talent that captures the people and the times!" She has degrees in journalism and communications.

Brock has often been described by Bodie as "an essential half of this writing team." With degrees both in history and education, Brock has, in his role as researcher and story-line consultant, added the vital dimension of historical accuracy. Due to such careful research, The Zion Covenant and The Zion Chronicles series are recognized by the American Library Association, as well as Zionist libraries around the world, as classic historical novels and are used to teach history in college classrooms.

Bodie and Brock have four grown children—Rachel, Jake, Luke, and Ellie—and five grandchildren. Their sons, Jake and Luke, are carrying on the Thoene family talent as the next generation of writers, and Luke produces the Thoene audiobooks. Bodie and Brock divide their time between London and Nevada.

For more information visit:
www.thoenebooks.com
www.TheOneAudio.com

suspense with a mission

TITLES BY

Jake Thoene

"The Christian Tom Clancy"
Dale Hurd, *CBN Newswatch*

Shaiton's Fire

In this first book in the techno-thriller series by Jake Thoene, the bombing of a subway train is only the beginning of a master plan that Steve Alstead and Chapter 16 have to stop . . . before it's too late.

ISBN 0-8423-5361-5 SOFTCOVER

US $12.99

Firefly Blue

In this action-packed sequel to Shaiton's Fire, Chapter 16 is called in when barrels of cyanide are stolen during a truckjacking. Experience heart-stopping action as you read this gripping story that could have been ripped from today's headlines.

ISBN 0-8423-5362-3 SOFTCOVER

US $12.99

Fuel the Fire

In this third book in the series, Special Agent Steve Alstead and Chapter 16, the FBI's counterterrorism unit, must stop the scheme of an al Qaeda splinter cell . . . while America's future hangs in the balance.

ISBN 0-8423-5363-1 SOFTCOVER

US $12.99

for more information on other great Tyndale fiction
visit www.tyndalefiction.com

THOENE FAMILY CLASSICS™

✪ ✪ ✪

THOENE FAMILY CLASSIC HISTORICALS
by Bodie and Brock Thoene
Gold Medallion Winners*

THE ZION COVENANT
Vienna Prelude*
Prague Counterpoint
Munich Signature
Jerusalem Interlude
Danzig Passage
Warsaw Requiem*
London Refrain
Paris Encore
Dunkirk Crescendo

THE ZION CHRONICLES
The Gates of Zion*
A Daughter of Zion
The Return to Zion
A Light in Zion
The Key to Zion*

THE SHILOH LEGACY
In My Father's House*
A Thousand Shall Fall
Say to This Mountain

SHILOH AUTUMN

THE GALWAY CHRONICLES
Only the River Runs Free*
Of Men and of Angels
Ashes of Remembrance*
All Rivers to the Sea

THE ZION LEGACY
Jerusalem Vigil
Thunder from Jerusalem
Jerusalem's Heart
Jerusalem Scrolls
Stones of Jerusalem
Jerusalem's Hope

A.D. CHRONICLES
First Light
Second Touch
Third Watch
Fourth Dawn
and more to come!

THOENE FAMILY CLASSICS™

✪ ✪ ✪

THOENE FAMILY CLASSIC AMERICAN LEGENDS

LEGENDS OF THE WEST
by Bodie and Brock Thoene

The Man from Shadow Ridge
Riders of the Silver Rim
Gold Rush Prodigal
Sequoia Scout
Cannons of the Comstock
Year of the Grizzly
Shooting Star
Legend of Storey County
Hope Valley War
Delta Passage
Hangtown Lawman
Cumberland Crossing

LEGENDS OF VALOR
by Luke Thoene

Sons of Valor
Brothers of Valor
Fathers of Valor

✪ ✪ ✪

THOENE CLASSIC NONFICTION
by Bodie and Brock Thoene

Writer-to-Writer

THOENE FAMILY CLASSIC SUSPENSE
by Jake Thoene

CHAPTER 16 SERIES
Shaiton's Fire
Firefly Blue
Fuel the Fire

✪ ✪ ✪

THOENE FAMILY CLASSICS FOR KIDS
by Jake and Luke Thoene

BAKER STREET DETECTIVES
The Mystery of the Yellow Hands
The Giant Rat of Sumatra
The Jeweled Peacock of Persia
The Thundering Underground

LAST CHANCE DETECTIVES
Mystery Lights of Navajo Mesa
Legend of the Desert Bigfoot

✪ ✪ ✪

THOENE FAMILY CLASSIC AUDIOBOOKS

Available from
www.thoenebooks.com or
www.TheOneAudio.com